# *R*emember to *B*reathe

## A Collection of Contemporary Erotic Romances

BY

## Jae El Foster

**DCL Publications, LLC**

**www.thedarkcastlelords.net**

*Remember to Breathe: A Collection of Contemporary Erotic Romances*
By Jae El Foster

First DCL Publications Edition: July 2023

DCL Publications
1033 Plymouth Dr.
Grafton, OH 44044

ISBN 978-1-7379237-7-0

This is a work of fiction. Names, characters, places and incidents are the product of the author's imagination, and any resemblance to any actual persons, living or dead, events, or locales, is entirely coincidental.

Cover Model: Vikkas Bhardwaj
Cover Design: Jae El Foster
Editor: Jean Watkins

PUBLISHED IN THE UNITED STATES OF AMERICA

# *Table of Contents*

# *Sheets*

She reached for his hand, but it wasn't there. Opening her eyes, she looked beside her and saw the right side of the bed was empty. Squinting, she lifted her head and looked around the bedroom. John was gone.

Olivia smoothed her hand down the sheet beside her and felt a slip of paper. Taking it, she brought it close and read the roughly scribbled note, thanking her for the fun and signed with John's first name. No last name. No phone number. A one-night stand, she realized. A sigh escaped her and she plopped her head back down onto her pillow, letting the note slip from her left hand and down to the floor.

"Just my luck," she muttered and pulled the covers up to her chin. "He was so cute too…"

She thought of their night of passion. They'd met at a bar while she'd been out with friends after work. She'd been timid at the bar at first, but once she'd had a few drinks in her, she'd loosened up and enjoyed the atmosphere. John had caught her eye around two hours in, and he'd sent a round of tequila shots to her table – one for her and one for each of her three co-workers. She'd looked over and thanked him with a smile, raising the glass to him before downing the shot.

By the persistence of her co-workers, she'd eventually stood from the table and wandered over to him, thanking him for the round of drinks. He asked her if she wanted another, and she'd refused. Then, a Hank Williams song came on the jukebox and he'd asked her to dance. That, she accepted. They'd danced to three more songs after that one before he finally told her his name and she conceded to another drink.

Two shots later, they were in his car, where he had one hand on the wheel, and one between her thighs. Olivia was fully wet and yearning for him by the time they reached her apartment building, and the race up the stairs had been heated. Once inside her apartment, they stripped each other of their clothing and he carried her to the couch, where he parted her legs and dipped her tongue inside of her aching womanhood.

She remembered screaming through the ecstasy brought about by his incredibly skilled tongue, and once he'd had his fill of her taste, he carried her into her bedroom, where he laid her on the bed and crawled up her body. As he looked into her eyes, he'd entered her fully, and he'd remained inside her throughout most of the night. His endurance had been incredible, and even after his first orgasm and her third, he'd shown no signs of slowing down.

Eventually, exhausted and in a state of nirvana, she fell asleep in the cradle of his arms. She'd believed they had shared something incredibly special – a deep satisfaction that had filled them both with undeniable electricity neither had experienced before.

Apparently, she'd been wrong. John was no longer beside her, and all he'd left her was a quick thank you, scribbled on a post-it from her bedside table.

Olivia lay in her bed for nearly another hour, contemplating the night and trying to shrug off the fact that she'd been only a lay to him – that their electrified night of intimacy had meant nothing to the handsome man. When her phone rang, she took it from the nightstand and glared at the caller id, wondering if it was him. Instead, it was Tiffany – her office assistant and one of her best friends.

Clearing her voice, Olivia answered the call and tried to sound as chipper as possible. "Hey, girl."

"Don't just 'hey, girl' me," Tiffany told her in a voice that was much too enthusiastic for Olivia to handle this soon after waking up. "How was he? I bet he has a huge pecker, doesn't he? Is he still there?"

Olivia chuckled. "He was *fantastic*," she admitted, "and yes, he was huge. But nope... he left in the middle of the night while I was asleep."

"Ugh!" her friend groaned loudly. "Did he at least leave a number?"

"Nope. Just a quick 'thank you' on a post-it. No last name either." She sighed and then yawned. "Ah well..."

"The bastard. Well... at least you got some?"

It was true, Olivia thought. She hadn't been sexually fulfilled by a sexy man in weeks... maybe months. And the sex *had* been fantastic. "Yep," she noted. "I'm totally going to have to change these sheets today."

Tiffany cheered so loudly that Olivia had to pull the phone away from her ear. She switched it to speaker and set it down on the nightstand.

"So, what are you up to today?" Begrudgingly, she threw the covers off her and sat up on the bed. Another yawn slipped through.

"Taking you to lunch," Tiffany told her. "Are you at least dressed and ready?"

"Lunch? What time is it?"

"Fifteen to twelve."

Olivia's eyes snapped open wide. She'd not slept past eight in… well, ages. "Crap!" she exclaimed and climbed onto her feet. "I way overslept."

"It's Saturday morning," her friend acknowledged. "You're allowed to sleep in on Saturdays."

"But not *this* late. This is too late."

"Take a shower," Tiffany continued. "Meet me in the lobby in a half hour. I'll pick you up."

"That sounds great. Can you take me back to my car after? It's still at the parking garage."

"Rode with him, eh?" She could hear Tiffany chuckle after the comment.

"How else was he going to finger me during the ride?" Olivia smirked and smiled. "I'll see you when you get here." She reached for the phone and ended the call.

In the shower, she cleaned exceptionally well and then stared down at her pubic mound. She wished she'd thought to trim it up a little before last night – maybe save some cool design or a landing pad into it – but she hadn't expected anyone to see it but her, especially a stud like John. Currently, it looked like an overgrown jungle and she wondered if he'd sifted through her wilderness while tasting her underused womanhood.

Even though she knew she'd likely never see him again, she trimmed her jungle down to a nice meadow and turned off the shower. Once dried, she brushed her teeth, combed her dark brown hair, and applied a little eye-shadow and lipstick. Then, she dressed in a comfortable pair of jeans, a light blue blouse, and wore a pair of black sneakers that had seen better days. By the time she grabbed her purse, locked up her apartment, and headed downstairs, Tiffany was in the lobby awaiting her.

"Finally," the blond woman groaned. I've been here well over thirty seconds."

"Oh, hush," Olivia said with a smirk. "Where are you treating me to lunch today?"

"Why is it my treat? You're the one that got laid."

"You're the one that invited me."

"Touché," Tiffany said and snickered. "How about the tea room? I'm in the mood for something a bit classier after that bar food last night."

"I haven't been to the tea room in months. It sounds heavenly!"

The sky was gray outside and storm clouds were plentiful. Thunder rolled through the heavens as they reached Tiffany's modest car, and as they started down the road, the rain began to pour.

"Just in the nick of time," Olivia noted. "Two more minutes and we would've been soaked."

When they reached the tea room, they discovered the parking lot was nearly full. They found a spot toward the far edge of the building and then rushed to the front door, where they were told they'd have a twenty-minute wait before they could be seated. Quietly, they debated over waiting for a table or finding another place to eat, but one glance at the storm building outside helped them decide to take a seat on the available bench and practice patience.

From where they sat, they could see into the eloquently decorated dining room. Olivia decided to people-watch for a bit while they waited to be seated. She looked at the finely dressed men and women that occupied each and every seat. They were dressed in suits and lovely dresses – the women in full make-up with their hair styled and expensive-looking jewelry covering their earlobes, necks and wrists. She looked down to her jeans and sneakers and sighed. She felt out of place here and wished that Tiffany had told her where they were going before she got dressed for the day.

Looking at her friend, she noticed Tiffany was dressed similarly out of place, and that helped make her feel a little better, but not much.

"You look glum all of a sudden," Tiffany noted as she caught her gaze. "What's wrong?"

"I don't think we dressed properly for this place," Olivia told her and then gestured toward the crowd in the dining room. "Look at them. They all look like they're dressed for a fancy dinner party."

"So what? They all look stiff and uncomfortable. Look at that woman over there." She pointed to a plump older lady seated at a table with a man with gray hair and a black suit. "See how she's sipping her soup from her spoon. She looks terrified that she'll spill it on her dress."

"So?"

"Do you know how much food I've spilled on this shirt?" For emphasis, Tiffany tugged at her brown button-down shirt. "Plenty. But it's wash and wear. If I spill something on it, who cares?"

She smiled and Olivia smiled back. She knew Tiffany was right, but that didn't make her feel any better about it. Still, she managed to relax a little and went back to her people watching.

That was when she noticed John, sitting at a table toward the middle of the room, cutting his food and smiling at a young woman who looked no older than twenty. John looked more handsome than she remembered him being, and he – like most of the other men in the place – was dapper in a suit and tie. The woman was wearing a red silk strapless dress with cleavage that made Olivia feel flat-chested.

She felt all the color drain from her face. Hard, she gripped Tiffany's wrist.

"What's wrong now?" the woman asked her.

"Its… him." Her eyes were large as she looked at John, who thankfully had not noticed her. "It's John, from last night."

"You're shitting me!" Tiffany exclaimed. "Where?"

"There." Olivia pointed a shaky finger in his direction. "With the Barbie Doll in red."

"Oh, wow! It is him!"

"With a date…"

"That bastard!" Tiffany began to stand but Olivia stopped her. "We should go over there. You could 'thank him' for last night and put him in his place. Let's see how that little tart likes her man after that."

"No…" Olivia muttered. "Let's just get out of here."

"But it's still raining."

Olivia looked at her with a pleading expression. Finally, Tiffany relented and they stood. Outside, they had to hurry to the car faster than they'd hurried from it, and they were fully drenched when they made it inside of it.

"Feel like a wet rat now," Tiffany commented as she started the car. "We weren't this soaked going inside."

"Thank you for letting us leave. I just can't face him right now... especially while he's with another woman."

"Screw that other woman," her friend said and snarled. "She deserves to know her man was with you last night."

"Maybe... but that's not my place to tell her. After all, we just had a one-night stand. I can't put a claim with a guy I don't even know the last name of."

"You're too damn kind, Olivia. You know that, right?" Pulling out of the parking spot and heading toward the street, she asked, "So, where to now?"

"Fast food," she told her. "I need comfort food, and we'll blend in just fine there."

"Okay, but I choose the fast-food joint." She winked and smiled and then headed to a burger joint. There, they ate quickly, stuffing their guts with cheeseburgers, fries, and cold sodas in paper cups.

Looking around the restaurant, Olivia saw she'd been right. Everyone here was sloppily dressed and soaked from the rain. She blended in perfectly and felt like she was finally able to disappear into herself, shielding herself from the memories of last night and from the man that had filled her first with pleasure and then with remorse. She'd never slept with a taken man before last night, and the realization of the action mortified her.

"Did he at least unload in you?" Tiffany asked as Olivia was sipping her soda. She nearly spat out the liquid when she heard it. "At least then he might have knocked you up and you can lord the bastard child over him."

She swallowed and waited a moment before responding. It took a second to compose herself from the shock of the question, but she didn't know why she was shocked. Tiffany had no censor button, and that was part of what she loved the most about her.

"No," she finally replied. "The first time was on my belly, and the second time was dessert," she admitted and blushed from the confession.

"Dessert, eh? How'd it taste?"

With a giggle, Olivia shrugged and blushed deeper. "Like cinnamon and slimy bliss."

Tiffany cocked an eyebrow. "So, why do you need to change the sheets?"

"Because I soaked the hell out of them."

After a brief moment of silence, the two women burst into laughter over the comment. It felt good to Olivia to laugh, especially after seeing John and his perfect girlfriend in the tea room. She'd never felt so embarrassed of herself as she had when noticing them, but she couldn't really understand *why* she was embarrassed. After all, she hadn't known he was taken. He'd come on to her, and he'd seduced her with dancing and drinks. If anyone was to blame, it was John, and now she wondered if Tiffany had been right. Perhaps she should have confronted him in the tea room, but now it was too late. Even if they returned there, he'd surely be gone by now.

Once they were finished with their meals, they emptied their trays into the trash can and headed outside. The rain had lightened up to a sprinkle, which was a wonderful change from the harshness of earlier. In the car, Tiffany cranked the engine and pulled onto the main road, heading away from the direction of Olivia's apartment building.

"Where are we going now?" she asked her friend, even though she really didn't care where Tiffany was taking her. Right now, the last place she wanted to be was alone in her apartment with memories of last night and thoughts of John and his pretty little tart.

"Shopping," Tiffany told her. "Payday was yesterday, and I noticed that little raise on my check."

"Little?" Olivia scoffed. "You got three more dollars an hour!"

"I didn't *mean* little when I said it." She smiled and took her eyes off the road long enough to blink. "After we kill some time at the outlet mall, I'll take you to your car."

Olivia had already forgotten she needed to pick up her car. The sight of John in the tea room had knocked the thought out of her. However, she was glad in the delay of retrieving her vehicle. Returning to the scene of the crime was currently at the bottom her list of things she wanted to do. She'd eventually need her car, but right now, the further away she was from things that reminded her of the one-night stand, the better off she felt she'd be.

When they reached the outlet mall, the rain had stopped completely and the clouds were moving on, allowing the sunshine to peek through. The air felt muggy, but at least they were no longer having to suffer being drenched.

"Where do you want to go into first?" Tiffany asked as they stood in the parking lot, staring at the expansive outlet mall. The place contained over seventy shops, and each one they could see had sale signs plastered in their windows.

"I've got two credit cards and my checkbook on me," Olivia told her as they began toward the mall. "Let's start at the beginning and just work our way down."

Tiffany looked at the massive outlet mall and added, "If we work the whole place, I may need to borrow one of those credit cards."

Olivia chuckled as they entered into the very first shop – a shoe store, and one of her favorites. Within, she tried on eleven pairs of shoes while Tiffany tried on seven. Even though Tiffany bought nothing, Olivia chose two pairs to purchase and began to feel a bit better. By the sixth store, she held two hands full of shopping bags and was fully elated. Before heading any further, they loaded their packages up in Tiffany's trunk and relaxed against the car for a bit.

"I can't believe you bought see-thru lacy panties," Tiffany told her as she lit a cigarette from her pack. Olivia hated the smell of smoke, but outside with the breeze blowing, she didn't mind it so much.

"Don't forget the matching bra," she said and snickered. "After last night's surprise hook-up, I decided my well worn pink cotton panties and sensible bras just aren't very sexy."

"Did he comment on your underwear?"

"No... but if I'd been wearing the red lacy ones I just got, I'm sure he would have." She shrugged and watched Tiffany smoke. "Besides, I had to throw last night's panties away. They got torn as he ripped them off my body."

Tiffany laughed so hard she dropped her cigarette to the wet ground and went into a coughing fit. Olivia joined her in the laugh.

"That cough comes from smoking too much," she pointed out.

"That cough comes from you cracking me the hell up!" Tiffany countered and then sighed pleasantly. "Tell me, dear friend. Did it hurt when he ripped your panties from your body?"

"Oh, yeah," she told her in an edgy sort of way. "It hurt oh so good!"

Tiffany cracked up again and Olivia joined her. After a moment of laughter, they caught their breath and resumed their shopping. By the time they were exhausted from it and had spent way too much money, they'd made it only through two thirds of the stores and decided to call it quits.

They filled up the rest of the trunk and then packed the backseat with their purchases. Then, they decided they were hungry again and hit up a small Mexican restaurant about a block from the mall. In the early evening hour, it wasn't as packed as the tea room and the burger joint had been, but there was still a twenty-minute wait for their food after they ordered. This gave them time to enjoy margaritas and chitchat about what they'd bought.

Tiffany went on and on about a crisp white pantsuit that she'd bought for work, but lamented over the fact that she hadn't found the right shoes to match it. Olivia pointed out that she had worn a pair of white pumps to work just last week, but Tiffany noted that high heels were not the most comfortable footwear in that office. Olivia quickly agreed.

"Don't they say 'fashion before comfort?'" she asked and sipped her drink.

"Screw that," Tiffany chided. "If that was the case, I would've dressed like a stuffy prim lady for that tea room."

Olivia smiled and sucked down the rest of her margarita. This was the second one she'd finished while waiting on their food, and she was ready for a third. Their server seemed to notice it too, and shortly after taking her glass, he brought her a fresh drink. He brought Tiffany a fresh one too, even though she wasn't done with her second one yet.

She was starting to feel tipsy, and while she enjoyed an occasional buzz, the lightheaded feeling reminded her of her mistake from last night. She hated that she considered her interlude with John as a mistake, and if he hadn't been with somebody else, she knew she'd have felt differently about it. Yet, the fact that he had a beautiful young woman in his life and had cheated on that girl with her made her feel miserable inside. For Tiffany's sake, she kept a smile on her face though, not wanting to ruin her friend's fun with more griping and carrying on about her misstep.

"I can literally see your brain working overtime," Tiffany told her as she finally finished her second drink and pulled the fresh one close. "You're thinking about *him* again, aren't you?"

Olivia sighed and shrugged. "Is it that obvious?"

"It's written all over your face. Come on, girl. Loosen up. Who cares if he cheated on his girlfriend, or his wife, or whatever the little harlot is? You got laid, and you said it was good. Enjoy that. Revel in it. I know I would be if I were in your shoes."

"You couldn't fit in my shoes," Olivia told her and chuckled.

"You do have big feet, but you know what I mean."

She did, and Tiffany was right. She had enjoyed the sex – much more than she'd enjoyed sex with the last few men she'd been with – and she needed to enjoy the memory of it and move on. But it didn't seem so easy to her. John had managed to find her emotional g-spot, whispering sweet nothings and beautiful compliments into her ear as they'd enjoyed their moment of erotic passion. He'd made her feel like a woman again, instead of the old maid that she'd begun to feel like.

At thirty-five, she found it ironic that she considered herself an old maid. Any magazine or lifestyle expert would have told her that she still had her best years ahead of her, but the truth of it was she was afraid of growing old alone. Even if she couldn't have John, she wanted somebody in her life – a man that would coddle her and love her and tell her she was beautiful even on days when she didn't feel like it. However, that man never seemed to come around, and when she felt like she might have found one, the situation blew up in her face.

The food arrived, and even though Tiffany ate heartily, Olivia noticed her appetite had abandoned her. She picked at her food and nursed her drink, but she felt like she was finally ready to claim her car and return home to her apartment, where she could change the sheets and lay in bed with the television on to numb her mind. Tiffany seemed to notice this, and when her meal was half through, she asked for their leftovers to be placed in takeout containers.

The server brought their freshly packed food to the table, along with the check. Tiffany reached for it, but Olivia snatched it away.

"Nope," she told her friend and took out a credit card. "You got the last one. This is on me."

"That was fast food," Tiffany countered. "I spent a whopping twelve bucks."

"I make more than you do."

Tiffany considered this and nodded. "You have a point."

Olivia paid the check, left a generous tip, and headed out to the car with her best friend at her side. She was thankful for Tiffany. The woman had done everything within her power to make her forget John and his woman today. Even if it hadn't worked, it was admirable.

"Ready to pick up your car?" Tiffany asked as they climbed into hers.

"Yeah... I'll need to transfer these packages over when we get to it," Olivia noted.

"I can't believe we bought so much stuff. It's like we were doing Christmas shopping, but for ourselves."

Olivia snickered. "That's the best kind of Christmas shopping."

"Agreed."

Traffic was heavy on this Saturday night, and they made it to the parking garage in just over a half an hour. As they turned into it, Olivia glanced across from it to the bar they'd been at last night. It was even more packed than it had been then, and she was thankful she was not inside there. She wondered if John was in there though, seeking out another dumb broad to whet his fleshy whistle. It wouldn't be her, she decided. She'd had enough of him, and for the moment, she was adamant to keep her distance from all men that she caught the eye of.

"You'll feel better in the morning," Tiffany told her. "The first day after an unexpected one-night stand is always the worst."

"I sure hope you're right."

They found Olivia's car and transferred her packages into the spacious trunk. Then, with a long hug, they bid each other goodbye. Once Tiffany's car was out of sight, Olivia finally cranked hers and pulled out of the space. At the gate, she paid the hefty fee for leaving the vehicle there for so long, but she didn't mind it. At least the parking attendant was just taking her money; not part of her soul.

She glared at the bar as she drove out of the garage, and she wished she could remember what John's car had looked like. But when they climbed into it, she'd been much too drunk to even notice the color of the vehicle. It didn't matter though. She was through with him, and he'd made it clear that he was through with her.

On her way home, she stopped by a liquor store and bought two bottles of red wine. They would help comfort her through the night, she decided. Then, she considered picking up a pizza, but she remembered her leftovers from the Mexican restaurant in the trunk with her packages. That would more than suffice.

At her building, she parked in her designated spot and popped the trunk. Looking into it, she became overwhelmed by the sheer amount of full shopping bags she'd accumulated while at the outlet mall. It was a ridiculous amount, and she imagined her credit card bill would be steep. Deciding to wait until tomorrow to unload it all, she grabbed only the leftovers and with them, the wine and her purse in tow, she locked up the car and walked to the front of the building.

There were a few tenants mingling in the lobby, most of whom she knew. They waved and smiled at her. She couldn't wave well with her hands full, but she smiled just the same – even though she didn't want to. Then, she faced the staircase that would lead her up to her third-floor dwelling. The building had an elevator, but she'd gotten stuck in it twice over the three years she'd lived there, and even though they'd insisted it was repaired and fully functioning, she didn't trust it. Thusly, she began up the stairs, hurrying as swiftly as she could while remaining cautious of her footing and conscious of the items she carried.

There was a door that opened to each floor, and when she faced the door to her floor, she had to set the wine down to open it. Once it was open, she picked up her wine and hurried through, letting it shut on its own behind her. Turning to the left, Olivia looked to her apartment door. There, she saw John sitting on the ground with his back against the door.

She nearly dropped everything then and there, as the shock of seeing him overwhelmed her with a world of various emotions. John noticed her immediately and hurried to his feet, smiling broadly at her image. He was still wearing the suit she'd seen him in at the tea room, and she wondered where his young lady was at.

"There you are!" he exclaimed brightly as she slowly – cautiously – approached. "I've been waiting here for a couple of hours now. I was almost ready to give up on you."

She began to fume as he spoke. How dare he show up at her apartment after leaving with nothing more than a quick scribble on a post-it note and having dined for lunch with another woman? She shook her head at his brazen arrogance.

"Aren't you going to say hello?" he asked her as she neared him. His smile was still there, but it seemed a little nervous now.

"I have nothing to say to you," she told him. He stepped aside as she set her wine and food down and sought her keys from her purse.

He looked at her with obvious confusion. "Did I do something wrong?"

"Ha!" she laughed and unlocked the door. Pushing it open, she gathered her things. "No. Not at all. You just did what every other jerk in the world does after a quick romp in the bed – left me alone with a quick thank you on a post-it and nothing more." Once inside, she looked back at him to see he was following her inside. "And then... went out with another woman!"

"Wait. What?" He shut the door behind him and stayed in that spot. "What are you talking about?"

Olivia placed her stuff on a table and turned to face him. "Don't treat me like an idiot, John. I saw you out with that other woman today, at the tea room. Who is she? Your girlfriend? Wife?"

She watched his smile grow again. The broader it got, the angrier it made her.

"I think there's been some sort of mix up here, Olivia," he protested and took a step toward her. She, in turn, took a step back and away from him. "Didn't you read my note?"

"Yeah!" she said. Her emotions were boiling within her. "I read it. 'Thanks! John.' Should I be impressed by that? Overwhelmed with gratitude that you thanked me for a one-night stand?"

"One-night stand? Olivia, I think you're missing something here. Come on. Let's go to your bedroom and we can figure this out."

She laughed again, even though there was no humor in its tone. "You've got balls, that's for sure. What's wrong? Couldn't that floozy at the tea room get your rocks off? You had to come back here for round two?"

John cocked an eyebrow, but he was still smiling. He walked toward her again, and then he walked on by her, heading toward her bedroom door. She watched through exasperated eyes as he opened the door, turned on the light, and stepped inside.

"Hey!" she called, following after him. "I didn't say you could go in there."

In the room, she found John standing beside her bed. He waited until she was closer and then pulled the sheet back a little on the side he'd been on. There, she saw two more yellow post-it notes.

27

"These must have gotten scattered as you slept," he said, taking the notes and handing them to her. "I didn't account for that. I should have left them on the table."

Still angry but now curious, she snatched the notes from him and read them. They were apparently the first two of three notes meant for her – the last one being the one where he'd thanked her and signed his name. On the first note, John explained that his sister was getting married today and he was taking her to lunch at the tea room before the service at three. The second note had his phone number with instructions for her to call her if anything came up. It also notified her that he'd be back after the reception.

Mortified, she let the notes slip from her fingers to the floor. Then, with panicked eyes and a slack jaw, she looked up at him. Now, she was more embarrassed than ever. John had been a true gentleman in his note – a note that had gotten lost between the sheets.

"I tried to wake you up and explain everything to you," he continued softly, "but you were out like a light. I figured you'd see the note when you woke up, and everything would be fine."

She was speechless, even though there were a million things to say rushing through her mind. John's smile widened a little and he approached her, putting his strong hands gently atop her shoulders.

"I'm sorry if you thought I was trying to be a player and use you for a one-night stand," he told her, massaging her shoulders to help loosen her up and relax her. "I wouldn't do that... not to you. I really like you, Olivia. I'd planned to spend the whole evening with you, getting to know you better."

"You – you like me?" she asked and wondered if she sounded ridiculous saying it.

He chuckled. "Of course, I do. I mean... wow! I had the best night of my life with you. I've been single for a long time now, and when I found you, I thought I'd struck gold. You're beautiful, funny, and sexy as hell."

"You think I'm sexy?" She couldn't believe her ears. No one – not one man she'd ever been with – had called her sexy before. It was a word she thought she'd never hear... at least, a word that she thought would never be meant for her.

"Incredibly sexy," he concluded. "The way you smell... the way you feel... the way you taste. I couldn't believe my luck when we met last night. It was the most perfect, passionate night of my life. All I've done today is crave you."

"I'm sorry you didn't see the rest of my note. Can you forgive me for leaving when and how I did?"

She stared into his stunning blue eyes and saw the hope and honesty that lay within them. Then, in lieu of a verbal reply, she put her hands to his chest and pushed him backward. John collapsed atop her bed with a soft thump. Olivia wasted no time as she joined him, climbing on top of him and straddling him. Sitting atop his lap, she leaned forward and placed her hands on either side of him. Then, she lowered her face to his so that their noses were only inches apart.

"Forgive you?" she asked in a breathy tone. "I'm ready to fuck your brains out."

John was about to reply, but she pressed her lips to his and kissed him with such intensity that she felt that familiar wetness build between her thighs again. He instantly fell into the kiss, letting their tongues connect and gently wrestle against one another. She felt him wrap his arms around her and pull her close, so that their bodies were like one. Even with his slacks and her jeans forming a barrier between them, she could feel his manhood growing and pressing against her.

Suddenly, John rolled her onto her back and pressed his weight against her, continuing the kiss. His tongue unlatched itself from hers and his lips began to work their way down her chin and onto her neck, where he focused his attention for a long moment. As he kissed her, he pulled his hands between them and began to unbutton her shirt. He broke the kissing long enough to spread her shirt open, and then he resumed kissing her, working his lips over her chest and the areas of her breasts that were exposed from her bra.

Olivia gasped as she felt him slide down her, kissing his way down to her belly and focusing on that area as he unzipped and unbuttoned her jeans. She lifted her hips as he started to tug them down. John stood long enough to pull them from her body and toss them to the floor. Then, he lowered himself onto his knees and wrapped his fingers around her pink cotton panties. Olivia propped herself up on her elbows and looked down at him. He locked eyes with her and smiled as he worked her underwear off and pulled them from his body.

He looked down at her pubic mound and then back into her eyes. "You trimmed up."

She smiled. "Do you like it?"

"Sure, but I didn't mind it before. I like a wild woman." He grinned mischievously and then lifted her legs, propping them onto his shoulders. He stared at her womanhood for a nice long moment and then pressed his thumb into her clit. She shuddered and gasped from the pressure. His touch was electrifying.

Lowering her head down to the bed, she closed her eyes and took a sharp breath as he began to tease her with his thumb, causing her heated wetness to grow.

"You're so beautiful," he whispered and then removed his thumb. Before she could open her eyes and look at him again, she felt his tongue replace his thumb as he took a deep, long lick up her slit. She could feel his tongue lap at her wetness, and a moan fell from her as he began to lick more heartily. His tongue flicked over her clitoris at a swift repetitive pace – a skill that other men she'd been with lacked severely.

She felt her hips begin to buck as she pushed herself toward him with each lick he took. When he paused, she relaxed a little, yearning for more. His tongue was replaced by his lips. They wrapped around her clit and began to suckle it.

Olivia's moan turned hoarse as he pleasured her. She crossed her ankles behind his neck, holding his face against her, allowing him to feast on her until he'd had his fill. She heard the sound of his zipper lower and realized his slacks had likely grown much too tight in the crotch for him to remain comfortable. Still, he didn't pause for even a second in pleasuring her. He feasted on her until her hoarse moans turned to gasps for air and finally a scream that arrived with the most intense orgasm she'd ever experienced. Throughout her orgasm, John continued his feast, ensuring none of her juices went to waste.

Eventually, she couldn't take it anymore. The electricity was much too intense. She unwrapped her feet from behind him and allowed him to come up for air. When he lifted his head, she looked at him through feverish and lusty eyes. He was still smiling – a smile that glistened with moist stickiness.

She lowered her legs onto the bed and watched as he shrugged his coat to the floor and undid his necktie. He left it around his collar as he unbuttoned his shirt and cuffs. Then, he pulled his shirt away, revealing his rippling muscles, delicious pecs, and impressive abs as he threw the shirt to the floor.

He seemed weak in the knees as he stood. She understood. After her orgasm, she felt weak all over. But as he stood and she saw his marvelous erection staring at her, she somehow felt reenergized. She stared at it for a long moment as John unbuckled and pulled free his belt, tossing it to wherever his shirt had landed. His pants and boxer shorts swiftly followed. Then, standing naked in front of her like a perfectly chiseled masterpiece, he licked his lips and winked.

"Don't just stand there," she told him and brought her knees up and parted them. With her womanhood exposed and ready for him, she added, "Come inside and play."

John needed no further invitation, and as he lowered himself down onto her, he slid inside of her welcoming entry way, filling her with every inch he had to offer. His lips landed against her and she wrapped her legs around his lower back, holding him in place inside of her.

He broke the kiss long enough to whisper, "You're everything I've ever wanted," and then he kissed her deeper than before.

She wanted to tell him that the feeling was mutual, but as he began to softly buck into her, she could mutter no words. Instead, she focused her attention on his kiss and on the blue eyes that were not closed but stared intently into her hazel orbs.

They spent several minutes in this position until John couldn't stand the pleasure any further. He pulled out of her in the nick of time and exploded across her stomach. With every burst, he gasped and moaned, twitching through his orgasm but never once breaking eye contact. She thought he was absolutely beautiful as he orgasmed. His smile seemed both sinful and angelic. He hadn't needed to handle himself as he reached his brink, showing Olivia that she was all the turn-on he needed. When he was done, he reentered her and pressed his stomach against hers, smoothing his juices between them.

He leaned forward to kiss her again, but she stopped him with a question.

"Can I ask... what's your last name, John?"

"Gunner," he told her with an almost animalistic tone.

Jonathan Gunner... It was perhaps the sexiest name she'd ever heard, and it belonged to the sexiest man she could have ever imagined. She grinned a smile large enough to match his and tightened the grip of her legs around his waist, holding him deep inside of him.

"Well, Mister Gunner... are you ready for round two?"

"Round two?" he asked and chuckled lightly. "Baby, we're just getting started."

She inhaled and took in his sensual and masculine scent. Then, she held on tight as he took her on the ride of her life – a ride that last deep into the night until the first rays of the sun began to light the world outside.

When their passion was exhausted and John drifted off to sleep beside her, Olivia kept her eyes on him, studying him... memorizing every inch of him that she could see in the dimness of her room. At seven, she stood and left the bedroom, entering the kitchen and making coffee. She drank a hot cup of black brew and checked the morning's headlines on the news apps on her phone. Then, she reentered the bedroom, finding John was right where she left him – slumbering between the sheets.

Utilizing her phone's app, she took a photo of him. It showed his rippling torso, muscular arms, and his sweet sleeping face. Then, she texted the photo to Tiffany with the caption: "Let's do a late lunch. I have a lot to tell you about." Once the text was sent, she climbed back into bed, rested her head against him, and felt his arm slip around her pulling her close. Even in his sleep, he was warm and considerate.

There, she finally drifted off to sleep, knowing without a doubt that this time when she awoke, he would be right there beside her... and he was.

### *End*

# *The Room Next Door*

If there was one thing Rebecca hated more than traveling for work, it was having to stay in various locations for several weeks to months. Her job allowed her to see all parts of the country – areas she never would have visited before – but it also kept her away from her home and family and thwarted her from finding a lasting relationship.

Because of this and so much more, she was bitter toward her work. Her job was to scout locations for new casinos and to stay in the towns from the start of development until the end of opening week. It had helped to make her a hardened woman over the years, but it was that hardness about her that her employers loved. It kept her on edge, on focus, and intolerant of mistakes or misbehavior at their properties. This made her an asset to a company that she wished she could afford to leave.

There were other jobs, she knew. Jobs that paid better, offered more benefits, had grander retirement packages... The problem with those jobs was that the work would be no less. If she took one of them doing the same thing she did now, she would remain in the same unhappy and bitter boat. Sure, she'd be able to reap the rewards, but she had seniority where she was at, and in a few more years – a few *long* more years – she would be able to hang up her development hat and be promoted to a nice cushy office job with a lot less work and more at home time. It was what she'd been working for, and it was currently why she was in this nowhere town of Sinclair.

It was her job to turn Sinclair into the new 'it' location for tourists and gamblers. She'd succeeded in doing this with other small nothing locations, and she knew she could do it again. She'd been here for fourteen weeks now, had purchased enough adjoining properties to build three hotels, two casinos, and a decent sized theme park. With their developments finally finished, all she had left to do was ensure the new staffs were well trained and that everything ran smoothly for the big extravagant grand opening and ribbon cutting that her employers enjoyed so much.

With any luck, she'd be out of here in less than two more weeks.

At most of her locations, she was housed in either a bed and breakfast or in a tiny rental house that she could call her own. On occasion, one town or another would have a decent hotel – usually 'historic' – that she could comfortably call her home with housekeepers to keep it tidy for her. In Sinclair, there were none of those options.

Well... there *was* a motel, and it was currently her newest short-term residence. It was called Sin Motel, and she despised the name nearly as much as she despised the dirty and ill-repaired room that she was holed up in. There were eleven guest rooms at the roadside dump, and they each had their own 'nifty' exterior entrance. During the weeks she'd been there, she'd seen 'guests' come and go plenty. More often than not, the people who checked into the rooms left a few hours after, having properly pleased each other or made some horrible drug deal during that time. There were three rooms, other than hers, that had long-term guests in them. One was the elderly parents of the motel's owner, Skip Weston. One was occupied by a disgraced husband who was on the outs with his wife, in a broken marriage that showed no signs of reconciliation. The third was the home of the motel's housekeeper Matilda. Of the three long-term rentals, she'd met only Matilda, and the housekeeper was the source of her knowledge for the other two rooms and their occupants.

Matilda cleaned each room three times a week, and she changed the sheets only twice a week – or after every nightly 'wham-bam' had checked out. She was a gossipy woman who looked rough and always smelled like cigarettes and bourbon, but in a way, Rebecca liked her. She was her only friend in this place, if she could be considered a friend. Perhaps 'acquaintance' was more appropriate, but after a while, 'friend' rolled more easily off the tongue.

Once thing she didn't quite understand was Matilda's obsession with her boss Skip. The housekeeper was maybe thirty… thirty-five, and on the few days Rebecca had seen her with combed hair and make-up, she'd been almost lovely. Skip, on the other hand, was a pig. He was fat, loud, smelled bad, was missing most of his teeth, picked his nose, farted when he walked, and had nothing good to say about anyone. He was forty going on asshole-ity.

Sin Motel was by far her least favorite aspect of Sinclair, and she wondered how it had managed to stay in business. Surely, it had to undergo county health department inspections, but she'd never seen an inspector on the property, and one was certainly needed. When Rebecca checked into her room, the first thing she found was a used condom on her pillow. Obviously, Matilda had not yet cleaned the room. When she called the lobby to report it, Skip had simply asked, "Well, did ya thrown the damn thing away?"

Rebecca had, indeed, thrown the condom away, along with the pillow that it had been stuck to. She drove immediately to the nearest department store and purchased three brand new pillows, four new sets of sheets, three new blankets, six new towels, six matching washcloths, and a DVD player, since the television operated on broken rabbit ears and picked up absolutely no stations.

Currently, it was seven at night and Rebecca lay top her bed watching a DVD of 'Never Been Kissed.' It was one of her favorite movies over all, and it was definitely her favorite Drew Barrymore flick. Few people knew of Rebecca's love for romantic comedies, as she kept it a secret from practically everyone. She couldn't ruin her tough boss reputation, after all. It was at her favorite scene – the climax of the movie – where Drew's character is standing on the ball field, waiting nervously for the love of her life to show up and forgive her. The first time she saw this scene, she broke into tears when the adorable Michael Vartan finally showed up to give Drew her 'first real kiss.' The second time she watched it, she cried even harder. Now, as she waited for him to show, she felt herself verging on tears once again.

From the room on the other side of the wall, right behind her head, she heard a man yell. Rebecca jolted upright off of her pillow and hurried to her feet, pausing the film as she did. That room had been empty for as long as she'd been here, and the sudden shout made her wary. With the movie silenced, she listened intently for another sound, another shout – another crying out from the room, but everything was quiet.

Perhaps, she thought, it was her imagination. She'd been working long hours for a while now, and she'd had little sleep to compensate for it. There was also the fact that this was the third night in a row she'd eaten fried food from the diner down the road. They had, she believed, the absolute worst food she'd ever eaten, but it was close and convenient, and at the end of a hard and long day, that seemed to be what counted more than the quality.

Settling back down onto the bed, she took the remote again to restart her film when she heard the same man's voice curse loudly. It was coming from right behind her, where the bed in the room next door would have been positioned. He sounded pained and in trouble, and this time, she knew she wasn't imagining things.

Rebecca hurried out of the room, throwing forward the

metal brace lock so the door wouldn't completely shut behind her. Then, she stepped down a few feet to the next door, where the curtains were half open. She wasn't sure if she should bang on the door, see if it was unlocked and barge in, or double check to make sure her imagination wasn't in overdrive. After a brief moment of pondering, she chose the third option and went to the window.

Peering in, she had to squint to see into the room's dim lighting. On the bed, she saw the source of the noise. It was indeed a man, even though she couldn't see his face. What she could see threw her for a surprised loop. He was lying naked upon the bed, masturbating ferociously. His body was twitching and convulsing through the actions, and she covered her surprised mouth with a hand as she heard him cry out again. With this cry, he began to orgasm, and hurriedly, she looked away.

"Oh… my lord…" she whispered to herself and was tempted to peek back into the window. Instead, she let a giggle slip out and went back to her own room, shutting and locking the door behind her – the image of what she'd seen burned into her mind.

Somehow, by the sound of his cries, she'd expected him to have been in mortal danger, but she'd been wrong. The man was alone in his room, whacking off, and being as loud as he could be about it. She could still hear him moan and grunt through his orgasm, and it made her giggle once again.

Eventually, his orgasmic tones silenced, and when she was certain he was done, she turned her movie back on. She was no longer teary-eyed, but seeing Drew and Michael kiss on that

ballfield still warmed her heart and gave her hope for true love –
just as it always did. When the movie ended, she put the DVD
back in its case and slipped 'There's Something About Mary' into
the player.

The movie was great – another of her favorites – but when
it reached the scene where Ben Stiller masturbated before his day
and Cameron Diaz met him at the door while he had his load
oozing from his hair onto his shoulder, she had to turn it off. After
what she'd witness through the window next door, it was way too
close to real life now. She could just imagine what would have
happened had she chosen to knock on the door while her new
neighbor was in the midst of his orgasm. Would the situation have
been similar? Would he have opened it, dripping with semen?

Unlike Cameron's character, Rebecca knew she wouldn't
have mistaken it for hair gel. Then again, she *had* mistaken the
sounds of a man in sexual ecstasy for one who was pained and in
trouble…

Once more, Rebecca let a snickered giggle slip out. At the
very least, her new neighbor had helped take her mind off of work
and this nightmare of a town.

With no more sounds coming from next door to disturb her
or to fill her mind with thoughts of humorous manly masturbation,
she popped in a DVD of Hitchcock's 'Rebecca' based on her
favorite novel by Daphne Du Maurier. It was also that Rebecca
that she'd been named for. The movie and film had also been a
favorite of her mother, who watched it every chance she could and

read it even more.

Halfway through, she dozed off, and when she awoke, it was do the drum roll alarm that always started her day.

She showered and dressed, choosing a black and white pinstriped suit with a ruffled collar white shirt and no tie. With it, she wore spiked black heels that helped give her the appearance of a hard and ruthless business woman. She wore no jewelry and only the most basic of make-up. Yesterday, she'd worn a similar suit but it had been navy blue, and her handbag had matched. Quickly, she transferred that bag's contents into her black clutch.

Opening her door, she wondered about breakfast and if she was even hungry. She didn't feel hungry, but she needed coffee. The coffee in the motel's raggedy lobby tasted like hot colored water to her, but she somehow felt that hot colored water still would have been stronger.

Rebecca ensured the room key was in her clutch and she closed the door, hearing it click and lock behind her. Even though the door required an old fashioned clunky key instead of one of the more modern key cards, it still locked automatically every time it shut. While inside, she could open it freely without the key, but when outside, a key was required. It was the only bit of security this place provided.

She got into her rental car and headed to the crappy diner with the greasy fried foods. Their breakfast wasn't much better than their other meals, but their coffee was fresh, black and strong – just how she liked it. Inside, she went to a far corner booth and sat by the window, looking out at the tiny town of Sinclair. Directly across from her were a hardware store, a pharmacy, and a post office – all in a connected strip of buildings. It wasn't much of a view, but it was what was there.

"Why, hello again," said the waitress – a middle-aged woman just a few years older than Rebecca. Her name was Wendy, and she'd been her waitress every time she'd come in during the morning shift. "You've been in town so long now, I'm surprised you haven't just bought a house and moved right in."

Rebecca outwardly cringed at the statement. "Please," she said and then sighed. "It's much too early for jokes. Can I get a cup of hot coffee, black, no sweetener, and one of those muffins like I got the other day?"

Wendy ignored the comment about her statement being a joke. Either it had gone right over her head, or she just refused to acknowledge it. Instead, she told her, "The muffins are long gone, but how about a piece or two of French toast?" She smiled wide. It was a sweet smile, but without coffee in her, it irritated Rebecca.

"Coffee and a piece of dry toast then," she replied. "I'm not very hungry yet."

Wendy jotted down the order. "When is that new park going to open?" she asked as she wrote. Then, looking at Rebecca, she added, "I'm not too thrilled about the casinos, but an amusement park would be fun."

"Tuesday of next week," she told her, "and a few days after that, I'm out of here and back home for a bit before they send me off to somewhere else."

Leaning forward, Wendy said in a hushed tone, "Skip will be glad you're gone, but don't tell him I told you. You just built some really big competition for his little motel."

"That motel is an absolute dump," she replied, not hushing her tone in the least. "Skip should be ashamed of it. Hell, this whole town should be ashamed of it."

Wendy cocked an eyebrow and left the table to put in the order.

A few minutes later, the coffee came just as she liked it, but the toast was smeared with melting butter. Rebecca already felt bloated and like she was gaining weight from the poor food choices this place had to offer; it was why she'd ordered her toast dry. Yet, Wendy gave her no chance to rebuke it as she instantly went to attend to another table of costumers – the local 'Liar's Club' as they proudly called themselves.

Nonetheless, she ate the toast and had to admit that it was better than dried hard bread. She sipped her coffee lightly until it cooled a bit, and then she drank heavily, finishing it in a matter of a few large sips. When Wendy passed by again, she ordered a refill, and once that was gone, she purchased a cup of it to go.

Her first stop of the day was to the freshly built training center that handled each of the casino's new employees, to check on their training. So far, everything had been going smoothly, but the locals were not exceptionally quick to pick up on new things. There had been a steep learning curve for them, and while Rebecca had little patience for the people around here, the trainers from corporate practiced patience as if it was the rule of the game. Now, as she peeked into the massive warehouse and observed the group of nearly a hundred new trainees and their coaches, she saw they were still progressing well. In fact, they seemed to be catching onto everything much better than the last time she looked in on them.

"Are they about ready?" she asked one of the trainers as she observed from the back of the room.

"About as ready as they'll ever be," he told her. "None of them are exceptionally bright, mind you, but they're all eager to learn, and everything's sinking in now. They'll be set by the grand opening."

"I hope so," she whispered and eyed the seated crowd as they endured a lecture. "The last thing I want is to remain here any longer than I absolutely have to."

"Have they told you where you'll be going next?"

She rolled her eyes. "They never do, but I sure hope it's somewhere a bigger than Sinclair... or an island. I'd be content with an island."

The trainer chuckled. "Wouldn't we all?"

She stayed in the training center long enough to go over the paperwork for the latest hires. Then, she took her daily tour of the casinos. Everything was falling into place beautifully, and a lot better and faster than she'd expected.

The same could not be said for the three hotels. None of

them had received beds for the guest rooms yet, nor had they received their computer equipment with the networked programs that were required to complete the staffs' training. On the basic trainings, they'd been taught everything else they could have possibly needed to know. Company policies, rewards policies, housekeeping standards, maintenance procedures, safety regulations... Uniforms were in place. The kitchen staffs were trained on the offerings. Bellhops had been trained on how to address and handle guests. Bartenders had been retrained for the industry standards...

Yet, without beds or a computer system to check guests in and out through, all three properties were missing the two essentials needed to operate. Rebecca had learned from her home office that each property was nearly at full capacity, but the reservations had been taken through the toll free line or over the internet. The properties themselves couldn't receive them and prepare until the computers were there.

So, she got on the phone. First, she called the company in charge of the computers, insisting they were due at the properties two weeks ago and informing the man on the other line that this was her third call and the final one before she flew over to their location and started castrating everyone in sight. The man put her on hold for nearly twenty minutes, and when he returned, he informed her that they were, indeed, on their way to Sinclair and would arrive by morning. A tracking number he provided to her confirmed this as she checked it on her phone. She ended the call with him abruptly and then dialed the number for where they'd ordered the beds.

"It was a huge order you gave us," the woman who answered said. "We're trying our best to get them all to you this week, but please have patience."

"I had patience," Rebecca replied, "a month ago when I put the order in. That patience is gone. Now, I just have anxiety, as we're scheduled to open in just over a week, and at full capacity."

"Let me see if I can work a little magic," the woman told her. Rebecca could hear her typing on a keyboard. "I see the processing is nearly complete. If I rush freight the order, they can be to you by Friday."

"Please see that they are," she informed her, "otherwise, this contract will be null and void, and my company will look into other suppliers for these three hotels."

When she hung up the phone, she was fuming. She called her corporate office and gave her boss a breakdown of the shit-storm happening around her. He told her to calm down and that he'd make a few calls and make sure everything was there and in place by the end of the week. He also informed her that the new manager for the amusement park had called him, wondering why she wasn't at their scheduled meeting an hour ago.

"Are you kidding me?" she spat. "Does he have *any* idea what the hell I've been going through today?"

"Apparently not. He'll be there all day though. Go see him when you finish up what you're doing."

Rebecca groaned and ended the call. Fortunately, the bar in this hotel was already fully stocked, and she helped herself to a shot of whiskey before leaving.

The amusement park was somewhat of a godsend after the trials and tribulations of the hotels. It was humorously named Sinclair City as homage to the town – something she hoped the locals would appreciate. As she looked at the large sign at the entrance, she thought of Skip and his naming of Sin Motel, which she thought was in poor taste. Even so, she had to admit it fit the majority of his clientele.

Most of the rides were up, ready, and functioning. The Ferris wheel spun as the attendant made a few adjustments. The roller coaster was at the track and ready to go; all it needed was patrons. There were booths of fun and games that would appease those old and young alike. There was also a carnival themed restaurant, as well as a few food stands located strategically around the park. The animals for the petting zoo hadn't been delivered yet, but the veterinarian on the site told her they would be in Saturday and assured her it was plenty of time for them to get used to their new surroundings.

At the park's main office, she introduced herself to the receptionist, gave her one of her cards, and asked to see the new manager.

"I know I'm late, but my job is hell and today was like dipping my toes into lava at the hotels," she explained.

The receptionist smiled. "It's quite alright. Mr. Davidson is on a call at the moment, but I'll let him know you're here, Miss Thorne."

"Thank you." She took a seat on one of the black cushioned waiting chairs that she'd ordered, thankful to see they'd arrived. Rebecca hoped there wouldn't be any major issues with this meeting – at least, not like the problems that had come up at the hotels. She wanted that sort of nightmare to be over for the day.

Her wait was around ten minutes, but it allowed her a chance to just sit and stop. At first, all she could think about were the day's problems and successes, but then she forced her mind away from matters of work. The thoughts about her movies – the ones she'd watched last night. She wished she'd finished 'Rebecca' even though she knew precisely how it ended.

Then, her mind drifted to 'There's Something About Mary' and to the 'hair gel' incident where she'd stopped the film. It brought back memories of what she'd seen in her neighbor's motel room window – only his lower torso laying on the bed as he whacked himself off into an explosive orgasm. The vivid and visual memory of it made her smile, although she didn't laugh this time... not in front of this sweet and somewhat elderly appearing receptionist.

The end of her wait was signaled by the receptionist's announcement that, "Mr. Davidson will see you now, Miss Thorne."

She stood and thanked the woman, and then stepped around the counter and through the door to his office.

Mr. Davidson stood to greet her, but he was not one of the people that Rebecca had hired, and this was their first meeting. Normally, she would have already known the management over one of her properties. If she had known this one, she would have already drooled over him.

He stood nicely over six feet tall with a sharp black suit, a crisp white shirt, and a black tie to match. His dark hair was slicked back and perfectly in place, and his sly brown eyes were intriguing but friendly. He had a smile that could have made any single woman – or married one at that – fawn over, and when he shook his hand, she felt his strength. To all degrees, he was handsome and rather debonair. He reminded her a little of an old Hollywood actor, back when actors had great looks, better wardrobes, courtesy and kindness.

"Miss Thorne," he said as the contact broke. Her toes curled when he said her name. His voice was deep and almost seductive. "It's a pleasure to meet you finally. I've heard many great things about you."

She, in turn, had heard absolutely nothing about him, except that he'd been hired from another theme park and had moved to this horrible little town just for this management position, which she knew offered great benefits and a fat paycheck.

"The pleasure is all mine," she replied, believing it to be the truth. She was grinning from ear to ear, and she couldn't break her eyes away from his gaze.

"Please, have a seat."

Even though his eyes left her as he took his seat, she kept hers locked on him as she took hers. Now, face to face with the desk between them, she wondered if her grin looked as silly as it felt.

There was much paperwork spread out on the desk, and Mr. Davidson wasted no time delving into them. He talked about projected sales, the total number of hires and their salaries, the budgets for foods, supplies, gift shop items, and animal and equipment upkeep, and he had the most detailed spreadsheets she'd ever seen.

Despite all of this, she found it hard to focus. They leaned in toward one another to look over the paperwork, and when that happened, she could smell him. He had the most deliciously manly scent she'd ever whiffed, and it made her head float above the stars. It was all she could focus on, and his words were nothing but background noise while she pretended to listen to everything he told her.

"In other words," he said as he placed the paperwork back into their folders and stacked them neatly on a corner of the desk, "we're in shipshape condition and more than ready for opening day."

"How – how long have you been in town?" she questioned. She knew it wasn't a response he'd expected, nor had she meant to ask it. She just… wanted to know.

Looking at his watch, he smiled. "Around twenty hours now, I guess," he said and grinned. She loved the way he grinned.

His eyes met hers again and she crossed her legs. "Not long, I guess. I've been working on all of this for weeks remotely while I settled my affairs in Orlando. This town will take some adjusting to. That's for sure. I've never lived somewhere so small."

"There is definitely a lot to be desired here," she agreed. "The only place with decent coffee is the diner, but that's about all that's good there... unless you want a ton of grease in your system."

He chuckled and folded his hands. "I'm vegan, so I'm sure it will be even harder for me to sustain my diet here. As for coffee, I've got a pot set up in the employee kitchen here. The coffee's the best on earth, ground from organic beans. Would you care for a cup?"

While a cup of *real* coffee sounded wonderful, and spending more time with him sounded even more so, Rebecca noticed the clock on the wall behind him and saw it was already nearing four o'clock. If she had more coffee now, she'd assuredly be up half the night. Thusly, she declined the offer.

"That sounds great," she said and stood from her chair, "but I really must be going. I have to go back to my office and journal today's meetings, and that'll take at least an hour. After that, I think I just want to go back to my room, kick my feet up, and relax."

"I understand," he told her and stood. His hand extended for another shake, and she accepted it. When she did, she noticed the lack of a wedding ring, or even a tan line from where one would have been. "Will I see you again tomorrow?"

Those were the words she *loved* to hear from a sexy man. Unfortunately, she knew this one didn't mean it in a romantic way. Still, she answered, "I'll make an effort to meet with you again tomorrow. You can bet on it."

His grin widened. Her heart fluttered. "I'm looking forward to it."

"As am I, Mr. Davidson."

"Please... call me Benjamin. Mr. Davidson is much too formal."

She considered his name and thought of how studious and alluring it sounded. "As long as you call me Rebecca, we have a deal."

"It's been a pleasure to meet you, Rebecca."

He broke the handshake and remained standing as she backed up from the desk and walked toward the door. Only when she reached behind her and felt the knob did she actually turn around to open it. As she stepped out and shut the door behind her, she wished she'd taken him up on the coffee offer.

"There's always tomorrow," she whispered.

She bid goodbye to the receptionist and stepped outside. The sun was bright and she had to squint, but she didn't mind. She was suddenly elated – a feeling she had desperately needed after the problems with the hotels. As she walked across the grounds, she noticed that she couldn't shake Benjamin Davidson from her mind. It had been quite a long time since a man had had this effect on her. It made her feel like more than just a corporate bully. It made her feel like a woman again.

In the small trailer that served as her office, just beyond the training center, she finished her journaling and the day's paperwork but found it hard to focus. Benjamin remained on her mind throughout it, and when she finally made it back to her dump of a motel room, she took her second shower for the day. It allowed her to cleanse away the negativity from the hotels' missing supplies, and it gave her the opportunity to pleasure herself with thoughts of Benjamin and what he'd do with her if she was his.

Restraining herself from screaming through the orgasm that was induced by her fantasy had been a chore, but she had learned from the guy in the room next door precisely how thin these walls truly were. If anything, she neither wanted to draw his attention with sounds of urgency like he had done to her, nor did she want to provide him with mental stimulation to help with his next wanking session.

She dried and dressed in her comfiest pajamas and considered rewatching 'Rebecca' on the television – not picking up where she fell asleep at, but starting it over from the beginning. Instead, as she sat down on her bed and then kicked her feet up, her head hit the pillow and she felt the long hours of the day and the drama over the beds and computers wash over her. Suddenly exhausted, she closed her eyes and drifted off to sleep.

"Ahh... yeah...!" the loud moan from behind the wall sounded and instantly awoke her. Rebecca's eyes opened quickly as she tried to place the sound, but it was distinct, and she remembered it from yesterday. "God... uhh...!"

He was at it again... the man in the room next door. She could hear the squeaking of his bed and the headboard grinding against the wall as he 'worked his magic' and toyed with his wand. Yesterday, she had giggled at the action. Tonight, it irritated her. Looking over at her phone beside the bed, she saw it was just after eleven p.m. She had been sound asleep and, even though she couldn't remember it, she was certain she'd been dreaming something wonderful.

Finally, the man in the next room screamed out a harsh and somewhat violent grunt, and whatever motions his orgasm was putting him through caused his headboard to slam with such force against the wall that it made the large framed print above her bed tilt and rattle.

"A boy's best friend is his hand," she muttered, playing off a line from Hitchcock's 'Psycho' – another of her favorite classic films by the master of suspense.

Now that she was awake, she felt the need to relieve her bladder. By the time she made it back to her bed and straightened the framed print above it, she grabbed the remotes and made herself comfortable. She finally started 'Rebecca' from the beginning like she'd earlier considered, and before she dozed off for a second time, she finished it.

Her sleep from that point was somewhat restless. She awoke a good forty minutes before her alarm was scheduled, and she went ahead and showered and readied herself for the day instead of just lying in bed like she'd wanted to. Remembering that she was to stop by and 'check in' on Benjamin Davidson again today, she decided to dress like a lady. So, she wore a white flowing dress with yellow and blue flowers speckled here and there, and a pair of comfortable white flats. This was one of only three dresses she'd brought with her, as her lifestyle rarely required them.

She took a little extra time with her hair and make-up as well, and to top off her look, she wore the pearl earrings and matching necklace that she'd inherited after her mother died. Looking in the mirror, she thought she did indeed look like a lady – and a lovely one at that.

Rebecca transferred the items from her black clutch to a padded white purse with a long shoulder strap, grabbed her keys and the room key, and headed out early. She considered stopping for coffee at the diner again, but this time she decided to try out Benjamin's organic brew at his office.

As she walked to her car and climbed in, she noticed the door beside hers open. Curiously, she paused and watched. She'd wondered what this heavy-voiced masturbator had looked like, and as he stepped out of his room, she felt her body flush and thought she would faint.

It was Benjamin Davidson, dressed for his day at the amusement park. It had been him that she'd heard masturbating behind her bed... him that she had watched ejaculate through the view of his window.

Suddenly, she felt more than flushed; she felt panicked. She had parked four spaces away from the car he was headed to, and thankfully he did not look her way. Frantically, she cranked her rental car and pulled out of the parking space. Then, with rather reckless speed, she hurried out of the lot and onto the street, causing some trucker to honk loudly at her as she darted carelessly in front of him.

Rebecca didn't care about the trucker or her speed; not right then. In fact, her panicked emotions turned and twisted on her, and suddenly, she was absolutely mortified. The man that she had the hots for... that had gotten her all worked up yesterday... Well, there was little left to the imagination anymore. Even though her view had been somewhat obstructed, she'd already seen his penis, and what came out of it. Granted, he'd had both hands around it at the time, double-fisting it as he brought himself to orgasm. Plus, there was the fact that he'd had on pants, so *everything* hadn't been seen. However, she knew precisely what he sounded like when he reached orgasm, and she knew exactly how hard and intense those orgasms were.

"No!" she cried out and slammed her hand against the dashboard. "This sucks! This *really really* sucks!"

She tried to control herself by taking into account that she couldn't blame him for masturbating. She'd done it last night in the shower, and many other times since finding herself mostly secluded in this small and rather worthless town. But Benjamin had been a new fantasy for her. She was attracted to him, and she had fantasized about him being this calm and sensual lover who knew how to treat her with love and respect – not as a man who banged one out as ferociously as he could.

Eventually, she decided against joining him for coffee and went to the diner instead. There, she placed her order to Wendy, asking for a giant stack of pancakes, slathered with butter and syrup and bacon between each cake. It was by far the most fattening thing she'd eaten in years, and she devoured every bite of it, trying to cool her emotions with a comfort food that had actually tasted better in her mouth than it had in her mind while ordering it.

Just as she finished it, her phone rang in her purse. Retrieving it, she saw it was her boss and answered.

"Yes?" she asked in lieu of a greeting.

"Hope I didn't catch you at a bad time," he said. His voice sounded somewhat excited. "I have good news. I pulled some strings and the beds and computers will all be there by two o'clock today. It took a miracle to work it out, but they're in route to you now."

"That's wonderful!" she exclaimed and was suddenly grateful for this new distraction that would keep her from having to keep her promised meeting with Benjamin.

"By the way, what did you think of the new manager for the amusement park?" Boom! Happy bubble shattered. "He's something, isn't he? First rate!"

"Yeah…" she muttered while still trying to show some

enthusiasm. "He's really good at those books."

"You sound tired," her boss continued, "but I know you've been working your fingers to the bone on this project. I probably shouldn't say anything, but I heard a rumor..."

Once more, her interest was piqued. "A rumor?"

"Yes... if this grand opening pulls off without a hitch, the people upstairs say they're going to promote you early. This might be the last development job you'll ever have to oversee with us."

This news was, most certainly, music to her ears. "Oh, wow! That's fantastic!" she exclaimed, not caring that her voice carried throughout the dining room. "I promise, I won't let you down."

"You never do." He bid her goodbye and ended the call.

"Good news?" Wanda asked as she set the check on the table.

"The best news, Wanda! The absolute *best*!"

She didn't explain to the waitress what this *best news* was, and instead, she paid her tab, left a more than usual generous tip, and headed back to the car. Thoughts of Benjamin and his peter were no longer at the forefront of her mind as she headed into work.

When she arrived, Rebecca went immediately to the trailer that served as her office and sorted through the morning emails, responding to what needed it and ignoring the rest. Just as she was about to stand from the desk and head to the casino training center to check on the daily progress, a knock sounded at the door.

The color washed from her face as she feared the visitor would be Benjamin. She was not prepared to see him yet, and she wasn't sure she'd ever be able to look at him with a straight face again. On the second knock, she finally stood, composed herself the best she could, and went to it to answer it.

It was Barbara, Benjamin's receptionist.

"Barbara," Rebecca said with a slight smile as she looked at the older woman, and then around her in search for Benjamin lurking somewhere. He was nowhere in sight. "What brings you by this morning?"

"I apologize for the intrusion," the woman began. Her smile was kind and her eyes were even more so. "Mr. Davidson called me as I was driving in to work. He said the two of you were supposed to chat today, but he's not going to be able to make it. I told him I'd just stop by on my way into the office and let you know."

"Oh…" she muttered and shifted her eyes to the ground. Within her, relief boomed like fireworks. "That's a shame. Is everything okay?"

"Yes," Barbara continued. "It's the strangest thing. He said some crazy person at the motel he's at sped off so fast that their tires spun gravel as they were taking off this morning. One of them got him right in the forehead. He says he'll be okay, but he's having it looked at just to be sure."

Rebecca sucked in a breath. She knew that he'd been walking to his car as she left, but she had no idea that she'd flung gravel while beating tracks out of there, nor had she known he'd been injured by a piece of it. Suddenly, she felt terrible for him.

"Please tell him to take it easy when you speak with him," she replied, her voice monotone as she considered what had happened. "I've got sixteen hundred mattresses and forty-odd computers coming in today, so I was going to have to postpone anyway. Tell Mr. Davidson I said there are no hard feelings and to take care of that head."

"Will do!" Barbara chimed and bid her goodbye. Rebecca shut the door behind her and went to her desk, standing beside it instead of sitting.

She was no longer caught up on the fact that she'd watched him masturbate, albeit without his knowledge. Now, her main focus was the injury to his head – an injury caused by her, no less. She felt terrible about it, and eventually, she knew he'd realize it was her that had caused it. There was no way around it. They were staying at the same crappy motel, and they were rooming right next to each other. He'd eventually notice her, and he'd notice the rental car she was in.

Glancing at her phone, she saw she still had a few hours before the shipments were due in. She called the managers of each hotel and alerted them that she would be there on time to sign for everything, but that she had some urgent business she needed to take care of in the next city. Once the calls were made, she hopped in the rental car and drove as swiftly but carefully as she could to where she'd rented it. There, she turned it in for a completely different model, insisting the car was fine but she was ready for something new.

The process took a bit of time, and when she returned, the delivery trucks were just arriving. While Rebecca believed this process of placing mattresses and setting up computers would have taken the rest of the day, she'd been poorly mistaken. It had taken nearly four full days to complete. During this time, she left for work an hour before her normal time, and stayed around two hours later. Although it had not been her sole intention, she'd managed to avoid Benjamin during this entire time.

By the time she went home on Friday evening, she had a pizza in one arm and a bag of fresh DVDs in the other. In her room, she opened a bottle of wine she'd bought earlier in the week and enjoyed it with her supper while watching a Tina Fey movie marathon. When the pizza was half gone and the bottle was empty, she opened a fresh bottle and set the pizza aside. She had to check on things at the complex tomorrow, but not at the usual early hour. Tonight, she could get drunk and enjoy it.

A little before one a.m., as she lay in the bed in her blue silk nightgown, watching the very end of a movie, she heard a familiar grunt come from behind her, in the next guest room. The picture above the headboard rattled slightly, and Rebecca smirked, realizing Benjamin was obviously feeling better.

Feeling the power of the wine surge through her, she sat up on her knees and pressed her ear to the wall. Listening carefully, she could hear him breathing hard and moaning. He wasn't being as loud as usual, but he was definitely feeling pleasure.

In this inebriated state, she started to become turned on a little by it. This gave her an idea that she would have known instantly was probably not a *good* idea, had she been sober. Staying in her upright position with her head to the wall, she slipped a hand under her nightgown and began to massage her clitoris. As she rubbed, she felt herself become even more turned on, and her inner sanctum became wet from excitement.

"Uhh..." she moaned, pressing on her clit as she stroked her index finger across it. "Yes...!"

"Oh, shit!" she heard Benjamin call out from the next room, but it wasn't out of surprise. His sensations were rising; she could tell by his tone. "Oh, God...!"

Rebecca pressed a finger inside of her, pretending it was him, as she toyed with her clit a bit more intently. Before, she had moaned intentionally. Now, as she worked herself and fantasized about the man in the next room, her moans and cries slipped out of her more loudly and unforced.

Every time she moaned... every time she whimpered or shouted, she heard Benjamin do the same. It became obvious now that he heard her – that he was listening – and this only added to her fantasy, pushing her closer to the brink of what she was certain would be one hell of an orgasm.

She began to talk dirty to her finger – to her fantasy... to the man in the room next door – as she masturbated, and he began to do the same. He began to answer her as if she was right there in the room with him, and he began to tell her sweet nothings like how sexy she was, how much he wanted her, and how she was the best that there possibly was.

Through this dual masturbation with nothing more than a wall between them, Rebecca and Benjamin somehow managed to reach their climax within seconds of each other. She hit hers first and screamed out from it, panting and shouting, cursing and trembling... causing the headboard to slam against the wall just as Benjamin had done last night. Hearing her climax must have pushed him to the brink of his, and his shouts were the most orgasmic that she'd heard come from him yet.

After a few moments, when her body had relaxed and her privates were too tender to touch, she slid down the headboard and lay back on the bed. She heard nothing more from Benjamin that night, and within twenty minutes, she was sound asleep and lost to the world.

The next morning, she awoke feeling refreshed and absolutely wonderful. It was like she was walking on clouds. She showered and then took her time dressing and getting ready for work. All the while, she wondered if Benjamin was as relaxed as she was... if their masturbation session had helped him forget the wound to his forehead.

Just as she was pulling up a pair of jeans, her phone rang. It was the petting zoo veterinarian, informing her that there was a problem with one of the animals.

"Is it bad?" she asked and slipped on her socks.

"It's pretty dire," the vet informed her. "Please get here as soon as you can."

Rebecca ended the call, threw on her shoes and a shirt, grabbed her purse and keys, and headed out the door. Outside, she noticed Benjamin's car was not in the parking lot. She knew then that he'd likely gotten the call first.

At the amusement park, she finally saw his car. It was parked at the gate to the petting zoo. There were several goats, pigs, a couple of donkeys, and a few fat chickens wandering around, safely contained but free to roam. There were two attendants with them, but the veterinarian and Benjamin were missing from the picture.

Instantly, she headed for the vet's office, where she found Benjamin first. He was sitting on the ground with his back against the wall. In his arms was a baby goat, dead. Benjamin was in tears as he held it.

All thoughts of last night's masturbatory fun were gone. That elated feeling she'd held this morning vanished. In the room was a still sense of mourning and loss, and she felt empathy for the manager. His tears made their way into her soul.

"He's been like this since he got here," the vet told her as he approached. "I can't console him. I've tried, but he handpicked each animal here, and this one had been his favorite. He named her Sarah after his mother."

Rebecca went to Benjamin and crouched down beside him. She placed a hand on his shoulder and looked at the small bandage over the wound caused by the flying gravel. He'd seemed so strong and on top of things when they'd first met, and during his masturbatory sessions, he'd seemed like a primal beast – sexy and savage. Now, she saw a completely different side of him, a sensitive side that was so strong it made tears well in her eyes.

He looked up at her and sniffled. She moved her hand from his shoulder and brushed his messy hair back and out of his eyes. He wasn't well groomed like had been. He was in a t-shirt and jeans that were worn out at the knees… fully unkempt.

She didn't speak. Instead, she sat beside him and rested her head on his shoulder, watching his hand as it stroked the top of the baby goat's head. After a few moments of this, he stopped crying, and the vet was able to take the goat from him and prepare her for burial.

"It's okay," she finally told him, making him look into her eyes. "She wasn't meant to last, but she sure was loved… by you. I'm sure she knew how much you cared."

They remained there on the floor for a bit longer before Rebecca stood. She offered Benjamin a hand, and after a moment of staring at it, he accepted it and stood with her.

"I just made a fool out of myself," he muttered as they left the veterinarian's office.

"No," she corrected. "Not to me, you didn't. You just proved to me how much of a real man you really are, and I think I appreciate you a lot more because of it."

He looked at her as if he was going to cry again, but he

didn't. Instead, he smiled and took her hand, walking to where they'd parked their cars.

"Is that your car?" he asked her as he eyed it carefully.

Rebecca cringed, feeling like the jig was up. "Yes. It's a rental, so I can't really call it mine, but it's mine for about another week."

"Funny... there's one just like it at the motel I'm staying at. It was parked two spaces from mine this morning when I headed out to leave."

She swallowed and considered what step to take next. Then, considering his current state of mind and the fact that a lie would only be uncovered eventually, she decided to be truthful with him and pray for the best. "One and the same," she told him and then smiled. Looking at the ground, she added, "I'm in the room next to yours."

Rebecca looked back up at Benjamin and watched his eyes widen. She recognized the embarrassment in them. It was the same embarrassment she'd felt when she realized he was the man she'd watched ejaculate. His face went red as he blushed, and he pulled his hand from hers and took a step back.

"Please... please don't tell me you're the woman I..." he let his voice trail off. She knew he was afraid to finish the statement. It was written all over her face.

"Yes," she confided, nodding her head slowly. "I'm the woman you... *communicated with* last night."

"No!" he cried out and tugged at his head. Briefly, he spun

in a circle through his fit. "No, please, tell me you're joking."

Stepping up to him, she leaned into him and whispered a terribly dirty phrase into his ear – a phrase she'd shouted out during her orgasm last night... the phrase that had made him climax with her.

He looked at her, blinking through a frozen and embarrassed expression. Then, when words returned to him, he asked, "How long did you know that was me?"

Hesitantly, she spilled the beans. She told him about how she'd heard him masturbating through the wall, and how – after they met – she saw him come out of that very room. Then, she told him about her freak-out and how she'd been the one who had sprayed gravel at him while trying to escape his line of vision. Finally, she admitted that she had become so turned on by him as he masturbated that she'd decided to join him. She didn't tell him about seeing him through his window though. That was her private dirty little secret.

"I've never felt so ashamed," she said and looked away. "When we met, I was somehow instantly attracted to you, which is something that never happens with me. Then, when I learned it was you masturbating right behind my head at night, I got really turned on. I'm sorry, Benjamin. It was terribly irresponsible of me, not to mention unprofessional."

He said nothing in reply. She refused to look back at him, knowing that she'd shocked him beyond belief. So, leaving him speechless, she got in her car, pulled out of the spot, and drove to her trailer by the training center.

Making her rounds seemed impossible. Her mind wasn't in the game. She had a grand opening coming on Tuesday, and this day was just blown. She called in her apologies to the casino and hotel managers and asked them to handle things today but to call her if there were any problems. They all told her the same – everything was going great. She hoped to God that they were being honest with her.

After about an hour of moping alone in her tin can, she got back into her car and returned to the motel. She noticed that Benjamin had not returned, and if he had, he wasn't there now. Perhaps he'd checked out, too embarrassed to face her after learning the truth. That was the most likely explanation. She only hoped he didn't quit his job because of it.

What really sucked was that she liked him – a lot. Despite her embarrassment over everything she'd confessed, and despite how terrible she'd felt after learning it was he that she'd watched orgasm through the window, she couldn't help the other emotions that came when she saw him or was with him… how she'd felt when orgasming to the sound of his voice through the wall. He'd made her feel like a sexual creature last night – not like some horrible boss that cracked a whip at every turn.

Rebecca had hoped deep down that she'd have been able to get to know him better at some point… that she could have experienced some truly intimate moments with him that didn't have a thin wall built between them. Now however, there was a much thicker and bigger wall there – an emotional wall that she feared she'd never be able to break through.

Sitting on the edge of her bed, she found herself wishing for Wednesday morning to come, when she could finally leave this place and return home. Benjamin had been the one fun and enticing part of this entire trip, and with that over, she was ready to pack up and go.

She heard a car pull into the parking lot, and as quickly as she could, she rushed to her window and looked out. It was not Benjamin. Instead, it was a chubby trucker and a girl that looked like a hooker entering the room three spaces down. She was thankful they weren't right next door, as she could only imagine the sounds that they would have made.

At four o'clock when he still had not returned, Rebecca grabbed her purse and keys and got in her car. She drove to the next down where she ate at a Mexican restaurant that served decent nachos and killer margaritas. After her fourth drink, she decided against a fifth, knowing she still had to drive. She wasn't ready to return to her room though. She was still too embarrassed over what had happened, and she didn't want to get there and find out that Benjamin really was gone.

So, she took in a movie. The theater was half full, and the film was a dud, but she endured it and tried her best to enjoy it. Perhaps her emotions had kept it from being good in her mind, but the day's circumstances were all that she could think of. When the credits began to roll, she stayed through the end of them, lost in thought.

Finally, at the beckoning of an usher, she left, got into her rental car, and drove back to Sinclair and the shitty motel that housed her shattered dreams. She was partly relieved to see Benjamin's car in the parking lot, but she became even more depressed upon seeing it. Glancing toward his room, she noticed the curtains were completely closed, even though she hadn't told him about her peeping tom incident.

Inside, she went through what had become her nightly process of taking a second shower and putting on her bed clothes. She wore a soft cotton nightgown this time. It was the most comfortable, and she needed its comfort right then.

Before crawling into bed, she put in a DVD of 'First Wives Club' and used it to remind her of why women didn't need men.

It didn't work.

Before the movie ended, she heard a knock at the door. Standing, she went to it and looked through the peep hole. It was Benjamin, and he looked frustrated. Was he there to yell at her? To tell her off and then tell her he quit? That was the most likely scenario and she hesitated opening up for him.

The knocking persisted. This time, it was accompanied by his voice. "I know you're in there, Rebecca. I can hear Bette Midler cackling on the television!"

*Busted by the Midler*, she thought and released a heavy sigh. Then, nervously, she unlocked and opened the door.

Benjamin stood in a fedora and a long khaki trench coat.

She ushered for him to come inside, and then she shut the door behind him.

"You don't have to say anything," she told him as she went to the foot of the bed and sat. "I understand if you never want to see me again and if you want to quit. I don't *want* you to quit, but I understand if you do."

He faced her and looked at her but said nothing. Then, he opened the belt of the trench coat and shrugged it to the floor. Underneath it, he wore nothing but his socks and shoes.

"I don't want to quit," he finally told her as her expression changed from disappointment to shock. "But I'm done masturbating through walls with you. If we're going to make each other orgasm, by God, we should do it the right way."

He smiled at her, and she giggled. Looking down to his crotch, she saw that he was semi-hard and ready for whatever she allowed. Through his window, she hadn't been able to see much of it – only the head as it erupted like a powerful volcano. Now, it was all right in front of her, and it was terribly impressive.

Looking back into his dreamy eyes, she asked, "Are you sure you want to do this?"

"I've had the hots for you since the moment you walked into my office," he confided, sounding no longer shy or embarrassed. "I admit, I was thrown for a loop to learn that you were the woman in this room – the one that I'd orgasmed with. But it didn't disappoint me. It pleased me – more than you could believe. I was just at a loss of words and couldn't tell you. I didn't know *what* to do."

Again, Rebecca giggled. "You have the hots for me?" she asked in an almost juvenile tone.

"Yep," he confirmed and took a step toward her, "but if you want me to put my coat back on and leave, I will."

Coyly, she began to pull the hem of her nightgown up over her knees. Her legs opened just a bit wider. "I don't want you to leave," she told him in a soft tone, "and I sure as hell don't want you to put that coat on."

She lay back against the bed, and he gently climbed on top of her. Their eyes met first, and then their legs. She felt him grow thicker and harder as he was pressed against her, and then she felt his hand run up her thigh and squeeze. She wrapped her arms around his waist and then ran her hands down to his cheeks, squeezing their ample firmness. Benjamin growled deeply from the action.

After a moment, he adjusted his hips a bit, and Rebecca felt the prodding of his tool push against her womanhood. She could feel the wetness growing within her, and she wanted him inside of her – fulfilling her in a way she hadn't been fulfilled in quite some time. Parting her legs a bit more, she allowed him her opening, and with a soft push, he entered into her.

"Talk dirty to me," he said, breaking the kiss and pushing in deeply. Her wetness allowed him greater strides, and she moaned loudly from them – not caring who heard.

Rebecca did, indeed, talk dirty to Benjamin, spilling off

every nasty phrase and slur she could in the most seductive and nasty tone she could imagine. Benjamin returned the favor, offering her some of that animal savagery that she'd enjoyed through the barrier of a wall. Their first time together did not last long because of this, and soon, she was screaming to God from an orgasm that sent him once again over the brink and into a state of sexual nirvana.

He stayed at her side throughout the night, and in the morning, he checked out of his room and moved into hers. For the rest of the weekend, they continued to explore and enjoy one another's bodies, but for Rebecca, it was bittersweet. She was growing too attached to him, and on Wednesday, she would be leaving him. She didn't want to leave him, but she couldn't exactly quit her job and stay in Sinclair. There was no other work here for her, and her job was important to her.

Yet, she told him none of this, as she wanted them to fully enjoy one another without that bittersweet reality taking over their minds and perhaps pushing them apart because of the knowledge.

On Monday, they drove to work separately, yet they communicated through texts and phone calls all day long. In the evening, they humped like animals all over the motel room, finishing in the shower and washing away the juices that they'd shared on each other.

Tuesday was the grand opening and nearly everyone from her corporate headquarters was in attendance. The hotels were fully booked, and most of Sinclair turned out for the ribbon cuttings. Parents and children flooded into the amusement park, making the most of every attraction it had to offer and ensuring Benjamin would not get bored. The casinos filled to capacity, with several winners, many losers, and hundreds of people having the good time that Rebecca had hoped for.

"You did great," her boss told her as they walked toward the emptied training center. "The men upstairs are impressed, and they've agreed to give you that promotion, effective tomorrow."

*Great*, she thought as he told her the news. *Goodbye, Benjamin...*

"That's wonderful," she told him, instead of voicing how she truly felt. "So, what's my new job? Do I get a nice cushy office next to yours?"

Her boss laughed and shook his head. "No," he said but his smile widened. "Taking on this location was your biggest success yet. It wasn't without its hiccups, but you proved yourself through it, and so the heads at corporate have decided to place you here permanently. We start construction on a new headquarters location this week, and we're going to build it right here in Sinclair. You are going to run it."

It was the worst news she'd ever heard and the best she'd ever heard, all at the same time. She was getting her promotion, but she'd have to move far away from her siblings, her dad, and her dearest friends. Yet, she was getting more than a promotion. She was being given the opportunity to stay with Benjamin, which was the reason she finally said, "That's the best offer I've ever had, and I graciously accept it."

At the end of the day, she broke the news to Benjamin, who was ecstatic, and throughout the night, they celebrated in their favorite and most intimate way.

"Tomorrow," Benjamin said as he thrust inside of her, "want to go house hunting?"

"It's like you can read my mind!" she exclaimed and then giggled as he quickened his speed and began to tickle her sides as he did.

"With our combined salaries, we should be able to afford a nice rental," he added in a panting voice.

"Screw that," she replied. "I make more than triple what you're making. We're going to find us a nice big house, and we're buying it."

"You want to stay in this town that long?" He was smiling but he sounded amazed.

"As long as you're here with me, I'd stay in Sinclair for the rest of my life."

Those words were enough to drive Benjamin into his orgasm, and as he started to pull out and cover her with his juice of life, Rebecca couldn't help but think he'd make an excellent father. So, locking him in place inside of her, she decided to find out.

### *End*

# *Say My Name*

She was married to a stripper who spent most every night shaking his junk in front of other women's faces. Fortunately for Tony, Isabelle trusted him. They'd been married for six years, and he'd been an exotic dancer for three of those. Every night, it was she that he went to bed with, made love to, and cuddled with. It also helped that she owned the club he danced at and worked every shift he worked.

Currently, she was minding the bar, serving up shots of tequila to screaming, giddy broads who were ogling her husband from the stools in which they sat. She smiled at them, taking pride in the fact that they were oblivious to the reality that the man they were drooling over was married to the woman pouring their shots. They paid, tipped, and returned their focus to Tony and his money maker.

Isabelle paused in her duties long enough to glance at Tony, who was watching her out the corner of his eye as he straddled a pole and did squats against it. He winked at her and grinned. She winked back and nodded up. It was sort of their own secret lingo – private greetings that let them know they were there for each other and would always be.

She began to giggle as he stood upright and snatched his

tear-away g-string off and waved it in the air like a tiny lasso. The roar of the crowd grew greater as they stared at his massive full monty. He flung the g-string off behind him on the stage and crouched low in front of one patron. Resting one hand on the floor behind him, he parted his legs wide and bent at the knees, flinging his manhood at her face.

"Ham..." Isabelle muttered through a chuckle. Then, she promptly returned her attention to the patrons at the bar. Still, she kept a coy occasional eye on the stage and on her husband, watching him earn his money as tips flew at him from left to right. When his song ended and he turned his back to the crowd, bending over to collect the cash and offering them a delicious moon, Isabelle noted that the stage was almost completely covered in green American bills.

"Give it up for Luscious Luka!" DJ Brazzy Bella said from her stand beyond the stage. Isabelle sighed, relieved that his show was over. The women in the club tonight where a more intense breed of hound dogs than usual. Three of the dancers had already been groped, which was blatantly against the rules. The guilty parties had been escorted from the club, but not without a shouting match. Only once though did Isabelle have to intervene. A flash of the gun at her hip had done the trick and the inebriated woman left without another word. Still, she knew that if one of these broads had pulled a stunt like that on Tony, she'd have knocked their lights out, and it wouldn't have been the first time.

Fortunately, no one laid so much as a finger on him, and as

he left the stage, Isabelle lifted her walkie-talkie and called Jameson back from his break.

"You ready to take back over?" she asked him and awaited his reply.

Static came from her device, followed by, "Yep. Just finished my burger. Let me hit the restroom and I'll be right there."

"Over," she remarked and grinned.

"And out," Jameson said.

In three minutes flat, he stood beside her and she turned the crowd of horny drunk women over to him. "They're all yours."

"Gee... thanks," he said in a sarcastic tone. "Ugh... Are they at least tipping better?"

"They drunker they get, the more green they slap on that counter."

With that, Isabelle left the bar and went backstage, where she passed Mikey – better known as Dick Cockerson. He was next up on the stage, and he wore a new outfit she'd never seen.

"I thought you were going to wear your angel costume with the wings?" she questioned, although she really didn't care what he wore as long as he looked sexy in and out of it.

"Someone spilled a cranberry vodka on the jockstrap last night," he told her. "I couldn't get the stain out, and I don't want to look like my pecker's bleeding."

Although he looked serious, Isabelle let a light laugh slip out. "I can't say I blame you there. Knock 'em dead, champ."

She found her husband in front of the full length mirror at

the dressing station. He was buttoning up his red flannel shirt and already had his jeans on. They were still open at the fly, waiting for him to tuck the shirt in.

"You killed it tonight," she told him and gave him a kiss on the cheek.

Tony returned the kiss with a full one on his wife's lips. "Those women are insane," he said when the kiss broke. Why do I put myself through so much verbal molestation night after night?"

Isabelle looked at the sloppily stacked amount of cash on the table in front of him. He'd racked in a few hundred bucks for a four minute dance. "So that you can buy me pretty things, of course," she replied.

He stared at her for a moment and brushed her hair back with his hand. "You're worth every penny of it too." After another kiss, he told her, "Someone threw a bottle cap at my butthole when I bent over to pick up the money."

Normally, she would have been fuming over something like this, and she partially was on the inside, but the way Tony said it made her outright laugh. "Did you catch it in your cheeks?" she asked, snickering through the words.

"Had I known it was coming, I probably would have tried!" He joined her in the laugh and hugged her close. "This is the weirdest job in the world. You know that, right?"

"You used to be excited about it," she whispered and breathed in his scent. He always smelled delicious. "You don't seem as enthralled with it lately though."

He broke the hug, rested his hands on her shoulders, and said, "I make more money here than I've made anywhere ever, but when we got married, I thought the only person that would be staring at my junk would be you. I know it's your club, and I know you love it, but it's really making me think I might want to try something else... something where I don't have to rip my clothes off and thrust my package at strange women's faces."

"But you thrust it so well!" She understood every word he was telling her, but it saddened her. She loved having him at work with her, and she didn't mind that thousands of women a night drooled over his impressive piece. He was hers and she was his and that had been all that mattered. Yet, his happiness mattered more, and she forced herself to remember that. "Okay then... how should we handle this?"

He sighed and looked up at the ceiling. She could practically see his mind trying to think of an answer, or if he already had an answer, it was trying to formulate how to say it. Finally, he stared back down at her, and with a smile, he said, "I quit."

She smiled back and nodded her head. "Okay. I can handle that."

"And I want you to quit too."

"Wait. What?" That came fully out of left field, and she was floored by the suggestion. "I can't quit. I *own* the club."

"Then sell it." His voice was a pleading one. "Please..."

She laughed again, but this time, it wasn't funny. "And do

*what*, Tony? I put everything into this club. My money, my time... my husband. I can't just walk away from it."

"Do you really love it that much? I mean, if you sold the club, we could do anything... go anywhere."

"What *anything* and which *anywhere* would this be? We have a nice apartment on the east side. You picked it out yourself. We decorated it together... made a home of it."

Tony held up a finger and reached for his jacket. From the inner pocket, he pulled out a brochure and handed it over. Isabelle took it and looked at it. Her eyes widened in surprise.

"Really?" she asked, looking up from the brochure to her husband. "Where in the hell is Wayfield?"

"It's a small town about ten hours from here," he replied. He was smiling, but she thought it was a nervous one. There are houses there for sale that are like a hundred times the size of our apartment, and the mortgages are half of what we pay here a month."

"A small town?" She swallowed, feeling a lump of fright in her throat. "You want us to leave the city? But I love the city. The city accepts me and loves me."

"The city will always be here, Isabelle. We can come back and visit, or if things don't work out in Wayfield, we could always move back."

"What would we do with a great big house?"

"We'd build a family in it." His smile was less nervous now and more hopeful. She stared into his dark brown eyes and saw herself reflecting in them. She sighed and narrowed her eyes to the floor. This deserved consideration, she thought. After all, Tony had been living her dream for years now. Wasn't it time she participated in one of his? Not to mention the idea of having children with him was more than just appealing. It had been a goal of theirs early on, but one they kept putting off due to work.

"Are you sure you wouldn't like to get a dog instead?" she questioned, even though she knew the answer. "Don't men like dogs?"

He chuckled and held her close. "Please, baby. Just try it… for me. For *us*. I love you, but I don't love *this* anymore." He broke the hug and gestured around at the building they stood in. "If someone is going to throw a bottle cap at my anus, I feel like that woman should be you, and only you."

Despite herself, she chuckled. Finally, after another pause of hesitation, she nodded her head and relented. "Okay, Tony. We can give this Wayfield a try, but if it sucks after a year, promise me we can come back to the city."

"Scouts honor!" he exclaimed and held up four fingers, separated in pairs.

"First of all, you were never a scout," she pointed out. "Secondly, that's a Vulcan greeting from *Star Trek*."

"Yep! To infinity and beyond, baby!"

"And *that's* from *Toy Story…*"

At the end of the night, she broke the news to her staff and dancers that she would be placing the club up for sale. She made a note that she didn't know how long it would take to move on the current market, but she would ensure whomever she sold it to would be kind and fair. Personally, she hoped it would take weeks for the right buyer to come around, but when her speech was over and the sad crowd of employees began to go about their end of the night duties, Jameson approached her.

"I'll buy it," he said with a somber expression.

Both Isabelle and Tony looked at him with surprise.

"Really?" Isabelle asked and raised an eyebrow. "How can you afford to buy the club? I pay you. I know how much you make."

He smiled and shrugged. "I don't work here for the money. I work here for socialization. My dad was a tech genius. He invented a lot of the apps used on phones today. When he and mom passed in that wreck, I inherited everything."

"You never told me any of this," she noted, "even that your parents were dead."

"You never asked."

She considered his words for a moment and smiled. "You've got me there."

The next day, the paperwork began, and by the end of the week, Jameson was the new owner of Stud Muffins, and Isabelle and Tony were officially both unemployed.

"I hope you know what you're doing," she told her husband as they sat in the car, buckled in for the long drive to Wayfield. She still wasn't sure this was a great idea, but she'd sold her club and they'd informed the landlord of their apartment building that they were looking for another house in another town and might want to break their lease. He had given them his blessing, but not without letting them know they'd be missed.

"Do I *ever* know what I'm doing?" Tony asked, keeping his mind on the road.

"That's not helpful."

They left a little before four in the morning, stopped for lunch and gas at around eleven at some seedy truck-stop with good food and nasty restrooms, and then they were right back on the road. When they finally reached Wayfield, it was nearing five o'clock and the sun was setting. They were greeted by a giant sign with a farmer and his wife, standing in front of a picturesque background of rolling hills, a barn, and a cow. In the sky, the words 'Welcome to Wayfield' were printed in big bold letters.

"See," Tony said, pointing at it, "even the sign is friendly."

Isabelle groaned and slunk down in her seat.

It was far too late to begin house hunting, but they found a charming bed and breakfast to check into. The owner's name was Myrtle and her husband Jack had died just a few years prior. That was the info she shared when introducing herself.

"He was a good man," she insisted as she stared at them through her glasses and with a warm smile on her face. "If only he hadn't spooked that darn horse."

In her mind's eye, Isabelle could visualize that scene, and she did her best not to laugh.

"How long will you two be staying here for?" Myrtle asked as she finally broke out the old fashioned guest ledger.

"Just a few days," Isabelle replied before Tony had a chance to give her a precise set of dates.

"We're house hunting," he added nonetheless.

Isabelle glared at him.

The kindly old woman's smile grew at the news, and she persisted to tell them the history of Wayfield. It had been founded in 1847 by Silas Wayfield, who had made his money on the railroads and then later in coal. The town had consisted of no more than a hundred people for many years, until Silas sold off chunks of land to investors who built new houses and commercial properties. The town square was erected in 1889, and by 1900, nearly four hundred people called Wayfield their home. Over the decades, some farmland was bought up and divided into lots, new houses were once again built, and a brand new schoolhouse was placed near one of the town's two churches. Now, many decades later, Wayfield had three schools – a high school, a middle school, and an elementary school – four churches, a large grocery story, and a dollar store. There were also three restaurants, a coffee shop, and several antique stores scattered around.

"It's absolutely booming," she added with excitement in her voice. "We're at around twelve hundred residents now, and steadily growing. In another fifty years or so, we might hit two thousand."

"What happens when you hit two thousand residents?"

Tony asked, obviously intrigued by her enthusiastic tale.

"Why, we'll have a parade of course – just like we did when we hit a thousand!"

Isabelle felt like she would be sick. What was so special about a parade, she wondered? In the city, there were parades throughout the year. She barely even noticed them anymore. It was always the same old floats, participants, marching bands and musicians. There was nothing *spectacular* about a parade – not anymore.

"I love a parade!" Tony exclaimed, and again, Isabelle glared at him.

After that, they were finally checked into a room on the second floor. They left Myrtle at the counter and carried their bags up, where the room instantly reminded her of one from her grandmother's house. It was incredibly old fashioned, with a handmade quilt and pillowcases on the bed, lacy curtains over the window, and large framed paintings of random scenic views that didn't seem to relate to one another. There was also a grandfather clock that didn't seem to be wound, a fireplace that probably didn't work since there was an electric heater parked in front of it, and a small dresser that would in no way fit all of the clothes she'd packed, not to mention what Tony had brought.

"Isn't there like a *real* hotel we could stay at, maybe in the next town?" she asked her husband, hoping he'd have a heart and take her away from this place.

"Come on, honey! Give it a chance!" he pleaded through a

hopeful grin. "We just got here, and that old lady downstairs promised us a hot breakfast in the morning."

"We could get a hot breakfast at a Pancake Shack," she reminded him.

Nonetheless, she changed into her nightgown and sat on the edge of the bed, looking at the paintings on the wall while her husband changed into his pajamas. When he joined her on the bed, they sat in silence for a bit, but only until Isabelle glanced at her phone.

"Okay, my life is over," she commented and huffed abrasively.

"What's wrong?"

"For starters, I don't have service on my phone."

"So we'd have to change carriers."

"Secondly, it's five-forty and we're dressed and ready for bed." Looking at him, she pouted. "We're now *old*, Tony. We're officially old, and we'll be *ancient* before we even turn forty."

He laughed and pulled her close to him. "There are other things to do in bed besides sleep," he said, nuzzling his nose to her neck.

"With that old lady downstairs? She'd hear every sound we make."

"Not without a *killer* set of hearing aids," he insisted. "I mean, come on. She asked for me to repeat our home address three times while checking us in."

"Nope," she said and pulled away from him, climbing up

the bed and resting her head on the pillow. "I'm old now and I'm going to sleep."

He chuckled and laid beside her. "Are you going to be like this the whole trip?"

"Like what?"

"Like you don't want to be here."

"I *don't* want to be here!" She sighed and rolled over so that her back faced him.

"Not yet, you don't, but if you give it a little time, this place might grow on you."

She groaned once more, closed her eyes, and forced herself to fall asleep at this ungodly early hour. When she awoke, it was at six a.m. – three hours before she normally climbed out of bed. Isabelle rolled over and looked at her husband. He was still sound asleep. She studied his face for a moment and considered he was lucky he was cute. Then, she got up and opened the room door, stepping into the hallway.

In the bathroom, she did her business and washed her face. Then, as she opened the door again, the fresh scent of coffee and bacon hit her square in the face.

Isabelle followed the scent down the stairs and to a dining room with a large table and eight chairs. Only two of the chairs had place settings at them. All over the table were platters of bacon, sausage, scrambled eggs, biscuits, freshly cut fruits, oatmeal, and most importantly, a carafe of coffee.

"Well, good morning, dearie," Myrtle said as she entered

the room from a kitchen, carrying with her a big bowl of fresh sausage gravy. "I hope you've brought your appetite. It's been so long since I've had guests that I think I might have overdone it a little."

"Good morning," Isabelle replied and offered her a smile.

"Where's your husband? What's his name… Tom?"

"Tony," she corrected, "and he's still asleep."

"Shouldn't you wake him before the food gets cold?"

Normally, Isabelle never would have woken Tony before he was ready to get up. He'd worked the same night hours that she had, and so he had a tendency to sleep in each morning. Today, however, she felt he more than deserved to get up at the crack of dawn. Perhaps it would be enough to make him realize this was not the type of life he wanted or that they needed.

"Yes… yes, I should."

She excused herself from the dining room and went back upstairs. On her way to the bedroom, she heard the shower running in the bathroom. She paused at the door and listened more closely. She could hear whistling to the tune of one of Tony's performance songs.

"Impossible…" she muttered and reached for the knob. Opening the door, she saw him standing in the tub, naked and wet with soap running down his body. He looked at her and smiled.

"Good morning, honey!" His voice was chipper and he sounded awake.

"I'm in the friggin' *Twilight Zone!*" she cried out and then shut the door, forming a barrier between the two of them. Before she turned away, she yelled, "Breakfast is served!"

At the table, Isabelle filled her plate with more food than she knew she would eat. Myrtle insisted she'd already eaten much too much as she'd prepared the food, and that the room was set for the two 'love birds.' Isabelle didn't quite feel like she and Tony were right for that phrase, and it was the first time she'd ever felt that way. The two of them had been practically inseparable since their first date. They fit each other like snug socks... usually. This venture, however, had thrown her for a loop, and somehow, it had also thrown an unexpected kink into their relationship.

When Tony came downstairs to join her, he was dressed for the day, while she sat at the table still in her nightgown. She avoided making contact with him as he filled his plate, and when he struck up conversation, she kept her answers as short and flat as she could.

"Hostile today, huh?" he asked after her third snippy reply.

"Not enough coffee in the world to prepare me for this town."

"I can make more!" she heard Myrtle reply from the kitchen.

Finally eying her husband, Isabelle noted, "I told you she could hear everything."

"What's that?" Myrtle asked and walked into the room. "I didn't quite hear that, dearie."

With a roll of the eyes, Isabelle set her focus on finishing her food.

After breakfast, she returned upstairs and took a hot bath, opting out of the shower. The last time she'd had a bath, she'd been in high school. Their apartment in the city had a walk-in shower, but no tub. It was relaxing to bathe in the warm bubbly water, even though she didn't want to admit it.

Her fingers began to prune and she pulled the plug, letting the water drain out. Then, she stood and grabbed a towel from the rack to dry off with. She wrapped the towel around her and went into the room to dress. It was a chilly day, and so she chose a red cashmere sweater that Tony had surprised her with last Christmas. Along with it, she wore black jeans and a pair of tough and comfortable sneakers.

"Look at this," Tony said as he stepped into the room, nearly scaring the life out of her. "This town has a local paper, and guess what's in it."

"Obituaries?" she said with a grimace.

"Houses for sale. There are some really nice ones. This can be our guide as we go on our hunt."

"Joy!" she exclaimed and hunted for her purse.

"Come on, Isabelle… You promised you'd try this. You could at least *pretend* to have fun. If nothing else, look at this as a vacation."

She sighed and straightened herself. She knew he was right. She had vowed to give this a shot, plus she'd already sold her club. There was nothing left to do *but* try.

"Okay" she whispered and forced a smile over her lips. "Show me the listings. Let's see what's out there."

"That's the spirit!"

Never the less, Isabelle rolled her eyes and snatched the paper from her husband's grip. She flipped to the classifieds and saw at least fifteen listings for houses for sale. Each had an address and a description; none had a realtor listed with it.

"No realtors?" she noted curiously.

"It's a small town."

"Okay then, I guess we're on our own." She lay the paper down on the bed and pointed at the first five listings. "We'll do five a day so we don't exhaust ourselves. Does that sound okay?"

Tony smiled and put his hand around her waist. "That sounds fantastic to me!"

With the paper in hand, they left the bed and breakfast and got in the car. The first house on the listing was on a road called Willow, and Tony noted it reminded him of that old movie from the eighties. Isabelle admitted she'd never seen it. The only fantasy she was interested in was that in the bedroom… or on the stage of her former club.

"No," she said immediately as they pulled up to the house. It was a brick build from the mid nineteen hundreds that looked like it had been through a tornado. The grass was waist high and brown from the winter, and the shrubs around the house concealed large sections of it. Several windows were broken out and the front door was hanging on its hinges. The house was massively exposed to the elements due to this. "This is certainly *not* a house I'm interested in buying."

"We could look inside," Tony nudged. "The door's open!" He laughed as he said this. Isabelle did not share in the humor. "Come on. The listing says it has an in-ground pool in the backyard. We can at least look at *that*. Maybe it'll make this fixer-upper be worth fixing?"

She didn't want to, but she relented and parked the car on the side of the road at the walkway. They didn't bother trying to enter the house. Instead, they walked to the back fence and pushed the gate open. The lawn there was in worse shape than out front. The pool looked like a murky green and brown pond. The stench of it made her feel sick.

"Uh uh," she said. "There's no telling what's living in that water."

"It's winter. I'm sure nothing's living in it."

"Fine… there's no telling what's *dead* in that water."

"Yeah… that sounds more likely."

He didn't argue her any further on this one, and they returned to the car and looked at the address for the next listing – one on Carter Street.

The house on Carter Street wasn't nearly as bad as the one on Willow had been. In fact, it was almost charming. It had a small front yard that had been taken care of, and the house itself was yellow with blue doors and shutters. Isabelle smiled when she saw it, and when they went to the front door and knocked, she was surprised when someone answered.

"Hi," Tony said to the old lady that answered. "I'm Tony and this is my wife Isabelle. We're wondering if we could tour the house. We're thinking of moving to this charming town."

"Well..." said the woman as she opened the door wider, "certainly. "Please, come in."

The house was indeed lovely, despite Isabelle's inner yearning to find something terribly wrong with it. There was one major problem with it that didn't involve bad smells or irreparable damage. It was so tiny! The living room was the biggest room in the house. The kitchen was half the size of their small kitchen in their apartment, and the bathroom was built large enough for only one person to have standing room at a time. Aside from that, it had only one bedroom. There would be no space to raise a family here.

She looked at Tony and shrugged. Tony obviously saw the issues with it that she did, and the thanked the woman for her time. "I sure appreciate you letting us in," he said, "but I think it's just a little smaller than we're looking for."

"Oh? Do you have children?"

"Not yet," he told her and smiled at his wife, "but we hope to start a family in Wayfield."

The house owner wished them the best and Isabelle and Tony returned to the car.

"Okay," Isabelle said as they cranked the engine. "I have to admit. That house was cute... but it was way too small for us. We don't need something smaller than our apartment."

"I agree," he replied and looked down at the paper. "Three more listings for today. Let's see if we can find something bigger and better."

The third property on their list took them almost to the edge of town. Even though the ride there was short, it was also wasted. While the house looked nice enough and the property size was decent, the For Sale sign on the front lawn had another sign tacked over it – one that said 'Sold.'

"How old is this paper?" Isabelle said with a grimace as she checked the date on the front. It was the paper's current issue, but they only published once every two weeks. With that knowledge now sinking in, she and Tony knew the rest of their hunt would be hit or miss.

The fourth listing was on the opposite end of town, and they drove through the square on their way. Isabelle noted the amount of shops on the square. From what she would see, there were three antique shops, two dress shops, an old bookstore, and – Tony's favorite – a comic book and collectibles shop.

"Care for a little break?" he asked her and pulled into a parking space.

"I'd love one."

While Tony wandered into the comic shop, Isabelle visited the bookstore next door. It was a charming shop with almost only antique and rare books. There was an old lady behind a counter who reminded her of a gypsy. Even with her age, she was beautiful.

"Welcome!" said the woman in a tender but vibrant tone. "Please, let me know if you see anything you like."

"I'm not a huge reader," Isabelle admitted, "but every now and then I find a book I can't put down."

"Maybe you'll find that special book here today," the woman noted. "Either way, just let me know, Isabelle. My name is Caroline."

"Thank you, Caroline." As she said that, it dawned on her that she'd never told Caroline her name. Puzzled by this, she asked, "How did you know my name?"

"It's a small town," Caroline said with a chuckle. "Myrtle at the bed and breakfast called me this morning and let me know she had visitors. She said you and your husband are a lovely couple, and for everyone to be welcoming to you – which is easy. We welcome strangers here like they're family."

"Huh." This was something strange for Isabelle, who had been born and raised in the city. Even if she frequented a store often, no one ever remembered her face or name. The staffs changed so quickly, and there were so many more customers to throw into the mix. It made her feel a little warm inside to be recognized, even by a woman who had never seen her before. "That's really nice."

"That's Wayfield."

She couldn't help the smile that formed over her lips, and as she browsed the dusty old books on the shelves, she did find one that caught her eye. It was an antique copy of Walt Whitman's

*Leaves of Grass.* Isabelle had always loved poetry, and she'd been a fan of Whitman's since having to study his work in high school. The price was in pencil on the inside – thirty bucks. That was cheap enough, she thought as she carried the book to the counter and pulled out her credit card.

Caroline rang up her purchase and put the book in a brown paper bag with the shop's name and logo on the front. As Isabelle took the purchase and started to walk away, the shopkeeper asked her, "Will we see you and your husband at the community picnic tomorrow?"

*Community picnic?* she thought and turned back to face the woman. *What is this? Mayberry?* "This is the first I've heard of it," she replied.

"It'll be at Wayfield Park starting at eleven in the morning. I sure hope you're able to make it. You'll get to meet everyone who's anyone here in town."

While it didn't sound like her usual idea of a good time, it did sound like a distraction from house hunting. She smiled, thanked Caroline for the information and the invitation, and left the shop.

Outside, Tony was relaxing against the side of the car, flipping through an old issue of *Action Comics* that he said he picked up for 'a steal.'

"If we're going to buy a house," she told him as the climbed into the car, "we can't go around spending all of our money shopping."

"You bought a book," he countered.

"Yes, but mine only cost thirty dollars. How much did that old comic run you?"

"Seven." His grin widened. She had way outspent him.

Just up the road, they noticed the coffee shop that Myrtle had mentioned last night. They both agreed they needed the extra boost of energy before checking out the last two houses on the day's list. Inside, the heavy aroma of fresh brew hit them hard, and they each ordered lightly sweetened lattes.

While parking, Isabelle had told Tony about the community picnic, but now she had to question it. She decided to present the question to the barista. "Could you tell me why there is a community picnic at the park tomorrow? It's winter, after all."

The barista smiled, and in a voice that was rich with friendly courtesy, she said, "Yes, ma'am. It's tradition in Wayfield. Everyone dresses for the cold, and there's a nice bonfire to keep warm by and roast marshmallows. Miss Henderson from the senior center makes her special hot apple cider, and the Davidson family brings their *famous* pulled pork – and plenty of it. Then, there are little games and contests all throughout. Once you get started, no one ever even notices that it's cold." Then, as if suddenly remembering something, she added, "And there's a hot dog eating contest! It's pointless to enter though if you're hoping to win. Winston Jones has won that contest six years in a row, and believe it or not, he's the skinniest guy in town."

"Wow!" Tony exclaimed. "That event sounds fantastic."

"I hope you'll be able to make it. I'll be going after my shift ends, so I might miss you, but there will be plenty of good folks there to keep you company."

At a table by a window, they sipped their lattes and each ate a bran muffin to give them an extra little bit of nourishment. They'd both eaten heavily at breakfast, but the muffins had been fresh and they were still warm from the oven – not to mention they were as delicious as they smelled.

When they finished and began to leave, the barista thanked them and told them to enjoy their day, calling each by their name. Outside, Tony asked, "How did she know our names? We didn't tell her, and we paid with cash."

"The woman at the bookstore knew who I was almost immediately," Isabelle replied. "Apparently, Myrtle has been giving everyone in town a head's up about us."

"Gotta love small towns," he chuckled.

"Do I?" She smirked and got into the car.

The fourth house on their list was actually a trailer – and it wasn't in good condition. It was missing half its roof and a blue tarp covered those sections. The trailer sat on wheels above the ground, and had a screen door with holes in it. All of the windows were tinted black.

"No," Isabelle said, refusing to leave the car. "I'm not a snob, but I refuse to even look inside that dump."

"I'm with you on this one," he said and backed the car out of the drive, having not even cut the ignition to consider checking it out.

The final house on the list was a late eighteen hundreds build with two stories and a nice balcony from the second floor. They both admitted it looked lovely, but like the third house on their list, it had a sold sign in the yard.

"That's that," Tony said and pulled out of the driveway. "What do you want to do now? Go back to the bed and breakfast? Go for a drive in the country? Shop more?"

Isabelle took her phone from the purse. She still didn't have service, but at least it kept accurate time. She was amazed to see that it wasn't even noon yet.

"It's eleven forty-three," she announced in a groan. "Time is creeping by!"

Tony put a hand on her thigh and squeezed. "We could go to that park and check it out a little early… see if it's something we would enjoy being at tomorrow with a crowd."

She sighed and nodded. "Okay, let's go take a look."

Wayfield Park was impressive. It had a pond with ducks, a little wooden bridge that went over it, and three different playground areas. There were picnic benches and tables scattered all around, as well as beautiful trees that still had colorful leaves from the fall. It had been so long since Isabelle had been in a park that wasn't surrounded on the outside by tall buildings and heavy traffic, or that didn't have homeless people sleeping on the benches or asking for a handout. It was almost tranquil, she thought, and she took her husband's hand and walked with him to the pond.

"You'd think the ducks would have migrated south," he said as they watched them float atop the water.

"I don't know if ducks do that," Isabelle remarked. "I'd look it up, but you know... no service."

"Who needs cell service right now? Look at this place, honey. It's just beautiful."

"Want to play on the swings?" she asked him and pointed to one of the playground sections. "They look pretty sturdy."

"Yeah, I do!"

They raced each other to the large and sturdy swing-set, and as they chose their swings, they competed against each other to see who could swing the highest. Laughter filled the air and as it did, Isabelle's worries and dreaded thoughts over leaving the city began to vanish. She hadn't let loose and played like this since she was a child, but all of that joy seemed to return to her now – in this place that she'd fought so hard against visiting.

When they'd had their fill on the swings, Tony began to chase her, threatened to tackle her to the ground and tickle her. Isabelle was incredibly ticklish and to her, it was the worst threat of them all.

Finally, when he'd chased her far from the swings, leaving the bulk of the park behind them, he caught up with her and tackled her, bringing her down to a soft pile of leaves at a grouping of trees. He lay atop her, tickling her hectically as she giggled and cried out, trying to push him from her. Finally, she succeeded and forced Tony onto his back. Looking into his eyes, she smiled at him and caught her breath. Then, she kissed him.

She felt his arms wrap around her as he held her close, and the kiss seemed to spark a flame within them that had been blown out that night at the club – the night Tony quit and asked her to sell. All of that was forgotten now, and they made out for a long moment, rolling around in the leaves and becoming disheveled by them.

"I love you so much," Tony told her and slid a hand down her hip.

"I love you too, you brute."

Tony stood and reached down, helping Isabelle to her feet. Yet, once she was up, she pushed him back down atop the leaves. "Hey!"

Looking around, she saw the place was pretty much abandoned, and a somewhat naughty feeling overcame her. She looked at her husband again and lowered herself onto her knees between his parted legs. Then, she undid his belt, unsnapped his jeans, and unzipped his fly.

"What are you doing?" he asked almost nervously. Still, he was smiling. "Someone could see us."

"There's no one here to see," she told him and grabbed his manhood through his boxer shorts. She felt it throb from her touch. "No one but you, me, and the ducks."

"Those ducks can be voyeurs, you know."

"Since when is a former stripper afraid of voyeurs?" As she asked this, she reached into the fly of the shorts, grabbed his manhood, and pulled it out. Squeezing it, it grew in her hand. Isabelle lowered her face toward it but kept her eyes locked with his. With a sinful smile, she took the head between her lips and suckled it.

Tony gasped and then rested his head against the leaves. As Isabelle sucked him, she stroked him, bringing his erection to its proud fullness.

"Yes..." he moaned in what was close to being a whimper. "Oh... baby..."

Pulling off him, she said, "Uh uh. Say my name."

He looked up at her again and grinned. "Isabelle..." She took him back into her mouth. "Oh, God... Isabelle!"

Through the excitement of their rather public display, Tony did not last very long. Isabelle drained him of every burst and drop that he had to offer, having almost forgotten how distinctly delicious he was. When she'd had her fill and he began to soften in her mouth, she tucked him back into his boxers and refastened his jeans.

Standing, she looked down at him and smiled. He looked spent, with his eyes closed and a humorous grin overcoming his post-orgasmic face. She didn't know what had overcome her and made her go down on him right then. The only times they'd done anything in public had been at her club, and even there, they'd contained themselves to her office. Perhaps it was the beauty of the park, or even the club that had caused this indecent but sensually heated moment. Either way, she felt good about it – and she felt good about herself. She was no longer in the agitated state that she'd woken up in. She was ready to conquer the world.

Extending a hand to him to help him up, she said, "Come on. Let's go look at some more houses."

"Yeah?" he asked, taking her grip and standing. "You mean it?"

She didn't speak, but she nodded with a grin that let him know she was serious.

As they headed back through the park, she realized Tony had finished just in time. Several couples and some with children were beginning to wander into it. Each that the passed waved at the new couple and greeted them – some by name. Neither Isabelle nor Tony questioned this anymore. They now assumed everyone in Wayfield knew who they were, and they accepted the fact.

Over the next few hours, they looked at and toured six more homes, and although none had been as bad as some that they'd seen, none seemed right for them. Either they weren't large enough to start a family in, or they were much too large to feasibly keep up. One of the houses was three stories with four outbuildings and several acres of land for farming. It was too much for them, as neither Isabelle nor her husband had any intention on becoming a farmer.

Finally, they gave up for the day and returned to the bed and breakfast, where they sat in the car for a moment. Glancing at her husband, Isabelle thought he looked a little deflated.

"This has been a bust," he said, shrugging but not looking

at her. "I'm sorry, Isabelle. I may have talked you into selling your club for nothing."

"Don't give up yet," she told him and put her hand on his. "There are still four listings we haven't tried, and maybe one of them will be perfect for us."

"Maybe," he said as he opened the door. "Or maybe you could start a new club when we get home. I'll dance for you again."

Isabelle knew that was the very last thing Tony wanted to do, but it warmed her heart hearing him saying that. In fact, it warmed it so much that she suddenly became determined that Wayfield would be their new home. She just didn't know how to make that happen without the right house.

Inside, they found Myrtle sitting at the counter, chatting on the phone. She hung up hurriedly when they entered, letting them know she'd likely been discussing them to one random townsfolk or another.

"Hello there, dearies!" she exclaimed in an overly chipper tone. "So, tell me... are you Wayfield's newest citizens? Did you find a house?"

"No, ma'am," Tony noted and headed right for the stairs.

"Not yet, anyway," Isabelle added. She watched her husband disappear from view and then approached the counter. "Tell me, are the houses listed in this paper the only ones for sale?"

Myrtle's smile grew. "There are one or two that haven't been listed in a few months, but as far as I know, they're still on the market. Would you like me to write the addresses down for you?"

"Myrtle, that would be a blessing. Thank you."

Quickly, the old woman jotted down a couple of addresses and handed the paper over. As Isabelle looked over it, her eyebrows lifted and her eyes widened. She looked at the woman and then grinned.

"Let's go in my office," Myrtle said. "I'll tell you all I know about them."

Later, when Isabelle finally made it back to the room, she found a somewhat defeated Tony lying on the bed with his eyes closed, rubbing his temples to rid himself of what she assumed was a headache. She didn't say anything to him at first. Instead, she curled up beside him, kissed his cheek, and rested her head on his shoulder.

"I love you, Isabelle," he told her in a saddened voice. "I'm sorry about all of this."

"Let's not worry about that right now," she replied. "Why don't we go out for supper? I'm not really in the mood to go to bed at five o'clock again."

"Tired of feeling old?"

"Let's just say I'm finally starting to feel like my old self again."

They ate at a meat-and-three diner called Ma's Place. Although it was not the typical type of food they usually dined on, they both found it delicious, and when two slices of fresh custard pie arrived for dessert, Isabelle noticed Tony was starting to feel a bit better. At the very least, he had an appetite, and that was a sign his mood was improving.

After dinner, they learned about a drive-in theater just outside of town that showed a double-feature nightly. Neither of them had ever been to a drive-in, and they decided to try it out. She'd seen drive-in theaters in movies before and remembered the patrons hooking on a speaker box to their open car windows. It was cold out, and she hoped that wouldn't be the case. To her surprise and delight, the theater had been recently remodeled. The movies were digital instead of old film, and the sound came from a special radio station that they were able to pick up without having to roll down the windows.

They had gone on what they learned was eighties night. The films shown were the original *Ghostbusters* followed by *Back to the Future*. The lightheartedness of each film, mixed with a bit of romance, mystery, and fun scares, helped them both forget their worries. Isabelle's former club and the apartment in the city were light-years away from her mind, and beside her, she saw that Tony looked like his usual handsome self. He laughed in all the right places, and twice in *Ghostbusters*, he winced at the scares.

When the films were over, it was late. They arrived back at the bed and breakfast to find Myrtle sitting in a chair in the lobby reading a book. She looked up from it and smiled at the couple. "Did you have a good time out?" she asked in the way a kindly grandmother would have.

"It was a blast," Tony exclaimed – a complete change in his demeanor from the last time they'd entered the place. "The drive-in is fantastic."

"I haven't been since they remodeled it," the old woman continued, "but I've heard some really nice things about it." As Isabelle and Tony started to the stares, Myrtle added, "Any requests for breakfast?"

"Just work your magic," Isabelle replied. "Everything you made this morning was wonderful."

In their room, they changed for the night and then lay on the bed. Isabelle sighed with relief.

"It's good to be home for the night," she muttered.

Tony looked at her and cocked an eyebrow. "Well, it's not home, but it's good to be out of that cold. It's freezing out there tonight."

She felt his hand slide up the hem of her nightgown and caress her inner thigh. His thumb smoothed over her clitoris, making her gasp.

"Mind if I pay you back for the park?" he asked her and then slunk down her body. He pulled her nightgown up over his head and gently parted her legs.

"That sounds *wonderful…!*"

She felt the warmth of his tongue on her and smiled. Tony was pretty skilled at pleasuring her this way, although that had not always been the case. When they first began dating, he'd been a little inexperienced and she'd had to guide him and teach him. He was a fast learned though, and over the years, he'd continuously gotten better.

Her body became heated as he nibbled on her rosebud. Isabelle trembled from his touch and clutched the quilt in both hands. When his tongue entered her, she sucked in a hard breath and then hissed it out. A curse slipped from her lips, followed by a growl deep within her.

"Ahh… yes…" she moaned and pushed herself more firmly against his mouth. "That's right, baby…"

He pulled away from her and lifted his head up and out of the nightgown. "Nope," he said with a devious grin. "Say my name."

"Mmm…" she muttered, loving it when he played her games against her. "Tony…! Yes, Tony!"

"That's right," he told her and then buried his mouth onto her womanhood.

As he penetrated her with his snaking tongue, she wrapped her legs around him, locking them in place by crossing her ankles together. Then, she began to buck against him, alternating her movements with his. When she reached climax, he fed on her more savagely, ensuring she felt as much electrifying pleasure as his mouth and tongue could possibly deliver. Isabelle nearly screamed out through her orgasm, but she muffled it, as the back of her mind was still conscious of the fact that Myrtle was still in the house.

Pulling another of her cards, he continued to feast on her until she was spent and exhausted, trapped in a state of blissful nirvana. Then, he crawled up beside her again and held her until they fell asleep.

In the morning, they awoke together, just a little later than the morning before, and showered one another clean in the bathroom. Once dressed, they went downstairs where breakfast and coffee awaited them. Myrtle sat at the far end of the table this time, reading a tabloid she'd likely gotten at the supermarket. Looking up from it, she greeted her guests with the usual friendly smile.

"Sleep well?" she asked as they began to fill their plates.

"Best sleep I've had in ages," Isabelle admitted and then smiled at her husband. Tony blushed.

When they'd had their fill of food and coffee, Tony asked, "Ready to look at some more houses?"

"Later," Isabelle replied, "after the picnic. I want to go by the grocery and see if I can think of something to bring to it."

"Something to bring?" he questioned and gazed at her with a sly grin. "Okay, who are you and what did you do with my wife?"

She smirked and shrugged. "You asked me to give this place a chance, so I am. Don't tell me you want me to go back to being bitter and rushed."

"Not in a million years."

"Myrtle," Isabelle asked as they stepped toward the front door, "you'll be at the picnic?"

"I'll be there," she replied. "You can count on it."

"Good." Isabelle winked, wondering if Tony had noticed. If

he had, he showed no signs of it.

At the grocery, she became a bit overwhelmed. Isabelle had never attended a community picnic before, and she had no idea how many people would be there or what she should bring. So, she decided to put her focus on the town's children, and she filled her shopping cart with dozens of bags of various candies.

"I hope this place has a dentist," Tony joked as they headed to the checkout counter. From behind him a woman answered his question.

"There are two," the stranger said with a smile on her face. "They're both fantastic." She extended a hand, which Isabelle accepted and shook. "I'm Sandy. My husband is Bernard. He's one of the dentists in question."

"It's so nice to meet you," Isabelle said warmly. "I'm Isabelle, and this is my husband Tony."

"It's great to finally meet you two," Sandy said. "I've heard lovely things about the both of you." She looked down at their cart and asked, "Are you getting an incredibly early jump on next Halloween?"

Tony chuckled. "Nah... It looks like all of this is going to that picnic today."

"Well, everyone around here does have a sweet tooth," the woman noted. "I need to get back to my shopping, but I'll look forward to seeing you at the picnic!"

"Well...isn't she lovely?" Isabelle asked Tony when Sandy was out of ear-range. "Everyone around here is so kind and warm."

"It sounds like this town is growing on you," he said. Then, in a lower tone, he added, "I just hope one of those last four houses works for us. Otherwise, this has all been for nothing."

"Earlier, you told me to look at this as a vacation," she reminded him. "Can't you do the same?"

He thought it over and then smiled again. "You're right... as usual."

"I love it when you say things like that."

They checked out and loaded up the trunk with their bags of goodies. Then, seeing it was nearing eleven, they headed straight to the park. There, the discovered the place bustling with much more activity than yesterday. It was almost like a fair was happening instead of a picnic. There were pony rides, people juggling, clowns blowing up balloons, and a magician was on a platform that hadn't been there before, performing tricks. Another platform had been erected not too far from there. On it was a band playing 1950's music.

The crowd was enormous, and the whole park smelled like a mix of the best of foods. They found a man in a top hat and suit who reminded Isabelle of the 'great and powerful' Oz in *The Wizard of Oz*. They introduced themselves, learned that he was Wayfield's mayor, and asked where to put the many bags of candy.

"Just leave the trunk popped," he told them with a giddy grin on his face. "I'll make sure it's all put out for you. You two kids go have fun and enjoy the festivities."

They wandered around for a bit and met so many new

people that the names began to all blend in together in their minds. Everywhere they turned was food, and Tony ate like a starved horse every chance he got. Isabelle was saving her appetite though.

"Aren't you hungry?" he asked her as they wandered over to a clown, who handed Isabelle a balloon.

"I've got my sights set on *that*." She pointed a few yards away, where several people were setting up the area for the hot dog contest. "I intend on giving Winston Jones a run for his money."

"Who?"

"The guy that always wins."

"You remember his name?"

"Sure," she said and grinned. "He'll be my competition, after all."

Before the contest began, there were other competitions. Of all of them, Isabelle and Tony chose the three-legged race to enter. They were one of about thirty couples who had entered this contest, and when they crossed the finish line, they learned they'd come in third in the race. They were cheered by the crowd, and excitedly, they shared a kiss to celebrate.

At the hot dog eating contest, Isabelle showed her husband a side of herself he'd never seen. There were eight competitors, including her and Winston Jones. The barista had been correct in her description of the man. He was middle aged and skinny as a rail. Still, he savagely out-ate most of the other competition, after a few minutes, it was just Isabelle and he remaining.

"You better eat up," she told him as she crammed another

dog into her mouth. Chewing it up fast and swallowing, she added, "Your winning streak is about to come to an end."

Winston took her challenge, but on his thirty-fifth bunned hot dog, he felt sick and had to vomit into a trashcan – which was against the rules. Isabelle managed to scarf down thirty-nine bunned dogs, and she stood victorious, albeit bloated and full.

She'd expected Winston to be angry over his loss, but he walked over to her on weak knees, shook her hand, and congratulated her. "Wow!" he exclaimed. "You're amazing. Welcome to Wayfield."

Isabelle beamed with a mix of pride and warmth. She'd entered this type of competition three times before, long before she ever met Tony. She'd won two of those competitions, and neither of the men she'd outlasted had been nearly this kind and courteous. It impressed her.

"Where in the *hell* did you learn to do that?" Tony asked when she returned to him with her little trophy. "More so, where did you put all of that food?"

She smiled and winked. "In my belly!" she said in a voice a monster might have used. Then, she added, "Let's see what they have here for dessert."

About a half an hour later, she spotted Myrtle, who waved her over. She excused herself from Tony and followed the woman to one of the playgrounds. Glancing back to her husband, she saw he had been brought into conversation by several new and friendly faces. She chatted with Myrtle for several minutes, and when they parted, she gave her a warm hug.

Returning to Tony, he asked, "What was that all about?"

"Just an old lady, needing someone to talk to," she said and shrugged. "I think I could use a nap. Ready to head back to the house?"

"Yeah…for a while, I thought I'd have to borrow a wheelbarrow just to get you to the car." He chuckled, and so did she.

At the bed and breakfast, they went up to the room, where Tony collapsed on the bed and Isabelle stared at one of the weird paintings on the wall. "This place could use some remodeling," she noted.

"I'm sure whatever house we end up with will need the same," he replied. "How are you still standing? You ate like a hundred hot dogs… and everything else."

"It's a gift," she told him. Pulling an envelope from her back pocket, she tossed it to him and added, "So is this."

He took the envelope in his hands and looked at it. It had their names written across it. "What is it?"

"It is the deed," she said with a smile that was larger than life, "for the bed and breakfast."

Tony's eyes nearly bulged out of his head. "What are you talking about?"

Isabelle sat down beside him and put a hand on his knee. "After you went to upstairs last night, I asked Myrtle if there were any other properties for sale that weren't listed in the paper. She told me about two of them, and one of them was this one. She has family in Florida – a daughter and three grandchildren – and she's been aching to move down there to be closer to them. We discussed it and decided this would be the perfect place for us to start *our* family. She signed the deed over to me last night, and I wrote her a check for her asking amount, leaving more than plenty left in the bank to do wonders with this old house."

"You're serious, aren't you? You're not joking?" He tore open the envelope and pulled out the copy of the deed. Sure enough, he saw both Myrtle and Isabelle's signatures on the appropriate lines.

"It's all ours."

"I – I don't know what to say," he remarked, and she could see he was becoming emotional.

"You could say, 'Sure, honey, we can hire movers to take care of our stuff at the apartment.' After all, we're going to have to be here to make sure the remodeling work gets done right."

His eyes still screamed disbelief, but his tone was breathtakingly somber. "Isabelle... wow... I love you."

"I know," she told him and edged her hand from his knee to his thigh. "And I love you too. What say we *christen* our new home?"

Tony put his hand to her cheek and leaned in for a kiss. When it ended, he whispered, "That sounds like the best thing I've ever heard."

Slowly, they kissed again, and this time much more deeply

as they fumbled with each other's clothes, stripping them away and dropping them to the ground. Isabelle pressed Tony against the mattress and straddled him. His erection was full as she took it in her hand and lined it up with her opening. As she sank onto it, he gasped and bit his bottom lip.

They were not worried about Myrtle hearing them this time, as she was not yet back from the picnic. Thusly, their cries and shouts went unheard by anyone but themselves.

"Yes!" Tony shouted, holding onto her hips when he climaxed inside of her. "Oh, baby, yes!"

"Uh uh," she noted and rolled her hips a little. "Say my name."

He obliged, saying her name with each upward thrust... each blast of his hot love juice that he spilled into her, and when he was finished, he continued on for a second round, ensuring he brought Isabelle to the greatest orgasm of her life – an orgasm that she scream his name through, over and over again.

### End

# The Layover

Her flight was scheduled for 11:35 a.m. and the airport was absolutely packed. Security hadn't taken nearly as long as she'd thought, which was a definite plus, but she worried about the crowd. Even though everyone in this part of the airport was either a ticket-holder or an employee, she was concerned about pickpockets. Although Maria had never been robbed before, she'd heard horror stories from other people who'd told her tales of how they'd arrived in the airport with their wallets or purses, but when they'd started to board their flights, those things had gone missing. Thusly, she clutched her purse close to her body and kept her single piece of carry-on luggage at her side and in her grip.

It was snowing outside, which was another thing she didn't care for. Normally, she wouldn't have minded the snow, but the idea of having it cover the ground as she was soon to board a plane frightened her. What if the runway wasn't properly cleared? What if the plane began to taxi down it and started to skid?

To make it worse, she was traveling further up north, where the weather was assuredly worse. This hadn't been in the plan when she'd scheduled this trip to visit her sister in New York. It was only the start of December. Why didn't the snow have sense enough to wait until Christmas like it was supposed to?

She found a seat near a window and made herself as comfortable as possible. From within her oversized purse, she took out a paperback romance novel that she'd purchased yesterday just for the flight. It was a trashy sort of novel according to the blurb, but that was just what she'd wanted. Love and lust – nothing mysterious or horrific. The idea of flying in the snow was horrific enough for her.

An hour and a half passed and several flights boarded and took off. She noticed that the waiting area had cleared out drastically, with only about thirty or so people currently lingering around. Her flight was the next one scheduled, and so she assumed that most if not all of these people would be joining her aboard. Coyly, she studied them, looking for anyone strange or suspicious. There were a few families – parents with children – and a several couples. There were also the solo travelers. They were easy to spot, as they mostly sat alone, spaced out from the rest with empty seats around them. She was one of those solo travelers, and there were five seats separating her from the nearest person.

Even though no one looked particularly suspicious or dangerous, there was one man that caught her eye across the room. He was seated by himself, also near a window and reading a newspaper. He too had only one carry-on bag, and it was parked beside him. He reminded Maria a bit of the love interest in her book. Likely around thirty years old, tall and slender, with dark brown hair and eyebrows that were well-formed above his thin black-framed glasses. He also reminded her a little of Clark Kent from the comic books, and she had to wonder how close to a superman he really was.

He looked up from his paper and noticed her glance. Embarrassed over being caught, she returned her eyes to her book, but not before she noticed he smiled at her. Coyly and refusing to make eye-contact, she smiled in return.

Over the top of her book, she studied him on and off until the boarding of their flight was announced. Then, she made sure to trail behind the group so that he was ahead of her. Even though she found him attractive, she didn't hope to start up a conversation with him. Men like him were for looking at and fantasizing about. Even though Maria considered herself attractive, she'd never been approached by such a specimen, and in turn, she never approached them. It was an unwritten rule of hers. She could look, but she didn't dare attempt to touch.

While she waited in the boarding line, she texted her sister to let her know she would soon be in the air. Then, she crossed herself and said a silent prayer that the snow wouldn't cause her flight to crash and burn.

She watched the attractive man with glasses show his boarding pass and then walk through the terminal and into the loading chute. Maria noticed his rear as he walked. It seemed to flex with each step, and she felt a bit of sweat form on her brow. She stood in a daze with that image dominating her mind before she heard the attendant call to her.

"Miss?" Distracted from her thoughts, she turned her focus

to the attendant. Only then did she notice everyone else in front of her had already passed through and was boarding. "You're next."

"Oh..." She stepped up to the uniformed woman and showed her ticket and identification.

"Have a wonderful flight," the woman said as she allowed her to pass.

"You too," she said, absently and lost in thought. Then, realizing what she'd said, she corrected herself. "I mean, you have a good day."

The woman smiled at her and then looked to the next person in line.

Maria boarded the plane, stowed her carry-on, and found her seat. She was in an aisle seat, with the middle seat next to her vacant and an elderly man sitting by the window. She didn't mind this arrangement. There was no one right next to her, and she hated sitting by the window. Looking out at the clouds so close disturbed her. It was a reminder to her that people were meant to be on the ground and on their own two feet. Flying was to be left for the birds.

Had her sister not booked the flight for her, she would have likely taken a train or rented a car, but with the snow falling so heavily now, she worried about those methods of transportation as well. Were they any safer than being in the sky? At least soon, she would be above the clouds and above the snow that fell. It was still landing that she was concerned with. Just waiting for the plane to take off, she noticed through a glimpse out the small window that the snowfall was heavier than it had been when she'd been inside the terminal's waiting area. What if it became too heavy and the plane couldn't land?

Or, worse yet, what if it tried to land and couldn't stop?

She looked away from the window closed her eyes, focusing on her breathing. Slow, deep and steady breaths always helped to relax her, and momentarily, she found it working. When she was calm again, Maria opened her eyes again and sighed.

The stewards addressed the passengers and went through the various safety precautions. Then, they heard an announcement from the plane's captain, letting them know they were about to take off. Maria checked her seatbelt and made sure it was secure. Then, she fished her book out of her purse and tried her best to focus solely on that.

Within a few minutes, she felt movement and looked up from the book and back toward the window. The plane was taxiing down the run away and preparing for liftoff. She watched with wide eyes as everything went horizontal outside. They were taking off, and the safety of the ground was gone from view.

When the plane was in the air and flying steadily, the passengers were informed they could unfasten their safety belts and were free to move about the craft. That, she thought, was the worst advice they possibly could have been given. There was no way she was going to unfasten her belt, nor would she stand up and move around this plane. She wanted it to reach her destination and safely land so that she could get off it – plain and simple.

"I wish I was in first class..." she grumbled beneath her breath.

"Don't we all?" asked the old man next to her, who was staring out the window watching the clouds go by. "Remember that old episode of *The Twilight Zone*? The one with William Shatner?"

She looked at the old man and shrugged. "I've never seen the show."

"It was a terrifying episode," he continued. "In it, Shatner was on a flight similar to this and in a window seat like I am. Looking out the window, he noticed a monster tearing apart the plane as it flew through the sky. It was the scariest of all the episodes."

Maria cringed and swallowed. "I'm glad I missed it then," she confided. The old man said nothing more, but all she could think about now was that some horrible monster had hitched a ride with them, just to sabotage the flight by dismantling the plane from the outside.

"Excuse me," she heard another man's voice coming from straight ahead. Looking toward it, she saw the curtain to first class part, and the handsome man with the glasses stepped through. "Pardon me," he said as he walked down the aisle, trying not to bump into anyone's knees or step on any feet as he did. "Please excuse me," he told one lady whose leg was stretched out into the aisle. "First class's restroom is *conveniently* out of order."

"Phooey for you," the woman told him and, with a bit of an

attitude, pulled her leg back in front of her.

Maria instantly buried her nose back in her book as he approached her. She hoped he didn't recognize her from before when he caught her staring at him. She wanted this flight to end with as little drama as possible.

Needless to say, he stopped right beside her.

"*Love Everlasting…*" he remarked, reading the title of the book. "Isn't it interesting when a man writes a bestselling romance?"

Nervously and almost bashfully, she looked up at him and then at the cover of her book. She hadn't noticed before that it was written by a man – Judd Williams. Offering a shrug, she replied, "I guess everyone has to make a living somehow."

"I suppose. Enjoy the book." He smiled at her and then continued on toward the small restrooms beyond the next curtain.

Once he was a few feet away, she sighed in relief. She hadn't wanted him to speak to her. He was supposed to be the object of fantasy, like Lois Lane dreaming about a romp in the bed with Superman. Fantasies like that weren't supposed to stop and talk to women like her. She was a school teacher, for crying out loud. The only men that paid attention to her were also usually school teachers as well, although sometimes she caught the eye of a chubby waiter or an older mailman. Most of the men she'd dated fell into the categories of geeks or losers – either unattractive men with good jobs or somewhat attractive men with no jobs who were with her for the financial security… if you could call a teacher's salary financial security.

She focused her eyes back on the pages of her book, but she refused to read another word until the attractive man made his way back up the aisle and into his first-class seat where she wouldn't have to see him again. With that thought, she was now thankful she'd been booked in coach.

Momentarily, he returned, and this time, he did not stop to speak to her. Yet, as he passed her by, she found her eyes drawn once again to his muscular bottom as it flexed with each sturdy step he took. Her mouth almost watered over the sight of it. She almost wanted to reach out and give it a good squeeze, but she didn't dare. That was the type of forward move that women like her just didn't make. The last ass she'd squeezed had been soft and as moldable as an out of shape pillow.

When he was back in first class and the curtain stilled, Maria was finally able to return her focus to her book. However, every time the hero made his appearance, all she could picture was that handsome, well-build man with the flexing bottom in the hero's place. He seemed to take over in the fantasy of the novel, and when the scenes became intimate, she found herself become heated from them. There was a tingling between her legs when the hero ripped his shirt off, and she could imagine that man in the glasses doing that very move.

Maria shut the book. If she read anymore, she knew she would grow wet between her legs. She was on an airplane with an old man two seats over. She had to retain her sense of decorum.

There were magazines in the back pocket of the seat in front of her, and so she tucked her book back into her purse and took a magazine in its place.

It was a catalog, offering various flight-oriented merchandise for sale. There was also a section on unusual and eloquent gifts that could be ordered. Each had such an expensive price tag that she thought her eyes would pop out of her head from the shock. Still, thumbing through the catalog helped to take her mind off of the handsome passenger, and she browsed slowly through each and every page until a message from the captain came over the speaker system.

"Attention, passengers," he began, and Maria wasn't sure she liked the tone of his voice. "It appears we are flying toward a blizzard and will be unable to land at our destination. We will be laying over in the small town of Frampton, in upper Illinois."

A layover? This was the second worst thing that she could think of happening. She had plans with her sister. She had a destination to reach. How could there be a layover? That was definitely not in her plan for this week.

"There will be a bus meeting us at the airport to take us to Frampton's only hotel. We've been assured that there are rooms available, and we will be there at least through the night until we've received word that it is safe to continue. I apologize for any inconvenience."

The speaker system silenced, but the crowd on the plane replaced the captain's voice with loud moans, groans and gripes of their own. Maria stayed quiet, but inside, she was both fuming and panicking. Fishing her phone from her purse, she tried to text her sister, but there was no service. Either she was out of range, or the snowstorm had seen to it that outside communications would be thwarted. Neither of those was pleasant, and she wanted to scream or cry or storm to the cockpit and demand that the captain continue on to their destination.

Yet, if he did, they would be in peril. She just *knew* it.

"This is why I hate flying," she finally muttered.

"At least there's not a monster on the wing tearing the plane apart," the old man told her. "At least, not yet." He smiled at her and then returned his eyes toward the window.

Maria swallowed down a lump in her throat and wondered if it would be inappropriate to smack an old man for trying to scare her. Even though she knew it would be, the idea was still tempting.

About fifteen minutes later, the sign to fasten seatbelts lit up. Maria barely noticed, as she'd never unfastened hers to begin with. Then, glancing past the old man to the window again, she noticed that the world was once more heading behind her in a diagonal position, only this time, the plane was moving downward, preparing for a landing.

At least, she thought, she would be in a hotel and in a private room, away from this chaos and the old man that was trying to terrify her. She would also be out of range from the hunky man in first class, and in time, he would be fully out of her fantasies… out of her mind.

Even after the plane landed, it was still a good twenty minutes before the passengers were allowed to leave it. When she finally stepped off, she noticed she was in the smallest airport she'd ever seen. There were only two terminals inside, and out the window, she could see only one other plane. It was small and rickety and had an old-fashioned propeller on the nose.

"Where the hell are we?" she whispered to herself, even though she knew exactly where they were. They were in some town called Frampton and far from New York City.

In the small lobby, she saw the man from first class sit at a seat near a window facing the front. He made himself comfortable and pulled a magazine out of his carry-on bag. From where she stood, she couldn't see the title of the magazine, but his glasses made him look intelligent so she imagined it was *Forbes* or *Newsweek* or something along those lines.

She sat on the opposite side of the lobby, as far from him as she could. With his nose buried in the magazine, she studied him for a bit longer. He sat with good posture and properly, without his legs crossed or kicked out lazily in front of him. She did not know why she was somewhat obsessed with him. Perhaps it was because he'd noticed her looking at him before, and he had smiled at her. Maybe it was due to the fact that he'd noticed the book she was reading and had commented on it... that he had talked to her. His voice had been smooth and suave... sexy.

Maria huffed and looked away from him. She fidgeted in her seat and wondered what to do. She didn't want to take her book out again. It reminded her too much of him. She looked around for a newsstand or a small bookstore, but there was nothing like that here. The most civilized thing she saw was a large coffee urn near the ticket booth. It was surrounded by stacks of white Styrofoam cups and packets of powered cream and sugar. This was a far stretch from the *Starbucks* that had been at the last airport.

Ignoring the coffee, she simply closed her eyes and tried to relax. Yet, the moment she calmed, she heard the announcement that the bus had arrived to take them to the airport. She opened her eyes and looked out the front windows. There, she saw a big yellow school bus waiting in the snow.

"A school bus?" she questioned aloud. "They sent a *school bus*?"

The passengers began to form a line at the door. She saw the man with the glasses was in the middle of it, and so she tailed behind at the end. The door opened and the line processed outside into the cold. She wondered where her big suitcase was, but she quickly realized that everyone's luggage was still on the plane.

One by one, the passengers climbed aboard the bus, filling the seats from the front and down to the back as instructed. Maria's seat was the very last one on the bus, and she was thankful to be hidden in the back. She reached for a seatbelt to fasten, but there was not one there. Then, she remembered that most school buses were still not equipped with them – something she'd protested over several times during her teaching career. At those times, she'd protested for the safety of her students. Now, she once again worried for her own safety.

A teenager was in the seat next to her. He seemed as put off by the situation as she was.

"This sucks," he muttered and groaned.

"Yes..." she agreed. "Yes, it does."

The ride to the hotel was lengthy, and when they arrived, she learned they'd been misinformed. It was not a hotel – not by any means. It was a roadside motel, with exterior entrances to the guest rooms and an appearance that reminded her greatly of the Bates' Motel in *Psycho*.

"Perfect..." she whispered. "Just flippin' perfect."

"This place looks creepy," the teenager replied. "Do you think anyone ever died here?"

She considered his question and then glared at the structure. "By the looks of this place, I'd say everyone that has ever stayed in it probably slept with the lights on... if they slept at all."

The bus unloaded, and as Maria was the last passenger on it to step off, she was at the back of the line to wait for a room. Along with many others, she waited in the snow. The lobby was the tiniest she'd ever seen and only fit a couple of people at a time. Slowly, the line began to move, and when she was halfway to the door, she watched the man with the glasses step from the line and hurry around the building. There, in the shadows of the building's side, she could see his silhouette. Maria didn't have to see him to know what he was doing. He was relieving his bladder, and it made her realize how full hers was. Although she'd not drank anything on the flight, she'd had four cups of coffee leading up to it, and her bladder was full and heavy because of them.

She wouldn't join him at the side of the building. That was something that just wasn't going to happen. She let her eyes move around the building's exterior doors and, at the far end, she finally spotted a restroom sign that the handsome passenger had obviously not noticed. Swiftly, she made her way to it, and inside, she found the room to be disgusting.

Lining the toilet seat with paper, she settled down and let her bladder release. When she was finished, she tried to flush the commode, only to discover it was out of order. The sink also did not work, which made it impossible for her to wash her hands.

"How is this place even in business?" she wondered as she stepped from the room and headed back to the line. It was much shorter now, but much to her disappointment, she found that she now stood directly behind the man with the glasses.

"Did you really use that restroom?" he asked her, not looking back at her.

"Unfortunately…" she muttered, feeling her anxiety soar from his communication with her.

"Brave woman."

That was the last thing he said, as the line moved forward again and just the two of them were left outside in the snowy cold.

It was the most awkward and uncomfortable that she'd felt yet. He stood directly in front of her, and even though he was in a full suit, she could do nothing but picture him naked, like the hero in her book had been in several of the scenes she'd made it through. She wondered if his bottom – the one that was literally now inches away from her – was as firm and beautiful as it appeared in those pants. Then, she wondered if he was really as strong and slender as he appeared once that shirt, jacket and tie were stripped from him. After a moment of contemplation, she averted her eyes from him and looked up at the falling snow. It wasn't coming down quite as heavily as it had been, but it was still falling pretty hard. The ground was fully covered, and for the first time, she noticed her shoes were in the same shape.

Finally, it was her turn to enter the lobby, and she followed the handsome man inside, nearly jumping out of her skin at the sound of the door closing behind her. Maria waited as patiently as she could as he checked in. Then, as he gave his information, she thought she would faint.

"What's the name?" the male clerk asked him.

"Williams," he replied. "Judd Williams."

*Impossible*! she exclaimed in her thoughts. *Absolutely impossible*!

Fishing the book out of her back, she opened the back cover to the author's bio. A photo was included, and seeing it nearly made her heart stop. The man in the picture was undeniably the man standing in front of her – the man who'd commented on her reading choice... the man she'd blown off with a simple and unimpressive reply.

*Perhaps they'll let me just stay in the school bus,* she

thought and started to turn away. But when she looked out the window, she saw the bus's headlights were on and it was starting to leave the parking lot. It would not be staying overnight with them.

"You're up," Judd Williams told her, stirring her attention. She looked at him with wild eyes, speechless and dumbfounded.

Judd stepped aside and ushered toward the counter. Hesitantly, Maria approached it and began to hunt for her wallet in her purse.

"Sorry, lady," the clerk told her in a gruff tone. "We just sold out."

"Wait. You just *what?*" She couldn't believe her ears. This was so much worse than what she'd expected. She'd expected to be put in a rickety old room with a shower and a curtain in front of it, and for some creepy man dressed in his mother's clothing to knife her to death. Being slaughtered by Norman Bates suddenly sounded much more pleasing than freezing to death in the cold.

"Sold out," the man repeated. "You know... it's what happens at places like this when all the room are booked."

"But that's impossible," she countered in an angst-ridden tone. "We were told you had plenty of rooms."

"No... I told the airport we had *rooms*. I never said anything about plenty. Now, if you'd like, there's a motel in the next town, but the bus station won't open until six and the first bus out is at seven-thirty."

"What am I supposed to do until then?" She began to panic

and to grow angry all at once. It was beyond her how this could happen, but it was happening, and it was horrible.

"There's a supply closet near the restroom," the man said. "I can give you a blanket and a pillow, but there's not much room to lie down."

She stared at the man for a moment, waiting for the punch line – for him to admit this was all a bit hoax and they had a room ready for her. Yet, he simply stared back. Finally, with no other option and nowhere else to go, she gathered her purse and her carryon bag and stormed out of the lobby and back into the snow.

She wasn't sure how far away that next town was, but she had no choice but to walk there. Two things would happen. She'd either make it to it, or she'd freeze to death trying. Either option seemed better than spending the night on the floor of a supply closet.

Behind her, she heard the door open and shut. Ignoring it, Maria continued on, but after a few steps forward, she heard a man call behind her.

"Hey, now!" the man shouted, drawing her attention. "Hold on there!"

Turning around, she saw Judd Williams hurrying after her. He was by far the last person she'd wanted to see right now. She'd already fully embarrassed herself in front of him – reading his book and having no idea he was standing there talking to her. Now, he was following her out in her moment of despair.

"Go to your room, Judd," she said in a firm tone and kept

walking.

"Only if you'll go with me," he told her, and his words stopped her in her tracks. "Otherwise, screw this place. I'll walk with you. If you want to freeze out here, the least I can do is keep you company and freeze too."

She stood still and quiet for a moment, keeping her back to him. She didn't know what to think. While his offer of sharing his room sounded like a wonderful fantasy straight out of his book, it also sounded quite impossible – like most fantasies. What did he want from her? Did he expect her to share his bed… to simply turn herself over to him as a thanks for keeping her out of the cold?

"My room has a sofa," he continued when she said nothing. "You can have the bed. I can take the sofa. Trust me; I've slept on plenty of them before."

She scoffed with a laugh. "You're a successful writer," she told him, still keeping her back to him. "You fly first class. I doubt you've ever had to sleep on a sofa before."

"I wasn't always a successful writer, you know. I wasn't born with a bestseller in my tiny infant hands. I had to make a lot of sacrifices to follow my dream, including spending a lot of nights on couches while crashing at friends' houses." He silenced for a moment, but she offered nothing in reply. Then, adamantly and almost abrasively, he added, "I'm a person, you know. Not just a celebrity. And right now, I'm freezing my balls off out here trying to help you. The least you could do is turn around and face me."

She considered Judd's words, and despite her better

judgment, she finally turned around and looked at him. Despite how adamantly he'd pleaded with her, he was smiling charmingly. Snow was building on his shoulders and in his hair, dusting his jacket in white.

"There now," he told her. "You faced me, and you didn't turn to stone."

She couldn't help but smile back, as the humor of his comment was obvious.

"If you try to hoof it to the next town, you'll never make it. Not unless you hitchhike, and in this snowstorm, I don't see much traffic coming through. It's already dark… probably because of the dark clouds and the early dusk, and if anyone picks you up out there… do you really trust whoever it would be?"

Not once in her life had Maria hitchhiked, but she'd heard the horror stories about rapists and murderers. Judd had a valid point, and she had no choice but to relent.

"Okay," she told him, almost bashfully. "I can't argue with you. I'm freezing and this whole scenario has exhausted me."

"So, you'll take me up on my offer?" His expression almost looked hopeful.

"I'm out of options," she admitted. "It's this or die, right?"

"Pretty much," he said. "I mean, I bet the wolves and coyotes are probably pretty hungry right now too."

"Okay, that one's pushing it a bit."

As she said the words, she heard a wolf howl in the distance. From the sound, she shuddered.

"Is it?" His smile widened. "Quit fighting me on this and just come with me. It'll be warm and probably more comfortable than standing out here in the snow."

Once more, she couldn't argue with him, and as she relented, she said, "Okay. Let's get inside. I'm freezing."

Still keeping her distance, she followed him to his room – number twenty-two. Inside, they discovered it was nearly as cold as the outside had been. Judd went to the thermostat to adjust it, but quickly discovered it didn't work. All it blew was cool air.

"There's no heat," he announced, and Maria thought she'd burst into tears. "But there are extra blankets in the closet... and another pillow."

He took two of the three blankets and spread them over the bed's comforter, ensuring it would be as warm as possible for Maria. She watched as he did this, noting the chivalrous gesture and feeling he was more like the hero in his book than she'd earlier thought. Judd then took the extra pillow and the last blanket and put them on the sofa.

"Should we watch some television? The sign outside read: 'Free HBO.'"

"You can if you'd like," she told him as she pulled the covers back on the bed. "I'm pretty exhausted. I know it's early, but I really just want to go to sleep and let the rest of this awful day slip away."

"I can't say I blame you." He took the remote and went to the sofa and sat. "If it's too loud, let me know." He powered on the television. It instantly shorted out and went black. "Or... maybe sleep is all that's in the cards tonight." With a toss, he flung the remote to the floor and sighed. "I hate cheap motels."

Before climbing into bed, Maria decided to try her sister again. She took her phone from her purse but noticed immediately that she still had no service. Frustrated, she set the phone on the nightstand and looked for a room phone, but this small roadside motel offered no such device in its guest rooms. *It figures*, she thought. This was the by far the worst motel she'd ever seen.

She looked over at Judd, who had dragged a magazine out of his bag and was flipping through its pages on the couch.

"Thank you," she told him, feeling she owed him that much, "for getting me out of the cold."

He looked up at her and smiled. "You're welcome, Miss."

"Maria," she said and smiled back. "Maria Barone."

His smile widened. "It's good to meet you, Maria Barone."

"Likewise." She smiled again, kicked her shoes off, and climbed into bed.

The room was quiet and chilly as she drifted off to sleep. Almost instantly, she began to dream. In her dream, she was within the novel she'd been reading and was playing the role of the protagonist. Judd was the hero – one who had already stripped down to nothing but his underwear and was enticing her with his lean but muscular and sinewy body. No words were spoken as he approached her, and when he kissed her, she felt such electricity that they began floating off the ground. Then, it occurred to her they had not been on a ground at all. They were on a ship in the middle of a vast ocean with blue skies and bluer water for as far as the eye could see.

When the kiss ended, they lowered back down to the ship's deck, and in turn, Judd lowered Maria onto her back. She'd been dressed when floating with him, but now she was almost naked, wearing only her panties and bra. Judd came down onto his knees and grinned hungrily at her as he wrapped his fingers beneath the waistband of her panties and tugged them from her body. Then, standing again, he took off his underwear and kicked them into the water.

She stared at his marvelous package – the most exquisite specimen of masculinity that she'd ever seen. It was fully erect and throbbing with its readiness. She parted her legs and spread her lips with her fingers, inviting him to venture inside of her.

Their eyes remained locked as he returned to his knees and crawled up as close to her as he could get. He propped a leg onto each of his shoulders and lined his tool up with her opening. Then, with a slight push, he entered her and filled her, working to satisfy her primal craving for him. He leaned forward to her so that they were facing one another, pushing her legs back and spreading her wider for full penetration. Just as he entered as deeply as he could go, she felt a coldness that shattered the moment. She blinked from it, and when she reopened her eyes, Judd was no longer inside of her and she was still in the bed of the crappy hotel room.

Taking her phone from the bedside table, she noticed it was

nearing one in the morning, and the room was absolutely freezing – likely just as cold as it was outside. She looked over to the couch. Judd was trembling fiercely beneath the thin blanket.

She couldn't let him freeze. After all, he'd ensured she wouldn't by bringing her inside and giving her the bulk of the covering. Maria tossed the covers from her and began to stand. Only then did she notice her panties were soaked from her dream.

It was an uncomfortable wetness, and so she tugged them off from beneath her dress and crammed them inside of her purse. Then, feeling the sticky remains of her moisture, she stood and walked to the couch.

Gently shaking his shoulder, he looked at her with sleepy but conscious eyes.

"Come to the bed. It's much warmer there," she said. "You're freezing."

He looked at the bed and then back at her. "Are you sure?"

Maria smiled and nodded. Then, she took his hand and helped him stand. In a moment, they were both beneath the covers with as much warmth as this hotel allowed them. Judd had even thrown on the blanket he'd had on the couch.

Their body heat helped to warm them, but Maria could not fall back to sleep. All she could think about was her dream and the fact that she had the dream's very specimen lying right beside her. His eyes were closed, and through the dimness of the room, she studied his beautiful face and watched him as he breathed.

He was still trembling, and so she snuggled up close to

him, wrapping an arm over his chest. He'd removed his suit jacket and white shirt and tie. All he wore was a white t-shirt and his black slacks. Judd opened his eyes and looked at her again, smiling.

"Thank you," he said, and then turning onto his side, he wrapped an arm around her as well. This brought them close together with their faces only a few inches from each other. Their eyes remained open for a bit. They seemed to get lost in one another.

Then, in a daring move and one she'd never normally try, she kissed him softly on the lips. She was prepared for him to withdraw from the kiss and perhaps throw a fit over it, but he did no such thing. Instead, he kissed her back with warm tenderness.

Maria began to grow brave, remembering her dream and kissing its hero. She ran her hand down his side and rested it on his hip. She could feel his left cheek beneath her fingers and she squeezed it. Judd followed suit, caressing her thigh through the thin fabric of her dress.

The room began to warm from the sudden heat of their newfound chemistry. She stopped squeezing his cheek and pulled her hand forward a bit, feeling a bulge growing beneath the fly of his slacks. With her eyes still locked onto his, she found his zipper and tugged it down. Slipping two fingers inside his fly, she caressed his manhood, noticing he wore no underwear, unlike in her dream. He sucked in a breath and then kissed her again.

Maria felt his hand leave her cheek and clutch her dress. He tugged it up enough to slip his hand beneath it, and she trembled as his index finger pressed into the vee of her legs and caressed between her lips. She was still soaking wet, and the wetness encouraged him to rub her with a deeper pressure.

Even as they kissed, she moaned deep inside. She unbuttoned his slacks and released his manhood – thick and lengthy. It felt like the biggest one she'd ever held. She squeezed it and ran a finger over its tip. Feeling its sticky secretion, she was encouraged to begin stroking it.

Judd inserted his finger into her opening as she handled him. Their kissing ceased as they gasped and moaned, but the break from the kiss was only a break. As he rolled on top of her and lined himself up with her opening, it resumed. The kiss was the only thing preventing her from screaming with ecstasy as he pushed into her, and the deeper he went, the more passionate the kiss became.

Their tongues met as he started to thrust inside of her. She parted her legs for him, allowing him deeper entry, and he accepted the wider spread with eagerness. With their tongues wrestling, he held a steady speed, pulling back until only the head remained in her, and then gently pushing his full length deep into her each time. She broke the French kiss long enough to ask him to do it harder and faster... to give it to her in the way that her body yearned for it.

Judd happily obliged, but he still handled her with care and tenderness. He didn't talk to her with a slur of curse words like they did in the few dirty movies she'd seen. Instead, he told her how beautiful she looked to him and how good she felt to him. He told her how much he'd wanted her since first noticing her in the airport lobby, and he whispered sweet nothings to her in the way that a longtime lover would have to their mate.

He gasped with a giant grin as he felt her wetness soak over his member… as he heard her whimper and tremble beneath him. He'd somehow managed to bring her to a full orgasm – the first one she'd ever received from anyone but herself. No man had ever been able to satisfy her in bed before. Judd was not just any other man though. He was tender and masculine all at the same time, and he devoted as much energy in pleasuring her as he did pleasuring himself.

He held steady inside of her throughout her orgasm. She clenched her muscles around him, contracting through her electric flood. Her moans were loud and hoarse, but she didn't care. She was in absolute bliss, and despite the freezing cold of the snowstorm, she was sweating and hot. Judd was sweating also. His t-shirt was absolutely soaked.

"I don't think I can last much longer," he whispered to her and then nibbled on her earlobe. It was true, she thought. She could feel him throbbing inside of her. He was close to orgasm, and she yearned for it.

"Fill me," she whispered back. "Please… give it to me."

He grunted and began to thrust into her again. The throbbing of his member intensified, and then he began to cry out.

146

She could feel herself filling with his juices as he fired off his rounds – an impressive amount, she thought. She tightened herself around him once more, helping him to contract through his orgasm, and then she wrapped her legs around him, holding him there even after he had finished.

"You're so amazing, Maria," he whispered to her and then kissed her again. This kiss was soft and tender, like the very first one they shared.

"You're pretty remarkable yourself, Judd," she admitted when the kiss broke.

They showered together, washing away the sweat and remains from their erotic interlude, and then they dried each other with the lone towel that the room provided. When they returned to bed, they did so naked, and in each other's embrace, they drifted off to sleep.

When they awoke, the storm had ended and the school bus had arrived to return them to the airport. They dressed in the clothes they'd stripped off last night, except for Maria's panties which were sticky and in need of washing. When they loaded the bus, they sat in the very back together and enjoyed each other's company.

"So, what are you going to New York for?" he asked her as the bus began toward the small airport.

"I haven't seen my sister in three years and tomorrow is her birthday," Maria said. "How about you? What's taking you to the Big Apple?"

"A book tour," he admitted but cringed when he said the words. "I was supposed to appear on a talk show this morning. It was my last stint on the tour, but I don't think I'll make it." His cringing expression lightened as he chuckled. "Are you going to stay with your sister?"

"Yeah, but it won't be comfortable. She has a tiny apartment with two bedrooms and three kids. I may grab a hotel room when we land."

He took her hand and caressed it. Looking into her eyes, he asked, "Would you like a little company? My schedule is clear for the rest of the week, and I'd really like to get to know you better. I've never met anyone who makes me feel quite like you do."

"Oh?" she questioned, brightening at the comment. "And how do I make you feel?"

"Like a real person," he admitted. "Like a real man. Maybe I can be *your* man for a bit... if that's something you'd like? I don't want this to be a one-night fling. I'd really like to see where this goes."

She squeezed his hand and blushed ever so slightly. "I think I'd like that a lot, Judd. I really do."

"I have one condition though."

"What's that?" she asked, almost afraid of what he might say.

"I get to pick the hotel. There's no way I'm staying anywhere without heat and room service after this layover."

She laughed at the remark and said, "Deal." Then, they

kissed again, and they continued to do so for the rest of the trip to the airport.

## *End*

# *R*emember to *B*reathe

Her name was Melody Campbell and she was as shy as she was beautiful. At twenty-four, she'd taken a job no one else in her small town seemed to want, that of head librarian at the public library. There were a few reasons why she considered it the perfect job. For one, it was a quiet place and Melody hated loud noises. When there was a raucous nearby, she would turn the other way. She was a peaceful young lady who wished for the world around her to be the same. In the library, peace and quiet went hand in hand.

Secondly, she was a lover of the written word. She always had a book in her hand, whether she was dining on a meal, walking down the sidewalk, or lying in bed. Books were the gateway to endless stories, unlimited universes, and the types of romances and intrigue that did not seem to exist in the real world anymore. The library was full of these books, and she had the distinct ability to order more every month to ensure her patrons were never at a loss for 'word.'

Thirdly, the library was a safe harbor away from young men who only had one thing on their minds – sex. The people who frequented the library were most often older women, young children, or teenagers that were being forced to read one book or another for school. Rarely did some man in his twenties wander in to browse the shelves. When they did, it was because they were looking for something to read, not because they wanted to crawl up Melody's skirt.

She had no interest in men that wanted her only for her body. If a man caught her eye, it was usually because they were interested in a book that she'd either read and enjoyed or that she too was interested in reading. Those were the men she enjoyed, and her communications with them were limited to the types of discussions one would have had in a book club.

Another reason the library was perfect for her was because of the children. Once a week, she got to host a story time, and small children would come and sit and listen to her read to them. She had a great way of narration, always voicing each character in a book uniquely and to fit their personalities. The kids were always enthralled, and their cheering and applause at the end fulfilled her in a way that nothing else could ever surpass.

Aside from all of this, she was not an incredibly social woman. She had few friends, all of which were females either her own age or older than she. Melody also had no social media accounts, as she believed her private life was hers alone, and she didn't believe in airing out her dirty laundry for all eyes to see. Gossip was her least favorite form of communication, and she steered from it like it was the plague. Over the years, she'd been the subject of many gossip hounds, who spread rumors that she'd slept with this guy or that one, but they had all been lies. Just because she was beautiful, jealous people had a habit of making up ugly rumors about her to taint her image.

The fact of the matter was, she not only hadn't slept with the men she'd been accused of; she'd never had sex with anyone. Melody was a virgin, and she was proud of the fact. Raised with old fashioned morals and values, she believed in saving her bodily temple for the right man, and the right man would be one who never insisted on sex before she was ready. So far, that right man had not come around.

She had dated several guys over the years, but none of them had lasted. They had either pushed too hard to enter into her sacred vestibule and she'd cut them loose, or they had tired of waiting for her and had cut themselves loose. Sometimes she was hurt by this, but always, she knew they were out of her life for the best possible reason: to preserve her for a man that would love and accept her beyond the physical beauty that she had to offer.

However it went, Melody was happy and kept her self-esteem high. She wasn't a prude by any means. She liked music, the occasional bad foods, and she really enjoyed margarita nights with her girlfriends. There were things she was terribly conservative about though. She did not cuss, she preferred to use the proper names for genitalia, and she didn't like to watch sex scenes in movies. Reading them in books was a completely different thing. In books, she could imagine the scenarios herself as fantasies and picture the characters how she wanted to see them. In films, she was watching two real people simulate sex, and she was not a voyeur. She believed their intimate parts were best reserved for those that they explicitly shared them with.

The bell over the library door dinged and Melody looked up from her latest read. It was Paul, a regular to the library. Paul was tall, slender, wore glasses, always dressed in a cheap but nice looking suit and tie, and had some acne, despite being only a year younger than she was. His nose was a little long, and his lenses were so thick that they made his eyes look a little strange behind them. He had a great sense of humor though, and he was incredibly intelligent. His taste in books was also pretty nice. He'd often ask Melody for recommendations, and he'd take those recommendations, read the books, and then talk with her about them later. Paul was one of her favorite patrons and she loved to see him walk in the door.

"Hey, Miss Campbell," he said in a cheerful voice as he approached her counter. Paul had never called her 'Melody,' even though she'd told him often that he could.

"Paul, you're looking dapper as always today," she said pleasantly with a smile. In Paul's hand, he held a copy of *The Great Gatsby* - her most recent recommendation for him. "Did you enjoy the book?"

He set it on the counter and beamed. "I did not expect that ending!" he exclaimed, a bit louder than he should in a library, but she loved his energy so much that she never corrected him on it. "It had everything though. Mystery, decadence, romance… murder!"

"Fitzgerald's description of the elite atmosphere, the

fashions, the houses and cars… that was what always got me the most in that book," she told him. It was one of her favorite books, and she was thrilled that Paul had enjoyed it.

"I finished it yesterday afternoon," he continued. "Then, I started researching it a little on the internet and saw it was playing at the classic movie cinema in the next town. Needless to say, I drove out and took in the movie. It wasn't quite as good as the book, but it was still really good!"

"There's a remake also," she offered. "It's a little different than the version you saw last night, but it's visually stunning. We have it on the DVD aisle if you're interested."

"Am I ever!" Excitedly, Paul left the book on the counter for Melody to check in and hurried over to the aisle with the movies.

She kept her smile as she watched him walk away. Paul was pretty close to being her ideal man, but she wasn't sure they would have made a great pair. She was average sized and voluptuous, while he was tall and lanky and had a little more energy in his little finger than she usually contained in her whole body. Either way, she thought he was cute and charming.

When he was out of her line of vision, she took his book, scanned it into the system, and checked it in. A glance to her watch told her it was nearing lunchtime and she was beginning to feel a bit hungry. She was allowed to lock up the library for an hour at lunch, and glancing around, she noticed Paul was the only patron there. As soon as he made his selection and was checked out, she was free to lock up and grab a bite to eat.

After a few moments, Paul approached with the DVD in hand. He had a big smile on his face – as usual.

"Wow! This cast is fantastic!" he told her as he set it down with his library card. She took both, pulled up his account with the card, and then checked out the movie.

"No book today?" she asked, finding his lack of a reading selection to be unusual.

"Not today," he replied. "I got to town early yesterday before the movie started and went to this really nice antique bookstore. I bought a first edition hardback of *1984*. I read it in high school, but figured I'd get more out of it with an adult perspective."

"Wow!" she exclaimed and handed him the movie. "That must have set you back a bit. I imagine a first edition of that book is pretty pricey."

"Do you know Bloomfield Industries?"

"I've heard of them, but I don't know too much about them," she admitted.

Paul's smile grew. "That was my grandfather's company. He passed it on to my dad when he died, and when Dad passed, I inherited it. I'm not much for running a company, so I sold it last year. The first edition didn't really set me back anything."

Melody's eyes widened. While she was not one to strive for fortune, she found Paul's inherited wealth impressive. "That's fantastic," she told him, and she was truly proud for him. "I bet your girlfriend is super proud."

"Girlfriend?" he asked and cocked an eyebrow. "Wow, don't I wish… I mean, look at me, Miss Campbell. I'm the town geek. If a woman is interested in me, it's only because she knows I'm rich. Otherwise, the females just look the other way when I walk by. I sort of prefer it that way though."

"Why's that?" she wondered aloud. Paul was a super guy. She couldn't imagine women treating him poorly or being after him just for his money, but she knew there were women like that out there. Those were the ones who gave females in general a bad name.

"I'm saving myself," he said proudly. "When Miss Right comes my way, I'll know. Until then, I'm more than happy to be single."

All of a sudden, she was more impressed by Paul than ever before. She was amazed at his values and at how the crueler people of the world did not affect them – because, like her, he wouldn't let them. This made him strong… it made him a man.

His eyes left hers and went above her head to the clock on the wall. Suddenly, he looked a little deflated. "It's lunchtime," he announced and took a step back. "Time for you to lock up and get some food."

"I suppose you're right," she said and shrugged. Then, she pleasantly added, "I do hope you enjoy that remake. Please, let me know what you think?"

"You can count on it, Miss Campbell." He smiled again

and stepped to the door. As he pushed it open, he turned his head back to her and added, "I'm so glad you're our librarian here. You're very easy to talk to." Then, he stepped through the doorway and continued on, letting the door shut behind him.

Melody watched him through the window until he reached his car. Then, she sighed – almost dreamily – and locked the library door.

Normally, she would have grabbed her purse and headed out the door, on her way to one restaurant or another for lunch. This time, she returned to her seat behind the counter and relaxed. She thought of Paul and his mention of the antique bookstore in the next town, and then she pulled up her internet browser and began to search for it. Quickly, she found it – a place called The Ancient Attic Books and Collectibles. It was a good half hour drive from here, and they closed an hour after the library closed. She would have to wait until tomorrow, when she was off for the weekend.

"I can be patient," she thought as she wrote down the address and name of the store and tucked it into her purse. Then, closing the browser, she stood, collected her things, and finally left for lunch.

As it happened, Melody walked into the very restaurant that Paul was dining at. He sat alone at a booth by the window, gazing out in an almost lost state. From a booth not far from him, three women were looking at him and whispering. On and off, they giggled, and twice, Melody caught them rolling their eyes at him.

They were teasing Paul; she could tell. Deciding to show

them up, she walked rather sensually to Paul's table and stood across from him.

Instantly, he noticed her and perked up. A smile crossed his lips. "Miss Campbell!" he exclaimed. "What a pleasure to see you here."

"Hi, Paul," she told him and glanced to the girls at the other booth as she flipped her bouncy blond hair over her shoulder. "Mind if I join you?"

She smiled at the girls, who promptly sneered and looked away.

"Oh, wow… It would be an honor. Please, order anything you like. My treat!"

She could see he was excited, but she had no intention of taking advantage of his good financial fortune. "Nope," she said and shook her head. "My treat. I insist."

"Really?" She could see the dumbfounded look that filled his eyes.

"Yes. Now, tell me what's good here."

Paul ordered a Reuben sandwich with a small salad, and Melody had the same. They each had water with hot tea to drink and opted out of dessert. As they ate together, they chatted about the usual – books and what they've read and wanted to read.

"Have you ever read *Lady Chatterley's Lover*?" Paul asked as he sipped his tea.

"No," replied Melody, "but I've heard the movie is nothing but softcore eroticism."

"Ignore the movie," he continued. "The book is a beautiful romance, although it was once on the banned book list in America. When the film rights got purchased, they took a wonderful novel and turned it into smut."

She smiled in consideration. "I might give it a read then. I'm guessing you've seen the film?"

"I made that mistake, yes," he admitted. "They made a sequel too with Adam West, but I opted out of that one after my disappointment in the first."

"I can't imagine having to watch Adam West in a dirty movie."

"Neither can I, and I hope I'll never accidentally stumble onto it when it's on television."

They chuckled over this comment and finished their meal. Then, before it was time for her to stand up, pay the check, and return to work, Melody got brave and asked him something she'd never asked any of the library's patrons before. "What are you doing tomorrow afternoon, Paul?"

He cocked his head to the side and smiled wider. "I don't know... I just bought a new car and was thinking of taking it out for a spin. Why do you ask?"

"I want to check out that bookstore you visited, but I don't really want to go by myself. How would you like to come with me?"

He looked at her for a long moment before replying, as if considering her words and unsure as how to respond. Then, he said, "I think that would be wonderful. I have just one condition."

"Oh?" she questioned and straightened in her seat. Her eyes showed her intrigue. "And what's that?"

"That I get to drive."

Melody chuckled and accepted his offer, and at one o'clock the next afternoon, they met in the library's empty parking lot. The car that Paul pulled up in was a classic 1960 Cadillac 62 convertible, red with a white top that was already folded down. He wore black sunglasses and smiled at her from behind the wheel. Melody felt her heart skip a beat. Not only was the car absolutely stunning and in pristine condition, but Paul looked like he'd just stepped out of the sixties, himself. He wore a vintage brown suit with a crisp white shirt, unbuttoned at the collar with no tie. It was the first time she'd ever seen him without a tie, and without eyeglasses on his face.

"Wow!" she exclaimed as she walked up to the car. "Is this the one you just bought?"

"Yeah," he told her with pride in his tone. "Do you like it?"

"Like it? I love it!" She climbed in and buckled the seatbelt. Then, concerned over the sunglasses, she asked, "Can you see okay to drive?"

He laughed and shrugged. "They're prescription. I have my regular glasses in the glove compartment for when we get to the store. The lighting in there isn't very bright, and if I keep these on, I won't even be able to read a book's title."

The sunglasses and the casual look of his unbuttoned collar

made Paul look less like an intelligent nerd – for lack of a better term – and more like some debonair playboy that reeked of money. She liked the change, although she still didn't care about his money. She was, however, beginning to care about Paul, and as they left the parking lot, that was all that seemed to matter.

They took a longer route into the next town, utilizing a country back road that he could pick up the speed on a bit and show off his new car. For Melody, it was a thrilling experience, and unlike any she'd ever had before. She squealed with excitement as they sped down the road, and she laughed with joy the entire way. All the while, Paul proved to be a cautious driver and kept both hands on the wheel and his stare to the road ahead.

The wind tussled with her hair a bit, but she didn't mind it. The ride was exhilarating, and when they finally pulled off onto the town's main road, she was a bit sad that the fast-paced thrill ride had come to an end.

When they reached the store, Paul parked right up front. He hopped out without opening his door, walked around to hers, and opened it for her. It was perhaps the most romantic gesture anyone had ever done for her, but she didn't know if he saw it that way. Perhaps he was simply being chivalrous. Either way, she appreciated it and thanked him.

He also held the door to the shop open for her. When she stepped through, she saw he'd been right about the lighting. It was dim, but manageable. The door closed behind her and she turned and looked for Paul, but he wasn't there. Then, through the window, she saw him back at the car, retrieving his eyeglasses from the glove compartment. When he put them on and came inside, he looked like the same Paul that came into the library almost every day. It was amazing what a change sunglasses to eyeglasses made.

Still, she found him handsome, even if it was in a goofy sort of way.

They were greeted almost immediately by a clerk that looked up from her book and said, "Twenty percent off all books a hundred bucks or more," and then looked right back down at what she was reading.

Melody looked up at the shelves around her – the seemed to stretch right up to the shop's ceiling, which must have been over twelve feet high. There were more books in this place than she thought were in her library, and she was impressed by it – but not by the clerk. The clerk seemed impersonal and in the wrong business, she thought.

Where there weren't books, there were busts, artworks, oddities that she didn't know quite what they were, and antique posters and framed documents. The books, however, were prevalent.

"This place is amazing," she said as she walked alongside Paul and glanced at the titles on the shelf nearest her. "I've never seen so many books in one place before."

"That's something, especially coming from a librarian," he noted. "Have a look around. Maybe you'll see something you like."

"I'm sure I will," she told him, although she doubted she'd be able to afford much of anything here. She coyly glanced at just a few price tags on the books nearest her and cringed. This was definitely a store meant for browsing, not buying. At least, that was the case for Melody. Librarians didn't make much. She was lucky to be able to afford her rent and utilities every month, with a little left over for some small treats here and there. Of course, buying Paul's lunch earlier had put a damper on anymore treats for a while, and she didn't dare use her credit card in this store. It would take all year to pay off the interest.

"See something?" he suddenly asked and startled her. "Hey, sorry... I didn't mean to frighten you."

Melody smiled and shrugged. "I'm easily startled, so don't feel badly about it. And no... I thought I saw a title I'd been looking for, but I was wrong." She lied. She rarely ever lied, but she didn't want to let on that she was as poor as she was. Her financial state was her own worry, and she didn't want to put a damper on Paul's fun.

"What title are you looking for?" he asked, and she sighed. Was he calling her bluff? She didn't want to lie again, but she'd put herself in that position. Now, she had to deal with it.

"Nothing in particular," she said, fudging it so that it wasn't a big lie and hopefully one that wouldn't require more lies to cover up.

"How can you see a title you've been looking for, but it

being a 'nothing in particular' title?'"

*Crud...* she thought and shrugged. "Okay... I lied. I'm sorry. I looked at a few titles, saw some of the prices, and I didn't want to admit to you that I can't afford anything here. It's a great store; it really is! And I'm so glad we came here. It's just a bit out of my price range."

Melody hung her head low and pouted. Paul put a gentle finger beneath her chin and lifted her face up again so that she could look into his lens-covered eyes. He was smiling, when she'd expected him to be offended.

"There's no shame in that," he told her. "Before I inherited the company and sold it, I wouldn't have been able to afford anything in here either. Besides, I didn't earn my wealth. I lucked out. Not everyone lucks out like that, and those people work hard for everything that they have. What you have, you've earned." His smile widened and she saw the humanity in his eyes that matched that of his words. She nearly swooned from it.

"So, you're not mad at me?"

"Mad?" He laughed – a single *hah*. "Not at all. I don't think I could ever be *mad* at you, Miss Campbell. You're like a beautiful spring day, full of loveliness and light. What's there to be mad at in that?"

His words were like poetry to her, whether he intended them that way or not. She didn't know how to respond with words, so she offered him her best smile instead.

"There's that smile I know so well," he said and then

looked around the shop. "This place is a little stuffy... and dusty." Looking back at her, he added, "There's a cute little ice cream shop just a few spaces down from here. I owe you for lunch yesterday anyway. What do you say? They make a killer banana split."

It was an offer she suddenly found she couldn't refuse. "That sounds wonderful."

"Let's go."

On the way out the door, they heard the clerk mutter, "Come again," in a low and somewhat distant tone.

The ice cream shop was indeed right down from the bookstore, and Melody decided to try one of those banana splits Paul raved about. He ordered one as well, and when they arrived, she thought it was bigger than her stomach could handle. It was absolutely huge, but both she and Paul made an effort to try and finish them. Neither succeeded, and when she couldn't eat another bite, she thought she would explode.

"You're going to have to get a wheelbarrow to get me back to the car," she told him and pushed the platter away.

"I think we both need a wheelbarrow," he joked. "We can get two brutes to push us and see who makes it to the car first."

Melody laughed, but she stopped quickly as it did nothing but push on her full stomach. She had a feeling that her size four waist had likely just jumped up two additional notches, but she didn't care. She was having fun, and with a guy who seemed to be having fun with her too. Most importantly, he hadn't made a single move on her. However, she wasn't so sure anymore that she preferred this. The more time she spent with Paul, the more she liked him.

"Have you ever gone to the observatory?" he asked her. She looked and saw he was staring out the window. "It's absolutely magical at night."

"No," she replied. "I've never really had the opportunity."

He looked at her again and his sweet smile widened. "It's open late tonight. I've gone stargazing there many times. They have the best view and the strongest telescopes around. If... you're not doing anything later...?"

"Well..." she said, considering his invitation, "I didn't have plans, but..."

"But?" His eyes widened with hope.

"But I think I have some now." She put a hand on his and wrapped her fingers around it. He grabbed her fingers with his. It was a kind, soft grip – gentle, as a man should have been with a lady.

"You'll love it," he told her, beaming with inner joy that was written all over his face.

Looking at the small watch around her wrist, she asked, "It's still a little early to look at the stars though. What will we do until then?"

"Well..." He thought the question over and then leaned into her just enough, but not too much for her comfort. "There was another movie playing at the classic cinema alongside *The Great*

Gatsby."

"Yeah? What is it?"

"*Breakfast at Tiffany's*," he replied with an excited grin.

Her smile matched his. "Audrey Hepburn, here we come!"

*Breakfast at Tiffany's* just happened to be one of Melody's favorite films of all time. She was also a huge fan of Truman Capote's book that it was based on. There was one distinct thing that made the movie a little better than the book for her though, and that was an appearance by one of her favorite actors, Mickey Rooney.

She'd seen the movie several times, but it was one she'd never tired of. As they sat in the theater and looked beside her at Paul, watching his expression as he watched the film, she saw that he was enjoying it too. She wondered if he'd read the book, but his whispered words answered the question.

"Truman Capote wrote some fantastic stuff," he remarked and pointed at the screen. "Usually, movies based on books don't live up to their source material, but I think this film is exceptionally good."

In that moment, Melody decided to let down the guard she'd long built up and she rested her head on Paul's shoulder, snuggling in to watch the rest of the film. He wrapped an arm around her and placed his hand on her shoulder. She felt no desire to pull away from his warm and tender touch.

When the film was over, he drove her to the observatory, which was located just outside of town. It was dark when they arrived, and the night sky was crystal clear. They stayed there for a good hour, while Paul pointed out various constellations and told her their names in both English and in Latin. She was impressed with his knowledge of astronomy, as he could even show her on the telescope what planets were what, although they all looked much like more stars to her. She didn't admit that she couldn't tell the difference. He was too much in his element for her to burst that bubble.

"I'm sort of a science geek," he admitted as they walked down from the observation deck. "My dad used to take me out stargazing when I was a kid. He bought me my first telescope when I was nine. I became hooked on it."

"The universe is beautiful," she told him, "especially when someone explains to me what's what as well as you do."

He grinned but didn't reply. Instead, they left the observatory and walked to the parking lot. In the car, he asked, "Is it time for home?"

She didn't really want the night to be over; they'd had so much fun together today. But she was exhausted, and part of that was likely to be blamed on that huge banana split and the dark cinema they'd sat in right after.

"Yes," she told him and fastened her seatbelt. "It's getting a little late."

"I'll take you back to the library so you can get your car."

"No…" she shook her head. "If you'd just take me home. I can walk to my car in the morning. It's only a couple of blocks."

"Are you sure?"

"Certainly."

He smiled and nodded, and in about forty minutes, they were back in their small town. He didn't speed as he drove her home, which gave her comfort. Night vision was different than seeing the road during the daytime. It showed her how cautious he was, at least when he was with her.

He parked the car in front of her building and left the engine running as he got out and opened her door. Then, he walked her to the door and smiled down at her. She smiled in return.

"Thank you for a really wonderful day," he said. "You're an amazing woman, Miss Campbell."

"Please, Paul," she whispered. "Call me Melody." Then, standing on her tiptoes, she leaned in and gave him a soft and quick kiss on the lips. When the kiss broke, she added, "Maybe we can do this again sometime."

Paul was blushing from the kiss and grinning from ear to ear. "I'd really like that. Have a nice night, Melody, and pleasant dreams."

She held her smile steady as he walked back to the car, and she watched him until he'd driven off and was out of her line of vision.

In her apartment, she went straight to her room and changed for bed. Then, laying atop her covers with her head on her pillow, she thought of Paul and the wonderful time they'd had together. She couldn't wait until she saw him again, and with his vision filling her mind, she drifted off to a nice, deep sleep.

When she awoke the next morning, he was still on her mind. The memories of yesterday helped her from her bed, and as she showered for the day, she thought only of him and what they would do the next time they went out together. She thought about calling him, but she realized she hadn't gotten his number, nor had he asked for hers.

She considered driving to the library and looking his information up on the computer system, but that seemed a little obsessive to her. She didn't want to hound him or stalk him. Then, she decided she would take this Sunday for herself, and she would place her focus on tasks around the apartment. If Paul was still on her mind tomorrow as heavily as he was now, then she knew they would enjoy another yesterday in the future. If he wasn't, she understood she was simple reveling in the fact that she'd been on her first date in ages, and with a decent man.

Sure enough, when Monday arrived, all she could think of was him. From the moment she woke until she walked into the library, Paul dominated her thoughts. She'd never been out with a man so charming, dapper, and chivalrous as he was, and just the thought of him lifted her up so much that she sometimes felt like she was floating just above the floor.

Melody opened the library for the day and welcomed her patrons as they trickled in, returned books or gathered books, and entertained her with light conversation. Patiently, she waited for Paul, to come in and chat with her about their Saturday out or about some book he'd read or a movie he'd watched, but by lunchtime, he had not made an appearance.

She ate at the diner they'd eaten at together on Friday, hoping he might have been in there, but he wasn't. When she returned to the library, she feared he might have stopped by and she might have missed him. Then, she remembered that he knew the library's schedule like it was stitched into his brain. He wouldn't have come during the lunch hour, knowing she wouldn't have been there.

At an almost painfully slow pace, the day passed and closing time arrived. Paul was a no-show, even though he'd never told her he would be in today. Still, she'd expected him to show. He always came in on Mondays, seeing as the place was closed every weekend.

She began to feel a bit depressed – a feeling that didn't hit her often. Melody worried about what might have gone wrong. Had her kiss goodnight been too forward? Had he not seen her like that, but only as a friend?

She began to worry that she'd ruined what was blossoming into a good friendship. He was probably the nicest man she'd ever been out with, and she'd come on too strongly for him – blown it with flattering remarks and a soft kiss at the end of the night. Melody suddenly began to feel like some of the men she'd dated before – the ones who had made moves on her when she hadn't wanted the moves to be made.

Fifteen minutes after she was supposed to close, she finally flipped the sign on the door to 'closed' and began to turn off the lights. When she locked up and stepped into the parking lot, she looked for his car, but only hers remained. Saddened by this, she climbed inside and drove herself home.

That night, she planted herself on the couch in front of the television with a big bowl of ice cream in her hands and an old movie on the screen. It was *The Day of the Locust* – a film that often messed with her mind and frightened her, but one she enjoyed. Yet, even as she watched Donald Sutherland unravel the odd occurrences around him, the film failed to distract her from her thoughts. Midway through, she turned off the television, put her bowl and spoon in the sink, and went to bed.

For the rest of the week, Paul was absent from the library. On Thursday, she quit looking for him and began to feel a little angry at him. If he had a problem with how they'd ended their night, she felt he could have been man enough to have come in and talked to her about it instead of just avoiding her. Paul *loved* the library. There was no reason for him to exclude it from his life simply because they'd gone on what had felt to her like a date.

On Friday, she wasn't mad anymore. She was just disappointed. Disappointed in him... disappointed in herself. She looked up his account on the computer system, wondering if he had anything overdue. If that was the case, she could at least call him and notify him. But no, his library record was squeaky clean and everything he'd checked out was already checked back in – everything but the DVD of *The Great Gatsby*, which wasn't due in until next Friday.

"Another week..." she groaned and clicked the X box on the screen to close it. "He'll probably leave it in the drop-off box outside, afraid to face me."

Over the course of the weekend, she did everything she could think of to keep Paul off her mind. She cleaned her apartment from top to bottom, organized all of her drawers and closets, and rewashed every dish that was in her kitchen. That took up all of Saturday, and on Sunday, she got in her car and drove to the park, where she spent the day feeding the ducks and watching families play with their children. She loved children and had hopes of having a couple of them one day in the not so near future. However, if she wanted to have kids the natural way, she'd have to have a man in her life, and that brought about thoughts of Paul again. He would have made a great father, but not for her children. She'd well scared him off for that to ever happen.

Frustrated by the return of him to her thoughts, she returned to her car and drove to the library, opening up and entering, promptly locking the door behind her. It took a few moments for the computer system to fully boot, and when it did, she pulled up Paul's information. His phone number stared boldly out at her, and she reached for the phone but hesitated.

Did she really want to call him? To check in on him? To touch base with him? To find out where she went wrong.

"Yes... yes, I do."

Lifting the receiver to her ear, she punched in the digits and listened as the line rang. It was answered on the third ring, and by a female's voice.

"Hello? Bloomfield residence," the kindly voice asked. Melody cringed. Had she been out with a taken man? No… that was impossible. He'd said he didn't have a girlfriend… that he was waiting on the Miss Right to come into his life. "Hello? Is anyone there?"

She wanted to hang up, but instead, she replied, "Yes. This is Melody Campbell from the public library. I'm just calling to check in on Paul. He hasn't been in at all this week, which is very unusual for him."

The woman on the line chuckled. "So, you're the famous Melody…" *The famous Melody*? she thought. *What was that supposed to mean?* "I'm sorry, but he can't come to the phone right now."

"Might I ask how you've heard of me?" she asked. Confusion exploded through her brain like fireworks on the Fourth of July.

"You're all he talks about," the woman replied. "He'll be so glad to hear you called. He's been pretty upset about not being able to talk to you."

This was most certainly news to her. "Might I ask why he can't speak with me?" She tried to keep her voice steady and pleasant, but it was the most difficult thing for her to do right then.

"Oh, yes… I'm sorry. Mr. Bloomfield suffered a seizure last Sunday morning. He's prone to them, and too much exposure to technology brings them on. He's got to have rest, but the doctor said he'd be back to his old self by Monday."

A seizure... Hearing that was a slight relief but it also made Melody feel horrible and frightened for him.

"He wanted to call you, but he didn't have your number, and he surely can't drive again for a while – not until he's sure the new medications make it safe for him to do so."

Melody swallowed and felt the shaking that came from her entire body. "I – I understand. Is it possible for me to pay him a visit? I know he needs rest, and I promise I won't stay long."

The woman on the line let a light laugh slip through. "I think he'd really like that. He's been terrible depressed. Yesterday, he swore up and down you'd never speak to him again. Do you need the address?"

She considered asking for it, but remembered it was on his account information. She opened the browser for the page to load. "I have it right in front of me," she said. "Please, let him know I've called and that I'll be over soon."

"I'll let him know you called," said the woman, "but I'll leave your visit as a surprise, if that's okay with you."

Melody smiled. "Thank you. Might I ask your name?"

"Oh, yes. I'm sorry. My name is Mary. I'm the house manager. I oversee the rest of the staff and ensure Mr. Bloomfield is well taken care of."

Suddenly, just by the description Mary gave her, Melody realized that money spoke in volumes much greater than she'd realized before. Now, she was a bit nervous about visiting him, but she now knew why she hadn't seen or heard from him, and she wanted so much to let him know she wasn't angry about it... not anymore, anyway.

"I'll be there as soon as I can." She thanked Mary and ended the call.

On her way to the address listed on his account, she stopped off and bought him a cheap balloon and a cute teddy bear that held a heart that read 'Get Well Soon.' It was corny, she realized, but she didn't want to show up empty-handed. She wanted to let him know she cared, and hopefully a teddy bear with a heart would get the idea through to him.

The address led her into the country on a road surrounded by trees on either side. Finally, she reached a large stone mailbox with the correct digits on it. Slowly, she turned onto the driveway and drove for around another mile or so before she reached a set of large iron gates with a small guardhouse located beside them. Pulling up to the gates, she saw an intercom on a post beside her and lowered her window.

Pressing the button, she gave her name, and in a moment, the gates opened. Now, she felt a little more nervous than before. This kind of entrance screamed the type of money that belonged to the type of man that would normally want nothing to do with a woman of her social standing. After she'd driven through, she looked in her rearview mirror and watched the gates close behind her.

Melody drove for another few minutes until the trees thinned and a great clearing opened up. At the edge of that clearing was a cul-de-sac driveway with an enormous brick manor on the other side of it. A man in a tuxedo and a woman in a simple black dress stood before the steps, seemingly awaiting her.

She parked in the drive in front of the house and stepped out of the car – a car that she just knew they were probably looking at as if it was an eyesore. Embarrassed by it, she walked up to the two people and said, "Hi. I'm Melody Campbell."

The man remained stiff and silent, but the woman extended a hand for a shake. Melody timidly accepted. "It's a pleasure to meet you," the woman said in a chipper tone. "My name is Mary. We spoke on the telephone."

Melody smiled, relieved that it was, at least, the person she'd earlier conversed with. "It's good to meet you," she told her and then followed her up the steps. The man in the tuxedo opened the door for them, and after they'd entered, he closed the door and stood at its side.

"That is Jensen. He's buttled this estate through three generations of the Bloomfield men now."

Jensen bowed slightly at the waist and asked, "How do you do?" in a voice that was prim, proper, and British.

"A butler…" Melody noted to Mary. "I didn't know they existed anymore."

Mary chuckled lightly. "He's grandfathered in. This is his home, and he takes his job quite seriously. I imagine he'll be the butler of this estate until he's ready for the grave."

"Oh… Well, I hope that's not any time soon."

"He's eighty-three now," continued Mary, "and he shows no sign of slowing down."

"I'm impressed," Melody commented. "When I'm eighty-three, I just hope I can still stand upright on my own."

"It's all in how you live," the house manager informed her and led her to a grand staircase in toward the back of the large and elaborately decorated entrance room. "We must be cautious when we reach the second floor. Harriett, one of the maids, just waxed the floors in that hall only an hour or so ago. They could still be rather slick."

*One of the maids…* Melody thought. How many maids did a single man need?

Upstairs, she saw the floor extended in both directions for quite a bit. Mary led her to the right, where they walked to the door at the far end of the hall. When they reached it, Melody felt her nervousness twirl around in her stomach.

Mary knocked twice and waited. Almost instantly, Paul's voice could be heard calling, "Come in."

With an acute slowness, the house manager twisted the knob and pushed the door inward just a bit. She then turned to Melody and held up a finger, beckoning her to stay where she was. Melody nodded, and Mary entered.

"I'm sorry to disturb you, Mr. Bloomfield, but you have a visitor."

"Ha!" he laughed, but not in a humorous way. "Who'd visit me?"

Melody could hear the depressed tone in his voice, and she immediately felt worse for him. He hadn't meant to avoid her, and yet she'd made no attempt to reach out until now. It was a simple case of misunderstanding, and she hadn't counted on him feeling as badly about this as she did. Yet, by his tone, she knew it was more than just the seizure and the bed confinement that had him down. Mary had said it already; he worried he'd never see her again.

Mary opened the door and stepped off to the side, allowing Melody to enter. When she stepped into the room, her heart sank deep into her gut. Seeing him lying on his bed, sad and lonely, made her want to weep. Yet, when he looked up at her, his eyes grew wide in disbelief, a smile grew over his face, and she smiled in return.

"An angel..." he muttered and sat up a little. "An angel has come for me. I must have died and am on my way to heaven."

There was that poetic way of speaking that she loved so much, and Melody hurried over to his side. "Paul... I just found out what happened. Are you okay?"

He chuckled and nodded his head. "Yeah, I'll be fine. They have me on the absolute *best* medication, or at least that's what they've told me." His expression softened and his eyes narrowed to the covers atop him. "I'm sorry I couldn't call you. I wanted so badly to, but the doctor ordered rest with no interruptions, and

Mary takes everything so literally."

Melody glanced at the house manager, who shrugged and smiled. "I swore to your father before he died that I would do everything in my power to keep you safe," she said. "You can't fault me on that."

"I can sure try." He smiled again and winked at her.

At his bedside, Melody pulled up a chair and sat. She took his hand into hers and squeezed gently. Looking at Paul, she thought how fragile he appeared without his suit and glasses, confined to a bed. He looked pale – a sign he'd not been outside in days. She stroked his hand tenderly as she held it.

"I'll leave you two alone," Mary said and stepped back to through the doorway, "but this visit should be kept short. Paul has to rest up and get well if he ever wants to resume his normal life. Until his body becomes used to them, the medications make him weak and tired."

"It's true," he said to Melody as Mary closed the door behind her, leaving them be. "I sleep almost all day." He looked at her hands holding his and added, "But I'm sure awake now."

Melody's emotions were getting the best of her. She'd been angry when she hadn't heard from Paul, and when she found out he'd suffered a seizure, she'd become terrified – terrified for him, and terrified of losing him. Still, even with all he was going through, he still found the energy to flatter her and make her feel special.

She fought away the urge to cry; he didn't need to see her

be weak right then. Instead, she put on her most stunning smile and asked, "Can I tell you something, Paul?"

"As long as you're not telling me goodbye, you can tell me anything."

His words brought back the swell of tears and one trailed down her cheek. Breaking free of her grip, he reached over and wiped it away.

"I don't ever want to tell you goodbye again," she said in a trembling tone. "I want you to get well so that we can have countless more days and nights like we had that Saturday."

Paul's smile grew so wide that it could have lit the moon. "What are you trying to say, Melody?"

Bravely, she spilled her emotions in the most non-chaotic way she could manage. "I'm trying to say that I think I've fallen in love with you."

He looked at her for a moment, raising one eyebrow. Then, he chuckled lightly. "I don't know if I have the energy for fun and games right now."

"I'm not teasing you," she insisted. "I'm being blatantly honest."

His stare held hers and his winning smile returned. Once more, he wrapped his hand around hers and squeezed. "Then, may I tell *you* something?"

"Of course."

"I *know* I've fallen in love with you. I've been in love with you for a long time now, but I never thought anyone as wonderful as you are could love me back."

It was like a scene out of one of those classic films that they loved so much, and Melody once again began to feel like she was floating toward the stars. Elated beyond words, she leaned forward and kissed him. This time, the kiss was not as soft and innocent as the one they'd shared that night in front of her building. This one was full of passion – more passion than she'd ever shown a man before – and she realized as Paul kissed her back just how good of a kisser he was.

When the kiss broke and they both took a breath, Melody prepared to say something else, but Paul did not give her the chance. Instead, he brought her into another kiss and held her close. This kiss was softer, tender, and enticingly passionate. It was broken only due to the sound of Mary opening the door and clearing her throat.

Taking that as her cue to leave, Melody stood and brushed Paul's hair away from his eyes as she smiled down at him.

"Promise me you'll visit me again soon," he asked in a voice that showed needed.

"Every day until you're on your own two feet again," she promised, "and then I expect you to visit me."

"What if they won't let me drive?"

Melody looked at Mary, who shrugged her shoulders. "Why not? I've been aching to drive that convertible since he brought it home." She smiled as Melody and Paul shared one more kiss, and then she escorted Melody back to the car she'd arrived in.

\* \* \* \*

Melody and Paul were married on Christmas Eve inside of a cathedral that was decked out for their Christmas Mass services. Outside, snow fell heavily, coating everything around with a blanket of white fluff. The cathedral was packed. Everyone that seemed to have any acquaintance with Paul was in attendance, and it looked like the rest of the small town's population had joined them. When the couple sealed their new marriage with a kiss, the cheering from the crowd was near deafening.

They rode home to their manor in the backseat of a stretched limousine, where they drank champagne, held hands, and watched the snow through the window. There was no reception following the wedding; they'd insisted on that. If it had been up to them, they would have eloped, but they had their friends, family and colleagues to take into account. Thusly, they had the wedding for those people. Everything following was just for Melody and Paul.

"We leave for Hawaii in two days," Paul said as they neared the estate. "I can't wait to walk barefoot along the beach with you."

"I can't wait to spend our first Christmas together tomorrow," Melody added. "Spending it with you will make it the most wonderful Christmas ever."

He smiled and kissed her, nearly spilling his champagne

but preventing it at the last second. They both giggled about it, and then they kissed more.

In their room, Melody sat at the foot of the bed and watched as Paul stripped away his tuxedo jacket, cummerbund, bow tie, and shirt. He wore a white tank-top that showed off muscles she hadn't realized he had. In all of their months dating, they'd never seen one another without their clothes on, or even being close to naked.

She stood and turned her back to him. Slowly, he unzipped her wedding dress and untied the bow at the collar and the waist. She let the dress slink off her shoulders and slip from her body to the ground. Softly, she stepped out of it.

Turning around to him and facing him in nothing but her white corset and underclothes, she grinned as he pulled his t-shirt off and tossed it to the ground.

Melody was nervous. She knew what was about to happen, and it would be the first time she'd ever shared her body in this way with another person. Still, despite the nervousness, she was giddy and excited.

Paul unfastened his belt and pulled it from his tuxedo pants. It landed on the ground with the other clothes. He pushed himself out of his shoes using alternating feet, and then unbuttoned and unzipped his pants. Melody saw the white of his boxer shorts and felt her pulse begin to race.

With delicate ease, Paul took her in his arms and kissed her as he lowered her back onto the bed. One hand was on her hip. The other caressed her cheek. Her hands held onto his back, keeping him close.

When the kiss broke, she looked into his eyes and asked, "What do we do?"

He smiled and replied, "What do you mean, what do we do?"

"I – I'm a virgin, Paul... I don't know anything about this sort of stuff."

"I'm a virgin too," he admitted, and it was the first time either of them had admitted this to the other. When it came to intimacy, they both agreed they had a barrier that was waiting to be broken by marriage, but neither had known the other was immaculate.

"So, how do we handle this?" Her words were breathy. She ached for him. She knew that she wanted him inside of her, but she was timid about it. She feared it would hurt, and she feared that he might not enjoy her as she hoped to be enjoyed. What if she bled? Would he shy away from her, afraid he'd injured her? Would he ever be brave enough to try again?

He stood upright and she stood with him. He undid her corset and let it drop to the floor. Then, he removed her garters and stockings. Finally, when she was only in her bra and panties, he unlatched the bra and pulled it from her breasts. Instantly, his smile widened.

"Are those beauties really mine?" he asked. She could see he was anxious and nervous, just like she was.

"And no one else's," she replied. She kissed him and distracted him as she lowered his boxer shorts and squeezed his bare bottom. As she did, a part of him stiffened and grew against her. She broke the kiss and looked down at his manhood. It stood up in full salute impressively. Melody wrapped her hand around it and squeezed. It was the first time she'd ever done such a thing, and the way he purred deep within himself made her realize they were on the right track.

"Your touch feels so good," he whispered and looked down, watching her squeeze him. "I'm so hungry for you."

Melody let go of his erection, stroking her fingers down his scrotum as she did. Then, catching his gaze with hers, she tugged her panties down. She took his hand and pressed it onto her heated virginal prize.

"Oh, wow!" he exclaimed and licked his lips. "You're so warm there."

She took a step back, letting his hand fall away from her womanhood. Then, she sat on the bed and spread her legs, showing him what was now his.

"Please," she said as she spread her lips with her fingers. "I need you in me…"

Paul lowered himself onto his knees and crawled up to her. He replaced her hands with his and gazed at her budding flower. Then, he pressed his tongue to her and took his first taste of female splendor. She heard him moan as he tasted her, but her moan was louder and nearly muffled his out. He began to lick her deeply, and she began to tremble from this brand new sensation – one she'd never expected to feel because she'd never truly known what to expect.

He was gentle as he feasted on her, but she whimpered and grasped the covers around her in an almost violent way. This seemed to be an encouragement to Paul, who pressed his tongue inside of her and tasted the sweet wetness that was starting to build.

"Oh, Paul..." she gasped and pressed the back of her head firmly against the bed. "Yes... oh, yes, Paul!"

He fed on her for several minutes, delivering the greatest pleasure to his new wife that she'd ever known. The feeling of his tongue exploring her most private regions was so exhilarating to her that Melody found another brand new feeling come over her. In a jolt, she raised her torso and put both of her hands around the back of his head, holding him in position. Then, a surge of unexplainable electricity raced through her and she began to cry out in deep, harsh moans as she shuddered and trembled. It was, she realized, her first real orgasm, brought about by the man that she loved more than anything. This orgasm caused Paul to feed more hungrily on her, tasting her fluids and working for more.

After a moment, she let go of his head and he pulled his mouth away from her intensely satisfied vagina. He looked at her with a grand smile and licked his lips.

"Wow..." he told her as he stood on wobbly legs. "That was the most... delicious experience of my life."

"Please, Paul," she begged once more, although it was hard to find her words. She was still shaking. "Please... be one with me."

Paul kept her stare as he took his member into his hand and pressed it against her opening. As he entered her, Melody felt a slight and sudden pain, as he broke through a barrier that no man had crossed before. He saw her wince and he held in place right where he was, cautious of moving any further.

"Are you okay?" he asked her and leaned forward to her.

She bit her lip and smiled. "Mhmm..." she muttered from the back of her throat.

Paul wrapped his arms around her and held her close. Then, as he pressed deeper inside of her, he kissed her with tender and loving passion.

Softly, he rocked into her, slowly going deeper with every new stride. She moaned through the kissing, feeling herself stretch and throb in ways she never could have fully imagined before. Sure, she'd read about moments like this in books, but the erotic scenes had never seemed so vivid and felt so real as what she experienced now. Having her new husband inside of her was something completely different. It was a form of nirvana that she'd never known possible.

"Remember to breathe, my love," he told her, breaking the kiss. It didn't occur to her until then that she had indeed been holding her breath. "Tell me if I'm hurting you."

"You feel like magic," she whispered and kissed him again.

That evening, as they gave up their most valued possessions to one another – their virginities – Melody and Paul became as close as a husband and wife possibly could. But it went deeper than that. They truly felt that their souls had bonded in ways neither had known possible, and it was a bond that they knew was meant to last until the end of their days and far beyond.

*End*

# *The Preacher's Son*

When her husband divorced her to be with a woman that he'd been having a three year affair with, Tonya had been devastated. She'd known he was cheating on her. There had been telltale signs. He'd come in from work much later than he'd told her he'd be. He's smelled differently than when he left – the scent of perfume that was not her own. In bed, he'd not wanted to do anything sexual with her, claiming he was exhausted. One, as she was doing the laundry, she found a hotel room key in his back pants pocket. Another time, she'd noticed lipstick on the crotch of his white briefs.

Perhaps Tonya would have been able to forgive all of this, had it not been for the fact that he'd been sleeping with her *former* best friend Sarah. Often, when Charles would let her know he'd be out late, having to work extra hours in the office, she'd call Sarah to see if she wanted to have some girl time. Sarah always refused, swiftly running off some tale or another over why she was busy and couldn't make it.

On one such occasion, Tonya decided to go out anyway and treat herself. She dressed nicely and went to a fancy restaurant, where she hoped to indulge in some bubbly champagne and a meal fit for a queen. Yet, as the waiter appeared to take her order, she noticed another couple being seated at a table not too far from her. It was Charles and Sarah.

She'd made a scene, leaving her table and marching right up to theirs. First, she slapped Charles hard against the cheek, nearly sending him to the floor. Then, she did the same thing to the woman who had claimed to be her best friend. She said nothing to them after that and hurriedly left the restaurant. The whole ride home, she'd cried hysterically – sobbing and mourning the loss of something she'd already known was gone.

That night, she put all of Charles's clothes out on the lawn, along with all of his sports memorabilia and anything else she could find that reeked of him. Three days later, he called and told her he was filing for divorce with claims that he was leaving an unstable marriage with an equally unstable wife.

Tonya refused to fight him in court, but she hired a lawyer, found a middle ground for the paperwork, and signed her name to it. Charles did the same, having the nerve to bring Sarah with him to the meeting. Once the papers were signed, she stood from the table and left the office, refusing to ever look back at him or on the horrible way he'd treated her.

Still, the process had been rough on her. She became depressed and withdrew from the outside world and into herself and the comfort of a new apartment, having lost the house in the settlement. She'd been able to prove the affair, and Wayne was required to pay alimony to her monthly. That check was enough to handle her rent, utilities, and food. There was little left for anything else.

There was little of anything else she actually needed. Tonya was an avid reader and she had a library card and an app on her phone that allowed her to check out and read most any digital book she wanted. That became her life – a life lost in fantasy and romance, mystery and horror, drama and war. The outside world was of no use to her anymore. When the two people closest to her had hurt her in the worst possible way, she lost her faith in the world… her faith in humanity.

Her phone rang, interrupting the eBook she was currently reading on it. It was Clara, her sister. She'd not spoken to Clara in a few weeks, even though the woman tried calling her almost every day. Tonya always ignored the call, but she knew if she did that much more, Clara would simply come knocking on her door, insisting on seeing her and speaking to her to make sure she was okay.

She hesitated and answered just before it would be sent to her full voicemail inbox.

"Oh, my God! You *are* alive!" Clara exclaimed in a sarcastic way. "I was about to send out the dogs to sniff the woods for your body."

"Hi, Clara," Tonya said, ignoring the comment.

"Are you okay? Everyone is worried sick about you. No one has heard from you, and if it wasn't for your almost daily book reviews on that app you love so much, we'd surely be fearing the worst."

Even though Clara couldn't see it through the phone, Tonya shrugged in reply.

When no verbal reply came, Clara continued. She began with an almost exhausted sigh and then asked, "How long are you going to put yourself through this, sis? It's been *months* since the divorce, and even longer since you learned Charles was having an affair in the first place. Don't you think it's time you got out of that apartment and started to live your life again?"

This time, Tonya answered. "I *am* living my life," she countered, "only it's not as sociable a life as I used to live. I have my apartment, and I have books."

"That *can't* be enough. You can't possibly be happy, Tonya."

"I thought I was happy before," she muttered, "and look how that turned out."

"Charles was a jerk!" Clara was nearly shouting now. "He didn't deserve you! Neither did Sarah. They deserve *each other* – two creeps… two *losers* who hurt the one good person they had in their miserable little lives! And if you think they're happy with each other… well, they won't be. Now they get to know what it's like to live with each other, and Sarah will get to see how it feels when Charles wanders in late every night with lipstick on his collar and another woman's scent all over him."

"I'm not a homebody because I'm afraid Charles and Sarah are happy," Tonya told her. "I don't care if they're happy or not. I'm a homebody because I'm tired of being hurt. I don't like the way it feels and I'm not going to let anyone do that to me again."

"Good!" Carla exclaimed. "Don't let another man, or another friend, hurt you like they did. But, for crying out loud, Tonya! Get out of that apartment and live a little."

"And do what? Hang out at bars? Shop 'til I drop? I don't have money for either of those things. I can barely afford noodles or rice for supper every night, much less anything else."

"You *need* socialization, hermit lady!" Carla quieted for a moment and Tonya wondered if she was about to give up and end the call. In fact, she prayed for that very thing. Instead, her voice reappeared and it was more energetic than before. "I have an idea!"

"I hate it when you have ideas."

"I don't care. You might like this one."

Carla paused and Tonya groaned. After a moment, she asked, "Fine... what's this idea of yours?"

"You are going to come to church with me in the morning," she said, and Tonya could almost imagine her face beaming with enthusiasm.

"I'm going to *what*?" She'd not been to church in years. After marrying Charles, they'd attended regularly for a few months, thinking it was the thing to do for married couples. It didn't last long though. He became a football fanatic – or a fanatic for any sports or action flicks that happened to come on Sunday television. She spent the time reading books and writing stories that would never see the light of day. Eventually, church became nothing more than a memory for the couple – so much so that she couldn't even remember the name of the one they'd attended.

"I really don't think that's the place for me. You know I'm not very religious."

"You don't have to be very religious to go to church," Carla told her. "Reverend Bob's sermons are kind and loving. He rarely preaches fire and brimstone. Not to mention, its great socialization in a place that is filled with really good people. Maybe you'll make new friends. Maybe you'll find a part of yourself that you thought you'd lost forever. Maybe you'll hate it so much that you'll never want to go back. You don't know until you go."

She couldn't argue that last part, even though she wanted to. Still, the idea of sitting in a stuffy church with a bunch of old farts on a Sunday morning did not sound appealing to her. Either way, she knew if she didn't agree, Carla would not let up. She'd keep calling and coming up with more and more suggestions – some that would likely be better, and some that would assuredly be worse.

Begrudgingly, she relented. "Fine…" she whispered like a naughty child that had been told to go to her room. "But I'm not going to Sunday school."

"Sunday school? We're adults. We have Bible study."

"Either way, regular service tomorrow – one time only – is all I'm doing. I'm adamant on that."

"Okay, it's a deal," Carla said in a tone that was happy and rather victorious. "Service starts at 10:40 in the morning. I'll pick you up by 10:15 so we get there in time enough to find a good parking spot and decent seats."

"Will you be bringing Dodger?" Dodger was Carla's boyfriend for the last seven years. Tonya wondered if they'd ever get married, but then she thought that Charles's cheating might have scared the notion out of her.

"Nah, he has to work tomorrow. It'll be just the two of us."

"Okay... I'll be ready."

"And wear something nice!" Carla added. "That's the Lord's house you'll be walking into."

"Mary Magdalene didn't need nice clothes, and Jesus loved her just the same," Tonya pointed out.

"Hey! You *do* know your Bible."

"No," she corrected, "but I know love stories."

They ended the call and Tonya cringed and moaned. She wasn't terribly excited over the idea of going to church. She remembered when she was little and her parents would make her and Carla go every Sunday morning. Most of what she remembered from those days was the other women in the congregation gossiping about anyone and everywhere. It hadn't seemed like a kind and loving environment. So, when she and Charles would go, they would get there right before service started and leave immediately after. That way, she didn't have to deal with the gossipers, and she didn't have to worry if she was the one being gossiped about.

Perhaps times had changed, she thought. Perhaps Christian

women behaved more Christ-like nowadays than they used to. She doubted it, but she'd promised her sister and so she had to chance it.

For the rest of the night, Tonya put all thoughts of church behind her and focused on her eBook. She managed to stay awake long enough to finish it, and when she was done, she changed into her comfy nightgown and crawled into bed.

She never set an alarm anymore to wake her. She didn't need to. Tonya was never up later than eight-thirty or nine at night, and so she always awoke by seven o'clock or so the next morning. On this Sunday morning, her eyes opened at seven fifteen, and she stretched across the bed, releasing a heavy yawn.

It took her a few minutes to remember that she'd agreed to go to church with Carla this morning, and as the memory surfaced, she buried her head beneath the covers, thinking she might be able to hide for the day. She knew better, but she could always hope.

Finally around seven forty or so, she threw the covers back and sat up. She was still a little tired, but a warm cup of her favorite blend of coffee was sure to help set her in motion. In the kitchen, she put the pot on to brew and then went to her laptop and powered it on. Internet was her biggest – and only – splurge each month, and by the time the coffee was brewed and in her mug, she settled down in front of the laptop and checked the daily news.

That lasted all of two minutes, just like with every morning. The first headlines of each day, no matter what site she went to, were always filled with turmoil, threats and devastation. She didn't even know why she bothered to check them. She had little to do with the outside world, and it had less to do with her.

After her third cup of coffee, she decided it was time to shower and dress for church. When she'd been married to Charles, in those early years when they went to church, she'd dressed light and ladylike, in flowing dresses that were of the softest hues and that accentuated her best assets. Today, she chose a long blue denim dress with long sleeves and a white lacy collar that fastened at the neck. It buttoned all the way down to the hem of the skirt and made her look almost like a librarian from the turn of last century.

Tonya opted out of her contact lenses and wore her glasses instead. She applied no make-up and pulled her hair behind her into a tight and full bun. Looking into the mirror, she thought she was the plainest looking woman that she'd ever laid eyes on – mousey and bookish. It was the exact look she'd strived for, and she'd succeeded.

After dressing, she finally considered breakfast, but she wasn't very hungry. The idea of being inside of a stuffy nave with a few hundred people sweating, singing, and shouting their 'amen's' or 'hallelujah's' made her a bit uncomfortable, and it killed any appetite she might have had.

Instead, she relaxed in her favorite chair, chose a new book from the library app to read, and got lost in the words and adventures of characters that were much more lively and sociable than she. Time passed all too swiftly as she read, and before she knew it, a knock was sounding at her door.

"Already?" she grumbled as she checked the time. With a huff, she stood and ambled to the door, unlocking and opening it for Carla.

Her sister looked her up and down and then over again. Her eyes were wide. Her nose was crooked and flared as she sneered.

"Is *that* what you're wearing?" she asked in a voice that was shrouded in distaste and near-embarrassment.

Carla was wearing a comfortable-looking but rather stylish pant suit with a yellow blouse open at the neck. She looked business casual but lovely.

"What's wrong with it?" Tonya replied. She knew precisely what her sister found wrong with her appearance, but she played dumb anyway. "Don't you like it?"

"What did you do? Dig up Granny and steal her burial clothes?"

Tonya rolled her eyes and stepped aside for her sister to enter. She offered no other remark than, "It's comfortable."

"Liar," Carla protested. "You look tighter than an old nun's snatch."

With a shrug, Tonya brushed off the insult and grabbed her purse from the table, dropping her phone and keys inside. Then, she walked back to her sister and cringed. "I guess I'm ready." Her voice was that of a child being forced into a doctor's office.

"Where's your Bible?" Carla questioned.

"Bible?" She shrugged and offered a half smile. "I don't

have a Bible."

"You *used* to have a Bible."

"Things change. I got divorced. A lot of stuff got scattered. What can I say?"

"How can you not have a Bible in all of the books in this place?" Carla walked to the shelves and began eying the titles. "Who doesn't have a Bible?"

"Atheists?"

"Are you an atheist?"

"No… but that was a good answer for your question."

Carla grunted headed back to the door. "Let's go. You can share mine if you need to."

Tonya hoped she wouldn't need to. If the preacher did his job right, she wouldn't need a Bible in her hands; he'd be reciting the verses for her and then telling her all about them like she was a kid listening to story time at a library.

In the car, Carla had the radio tuned to rockabilly music – something Tonya wasn't a fan of. Still, she felt she had no right to complain about it, and for the length of the ride to the church, she gritted her teeth and bore it. When they reached the church, the parking lot was swamped with vehicles and well-dressed people – couples, families with children, people who were by themselves… The church itself was not as small as Tonya had imagined it to be either, although it wasn't one of those 'mega churches' by any means.

Carla parked in a space that was midway from the parking

lot's entrance and midway to the church's front door. When she killed the engine, she looked at her sister and asked, "Are you ready for some worship and socialization?"

"No," Tonya replied, not even needing to think about it – even a little. "I'm ready to get this done with and get back to my apartment. I was in the middle of a really good book when you arrived."

Carla rolled her eyes and stepped from the car. Slowly, Tonya followed suit.

Immediately, Tonya noticed how well-known and popular her sister was here. The second they began heading toward the building, people began to call Carla's name, wave at her, and yell flattering remarks about her attire.

Tonya received some attention also – from sets of eyes that noticed her dress, glasses and hair, and either gasped, huffed, or cringed upon seeing her. With any hope, they would dislike her enough that they'd ask Carla to never bring her back here again.

At the door was the church's preacher, greeting his congregation and shaking their hands as they entered. He was wearing a dark brown suit with a crisp white shirt and a brown necktie to match. His hair was graying at the temples but mostly black, and it was slicked back without a strand out of place. His smile was wide and friendly. Tonya thought he was handsome, but she knew that wasn't the first thought she should have had. Were preachers allowed to be handsome to those that attended service? Was it a sin to have even *thought* it?

It was one thing she detested the most about any religion – all of the rules to learn and abide by. There were so many and it was all so confusing.

"Carla!" the preacher exclaimed as she approached with her sister. "You look absolutely lovely this morning!"

"Why thank you, Reverend Bob!" Carla exclaimed, and Tonya noticed her bashful blush.

"And who might this... er... young lady be?" the preacher continued. He was still smiling, but his eyes seemed uncertain as he looked at Tonya.

"This is my sister Tonya," Carla told him. "She just arrived in our present day from her time machine. It brought her here all the way from 1900!"

Reverend Bob chuckled at the comment and extended a hand to Tonya. "Tonya, welcome to our humble church. It's a pleasure to meet you."

Tonya shook the hand, which was firm but nice, and replied, "I've been a homebody lately. Carla insists this type of socialization will be good for me."

"There's nothing wrong with being a homebody," he told her, "but being a hermit should be left to those tiny crabs. We're glad you're joining us today."

With a nudge, Carla urged her forward and past the preacher, into the building. "Come on, sis. Let's find us a seat."

Looking once more at Reverend Bob, Tonya said, "Thanks for the welcome."

Inside, it wasn't nearly as stuffy as she'd thought it would be. In fact, it was air conditioned, and there were many more pews than she'd expected. Carla began to lead her toward the front, but Tonya tugged on her arm and motioned to a pew at her left – not quite in the middle, but not too close to the front either.

"Ugh..." Carla groaned. "Fine."

They sat at the end of the pew near the center aisle and were quiet as many more members of the congregation filled the pews around them. As the seats began to fill up, Tonya heard the front door close. Out the corner of her eye, she saw the preacher walk up the aisle to his lectern. He held a large leather-bound Bible in one hand, coupled with a spiral notebook beneath it. As he readied himself, the chattering of the congregation slowly silenced.

Tonya remembered being new with Charles when they chose a church to attend after marrying. The preacher there had made a note of them and addressed their freshness to the congregation. She worried this preacher would do the same, and she didn't want to be the center of attention. That was part of why she'd dressed as plainly as she had – so that she could somewhat disappear.

Instead, when Reverend Bob began to speak, his words filled her with a different kind of dread. "What say we open our hymnals to page eighty-six and start this morning by singing to the Lord?" His smile widened, and the sound of a couple hundred people gathering their hymn books from the backs of pews filled Tonya's ears.

"Oh no…" she whispered to Carla. "I forgot about this part. You know how I hate to sing."

"Then just pretend to sing and mouth the words," she instructed and handed her a hymnal.

All at once, everyone around stood from their seats with their hymnals in hand, including Carla. Tonya was the last to her feet, and she fumbled through the pages looking for page eighty-six. By the time she found it, everyone had already begun to sing, and it took her a bit to locate the line they were currently on.

She followed her sister's instructions, mouthing the words without a sound coming from her lips. She was a self-confirmed horrible singer, and she was thankful for Carla's advice. Singing in unison, the congregation sounded like a group of heavenly angels. Tonya felt she surely would have destroyed that mojo with her croaking voice.

Her eyes shifted to her left, looking at the elderly woman beside her and making sure she didn't notice she wasn't singing. The woman was fully dedicated to the hymn though and not once glanced her way. When the song was over, relief swam across Tonya and she hurriedly took her seat. She wondered if anyone would notice if she took her phone out of her purse and read a little of her book, but she decided that would be pushing it. She didn't want to be called out not only as the new person but also as the one paying no attention to the service.

Reverend Bob promptly began his sermon, and it was one that discussed the joys of loving God and being loved *by* God. She thought his words and the scriptures he read from related to much more in life than just God – they related to *her* and how she'd been forgetting something important... loving herself.

She smiled at the thought. Naughtily, the idea of loving herself brought about thoughts of masturbation, and she fought to rid the notion from her mind. Church was most certainly not the place to think about such things. It was a place of pureness and goodness, not a place to consider when she'd last replaced the batteries in her vibrator.

These thoughts and the battle over them filled her mind as everyone around her began to stand again. She'd missed something, but what? Then, suddenly, she realized they were singing another hymn. Carla nudged her and Tonya stood, shrugging at her sister with eyes that screamed, "Oops!"

"Pay attention!" Carla scolded her in a hushed tone, barely audible over the sound of the singing.

Tonya didn't bother with a hymnal this time. Instead, she looked onto the copy her sister held and pretended to sing along.

After the song, several donation trays were passed through the pews. Carla dropped a twenty into the tray and handed it to Tonya. All she had on her was a fiver and she hesitated to part with it.

"I'll give it back to you later," Carla whispered to her, and so Tonya parted with the only money she had, hoping that her sister wouldn't forget to replace it.

Money was a rare commodity for Tonya these days – even

if it was only a five dollar bill. She hated giving it away, especially to an organization that she didn't belong to, but it was done. The tray was nearing the far end of her pew, and all she could do was hope it would be put to as much good use as five dollars could do.

With a sigh, she tried to direct her focus back to the preacher, who was gearing up for another round of sermon. She became antsy in her seat, starting to feel that stuffiness she'd thought she'd feel despite the air conditioning. Opening her purse a little, she saw her phone and punched a button. There was still a half hour left.

"Did you just groan?" Carla asked her, and Tonya didn't even realize her groan had been a vocal one. She'd imagined it was just in her head.

"Must be my stomach," she lied, despite being in the house of the Lord.

"Did you eat breakfast?"

"No..." At least that part, she could be honest about. In the quietest whisper she added, "Where are you taking me for lunch?"

"Lunch? Why do I have to buy lunch?" Carla whispered back.

"Because you made me give my money away," pointed out Tonya.

From their left, the little old lady beside them shushed them. "Quiet, heathens!"

Upon receiving the warning, Carla glared at Tonya, who smiled somewhat mischievously in reply.

Twice more, everyone stood and sang. On the first of these instances, Tonya stood and joined them, mouthing the lyrics as her sister had suggested. On the second instance, she became distracted. The door behind them opened and closed. She probably wouldn't have noticed, except it changed the lighting – brightening the room and then dimming it back to its regular light. Out the corner of her eye, she saw a man in a black suit with no tie and an unbuttoned shirt collar hurry down the center aisle, wearing sunglasses, and sitting promptly at on the inside edge of the front pew. He waved at Reverend Bob and then slumped down in his seat, relaxing his head back like he was sleeping.

She looked to Reverend Bob, who looked at the man and raised an eyebrow in what looked like a warning. Then, with obvious disappointment, he shook his head and returned his attention to the song being sung.

Tonya wasn't sure what was going on, but she found it intriguing – entertaining in a place where she'd quickly become bored. She smiled wider and focused her attention on the latecomer. Walking down the aisle, she'd noticed he was tall and in what appeared to be decent shape. His jacked was unbuttoned and not an ounce of fat showed through his dress shirt. His dark hair was messy and longish, and she thought he was kind of cute. She just wished she could get a better look.

"I see you looking at him," Carla whispered as the song ended and everyone sat. "Don't even think about it."

"Think about *what*?" she asked, even though she knew

good and well what her sister meant.

"That man's got a bad reputation with women."

"What man doesn't?"

"He's also Reverend Bob's son."

She thought she'd noticed a resemblance but hadn't really considered it. Now, knowing the truth, her smile was full and her eyes stayed on him.

"Is he single?" she asked, only to be elbowed in the side by the old lady next to her.

"I said to shush!" the woman told her and then looked back to the lectern.

Tonya quieted down but couldn't help considering this strange and apparently dangerous man. A preacher's son... She had sworn to herself after Charles cheated on her, and again after the divorce, that she'd never so much as look at a man in 'that way' again, and so she couldn't understand why he intrigued her so much. Perhaps it was the fact that she was sitting in the holiest of buildings and he had come in with an aspect of thrill that had distracted her from it. Perhaps it was the fact that she'd been thinking about her vibrator and masturbation not too long ago. It had been a while since she'd pleasured herself, but it had been so much longer since she'd been pleasured by a man. Tonya found herself suddenly missing the way a man touched, the way one smelled, the way one tasted...

She found herself fantasizing about him for the rest of the service. She wondered if he was a good kisser or a good lover. She wondered what his tongue would have felt like if he'd flicked it between her thighs. Coyly, she crossed her legs as a once familiar but long missing throb came from her womanhood.

"Quit fidgeting," Carla told her and then readjusted her seated position.

"I'm not fidgeting," Tonya protested.

"Then quit thinking about *him*. I know that's what you're doing."

"How do you know what I'm thinking?"

The old lady beside her cleared her throat and started to nudge her again. Tonya held a finger up to her.

"If you so much as touch me, I'll rip those dentures right out of your mouth, old lady," she told the woman. With a gasp, the woman scooted down a good foot and turned her nose up at her.

"Tonya!" Carla scolded in a slightly higher tone. "See. Damien is rubbing off on you already!"

*Damien...* she thought, finding his name to be both sexy and humorous. What were the chances of a preacher's son being named for an antichrist out of a fictional novel? She'd read *The Omen* twice when she was a teenager and then again after her divorce. While she was certain that this man in the front pew was definitely not the antichrist, is name did help add an additional certain edge to him.

Perhaps she'd been good enough, she considered. She'd been confined to her apartment day in and day out almost every day since the divorce was finalized and she'd had to find a new home. She'd been passive and complacent to her situation, deciding her solitude and loneliness were what were best for her. Yet, just knowing there was a rebel in the front row and that the rebel was the spawn of the preacher reawakened something inside of her – stirred away the inhibitions that she held so dear. She felt a little wild, even if that wildness was confined to her thoughts and imagination.

Coyly, she reached up to her collar and unfastened the top two buttons of her dress. She was getting terribly hot, and she certainly couldn't blame it on the temperature of the room itself.

While Reverend Bob finished his Sunday sermon, Tonya noticed that his son's head was now slumped down… his body, too relaxed. He had fallen asleep; she could tell and she found it hilarious. Reverend Bob refused to even glance at Damien for the rest of the service, although she could tell he'd become frustrated by the lack of respect his son was showing him.

There was likely a good excuse that the young man had been late, disheveled, and had fallen asleep. Tonya just couldn't figure out what it was. The most likely excuse was that he'd probably been out all night, partying at the bars and clubs and maybe dipping his tongue into the moist regions of a one-night stand.

She wondered what a one-night stand would have been like with him. He was probably an animal when in the heat of ecstasy, drilling away at a woman's nether regions while growling the absolute naughtiest things to her, pushing her into the brink of an orgasm that would make her scream like a banshee in heat.

Tonya uncrossed and then recrossed her legs, spreading a warm moisture over her inner thighs. She wanted to scream out like a banshee in heat, brought to an orgasm that would make her eyes cross and her hair stand on end. Even when she and Charles had made love – or even endured a quickie – he'd usually been the one to benefit the most from it. Sometimes he'd take her to the edge, but that was usually where he had finished and stopped, leaving her to take care of herself after he'd fallen asleep out of masculine exhaustion beside her.

For the first time in years, she wanted somebody else to take care of her sexual desires, and she wanted it to be the preacher's son.

"After service ends," Carla whispered to her, stirring her from her thoughts of arousal and climax, "I usually chitchat in the parking lot with some of my friends here. I'm glad to introduce you to them."

"Uh..." she said, trying to find words through her heated desires, "sure."

Tonya didn't want to meet her sister's church friends. All she wanted to do was go home, think about all of the nasty things Damien would do to her, and see how close to a banshee she could actually get her screams to sound when she soaked her sheets.

Eventually, service ended and Reverend Bob thanked his congregation. He rushed his thanks, obviously hoping for the room to clear out so that he could awaken and properly scold his son. As everyone started to stand around her, Tonya remained seated.

"Alright, you've endured it... Let's go," Carla said and smiled at her.

"I need to use the restroom," she noted and looked up at her sister. "Where is it?"

Carla pointed near the front of the worship room to a brown door that was at the far right side of the lectern. "Go through that door, make a left, and it'll be on your right."

"Thanks," she said and smiled. "I'll be out right after."

She waited for the bulk of the crowd to leave, including Carla, before she stood. Then, smoothing down the back of her prudish dress, she walked up the aisle and met with the reverend as he was stepping down to approach his still sleeping son. She smiled at Reverend Bob and thanked him for allowing her the pleasure of the sermon.

He was gracious but obviously distracted. "I hope to see you again," he said, smiled, and walked over to his son.

With a side glance, Tonya watched him shake Damien's shoulder, stirring him from his slumber. Then, she smiled and opened the brown door, stepping through.

She found the restroom pretty easily, but there was a short line to enter it and she was at the back of it. She honestly didn't have to use the restroom, but she was killing time while Carla got all of her chitchatting out and her church friends went their own way. When it finally came her turn, she walked in, locked the door, and went to the mirror. Gazing at her reflection, she decided she was not the type of woman an exciting man like Damien would have taken a second glance at, if he even took a first.

She unbuttoned her dress one more notch below what she'd undone earlier. Then, she unfastened the four buttons at the bottom, allowing her legs to move more freely but still remaining somewhat conservative and not showing off more than just a slight tease of what was beneath. She wished she'd worn her contacts, but there was nothing she could do about that. The glasses would have to stay, or else she wouldn't be able to see more than a few inches before her. Her bun, however, could go. She pulled out the pins, watched it fall, and then shook it out. Letting her hair loose helped her look less like a prude and more like a milf, she thought, and even though she wasn't a mother, the milf look would have to suffice.

Tonya always carried a tube of lipstick in her purse, and she reached for the bag to find it when she realized she'd left her handbag in the pew. She cursed this fact, fearing that someone might have stolen it or taken it mistakenly. Perhaps even the old bat beside her had grabbed it just to spite her.

Hurriedly, she left the restroom and returned to the nave, where she found the room vacant – except for Damien. He was sitting on the edge of the pew with his knees parted and his hands fisted together between them. His sunglasses were still on, but as he noticed her approach, he broke the fisted hands and used one to lift up his sunglasses. He gave her the once over and then smiled.

"You certainly must be new here," he told her in a voice

that was as sexy and exciting as he appeared.

"Yeah," she said, knowing she was starting to blush. "My sister talked me into coming."

"Did you enjoy it?"

His question was a general one but one she wasn't sure how to respond. Service had been okay at first, but she'd quickly grown bored with it – until he walked in and fully distracted her from everything his father was saying. That wasn't an answer she was prepared to outright offer him, and so she kept it simple.

"It was okay, I guess. This really isn't my scene."

"Oh?" he answered. His smile widened a little. "What's your scene?"

She shrugged and hesitated. She really didn't have a scene anymore – not since before she'd married Wayne. Now, her scene was at home in her tiny apartment, reading books and getting lost in other people's fictitious fantasies.

"I'm more of a homebody," she admitted and shifted her gaze to the floor. "I guess I really don't have a scene."

"That's a scene," he replied and she moved her eyes right back to his. "It actually sounds pretty good. I'm only here because my dad's the preacher and he considers this to be my only hope of salvation or redemption... or something like that."

"Redemption from what?" she questioned, feeling it was her turn to ask.

In turn, he shrugged and hesitated, just as she had done before. Taking his sunglasses off, he propped them on his leg. "I have a little PTSD from being in the military. I joined the army when I was eighteen and dropped out of high school the day I enlisted. It sounded like an easy way out, but it was far from that. After basic training, I got shipped off to the Middle East. Everything was fine at first. Hot, but fine. Then, as we were riding down the road, we got sabotaged. Two of our vehicles got blown up, a lot of my buddies got killed, and I walked away unscathed... I was lucky, but I didn't feel lucky."

"As terrible as that is, I don't see why you'd need redemption for that," she told him in as sympathetic a voice as possible. "It wasn't your fault those men died."

"That's not what I need redemption for," he explained. "I got shipped home and released of my duty. I couldn't shake what had happened or what I saw... became a huge alcoholic. Stayed out all night long at clubs and in the apartments of strange women. Got hooked on some bad stuff for a little bit, but I've been off that for almost a year now. Dad says I went from being a possible American hero to a sinner, just like that." He snapped his fingers for emphasis and sighed with an obviously heavy heart.

"So, you're a party boy?" she asked, wondering if it was the right thing to mention.

"Nah." He smiled and looked deep into her eyes. "Not for a while now. I know I look like crap, but I'm sober and working two jobs to keep my little studio apartment downtown. I'm only half awake because my second job is working the grave shift at a full service hotel. I'm a bellhop. It's kind of embarrassing to say it out loud."

Tonya smiled warmly. He didn't seem nearly as bad as Carla had insisted. He was just... misunderstood.

"I've got a reputation now though," he continued. "No woman of any quality wants to be seen with me."

"I don't know about that," she replied. "I wouldn't mind being seen with you."

Damien smiled again and his eyes brightened, a nice change following his tale of tragedy. "You seem like a really nice person."

"I have my moments." She blushed again and giggled lightly. "Look, my sister is out there waiting on me, and I think I left my purse in the pew... but I'd like to talk to you again, Damien."

"Really?" He stood, and she stepped back to give him room. "I'm listed in the church's directory on the website. My title here is 'Floor Sweeper.'"

"How sexy!" She smirked.

"Not at all."

"No... no, it's not." They shared a light laugh over this, and then Tonya cleared her throat and looked over to the pew she'd been seated at. She could see the strap of her purse awaiting her. "I've got to get going, Damien, but I promise – I'll be in touch."

Damien sighed, his smile half faded, and he nodded his head. "Sure thing," he said in an unconvincing voice. "Have a great rest of the day."

"You too," she offered and then walked toward the pew with her purse. As she took it and started to the door, she heard him stop her.

"How is it," he asked and she turned to face him, "that you know my name but I have no idea what yours is?"

"I'm Tonya," she said with a grin, walking backwards toward the door. Then, as she felt the door behind her, she blew him a kiss, saw his eyes brightened, and stepped outside.

Carla was waiting in the car at the walkway – engine running. She looked irritated, but Tonya didn't care. She, herself, felt elated.

"What's that smile for?" Carla asked as Tonya climbed into the passenger seat.

Not wishing to tell her sister the truth, she said instead, "I guess I just feel good right now. Let's eat."

They ate at a coffee shop, dining on artisan sandwiches and iced lattes. The lunch was quick, as Carla was eager to get home. When she dropped Tonya off, she slipped her a fifty and told her not to blow it on something stupid.

"What stupid thing would I go and blow this on?" she asked, somewhat defensively.

"Books," Carla told her. "You read too many books." Then, with a smile, she drove off.

In her apartment, she immediately went to her laptop and found the church's website. She hadn't intended on doing this first thing, but Damien had stayed at the forefront of her thoughts since leaving church, and she couldn't shake him. Not his image, not his voice, and most certainly, not his back story.

Sure enough, in the church's directory, she found him. A laugh escaped her as she did indeed see 'Floor Sweeper' beside his name. There was a phone number listed beside his picture – a photo that looked a couple of years old. Taking out her phone, Tonya saved his contact information and considered texting him. It felt silly to do it – he was a sweet guy and strikingly handsome, but he was a fantasy. She was afraid if she got to know him better, the fantasy would be over and reality would kick in. Would she like him just as much if she knew more about him?

"Only one way to find out," she said bravely and opened up her messenger. Her fingers froze, as did her mind, when she began to type out a message. Suddenly, she realized she didn't know what to say. What was she going to do? Come on to him? Invite him to her apartment? What if he was working, or what if he had expectations due to his past? Worst yet, what if he had *no* expectations and didn't want to get involved with anyone, trying to shake his reputation of a bad boy?

She grunted but decided she owed him some kind of contact. After all, she'd said she would. She decided to be humorous with it, and so she typed: *Hey, it's Tonya from Church. I saw your photo on the website. It's kinda goofy. I like it!*

Reading it over, she realized how stupid it sounded, and she was about to delete the message when her finger punched the wrong button, causing it to send.

"Crap..." she said as she winced. "I shouldn't have done that."

Setting the phone down, Tonya paced the room for a moment and then walked to her small kitchen, where she ran some tap water into a glass. She drank it quickly, quenching a thirst that she really hadn't even noticed was there. All the while, she listened for a ding to come from her phone, but with nothing but silence filling the air, she believed it to be best if he didn't reply. As sexually exciting as she'd found him, she didn't want to be a one-night stand for him. That, like most of what she saw in Damien, had been fantasy. She also didn't want to lead him on. Wayne had left her in a dark place – emotionally scarred and somewhat unstable. She wasn't ready for a relationship, and she didn't think Damien was either. He was working on himself, and that was admirable. It was also what she needed to be doing.

She sat at her tiny table and propped her cheeks onto her hands. Looking at the table's light brown coloring, she tried to rid her mind of the preacher's son. Just as her brain began to relax from thoughts of him, she heard her phone ding in the living room.

With a start, she bolted upright from her seat. At first, she wondered if it was him, replying to her corny message. Then, she considered the most obvious choice – that it was from Carla, bugging her again for something or other.

With a huff, she left the kitchen and approached her phone, pausing when she reached it. The screen was black. She wouldn't be able to see who the message was from until she punched the big round button at the bottom. Again, she hesitated and became nervous.

"Oh, grow up!" she told herself and snatched up the phone. Hitting the button, she read the words 'New Message from Damien Floor Sweeper' and suddenly felt elated again.

Opening the message, she noticed first the photo. It was of Damien in his army clothes. He looked sexy, heroic... even dashing. She stared at it for a long moment, studying his stone-faced expression... the look in his eyes... the lips that she could just imagine kissing. Then, she looked below the photo to the attached message and read.

*It is definitely a goofy photo. I prefer this one though. I hope you like it! Care to send one back in reply? I'd love one to remember you by. Great meeting you today. I hope to hear from you soon. ~ D.*

Her body flushed with warmth as she read, and when she was done, she began scrolling through her photos for just the right one. Yet, after seeing his studly army photo, all of her selfies looked boring and amateurish.

She decided to take a fresh one, but not in this dress or the glasses that rested atop her nose. In her bedroom, she stripped down and put on just her faux fur-lined robe. Then, in the bathroom, she put on her contacts and positioned herself at the bathtub with one foot resting on it and one on the floor. Holding the phone as far out from her she could, she took several shots with several different facial expressions. When she figured the right one was in there somewhere, she relaxed and scrolled through the images.

Most of them had seemed mundane. Boring. Yet, there was one that she thought flattered her nicely, and made her look fun *and* sophisticated – at least, as sophisticated as a woman could look climbing into a bathtub with her robe on.

She texted it to him with the message: *Time for a little relaxation. I hope you're taking it easy tonight too. That army uniform was sexy. ~ T.*

As she sent the message, she couldn't believe she'd used the word 'sexy' in the text. Was it too early in their new friendship for something like that? Had she gone overboard wearing the robe in the photo? The shot she chose had one shoulder exposed, as well as a hint of cleavage. She didn't want to come across as easy or slutty, and she prayed to the heavens that he wouldn't see it that way.

The message sent, and the word 'delivered' changed to 'read.' She waited patiently, staring at the screen and hunting for the '...' that let her know he was typing. Yet, as no such symbol appeared, the screen faded and then turned black.

"Figures," she grunted and set the phone down. "I either don't come on to men at all, or I come on too strong. I should just give up and go back to my book..."

Maybe she thought that her gripe would have made a reply come through, but it didn't happen. She picked up her phone again, closed her messenger, and opened her library app. Tonya hunted through her borrowed books list and found the one she'd been reading. It opened slowly, but it went right to where she'd left off when it did. She carried the phone to her comfy chair, settled in, and began to read.

She was nearly done with a chapter when the phone dinged and alerted her that she had a new message waiting. When the notice came on, she nearly dropped the phone, startled.

With clumsy and all too fast moving fingers, she minimized her app and opened her messenger. There it was – a new message from Damien. Tonya hesitated to open it, but there was a 'new photo' alert next to his name. Knowing that he'd sent her another photo further elated her and made her less worried over the tastefulness of the one she'd sent. Quickly, she slid right and opened the message.

This photo, unlike the last one he'd sent, was a selfie and not one that featured his army uniform. In fact, aside from some blue jeans that seemed to cover his legs like skin, there was no clothing at all. No jacket, no shirt, no sunglasses. He was also smiling in this one – that sexy and slightly dangerous grin he'd had in church.

She studied the photo like she was studying fine art. At first, she studied his smile and his wide and happy eyes. Then, she noticed his muscular chest, delicious pecs, and the six-pack that instantly made her mouth water. He was incredibly fit and looked absolutely delicious. For a long while, she gazed at the photo, nearly forgetting to check the message below it. Finally, she scrolled down a bit, letting her eyes leave the photo to see what he'd written.

*I forgot how beautiful you are. Thank you for reminding me. I'm at home, working out... I hope you don't find the pic to be in bad taste. Yours was so sexy... I know mine won't even come close. ~ D.*

"Ha!" she laughed. "If I look at it any longer, I'll be the one coming close." She chuckled harder as she spoke the words, having not meant to say them out loud.

Before she could even think of what to reply, another message came through from him.

*Do you like coffee?*

"I *love* coffee!" she exclaimed, even though he couldn't hear her. Realizing this, she typed the words into a new message, along with: *Did you paint on those jeans?*

After pressing send, she scrolled back up to the most recent photo and looked at those jeans, at his impressively defined abs, and then at his all too perfect smile – one that made her heart skip a beat.

Much more quickly than before, Tonya received a new reply.

*No, but that would be a lot cheaper than buying clothes. I'll have to try it sometime. I just put on a fresh pot of coffee, if you'd like to join me. 112 Wilmington, Apt. 35.*

Following this message was another picture – one of coffee brewing in a pot.

Tonya loved the photo of Damien working out, and she absolutely adored the fact that he'd shared with her his address and an invitation to join him for coffee, but she wasn't sure if she should accept. She thought about her sister and wondered what advice Carla would give if she let her know the circumstances, without letting her know who the man was. Knowing Carla, she'd tell her she'd been single and lonely much too long and to live a little… to take the man up on his offer for coffee. If she knew it was Damien, Tonya had a feeling the advice would be completely different.

As she considered things, her phone dinged with another new message. It was from Damien and included a new photograph. The image was him in the shower, from the waist up. Water ran seductively down his body, and his hair was soapy with shampoo. He had a silly grin on his face that absolutely tickled her. The image also made her more than a little hot.

She fought the urge to become too much more enticed and scrolled down to the message below the image.

*In the shower and freshening up… just in case I have someone to talk to this evening. It's been a long day and I found you so easy to talk to. Hugs, D.*

Now, Tonya knew that she couldn't refuse his offer. While his photos were sexy, his message was more flattering and heartfelt. She decided to take a chance – something she never did anymore – and in her bedroom, she dressed in a sensible skirt, a black blouse that matched it, and some black flats. She took her purse, keys, and phone and walked to the door. Stepping outside, she closed the door and stood in front of it, facing away from it. Utilizing her phone's camera, she took a picture of herself, smiling with the apartment number on the door visible behind her.

*On my way,* she texted back and included the image. *Keep the coffee hot!*

As she reached the stairs, she received a quick reply.

*It's always hot around here.*

There was that warm feeling between her legs again, only this time it wasn't brought about by fantasizing over Damien or by thoughts of masturbation. It was caused by only his words – and in text, at that. She smiled and headed down the stairs, out the building, and to her humble but working car.

Within fifteen minutes, she was parked in the garage across the street from Damien's building and looking at it, wondering what his apartment would be like. Being the pad of a single man with a reputation, she envisioned it messy at first, then with some sort of naughty sex chamber, and then with very little furnishings at all – as all he'd mentioned having so far were workout equipment, a coffee maker, and a shower.

Tonya quickly left the garage and crossed the street to the building. Opening the door, she found herself in an empty lobby with a door to a stairwell, a small elevator, and a bunch of mailboxes with apartment numbers and tenant names on them. She decided to take the stairs, as elevators had always frightened her. On the third floor, she stepped through another door and found herself in a long hall with thinning brown carpet and blah yellow walls.

"Ugh..." she groaned as she sniffed the air. It smelled like a mix of urine and body odor. For a moment, she thought she'd be sick from it. The consideration of turning around and leaving came to her. If the hallway smelled this badly, she could only imagine what the apartments smell like.

Then, she considered Damien. She'd told him she was on her way, and seeing as they'd just met, she didn't want to dampen their budding friendship with being a no-show. Holding her hand over her mouth and nose, she looked at the numbers on the doors and saw apartment 35 just a few doors down from her.

Hurriedly, she went to it and knocked. However, the second her fist hit the door, it opened. She realized that it hadn't been shut completely, and when she pushed it open the rest of the way, she found the place dark. Reaching to her right, she found a light switch and flipped it up, illuminating the space. Tonya shut the door behind her and looked around.

The first thing she noticed was that the stench inside wasn't nearly as bad as it was in the hall. That was a godsend. The second thing she noticed was the large amount of furniture that filled the small living room. A sectional sofa, an old box television, a stereo system with two guitars – one electric and one acoustic – on stands next to it... There was a recliner, an ottoman, a bookshelf with no books but plenty of VHS tapes and DVD cases. Two lamps were on two end tables. The only thing the room lacked for cluttered comfort was artwork or photographs on the walls… and Damien.

"Hello?" she asked, stepping deeper into the room. She looked ahead and saw a dim room that must have been the kitchen. There was also a small hallway that likely led to the bathroom and a bedroom. The smell of fresh coffee wafted out from the kitchen, and so she went to that first.

Flipping up the switch, she saw the coffee was ready but there was no one in there to drink it. She also noticed that the place was relatively clean with no dirty dishes filling up the sink.

Tonya left the kitchen and headed toward the hallway. There were two doors – one to her left and one to her right. She opened the door on the left first. It was dark like the other rooms had been. She turned on the light and found it to be the bedroom. Damien wasn't in this room either. However, the bed was made and there were no dirty clothes piled on the floor. Even though he had a lot of furniture, it appeared he wasn't a messy housekeeper. She smiled at this, but she still felt strange. Something was off, considering the host was missing after she'd openly been invited over.

She left the bedroom and shut the door behind her. The last place to check was the door across from her – obviously the bathroom. As she neared it, she heard water running. It sounded like a shower, which she found unusual, seeing that Damien had been in the shower when he texted her before she left. Hesitantly, she reached for the doorknob and opened it with caution.

The light was on in the bathroom, and a shout slipped from

her mouth as she saw Damien, folded over the side of the bathtub with the water steadily pouring down on him from the sprayer. In a rush, she went to him and felt the coldness of the water. It was like ice. She turned it off and then took his face in her hands. Lifting it to where she could see it, she noticed his eyes were closed and there was a gash across his forehead, bleeding. She then saw his cell phone across the floor against the wall beside the door. He'd apparently dropped it and it had slid over that way.

First, she checked his pulse. It was there, but she was no doctor or nurse and couldn't tell if it was weak or regular. She began to pat his cheeks and call his name, trying to wake him. When he didn't respond, she took out her phone and called for an ambulance.

\*\*\*\*

For three days, Damien was in the hospital. He'd slipped in the shower after texting her the picture, and when his head hit the tub, it had knocked him out. From the wound, he suffered a severe concussion. During this hospitalization, Tonya remained at his side, holding his hand, telling him funny stories, helping him eat, and even reading to him from the books on her library app. They shared intimate secrets, family dramas, and she even told him about losing her virginity to her high school's brainiest nerd just so he'd write her term papers for her.

On the third day, the doctor made it known that Damien

would have to have someone around to take care of him during the rest of his recovery. Tonya volunteered, insisting he could stay with her for as long as he needed. She made a point to call both of his jobs, as well as his father, and give everyone an update on what was going on. Then, as he was released, she wheeled him out of the hospital to her car, loaded him up, and took him home with her.

It took nearly a full month for the most extreme side effects of his concussion to fade away. These included blinding migraines, terrifying seizures, temporary losses of vision, and heavy numbness in his fingers and feet. Eventually, the migraines became mere headaches, the seizures tapered off, his vision became blurry but didn't fade in and out, and the numbness disappeared.

During this time, she'd given up her bed for him, insisting she was comfortable sleeping on her couch or in her favorite chair. He protested this almost nightly, telling her the bed was big enough for two. She eventually moved her favorite chair into that room and parked it beside the bed, falling asleep as close to him as she could get without fear of somehow pushing the boundaries in her sleep. Finally, one night as she curled up beside him to read to him, she drifted off with him, and when she awoke the next morning, his arm was wrapped around her, holding her close. She stayed in that position for a long while with a content smile on her face until she pulled herself up to use the bathroom and make coffee.

"How are you feeling today?" she asked him as she brought him a fresh cup of coffee to help him out of the groggy post-waking state.

"Like a million bucks... or a million pennies," he told her with a smile and took the cup, sipping lightly. "You make better coffee than I do."

"Your medical leave ends after this weekend," she continued, settling onto the bed beside him to enjoy the coffee and finish waking up. "The doctor said some side effects may take longer to go away – if they ever go away completely – but the ones he was concerned about are gone. You can return to your day job on Monday."

"Day job..." he groaned and stretched. Through a yawn, he added, "And the night job."

Tonya set her cup down on the bedside table and then took his hand in hers, gentle squeezing it. "You don't have to go back to both jobs, do you?"

He laughed, roughly. "Yeah... if I want to keep my apartment, anyway. It's the only way I can afford it." He looked at her and forged a smile. "Can I tell you something?"

Tonya chuckled. "Of course, silly. You can tell me anything."

He squeezed her hand and cleared his throat. "You're my best friend."

Her heart warmed with the words and she felt a little teary eyed, although she refused to let them fall. It had been a long time since anyone had called her a friend. Honestly, she replied, "You're my best friend too."

"I – I think…"

When he paused, she raised an eyebrow. "You think *what*?"

He gazed into her eyes and she saw nervousness in them. Then, his gaze shifted from hers and trailed down to the covers. "I think you might also be the love of my life."

Tonya couldn't believe her ears. He was telling her something that she'd been feeling this whole time while she'd cared for him. In the three days with him at the hospital, she'd fallen for him, and after the first week of having him in her apartment, she knew she'd loved him. She just never expected the feeling to be reciprocated. She had believed that Damien looked at her only as a friend, but now she understood differently. Now, she had that elated feeling that only he could bring to her, and it rippled throughout her body like a surge of electricity.

"I've wanted to tell you I love you for a while now," she admitted, still blushing after all these weeks. "And I do." Tenderly, she leaned into him and kissed him softly – a kiss that he returned with care and warm passion… their first kiss.

When it broke, he looked into her eyes again and whispered, "I love you, Tonya. The first time I saw you in my dad's church, I thought to myself, 'This could be her… this could be the woman I've been waiting for.' And you are."

They kissed again; this one, instigated by him. Their second kiss lasted a bit longer than their first, and when it broke, Tonya had to catch her breath.

"Do you really have to go back to that nightshift?" she asked. She was flushed from the kiss. It had been the most splendid and loving kiss she'd ever had, even counting the ones she'd shared with Charles. She realized in that moment that her ex-husband had never truly loved her. She could feel that Damien did.

To her question, Damien shrugged. "I guess so. I mean, I'll lose my apartment if I don't. The landlord has given me over a month's slack already. I don't know how much longer he'll do that."

"Screw the landlord," she exclaimed with a broad smile on her face. "That building smells like pee."

Damien chuckled and nodded. "Yeah... yeah, it does."

"So..." she began and nuzzled close to him, "lose the second job, and lose the apartment."

He laughed again, like he thought she was joking. "And do what? Move in with my dad?"

"No... move in with me."

Damien didn't laugh this time. Instead, he looked at her with curious eyes, as if studying her... as if in disbelief. "Are you serious?"

"Why not? You've lived with me for over a month now, and I've gotten kind of used to having you around." She ran her fingers through his dark hair, smoothing it down from where his sleep had disheveled it. "I love you, Damien, and I want you here with me."

He smiled softly and kissed her. When it broke, he said,

"You don't have to keep taking care of me, you know. I'm about as over this concussion as I think I'll get."

"I'm not talking about taking care of you. I'm talking about being in a relationship with you – a *real* relationship. One where you come home from work at the end of the day and I have supper ready and waiting. One where we watch movies together and read together... where you play me songs on your guitars... one where we go to bed each night together and..."

"And make sweet passionate love?" His voice was a little excited as he said this. It even showed in his eyes.

"Yes. Exactly." She rubbed her nose gently against his and held it there as she stared into his gaze. "What do you say?"

He took a moment to reply, but it was a short moment. He kissed her and whispered, "I think the hotel can hire a new bellhop."

Tonya's smile stretched nearly the entire width of her face. Coyly, she put her hand on his chest and stroked it up and down. "It only makes since. After all, I've seen you naked plenty."

"The doctor said you had to bathe me," he insisted through is grin.

"For the first few days," she admitted. "After that, I just enjoyed it."

"You sneaky little vixen."

"You walked in on me while I was in the shower... more than once, might I remind you?"

"I was just sneaking a peek," he said and gave her another

soft peck of his lips. "You washed my genitals."

"Yes, I did." Pride beamed through her voice. "Did you like it?"

"Your hand on my crotch? I *loved* it."

Not so coyly, Tonya slid her hand down over his abs and onto his crotch, squeezing it through his boxer shorts. She felt it respond instantly to her touch. "It seems like you still kind of love it."

He moaned as she continued to squeeze. His right hand left her back and trailed down to her thigh, where he returned the squeezing gesture. "More than words can describe."

Once again, they kissed, but this time it was a more intimate one, and one that lasted much longer. Tonya slid her fingers through the open fly of his boxers and took his manhood into her hand. She pulled it out of the fly and felt it grow from her touch. The hand on her hip began to work at her nightgown, pulling the hem up her legs and over her hips. Damien let go of the garment and began to squeeze her bare bottom.

"Not wearing underwear today?" he asked through the kiss.

"Never when I sleep," she replied.

"Good to know."

The kiss resumed, and from Damien's touch, Tonya felt the heat between her thighs grow. In her hand, he was fully erect – the first time he'd allowed himself to get this way with her, even when she'd bathed him. She squeezed him and stroked him and then pulled one of her legs over his, allowing him access to her warmth.

His fingers grazed her lips and stroked over her clit, teasing her and making her tremble.

"You're already wet," he muttered, almost proudly.

"You make me wet," she remarked, and to make sure the conversation didn't control the moment, she pressed the tip of her tongue against his lips. He parted them, letting his tongue come out and play with hers.

After a moment, she felt her body heat rise to a plateau that she hadn't felt in years... if ever. Damien pressed a finger against her vestibule, stroking her opening. She pushed down against it, taking his finger inside.

They handled one another for a long moment until Tonya slid her body onto his. She guided his member into her and sank down onto it. Damien's moan was music to her ears. He put his hands around her waist and she leaned into him. Instantly, their kissing resumed. Softly, she began to bounce against him, offering him full but gentle penetration. He alternated soft upward thrusts with her bounces, heavily increasing their pleasure.

"Is this okay?" he asked her as she lifted upright and pressed the palms of her hands against the mattress. "I'm not hurting you, am I?"

She gave him a catlike grin and whispered, "You're the only man who's ever found this spot." She began to moan and bounced a little harder.

"What spot?" he asked. He groaned as her speed quickened.

Through a pant, she gasped and said, "My g-spot!"

Neither Tonya nor her new love lasted long during that first encounter. Shuddering through an intense and blissful orgasm, she held him inside of her as he filled her with his juices of life. He'd been hesitant to do so, asking, "What if I get you pregnant?"

She responded with, "We'll make gorgeous babies, then."

And it was true. Tonya became pregnant after their third encounter, but their wedding wasn't due to the promise of a new child. He proposed to her the day he moved his stuff in with her, and she'd excitedly accepted. Like with all marriages, things were never absolutely perfect between them. They had little spats here and there. Every now and again, one would be temperamental and hurt the other's feelings. The money situation changed after the marriage, as her alimony from Charles ended the moment the marriage certificate was signed. But these were all minor things in the long run. Tonya took a part-time job with Damien's father's church, and she earned extra income editing novels for a small press in her spare time. Somehow, it was enough. Most importantly, she and Damien truly loved one another, were faithful to one another, supported one another on everything important and even the little things, and they raised their child with tender care and joy.

Because of all of this and so much more, they lived happily ever after.

*End*

# *Unmasked*

She wasn't much for costume parties, especially now that she was single. In fact, it had been well over a year since she'd been to a social gathering of any sort, and it had been the last one with her ex-fiancé Brandon. It was that party that had broken their engagement. She'd caught him on the receiving end of oral sex in the bathroom, pleasured by the hostess of the party who had invited them. In a way, Kim was happy she'd seen it. Otherwise, they would have been married by now and he'd surely be cheating on her still, just as he had then.

Kim knew that all men were not like Brandon; they weren't *all* scumbags, but catching him in the act had left a bitter taste in her mouth, and she was still recovering from it.

Regardless, this party was being hosted at Angela Buford's house, and Angela was her longest and closest friend. She couldn't refuse, and even if she tried, she knew Angela wouldn't let her. In fact, something told her this party had been scheduled just for her benefit, as Angela was not known to host parties of any sort... ever.

It was the week of Halloween and the party was scheduled for Halloween night. This was her least favorite holiday, as she hated not being able to tell who was whom when everyone was masked and in costumes. She felt uncomfortable talking to people on Halloween night, because she never knew who she was talking to. If it was someone she knew, she usually figured it out during the conversation, but if it was a stranger, she liked to place a real face with a voice when first meeting them.

Either way, she had to think of a costume to wear. She would have to go shopping to do this, as all she had in her apartment were regular everyday clothes. While Kim loved a good shopping venture, she never knew how to pick out a Halloween costume that wouldn't make her look stupid or creepy. Thusly, she grabbed her phone and called up Angela, since this was all her idea and her fault.

"Are you excited?" her best friend asked as she answered the phone, not even offering a 'hello.'

"You know this isn't my sort of thing," Kim replied and sighed, "but I'll go willingly. Otherwise, I know you'll just come over and make me go."

"Damn right. What are you wearing?"

"I have no idea. Will you go shopping with me and help me pick something up?"

Angela's voice grew greatly in volume. "Hells to the yeah! Want me to pick you up?"

"Yes, please. You know where all the good places to shop are anyway."

They ended the call and Kim got dressed and ready. Looking in the mirror, she didn't feel very pretty anymore, even though she was. Her self-esteem had been somewhat crushed by Brandon's cheating, and it only seemed to get worse. Because of this, she dressed in a baggy sweatshirt and a pair of loose jeans, keeping her look to match her current state of mind.

She waited outside the building for Angela to arrive. When she got there, Kim climbed into the passenger seat and buckled up.

"Thank god you asked me to go along," Angela said as they started off. "They way you're dressing lately, I can't begin to imagine what you would have picked out by yourself."

"Who's there to get all dolled up for?" she asked and shrugged. "Where are we going anyway? To the department store?"

Angela laughed. "No. Never. I don't even shop there for toothpaste. That place is a karma killer. We're going to Exquisite Looks. They have the *best* variety of Halloween costumes in the city."

"Exquisite Looks? I don't even think I can afford to walk inside that place."

"You can owe me then. I *insist* you look good at my party."

"Can't I just go as a witch? Paint my face green? Stick a wart on my nose?"

"Sure… if you're going to someone else's party. Didn't you read the bottom of my e-vite?"

Indeed, Kim had not. "You listed rules?"

"Just one. Nothing scary and nothing gross."

*Isn't that the point of Halloween?* Kim thought, although

she didn't ask the question. Instead, she sat quietly while Angela turned up the radio and sang along with whatever song was playing. Kim wasn't a fan of modern music, so it wasn't just the artist she didn't recognize. She simply couldn't grasp the electronic mess that was considered music nowadays. Her love for music lay within the elements of classic blues, artists like Muddy Waters, Sippie Wallace, B.B. King and Memphis Minnie. Those were crafters of true musical artistry in her opinion, and it was the only type of music that could both relate to her emotions and make her feel *their* emotions.

They arrived at Exquisite Looks in less than twenty minutes, and the parking lot was nearly full. Angela chose a space near the far end of the gigantic store, and by the time they reached the entrance, Kim felt like she'd walked a mile uphill.

Inside the shop was more packed than the outside. Not only were the racks of costumes plentiful and close together, but it looked like perhaps a half a dozen people or more had arrived in each vehicle outside. Kim instantly felt uncomfortable and more than a little claustrophobic.

"Are you *sure* we can't go to a department store? This place is a zoo," she pleaded to her friend.

"Take a breath and start looking at the costumes," Angela told her. "You'll be fine, and when we leave, you'll have something that'll make you really stand out as the beauty you are."

While Angela began to browse, Kim tried to disappear. She kept to herself, ignoring attendants and the other shoppers.

Casually, she glanced at the different racks. Nothing instantly popped out at her, and she didn't bother shifting through the different costumes and styles that hung from them. Eventually, she just found herself wandering and not really looking at anything at all. When she came out of this daze, she sought out Angela but couldn't find her.

There was a large back room in the store and she went to it, wondering if her friend was in there. The second she stepped into it, she regretted it. It was like walking into a haunted house. Every step she took, some piece of scary merchandise moved or spoke or lit up. Twice, she screamed as automated limbs reached for her. Hurriedly, she left the area and nearly ran smack dab into Angela.

"There you are," her friend said. She was holding in her arms a stack of costumes. "I've been looking everywhere for you."

"Don't go in there," she insisted, pointing at the back room behind her. "That place is terrifying."

Angela chuckled. "When did you become such a chicken? Come on. Let's sort through these and see which one screams *Kim!*"

She had to admit that Angela chose some *interesting* looks for her. The first three were easy for her to eliminate. They felt a bit too slutty to her, and seeing as it would be chilly on Halloween night, she wanted more on than a pair of panties, a corset, and some fishnet stockings. The next one Angela held up was a fairy costume, but there wasn't much fabric to it either, although it did offer a ruffled skirt over the built in bloomers. Finally, she showed her a cat suit that was reminiscent of Cat Babe from the *Bat Stud Returns* movie. She'd always loved Michelle Pheiffer's look in that. She could see herself being Cat Babe. It was a sexy, skin-hugging costume, but no one would get to see too much flesh and that made her happy.

"I like it," she admitted and saw Angela smile. Then, she looked at the price tag and grimaced. "But I don't like it at a hundred and thirty bucks."

"I told you'd I'd buy," Angela reminded her. "Let's get it rung up."

In the car, she still couldn't believe the price of the costume, but it would look decent on her and buying it for her seemed to have made Angela happy. She didn't want to disappoint her best friend. Angela worked hard to keep her included in things and to make sure she felt loved and appreciated. Kim knew she owed her the same in return.

"You bought the outfit," she told her, turning the music down as she did, "so how about letting me buy supper?"

"Supper… how European of you. But sure, that would be great."

Kim grinned. "Tacos and margaritas?"

"That sounds awesome! But not too many. Otherwise, you'll never squeeze into this costume."

Kim limited herself to two soft tacos and two margaritas, but she still felt full and lightheaded when Angela dropped her off at her building. In her apartment, she took her costume out of the bag and placed it on the bed. For a long while, she eyed it, almost itching to try it on. If she tried it on and it looked horrible on her, there was still time to return it and choose something else for the party.

Giving in to the whim, she stripped away her jeans and sweatshirt and tried to pull the costume up. There was one thing keeping it from fitting properly – her underclothes. She removed the cat suit and then stepped out of her panties, kicking them off into the room. After dropping her bra to the floor, she tried once more. It zipped up this time and truly fit her like a glove.

She walked to the mirror and took a long hard look at herself. It was hard for her to admit it, but she knew the suit looked stunning on her. The only problem was her face stuck out like a sore thumb. She took the mask from the bed and pulled it over the top her head, working it over her hair and positioning it properly atop her nose so that her eyes were in line with the openings. Now as she gazed into the mirror, she truly did feel like she looked stunning… stunning and dangerous.

"Meow," she said to her reflection, practicing Cat Babe's signature word. It sounded silly coming from her, and so she practiced it until she thought she had it right. Then, just for kicks, she worked on her purring. That was easier for her, as she'd always purred when Brandon had gone down on her.

Kim wished she'd grabbed an accessory. All she was missing was a whip. The outfit also didn't come with boots, but she had a pair of long black stiletto boots in her closet that she'd stored away for an occasion to wear them. The occasion had not come... not until now. Eagerly, she pulled them out, slipped them on, and zipped them up. At first, she was wobbly and unbalanced in them, but she practiced walking in them and noticed that when she did, she walked in a slinky, catlike fashion. They were absolutely perfect.

Taking out her phone, she took a selfie in front of the mirror and texted it to Angela. In a moment, she received a reply: *OMG! You look AMAZING!*

Kim didn't reply, but she did smile and giggle over Angela's response. It had been a while since anyone had called her amazing, but it had also been a while since she'd given anyone a reason to do so.

Deciding she didn't want to risk damaging her outfit by strutting around in it, she stripped it off, carefully folded it, and put it back in the box they'd placed it in at the store. Part of her wanted to put it back on and wear it out, maybe fight some crime like the 'real' Cat Babe. Another part of her remembered how winded she got just walking from the parking lot into the costume shop. Besides, she'd had enough adventure for the day. She'd gone out, browsed a store that was filled with a hoard of shoppers, and had margaritas and tacos. That was enough for one day.

The hour grew late, and as she went to bed and slept, she dreamed of her new costume. In her dream, she was acting out the fantasy she'd had before going to bed, creeping atop the rooftops of the city and looked for trouble. From high above, she looked down on an alleyway where a mugging was taking place, and she leapt down in a true catlike fashion, landing sturdily on her feet.

The muggers hadn't known what hit them. She clawed and kicked her way through the brutal battle, and when she was finished with them, she rushed to the man they'd been mugging. He was absolutely gorgeous – an Adonis of dreamland. No words were spoken, but they shared a kiss – one that ended only because of her alarm clock.

Still, because of her action-packed dream, she awoke energized and more refreshed than she'd been in ages. For the first time in a long time, she felt like going for a run. She dressed in running shorts, a tank top, and her best sneakers and headed out the door. Outside, the morning air felt fresh and exhilarating. It pushed her forward as she started into a trot, then a jog, and finally a nice steady run. She didn't have the same endurance she'd held a year or two ago. Laziness and depression had seen to that, but the cool air helped to push her forward. She kept imagining herself as Cat Babe, and considering the fact that the anti-heroine had never been a quitter. With that thought, Kim pressed on until her calves were simply too sore for her to run any further.

She rested on a bench across the street from a coffee shop and gazed through its windows at the patrons. Her breathing began to return to normal, but her heart began to flutter as she saw the door open and watched the most handsome man step outside. He was tall, blond and handsome, wearing a dark suit with a cranberry shirt, open at the collar. In one hand, he held a to-go cup. In the other hand was his phone. She watched him for a moment as he watched his phone and walked. Then, she suddenly realized that he was about to walk into the street, and there was a car speeding down the road toward him.

By sheer adrenaline-driven impulse, Kim leapt off the bench and rushed across the street, tackling the man to the sidewalk and moving him out of the way of the car, mere seconds before he would have been hit.

"Watch where you're going, asshole!" shouted the driver of the car through his window, raising a fist as he hurried away.

"Jesus Christ!" the man she'd tackled exclaimed. He was on his hands and backside, visibly shaken by what had just happened.

"I'm so sorry," Kim fretted and stood. She grabbed his phone off the sidewalk and handed it to him. His coffee was a goner though.

"Sorry?" the man asked, standing and dusting himself off. He looked at his phone and tucked it into his pocket. "You just saved my ass. I had no idea that car was coming so fast." He smiled at her and then exhaled a heavy sigh of relief. "Thank you."

Looking at him up close, she couldn't help but think he looked like the man from her dream last night, but that was impossible. It was most likely a trick from her imagination, and she brushed the idea away.

"I'm just glad you're okay," she replied, blushing just a bit.

"I'm just lucky you were around."

"Think nothing of it," she said bashfully as she smiled and looked away from his piercing blue eyes.

"Can I buy you a cup of coffee?" he asked and gestured down to the crushed cup, emptied onto the sidewalk. "I need to grab another one, and I'm happy to treat you. It's the least I could do."

She considered his offer for a moment, but she still had to go home and clean up for work. Shaking her head, she said, "No... I'm afraid I'm in a rush, but I do appreciate the offer. Just... look both ways before crossing the street next time, okay?"

He chuckled at the advice. "I promise."

With that, she turned from her implausible dream man and began to jog home. Behind her, she heard him shout after her.

"Hey! I never got your name?"

Looking back at him, she yelled, "Cat Babe!" and then continued her run back home.

Halfway home, she hated the fact that she'd lied to that man on the sidewalk. She wasn't Cat Babe, but at that moment, she'd sure felt like she was. Besides, it had been a fluke – a chance encounter, and the chances were high that the two would never meet again. If they did, she doubted she'd be as brave as she was today. Wearing that cat suit last night had done something to her, but she knew this newfound fearlessness would soon fade and she would again become the meek and timid Kim that she knew herself to be.

Nonetheless, she stripped her clothes off and kicked them

onto her bathroom floor the second she got home. In the shower, she thought of the handsome man she'd saved and the way he resembled the Adonis from her dream. Thoughts of them – or of *him*, as the two melded into one in her fantasy – brought about a heat within her that had been missing for quite some time. So, as the shower water sprayed down onto her, she took the opportunity to pleasure herself and allowed herself to orgasm for the first time in ages.

When she stepped from the shower, feeling refreshed and walking on clouds, she noticed a text had come in from Angela: *One more night! I can't wait to see you in that costume in person tomorrow!*

She texted back with a cat emoji and a simple 'meow.' Then, she dressed for work.

Kim was an office assistant at a design firm just a few blocks from her apartment. Her job was tedious and consisted of making coffee, running off copies of various reports, filing paperwork, and delivering files from one office to another. It kept her busy, but it wasn't fulfilling. Still, it paid the rent and that was what mattered.

At the end of the day, she texted Angela and asked her to meet her for a drink at their favorite after work bar. Angela declined, insisting she had to get stuff ready for tomorrow night. She invited Kim to join her, but then Kim returned with a rejection of her own. She loved her bff but she wasn't in the mood for cleaning Angela's house or hanging decorations. Instead, she went to the bar alone and treated herself to a martini – something she rarely drank but loved greatly.

When she'd had two, she paid up her tab and headed outside. She'd had to park on the street about a half a block away, and it was dark and chilly out. Behind her, she heard footsteps trailing not too far away. When she quickened her pace, so did whoever was following her.

Quickly, she turned around and came face to face with a young brute dressed in black with a stocking cap on his head. He looked smug and tough.

"What's the hurry?" he asked as he walked right up to her. "I wanna have a little fun with you."

The fearlessness from her cat suit had not quite worn off, and in lieu of a verbal reply, Kim pulled her fist back and punched him in the face, breaking his nose on contact. With a shout, the man covered his face and collapsed to the ground. Her eyes widened as she saw blood run through the openings between his fingers.

"Bitch!" he shouted and looked up at her. "You broke my nose!" She watched his hand move to his pocket, where he withdrew a knife. "I was gonna be easy with you, but not now."

She didn't give him an opportunity to stand. Swiftly, she kicked his hand, knocking the knife out of his reach. Then, she offered him one more kick, one that landed on the side of his head. On the sidewalk, the man held his head and rolled a bit, trying to pull himself away from her.

Kim marched up to him and crouched down beside him. "You should be careful how you treat women," she told him in a calm, steady voice. "One of these days, we're likely to claw your eyes out."

Standing, she strutted away and went to her car, where she buckled up and headed home.

In her apartment, she couldn't help but be excited over what had happened, even though she knew there was a great chance it could have gone the other way – a way that was much less to her advantage. When she thought of how she'd broken his nose and how she kicked the knife out of his hand, she started to giggle. She knew this sudden burst of confidence – this remarkable bravery – was psychosomatic and all in her head. She understood that it was brought about by a bit of cosplay exuberance as she'd pranced around in her new cat suit last night. Still, she couldn't share the reality that she had not only saved one man from danger, but she had thwarted a thug as well.

Kim considered calling Angela and telling her about what had happened, but she knew how her friend would react. While she'd be proud of her for defending herself, she'd also warn her how dangerous the streets could be for a woman by herself. She wasn't in the mood for a lecture, even though she knew Angela would have been right.

On the couch, she turned on a movie and settled back to watch. Her attention faded from it as she further considered the day's moments of bravery. She'd given credit for her new confidence to the cat suit, but when she thought about everything, she wondered how true that really was. Who wouldn't have tried to rescue someone that was about to walk out in front of a car? And what woman wouldn't have at least tried to defend herself against a man that wanted to take advantage of her and then threatened her with a knife?

What she'd done wasn't so much remarkable as it was instinctive. This realization did nothing to shake her confidence though, and knowing it had come from within her instead of her ownership of a new suit made it somehow even better. To reward herself, she decided to replay an event from the shower, and moving to the bedroom, she stripped down, grabbed a toy from her drawer, and spent some time playing with her kitty.

After her second outstanding orgasm for the day, Kim closed her eyes and drifted off to sleep, where she had a similar dream as the night before. This time, she was in her cat suit again, but she was the one in mortal danger. She was falling, and not in a graceful style like before. Her legs and arms were flailing about, and below her, the ground was growing closer by the millisecond. Then, just before she hit, she was caught in the arms of the handsome man that she had saved earlier in the day. He carried her off to safety and laid her down on top of cool grass. She smiled at him and purred, and then he kissed her. When the kiss broke, he reached for the mask to remove it, but as his fingers grazed its faux leather side, Kim woke up.

Despite the fearful fall from wherever she'd fallen from, all she would focus on was being kissed by that handsome stranger, and she lay in her bed for a long while with a rather silly smile on her face. When she finally sat up and looked at the time, she didn't much feel like a run this morning. Her legs were stiff and a bit sore from yesterday. She also didn't feel like going to work. There was a party tonight, and despite how she'd felt earlier about it, she was now anxious for it – anxious to wear her cat suit again.

In the shower, she decided she really wanted a whip to match the suit, and so she called in sick to her job and readied herself to go on the hunt for her accessory.

She thought of western outlets, sporting goods stores, and toy stores, but somehow, she ended up at a sex supply shop. The place was nearly as large as the costume shop had been, but somehow, this she found this store much more appealing. Not only was it less crowded with only a few customers and one associate dawdling around, but it reeked of excitement, and excitement was an emotion that at reverberated through her veins over the last couple of days.

"Looking for anything in particular?" the associate asked in a friendly tone. She was a young, goth-looking woman with green hair and several piercings on her lips, nose, ears and eyebrows. Once upon a time, Kim might have been intimidated by someone who looked like she did, but now, she found her presence to be unique and intriguing. In fact, she rather liked her.

"I need a whip," she told her with a smile on her face, "like Cat Babe would carry."

The associate grinned and nodded. "We've got just the thing."

She led Kim to an area that was set-up with all sorts of cosplay goodies. On a long wall, there were several accessories, including a selection of whips. She took one in a box and handed it to her.

"It's from the Cat Babe line."

Kim looked at the image on the box – a woman in a cat suit just like hers, cracking the whip. "It's perfect!" she exclaimed and had her ring it up.

When she arrived home with it, she immediately took it from the box, pushed all of the furniture back in the living room, and began to practice. It took a while longer to learn how to use it, unlike the few short minutes it had taken her to practice her meowing. Once she finally learned how to properly crack it, she practiced her stance with it. Legs parted and knees partially bent. One hand up like a cat bearing its claws. Head forward a bit with a look of mastery on her face. She worked the whip in this pose for quite some time until she felt she finally had it right, and then she sat down and relaxed.

At lunchtime, she decided she needed to leave the apartment again – to step away from her new toy and from the excitement that was building over getting to wear her cat suit again tonight. She got in her car and went to a small diner, where she ordered a grilled chicken salad and a side of fried okra. She really wanted their daily special – a Salisbury steak with a baked potato and green beans, but she remembered how tight that costume was. If she ate too heavily, there was a good chance it wouldn't zip up later.

Even so, her salad was great, and the fried okra made up for the calories she missed not having the baked potato. She declined a dessert when a selection was offered by her waitress, and before she changed her mind, she paid her check and turned to leave.

Just then, the man of her dreams – literally – walked in the door. It was the handsome blond man that she'd pushed out of the path of the speeding car... the man who had kissed her in her dream and tried to remove her mask.

She caught his eye immediately and he smiled at her as he approached. His smile, like the rest of what she could see, was absolutely flawless.

"It's you again!" he exclaimed with a hint of excitement. "I've been hoping we would run into each other again."

"You have?" she asked and then added, "So have I."

"I want to thank you again for saving me yesterday. That was really... heroic of you, *Cat Babe*." He said the name as if he was questioning it. Kim blushed as she considered she needed to come clean and share with him her true 'secret identity.' "Say... are you doing anything tonight?"

Her eyes brightened and her smile widened. Was he about to ask her on a date? As much as she'd fantasized over him, she hoped so. Then, just as she was about to say no, she remembered that she *was* doing something tonight. She was going to Angela's party, lest Angela hunted her down and killed her for being a no-show.

He seemed to notice her expression change as it went from excitement to regret. His voice followed suit. "I'm sorry. That was a bit forward of me. It's Halloween, after all. I'm sure a beautiful woman like you has plans."

*He called me a beautiful woman!* she squealed within herself.

Before she could reply, his cell rang in his pocket and he pulled it out to answer it. She noticed the phone was different than the one that had dropped yesterday, and she realized it must have broken in the fall.

"Can you excuse me for a minute?" he asked, looking at the screen. "It's my office."

"Sure," she replied and watched him step away as he took the call.

Just then, her own phone dinged within her purse. It was a message from Angela, pleading for her to call.

Kim hit the call button and walked outside so she wouldn't interrupt anyone else. When Angela answered, she was nearly frantic. "Early! I need you here early! Please!"

"What's wrong?" Kim asked, walking away from the restaurant.

"My dress!" her bff screamed. "I tried on my dress and it was too long. I stepped on the hem, tripped, and tore it! It looks bad, Kim. Like, *really* bad!"

One of Kim's most honed skilled was sewing. She would sew anything that needed sewing, and more than once had she come to Angela's rescue over something ripped or torn.

"Okay, I'll go home and get my kit and be right there," she promised.

"Bring your costume," Angela insisted. "It's a *big* rip!"

She ended the call and turned back toward the diner. Hurriedly, she returned to it and stepped inside. Her eyes scanned the place, looking for the man who had just called her *beautiful*. Sadly, he was no longer there.

"Just as well," she muttered as she stepped back outside. "He'll have to stay in my fantasies until we meet again... *if* we meet again."

At her apartment, she gathered her sewing kit, her cat suit, her black stiletto boots, and her brand new whip and loaded them all into a duffle bag. She also grabbed her make-up kit so that she could make sure her eyes and lips were lined and colored just right to go with the costume. Five minutes later, she was out the door and en route to Angela's house.

Angela was sobbing when she arrived. The dress she'd torn turned out to be her grandmother's wedding dress. She had decided to be the Bride of Frankenstein for the party, and she'd thought the vintage wedding dress would have been perfect. She hadn't counted on ruining it.

"It's not ruined," Kim insisted as she observed the damage. "It's just old, fragile, and torn. I can stitch it up, and it will last you for the night, but come Monday, you'll want to take it to a professional who can repair it properly. Otherwise, it'll never be the same."

"I wanted to badly to wear this on my wedding day!" her friend sobbed. "Now, I've *destroyed* it!"

"Go have a drink, try to relax, and finish setting up for the party. Give me twenty minutes and it'll be alright."

"You're just so wonderful!" Angela told her. "I don't know what I would do without you."

"Just consider it a partial payment on that cat suit you bought me," Kim said and winked.

"Consider the cat suit paid off!"

Stitching up the tear was a little more difficult than she'd counted on. First, she had to cut along the tear where the fabric had frayed when ripped. It hadn't ripped in a straight line either, which things rarely did. Moving slowly and carefully with small-spaced stitches, she began to repair the dress. It was a painstaking job, but she did it without error and in a way that made the new seam as unnoticeable as possible. When she was done, she raised the hem a good two inches to prevent Angela from tearing it again.

Once the dress was finished and ready to be worn, she helped Angela finish up preparations for the party. Then, she minded the trick-or-treaters as Angela got ready upstairs. When she came back down, she was the spitting image of the Bride of Frankenstein.

"You look amazing!" Kim exclaimed and took a few

photos of her on her phone. "I can't believe that hair!"

"It's a wig… thank god! I never would have been able to get mine to stand up like that." Angela posed for a couple more pictures and then said, "Go upstairs and use my bathroom to get ready. People should be arriving soon, and you'll have privacy there until you're ready."

"That sounds great! Mind if I use the shower?"

"By all means!"

Kim didn't exactly need to take another shower, but she wanted the opportunity to hide for a while longer until enough people had shown up so that she could disappear in the crowd. It was still a couple of hours until the party was scheduled to begin, but she knew how parties were. There were always those that arrived early, despite being told what time to get there. They were the ones that liked to sit down, relax, and make conversation. Those conversations often became intrusive into private lives, and she was not welcoming to that sort of intrusion.

The private bathroom that attached to Angela's bedroom was bigger than the bathroom in Kim's apartment. She locked the door behind her when she entered and then put the lid down on the commode so she could sit and check her phone. No texts. No missed calls. This made sense, as Angela was usually the only person to call and text her. Before her breakup with Brandon, Kim had been a lot more popular with a fair amount of people to converse with. Now, since become a reclusive, those numbers had dwindled drastically.

She had only one social media account left and she went to it to upload some of the shots she had taken of Angela in her Bride of Frankenstein costume. There were still a few hundred people following this account, but at one time, there had been a few thousand. Kim rarely posted anything anymore, which was part of why those numbers had also decreased. She chose three of the most flattering shots of her best friend and added them to her page, tagging Angela in each. Within moments, they began to get likes and comments, although each of those were from Angela's followers, not hers.

With a sigh, she pushed a button and the screen went black. She set the phone on the back lid of the toilet and stood, looking at the separate shower and bathtub, trying to decide which to use. A nice relaxing bubble bath sounded great, but she didn't want to completely dominate the room for too terribly long... even though she *did* want to. She opted for the shower, undressed, and turned on the water. When it was warm enough, she stepped in, drenched her hair, and used Angela's rose-scented body wash and shampoo. Angela had far superior grooming products to hers, but she also made a lot more money.

She stayed in the shower for as long as she could, until the water got too chilly for her to bear it, and then she stepped out and dried with one of the softest, fluffiest towels she'd ever held. At that moment, she heard a twisting of the locked doorknob, followed by a knock.

"Hey, Kim." It was Angela. Wrapping the towel around

her, Kim walked to the door and unlocked and opened it. "I brought you something." In her hand, she held out a glass of red wine, and Kim smiled seeing it.

"Just what the doctor ordered," she told her, taking the wine and sipping it.

"If you need my curling iron, you know where it is. You don't want flat hair coming out from under that cat mask."

Angela closed the door as she left, and Kim hadn't even thought about curling her hair. Yet, she thought long, curly, bouncy hair *would* look nice with the costume. After blow-drying it, she gave the curling iron a try and was pleased with the results.

It didn't take her very long to apply her make-up and get dressed. She stood in front of Angela's full wall-length mirror and gazed at her reflection. Cracking her whip, she meowed and then purred as lusciously as she could. She looked sexy; she had to admit it to herself. Not only did she look sexy, but she looked provocative and dangerous as well. Once again, she felt like she could have climbed out the window, leapt down to the ground, and went on the prowl looking for trouble.

It was amazing what a simple costume did to inflate her self-esteem.

She heard the doorbell ring downstairs and caught a whiff of Angela's enthusiasm as she welcomed in some guests to her party. They were starting to arrive, Kim thought, and soon, the house would be packed with people in various costumes and masks to shield their identities. She had to question herself over why the idea of masks still bothered her, as she was also wearing one and she was pretty sure no one but Angela would recognize her. Still, it was the factor of being on the receiving end of the unknown – conversations with strangers without being able to see their facial expressions as they talked to her. Perhaps she could solve that by simply not talking to anyone. Maybe a few purrs and an occasional meow every now and again would suffice.

She doubted it, but she could always hope.

Sitting on the bed, she slowly finished her glass of wine before heading downstairs to the party, and even then it was at the insistence of Angela, via a text: *Get down here! The crowd is getting thick!*

Kim cringed and stood from the bed. She took her whip, rolled it up, and attached it to the fake leather belt that came with the costume. Opening the door, she could hear the crowd meld with the music from downstairs. She hadn't heard the doorbell ring but a couple of times, and there were so many more people there already than she had imagined. That single glass of wine did little to prepare her for this sort of social interaction.

Downstairs, she stood on the last step and looked at the many people that were gathered around in groups – some talking, some dancing, and most drinking. There were costumes of all kinds from clown to cowboys to princesses to cavemen and roman leaders. She saw a Cleopatra who looked so realistic that she could have been the real thing. There were two astronauts in helmets that she couldn't see through to know who they were. Several others wore masks as well, and they made her cringe.

One costume that stood out was a man dressed as the Bat Stud – Cat Babe's arch nemesis and occasional love interest. He stood tall and brooding in his sexy costume and a mask that concealed everything but his eyes and lips. He was next to the liquor bar, sipping a drink, and looking around almost disinterested at with the party. Suddenly, he looked over and caught her eye. Kim was thrown by this and she looked away, down to the floor as she walked from the final step of the staircase. She avoided his gaze as she pushed through the crowd and into the kitchen, where she saw Angela's tall green wig from across the room, towering high over the other heads that were around her.

"There you are!" Angela all but screamed when she saw her. She had two drinks in her hands – not wine this time – and handed one over to her. "I've been waiting *forever* for you to come downstairs! You look so great!"

Kim knew that tone. Angela was drunk, and rightfully so. She'd worked hard on this party, and she'd probably been drinking since before Kim arrived to fix her dress.

"Everyone, meet the sexiest Cat Babe around!" she announced, and Kim blushed beneath her mask.

The room was mostly guys with a few women present. The women squealed and applauded, while the guys whistled and made cat calls at her. With her cat suit on, Kim had somehow expected to be the sexiest woman at the party. She didn't know if she actually was or not, but the sounds the crowd made at her surely made her feel like it. Worse yet, it only embarrassed her instead of making her feel like she was on top of the world, which was what it should have done.

She downed the drink that Angela handed her and waved at everyone in a shy way. Then, she handed the empty glass back and excused herself, returning to the large living room and the huge amount of people gathered there. Looking off to the bar, she no longer saw Bat Stud. Perhaps he had gotten bored enough with the scene and left. Part of her hoped so, but another part questioned this. Although she'd been a bit shy and embarrassed when he'd caught her looking at him, she found he was perhaps the most intriguing man there. Still, she wasn't in the mood to flirt with strangers, and she headed to the downstairs bathroom, only to find it locked.

Kim didn't need to use the bathroom; she was looking for an escape – a place to hide. She decided to walk through the dining room, which was also becoming crowded, and head out the sliding glass door to the patio. There, she spotted the Bat Stud. He held a glass in his hand and was staring off into the dark yard.

Quickly, Kim turned away and instantly collided with one of the dining room chairs, toppling it over. She clumsily stood it back up and glanced over her shoulder to see Bat Stud staring at her again. In an embarrassed panic, she rushed through the crowd and out of the room, squeezed her way through the living room, and headed upstairs. There were a few people mingling here as well, but when she checked in Angela's bedroom, she found it vacant and closed herself in it to hide.

It took her a moment to catch her breath and calmed her nerves. For a moment, she felt like the 'real' Cat Babe, running from a Bat Stud that was trying to apprehend her. Even though this Bat Stud had made no such move, she didn't want to give him any opportunity to try.

She knew she had to get a grip. It was a party, and he had obviously been invited. She considered finding Angela again and asking her who was behind the mask, but she didn't want to go downstairs again right then. She knew that if she did, she'd surely see him again, and he would see her.

A flush came from the adjoining bathroom and she nearly leapt out of her skin. When the door opened, she saw it was Angela and sighed a long breath of relief.

"What are you doing back in here?" Angela asked with a curious smile.

"Just needed some peace and quiet for a moment," she told her. "You about scared the life out of me."

"Fortunately for you, cats have nine of those," she joked and chuckled. "Come downstairs soon though. There are people I'd like for you to meet."

Kim considered protesting that, but she knew it was pointless. This was Angela's house, Angela's party, and Angela certainly wouldn't let her hide in here all night.

After a decent amount of time had passed, although not nearly enough, she stood from the bed and opened the door.

Peeking out, she saw a few people standing in the hall, chatting by the railing, but Bat Stud was nowhere to be seen. Relieved, she walked back toward the stairs, hearing the bathroom door open behind her. She ignored it, and as she took her first step down, she felt the long heel of one of her stilettos break.

Immediately, she began to fall forward, but miraculously, someone caught her.

"There now," said the voice with his arms around her. "I've got you, Cat Babe."

Looking back, she stared into the eyes of Bat Stud. He was smiling at her as he held her in his strong hold, and she swooned from it.

"You can't walk around here with just one heel," he told her, and suddenly, he lifted her into his arms and carried her into the bedroom. Behind them, people began to make jokes about it and one girl meowed in a way that Cat Babe would have done. Kim smiled and continued to gaze into the eyes of her rescuer.

In the room, he kicked the door shut behind them and laid her on the bed. Then, with gentle ease, he unzipped and removed both of her stiletto boots.

"My hero," she said and purred, even though she hadn't intended to.

"I think catching Cat Babe is one of Bat Stud's favorite pastimes," he replied and winked. "Are you okay? Did you hurt anything?"

She moved both of her feet, and they both felt fine. "No... I don't think so."

"Good. Such a beautiful cat suffering an injured paw would be awful." He sat down beside her and looked down at her. His smile... his eyes... they entrapped her.

"So... what's your name?" she asked, wanting to know who her rescuer was – who was behind that mask.

"I'm Bat Stud," he said in a very serious voice, and then he chuckled. "I guess if you want to know my true secret identity, you'll have to unmask me."

Her smile widened. "That sounds like an invitation."

"Maybe," he offered, "but only if I can unmask the infamous Cat Babe as well."

Kim considered his proposition, and even though she'd been uncomfortable and embarrassed by him at first, she discovered those feelings were gone. He'd saved her from what could have been a deadly fall down the stairs. Halloween costume or not, this Bat Stud was her hero, and she was aching to know who he was.

She sat up and faced him. Her hands timidly reached for his hooded mask, just as his did to hers. Slowly, and in near unison, they unmasked one another. When their identities were revealed, they both looked at the other in almost gleeful surprise.

"It's *you*..." she muttered, staring at the face and into the eyes of the handsome man she'd pushed out of the path of that speeding car... the literal man of her dreams.

"Holy cow..." he whispered and brushed a gloved hand

delicately over her cheek. "You weren't lying. You really *are* Cat Babe."

She giggled and blushed, looking down at her hands as her dream man took one of them in his. "Not really... My name's Kim."

"Kim," he said in a delicate and all too sexy tone, "my name is Ransom."

It was perhaps the sexiest name she'd ever heard, and she found it fitting. "It's good to meet you, again." Then, remembering his daring rescue as she began to fall down the stairs, she added, "Thank you for saving my life."

"You saved mine first," he told her and tenderly squeezed her hand. "I find this incredibly amazing. When I saw you in the restaurant, this was what I was going to invite you to. I had no idea you'd be here."

"Angela's my best friend," she told him and shrugged. "If I didn't come, she would have killed me. I hated not taking you up on your offer, but it looks like the fates had plans in store for us. How do you know Angela?"

"She works at my tech company. I'm one of her bosses. Would you believe she called in sick today, even though she knew I'd be here at the party?"

"Yes..." she said, thinking of how she too had called in today. "That is a very Angela thing to do."

"She wanted me to meet a friend of hers here – some single girl, beautiful, a great personality... I really wasn't in the mood to be set up with anyone, but I didn't want to disappoint her. I waited for a while to be introduced to this mystery woman, but it never happened."

"I have a feeling you're sitting on the bed with her right now."

They looked at each other for a moment, and then they laughed at the situation. After a moment, Ransom cleared his throat and said, "I'm not really one for large parties... Would you like to get out of here? We could grab a bite to eat... maybe take in a movie? I'm sure the city would get a kick seeing Bat Stud and Cat Babe out on the town together."

"I think that sounds absolutely purrfect."

\*\*\*\*

After the third date, their sexual chemistry became too strong for either of them to ignore. When Ransom dropped her off at her building, she invited him up for a nightcap, but as she shut the door behind him, Kim practically pounced on him and tackled him to her carpeted floor. They began to kiss in a most primal and animalist way, and their passion became heated.

He was dressed in a t-shirt that she hurriedly pulled from his body. It was her first look and feel of his torso. He was beautifully built, and his body was hard as a rock. She wore a button-down blouse that she would eventually have to sew the buttons back onto, as Ransom tore it opened and tugged it down her arms and back. The popping buttons flew everywhere.

This was the first time Kim had been with a man since Brandon, and she'd swore to herself that the next man she made love to would be the man she'd spend the rest of her life with. Even though she'd known Ransom for only a week and a half now, she could see that possibility in him, and making love to him now was a chance she was willing to take.

"Are you sure you want to take this step?" he asked her as she stood and pulled down her jeans.

"If you don't take those pants off, I'll rip them right off you," was her response.

Eagerly, Ransom obliged.

When they were in nothing more than their birthday suits, Ransom lifted her into his arms just as he'd done that night when catching her as she began to fall. He carried her to her bedroom, and once again kicked the door closed behind them. Laying her atop the bed, he climbed up between her legs and lifted her legs onto his shoulders. His tongue felt like magic to her as he began to explore her femininity. She moaned hard from his hot touch and writhed against her covers. When his tongue entered her, she purred deep within herself – the purr of a cat in heat.

He feasted on her until she begged him to stop. He was pushing her over the edge, but she wanted to hold out for as long as she could. Kim wanted her first orgasm with him to be with him inside of her, and so she pulled his face up to her, looked him in the eyes, and kissed him. He relaxed on top of her, and with her legs parted, he entered her.

Ransom was by far the largest endowed man she'd ever had. She felt him fill her in a deepness and with a girth that Brandon never could have accomplished. As he thrust into her, she knew he was the man she'd been waiting for... the man she needed, and she no longer cared about her ex or the way he'd cheated on her. She'd found a new man, and he was one who focused on pleasuring her instead of hurrying to climax.

"Is this okay?" he asked her as he pressed into her with tender care.

"It's *purrfect*," she whispered and kissed him deeper.

That night, what had begun as unbridled and lusty passion quickly transformed into an act of true love making. It was the start of a whole new chapter in their relationship, and it would become the best relationship that Kim could have ever hoped for. In three months time, she gave up her tiny apartment and moved into his much larger house on the far end of town. She kept her job until they married, and afterward, she focused on her health and taking care of the child that grew inside of her.

Ransom was dedicated to her in all ways possible, just as she was to him. If a cat truly did have nine lives, Kim believed she was living the best possible one because she was living it with him.

*End*

# Train Ride to Heaven

"You look nervous." Don remarked to Samantha as they waited in the station lobby. "Is everything okay?"

"I guess I'm just a little worried about this trip," she admitted and looked at her husband. "Couldn't we have just driven, Don?"

"What's wrong? Don't you enjoy a train ride?" He smiled and put a hand to her knee, gently caressing it. "Besides, driving would have taken probably twice the time. These trains move pretty fast nowadays."

She huffed. "That's what I'm worried about."

Don's smile widened and Samantha rolled her eyes. He cleared his throat and added, "I understand now. I get it. You're afraid of trains, aren't you?"

She crossed her legs and looked to the side, closing her eyes and turning her nose up at him. "No," she snipped. "I'm *not* afraid... I'm *nervous*."

"It'll be okay, Sam! It's just a train. You *have* ridden a train before, right?"

She said nothing at first, as she wished he'd just stop questioning her about it. When he'd told her they were going on vacation, she'd assumed they'd fly or drive. Don had said nothing about a train.

"Sammy?"

"Ugh!" she groaned and looked at him again. "Fine. No, I've never ridden on a train before. Are you happy?"

"Well, yeah, but you're not." He wrapped his arm around her and pulled her in close. "It'll be a great, honey! You'll see. I mean, trains have been around practically forever, and they've surely been upgraded over the years. There's nothing to worry about. They're probably the safest form of transportation there is."

"How can you say that?" she demanded and loosened herself from his grip. "It's a gigantic set of cars balancing on two skinny little rails on the tracks. What if it topples over?"

"It won't topple over."

"What if a deer runs in front of it... or a car stalls on the tracks?"

"Nothing is going to run in front of it, and nothing will stall on the tracks."

"What if a bridge is out and no one knows and we just go right off it, straight down to the jagged rocks of a rushing river?"

On that one, Don chuckled. "You've been watching too many movies, my dear. The conductors on these things are pros. Once we get going, you'll barely even know we're moving. Plus, there's a dining car for us to eat at, and a bar."

"Well..." she began as she shifted in her seat, "a drink *would* be nice." Then, her eyes grew big as new thoughts of possible disasters arrived in her head. "But, Don...!"

He put a finger to his lips and said, "Ssh... No more talk about devastating things, okay? We'll be fine. I promise. If not... if we crash and die, you can come back from the grave and revive me and kill me all over again for it, okay?"

"*Humph!*" she sounded, turning her nose up again. "That's not even the least bit funny."

Out the corner of her eye, she watched her husband look around the lobby, wondering what he was up to now. Then, quite suddenly, he pointed at a woman sitting by herself reading a magazine. "Look!" he exclaimed. "Look at her. Does she look worried? Frantic? Terrified that we might coast off the tracks and fall to our deaths? No... not at all. See how she smiles as she turns the pages of that magazine? She's ready for a nice and pleasant train ride."

"She's blond with big boobs and a two inch waist. I doubt she's even aware how one of these trains operates, much less the consequences if something goes wrong."

"Then she's blissfully oblivious. What's wrong with that?" He looked at Samantha again and kissed her cheek. "Besides that, no one's boobs are as beautiful as yours."

She glared at him and folded her arms. "Does your mind *live* in the gutter?"

"Hey, you're the one that mentioned boobs. I just commented yours are the best. What's wrong with that?"

She was just ready for this train ride to be done and over with. She'd done some research when he broke it to her how they would be traveling, and even though most of the research promised trains were safe to ride, others had recalled some serious and devastating accidents. There were even trains that had exploded or been hijacked. The possibilities for a ride like this to go wrong were endless. She wouldn't be comfortable until they were safely at their destination… if they made it there.

"Did you bring anything to read while we're on the train?" he asked when she'd gone silent for more than a moment. "I can go to the newsstand and grab you some magazines or a couple of books."

"I have plenty to read," she answered in a softer tone than she'd been using, "but thank you. I'm just ready for the ride to be over and for us to be in our hotel, safe and sound."

"And we *will* be," he ensured and kissed her cheek. "Everything will be perfect."

The truth was that Samantha's nervousness had not been quite this bad until they arrived at the train station. Before that, she'd given consideration to the possibilities of things going wrong, but they hadn't stricken the horrible fear in her that currently riddled her mind. She wished that Don would change his mind and opt for a rental car instead, but as she heard the horn of the train approaching the station, she knew that would not happen.

"Here we go," he said and squeezed her hand. Then, he stood and offered her his grip in assistance. She accepted it and climbed up on jittery legs. "Trust me, by the time you're settled in, you'll find the ride really enjoyable."

"And if I don't?" she asked as they walked to the boarding door.

"Then we'll get enough liquor in you until you *do* enjoy it."

They approached the entrance to the train and showed their tickets to the checker. He let them board, but Samantha had hoped he wouldn't. Nonetheless, she followed her husband to their seats and chose the one that wasn't beside the window.

"It doesn't look like too many people will be joining us," Don noted. Samantha stared at the scattering of empty seats all around.

"How many cars are on this train?" she questioned.

"I didn't really notice," he admitted. "I could ask someone."

"No... it's not that important." She shifted in her seat and fidgeted. "Where did you say the bar is?"

Don chuckled. "Let's wait for it to get rolling first. We'll need to go up top to cross through to the dining car and it's best to do that while it's already in motion so we don't get jolted."

"Up top?" She nearly froze. "On top of the train."

His chuckle turned to a laugh. "No, right above us, on the second level. It's perfectly safe."

Soon, the whistle blared and the train began to move. Samantha felt her fingernails digging – one set into the seat; the other on her husband's knee. Don took that hand and held it in an attempt to comfort her. Yet, there was no comforting her. As the train picked up speed, she grew tenser and restive.

"How fast does this thing go?" she asked, even though she wasn't certain she wanted to know.

"Not as fast as a car, or a plane," he pointed out. "Maybe sixty miles per hour at top speed... somewhere around that."

"What do I do if I have to use the restroom?"

"You go to the restroom, and you use it." His grin was a little cocky, and if she were in a tougher state of mind, she'd have likely smacked it right off his face.

This was no way to spend a tenth anniversary, she thought as she looked over her husband and out the window, watching the scenery pass by her at a steadily increasing speed. For a tenth anniversary, he could have flown her to a tropical island or to Greece or Paris. Heaven knew they could afford it. Don was a successful and highly recognized architect, and she was a bestselling author who wrote under a pen name that protected her true identity. Why he'd chosen a train for this vacation was beyond her. A cruise would have been nice... yachting maybe. Hell, at this point, she would have settled for a country club and a golf course.

She wished she'd thought to visit her doctor and have him prescribe her some valiums. Anything to relax her... Thinking again of the bar, she needed that drink and the distracting setting of the bar. Yet, the idea of crossing over from car to car terrified her.

Ahead, she saw an attendant with a friendly face checking on the people just a few steps ahead of her. The attendant glanced at her and cocked her head to the side, still smiling. She looked down at the guests once more and said something that Samantha couldn't make out. Then, she started toward her.

"Is this your first train ride, ma'am?" the woman asked in a southern and chipper tone.

"Is it that obvious?" Samantha replied.

"You look a little tense, but I assure you, our trains are perfectly safe. Now that we're safely moving, perhaps you'd like to visit the observation car? There's a snack bar on the way there. Maybe some yummies will help."

*Did she really just offer me 'yummies?'* Samantha thought and cocked an eyebrow. "The bar. How do I get to the bar?"

Beside her, Don chuckled. "She'd been nervous since before we even boarded. I think a drink would definitely help her."

"Of course!" the attendance cheered. "If you'll both follow me, we'll go upstairs and I'll guide you to that car."

*Upstairs?* she thought. *I have to cross cars?*

"Come on, honey!" Don said and patted her thigh as he stood. "Let's go get a couple of drinks in us. Maybe it'll help you relax and enjoy the ride."

"The bartender has a supply of signature wines, aged bourbons, imported vodka, and even craft beers," the attendant told them. "There is also a dining car next to it, but they may not be ready to serve yet. It's still a bit early in the trip."

She was still a little afraid to move from her seat, but if she wanted a drink, she'd have no choice but to stand up and follow along. Samantha was led through a door to a set of stairs that took them to an upper level. There, they entered into another passenger car and followed the attendant to a door at the end. Samantha watched as she pushed a button. The door opened and she stepped through, with a second door opening right in front of her. Don followed next, holding Samantha's hand and helping her through.

She was absolutely trembling as she crossed through those doors, but when she made it safely to the next car, she did so unscathed and released a heavy sigh of relief.

"See now? That wasn't so bad," her husband told her and kissed her cheek.

"Only three more cars to go," the attendant added, and Samantha wondered if she would faint.

Finally, they made it to the bar, where they were the only guests for a bartender who was dressed to the nines. They stood before him and Don gave him the order – a craft beer for him and whatever his strongest drink was for Samantha.

"Jittery, eh?" the bartender asked and smiled at Samantha. "I'll make you something that'll fix you right up."

She wasn't sure exactly what he made for her, but it was delicious and strong. Samantha drank it down quickly, put the glass back on the counter, and said, "Hit me again."

After two more of those mysterious but wonderful drinks, she began to relax. The bartender poured her another and popped a cap off another beer for Don. Then, the two went to a table at the corner by a window and sat down to enjoy their beverages at a slower pace.

"Feeling better?" Don asked.

"A little bit," she admitted. Her eyes were focused on the window and the scenery outside of it. From this elevated window, the view seemed much more scenic than it had below. "I think that guy put a *lot* of vodka in this."

"Good."

Samantha chuckled. She hated that she'd been so nervous during this trip. It would only be a few hours before they reached their destination, so it wasn't a terribly long train ride. Perhaps it was the horrible things she'd read in her research that had made her scared, but she finally admitted to herself that the trains in that research were horribly outdated. The one she and Don were on was a state of the art, modern model. Surely, it was incredibly safer than those that had crashed or rolled off their tracks or even fallen off out bridges that had collapsed.

She stopped thinking about it before she became nervous again. Casually, she sipped her drink and looked outside, watching the trees as they passed.

"Come sit beside me," she told Don and patted the seat beside her. She wanted to be closer to him, to show him some warmth and to make up for how she'd behaved.

"Alright." He stood from his seat and moved to the one beside her. "I'm glad you're feeling better about this." Checking the time on his watch, he added, "Just a few more hours, and we'll be on solid ground again."

"I'm looking forward to that."

Looking over, she saw the bartender was now engrossed in

a book. She considered asking for another drink before he got too engrossed, but she was only half through with this one. It, like the others, was pretty strong, and she wanted to make sure she could handle another one before ordering it.

"I love you so much," Don told her, distracting her eyes from the bar and pulling them to his. She smiled fondly at him as he raised his beer bottle up and said, "To ten more fantastic years with you."

Samantha raised her glass to him. "I'll drink to that." Glass to bottle, they clinked, and then they drank. As she lowered her glass, she felt Don's free hand rest on her thigh.

"Exactly how relaxed *are* you?" he asked as he slid his hand between her thighs and began to rub her.

"Don!" she scolded in a hushed tone. Whispering, she asked, "What if the bartender sees you doing that?"

"Then he'll have something to stroke off to later," he told her with a smile.

Samantha giggled and took another swig of her drink. Her husband was feeling adventurous, and while she found his actions to be erotic, she always worried about being seen. True, his hand was on her, but underneath the table. The chances of the bartender noticing were pretty slim, but what if others were to enter?

As she had the thought, she felt his fingers begin to collect her skirt, bringing it up over the knees so that his fingers could graze her womanhood through the thin cotton of her panties.

"I wish you hadn't worn underwear," he told her, but

282

despite the panties, she felt him work a finger beneath them. "Easy access is always preferred."

"You're being absolutely naughty."

"I'm hard as hell in these slacks," he admitted. "Bartender or not, I'm just another swig or two of this beer from taking it out."

Samantha gasped, albeit while smiling. "Don't you dare!" she threatened, but she also couldn't help but wonder if he actually would. Her smile became an 'O' as he pressed his finger inside of her.

"I feel you tightening up around me," he whispered and pushed his finger in a little deeper. "I also feel how wet you're getting."

She looked from his eyes to his lap, where she could see his full erection pressing against his slacks. His finger wiggled inside of her and she gasped. Quickly, she looked at the bartender again. His eyes were still locked onto his book.

"I want to be inside of you so much right now," Don whispered into her ear. Then, he kissed her earlobe.

"You *are* inside of me," she corrected and clenched her femininity just a bit tighter. "Don, we're going to get caught. Someone is bound to walk in here."

"Let them catch us," he told her. "They can't very well kick us off a moving train, now can they?"

"With my luck, they most certainly would." She adjusted in her seat enough to where some of his finger pulled away, leaving it in only to the first knuckle. She heard a zipping sound and looked back down to Don's crotch, where his other hand was easing down the fly.

"I could take it out right here," he said and grinned a bit wider, "or you could reach inside and give it a squeeze. Your choice."

She rolled her eyes at him but smiled nonetheless. Another moan escaped her as he pressed his finger deeper inside of her again. "Is this why you brought me on a train… to seduce me?"

"We've already joined the Mile High Club. In fact, after our last few flights, I'm pretty sure we're lifetime members by now."

Samantha smiled and purred deep within her. "And remember that time we took that three day riverboat cruise up the Mississippi?"

"We turned that fresh water river into salt water; I'm certain of it."

"Fish need their protein."

"There was that time in Jamaica on our honeymoon…" Don raised his eyebrows and gave her a boyish grin.

"We got kicked off the beach that time," she pointed out.

"Only because someone yanked the blanket off us. Otherwise, no one could see what we were doing."

"They didn't *have* to see. You were moaning louder than a trauma patient!"

"Just because you feel so good inside." He wiggled his finger around a bit and she parted her legs wider. "I'm sure that sense of adventure is still inside of you."

"You're just saying that because *you're* inside of me." She rolled her eyes but still kept her smile. Her smile changed as he began to thrust his finger into her and she bit her bottom lip. Once more, she looked at the bartender. He still had his book in front of him, but his eyes were on Samantha and Don. When she noticed him, he quickly looked away. "He just saw us," she whispered to her husband.

"Good," he replied. "You know that just makes it hotter for me."

"Didn't you go to Catholic school?" she teased.

"I'm why two of the nuns got kicked out," he answered.

Samantha felt his finger withdraw and she sighed from a mixture of relief and disappointment. While she was nervous about this particular public display, no one knew how to please her like her husband. He began to tweak her clitoris, emphasizing that notion. She looked at the bartender again; his back was to them now, and ever so coyly, she slid a hand into Don's open fly and squeezed his manhood. It throbbed powerfully in her grip, letting her know it was thankful for the attention.

"So, you *do* want to play…" he said through a shuddering breath.

"Maybe just a little." She watched the bartender to make sure he didn't turn around as she worked her husband's tool from his fly. Then, she softly began to stroke it. She ran a thumb over the tip of the head, finding it already sticky with secretion. "You're really turned on by this, aren't you?"

He squeezed her clit between his thumb and index finger and asked, "Aren't you?"

The door opened to the car behind them, and just as the bartender turned back to see who was entering, Samantha released Don and felt him do the same with her. She noticed as he covered his erection with his jacket, hiding it from prying eyes.

A crowd of six passengers entered into the bar – mostly elderly people – and gathered around the counter to place their drink orders. Samantha caught the bartender's eye as he looked back over at them and shrugged. Then, he greeted his new guests and welcomed them to the bar.

"I wonder where that observation car is?" Don asked and, as discreetly as possible, put his penis back into his pants.

"Oh?" she questioned in a tone that was meant to tease. "And just what are we going to do there? See the sights?"

"Sure," he told her. "You can see the sights… while I have you pressed up against the window, taking you from behind."

Despite herself, the thought of it made her clit throb. "I imagine it's through one of the cars behind us," she said and looked back at the door. "We can always go explore and find out."

Don said nothing in reply, but he stood, straightened himself, and then offered her his hand. Samantha accepted it and stood with him, and they headed through the door and into the next car, which was filled with only a handful of passengers. They smiled and nodded at each one; some smiled or nodded back, while two were focused solely on the view out their window.

In the next car, they found no one. Samantha began to lead her husband to the door at the end of it, only to feel his tug on her arm as he turned her toward him. Almost savagely, he began to kiss her. His body pressed against hers, and through the thin material of his pants, she felt his hardness.

As they kissed, Samantha let go of her inhibitions and unzipped him. She worked his manhood out of the fly and gave it a nice, firm squeeze. Don's hand was already working up the hem of her dress, and so she pulled up a leg and wrapped it around him. She felt the head of his prick push against her panties, teasing her opening with notions of what was to come.

He held her hem in the hand that was wrapped onto her back. With his other hand, he pulled her panties away from her slit and pushed his member against it. Samantha didn't mean to cry out, but as the head entered her, she couldn't hold the sound back. It broke their kissing and she found herself staring off at the door across from her while Don rested his face onto her shoulder and began to thrust into her. When he was several inches deep, he quickened his strides, bringing another shout from her lips. Then, falling into his groove, she moaned deeply with each push of penetration.

Don was well-endowed and somewhat thicker than the other men she'd been with before him, and he filled her in such a way that made her thankful for elasticity. She loved the way he took her... the way he teased her... the way he made her cry out when he'd bury himself deep inside of her and open her up in ways that no other man could. She felt his strides quicken with her ever-building wetness, and she heard him growl as he began to kiss and suckle on the side of her neck. She could tell he was close, and she was too. There was nothing Samantha wanted more right then than to have his seed inside of her while they held each other throughout what was certain to be earth-shattering orgasms.

Then, he pulled out and released his grip on her. She lowered her leg and took a step back as she smoothed down her dress.

"I know you haven't finished already," she told him with a curious gaze.

"Samantha, we're just getting started." He pushed his erection back into his pants and zipped up. "This was just a little interlude."

"An interlude? That was a hardcore…"

"Ssh…" He held a finger over his pursed lips. "See that sign?"

She followed his stare and realized the next car was the dining car.

"The observation car can't be too much further," he said in a hungry tone, and she knew he wasn't hungry for the food the dining car had to offer. He was hungry for more of what he'd just dipped into, and he was set on feeding that hunger in the observation car.

In the dining car, there were a few people sitting at a table, even though food was not being served yet. Samantha realized that they could have, once again, been caught in their lusty public display of eroticism, but she was still feeling the effects of the alcohol and so she didn't really care. Still, she didn't *want* to get caught. She wanted to play with her husband and have such an orgasmic climax that it made her toes curl up inside of her, and if they got caught in the middle of their playtime, she knew that wouldn't happen.

Casually, they walked through the dining car and greeted everyone they saw. Samantha was smiling, and she wondered if her smile looked silly. Then, she wondered if these people could tell what she and her husband had been doing. Could they see that Don was still erect in his pants? Was her skirt wrinkled from being gathered up? Did he leave a hickey on her neck from where he'd passionately kissed her there?

No one seemed to look at them strangely, and everyone was incredibly friendly. She relaxed a little, knowing that their erotic escapade was a secret only the two of them knew.

"Do you know where the observation car might be?" Don asked one of the people seated at a table. "My wife and I would love to sit there and enjoy the sights."

"Two cars down," said an old man who was seated with a woman, presumably his wife. "You can't miss it."

"The view is lovely there!" added the woman.

Don thanked them for the information and took Samantha's hand, leading her to the next set of doors. The next car they entered into was another passenger car, but it was empty of passengers. Samantha wondered if he would take her here like he had in the last one, but instead they kept walking until they reached the next door.

The observation car was impressive to her. It had large windows that curled inward toward the ceiling, and the chairs were spacious and faced each window, allowing for an optimal view of the scenery. There was a woman sitting in one of the seats to Samantha's left, gazing at a book as the world passed her by through the most tremendous view.

Don led Samantha to one of the seats on the side opposite of the passenger. There, Samantha sat, with her husband taking the seat beside her. Glancing over her shoulder, she saw that the passenger was paying them no mind; she had her nose in her novel like she was studying for an exam.

Then, she felt Don's hand return to her crotch. Looking down at it, she watched him gather up her dress and pull the front of it up onto her thighs. His fingers resumed their fondling. She noticed his other hand as he unzipped himself and pulled out his tool, which was still thick and hard. Samantha didn't need any guidance this time. She was in the mood and feeling the adventure. Softly, she lowered her face down to his lap and took him into her mouth.

Don's hand stopped grazing her femininity and went to the back of her head, where he caressed her hair as she suck on him with a skill long mastered.

The taste of his early bits of secretion filled her senses. Samantha loved the taste of her husband, and what she now tasted had her craving for more. She began to suck him harder and more deeply, feeling his hips buck with her strokes.

"Mmm..." he moaned from the pleasure his wife was delivering to him. "Oh... my..."

She pulled her mouth away from him and shushed him. "Quiet..." Promptly, she returned to the task at hand.

Samantha came to a halt with her lips wrapped around him as she heard something from the row of seats across from her. Cautiously, she pulled up and off of Don's member once again and looked up over his seat. The other passenger had closed her book and was standing. As quietly as she could, Samantha slipped back into her seat as if nothing had been going on. When the passenger stepped into the aisle, Samantha looked behind her and smiled at her. The woman smiled back and headed for the door.

She waited until the door opened and closed and the passenger was gone before looking at her husband and giggling.

"We almost got caught... again," she told him.

"*You* almost got caught," he corrected with a sly grin. "I was just sitting here."

Samantha cocked an eyebrow and smirked at him. She took his prick into her hand and began to squeeze and stroke it as her eyes went toward the window in front of her. "This view really is magnificent," she admitted.

"You're not afraid of the train ride anymore?"

"I'm too drunk to be afraid of the train ride now," she said and giggled once more.

"You almost made me blast off a minute ago," he told her. "That woman surely would have known what was happening then. You know I'm not quiet when I orgasm."

Samantha shrugged and let go of him. "When *are* you quiet, my dear?" she questioned with a smile. Then, she stood and took a couple of steps closer to the window. She held her smile steady as she heard Don stand as well and come up behind her. He wrapped his arms around her, pressing his manhood against her.

She pressed her hands against the window and relaxed a bit as Don pulled her dress up in the back and tugged her panties down. He lowered down onto one knee and fully removed her underwear. Once they were off, Samantha widened her stance and arched her back.

He was in her again before she could take another breath. When she did, she sucked it inside of her in a gasp and then hissed it back out. His hands went to her hips and he held onto her while he entered her with his full length.

With short and steady pumps, he began to thrust inside of her again. No one else was around here, and Samantha let her whimpers and moans flow freely from her lips. She felt herself grow wet inside once again, and the wetter she got, the faster her husband penetrated her. Every full pump hit her special spot – something she loved about Don and his endowment. He never had any trouble finding her g-spot. The more he pressed against it, the closer she felt her orgasm. She could tell he was close too. They'd been teasing one another for a while now, and even though he had good stamina, there was only so much he could take before releasing his seed.

"Yes..." she whimpered as tremors raced throughout her body. "Yes, Don... harder!"

"Yeah?" he asked and began to oblige. "Like this?"

Her reply was a gasp, followed by a shout. Her orgasm arrived at that same moment, and she pressed her face against the window and it shattered within her. She cried out as it happened, and then she felt Don collapse onto her back. He pulled her hips firmly against him and muttered something incoherent as his thrusts became erratic. Suddenly, she felt it – the unleashing of his seed, filling her in the most intimate and erotic way. He began to curse, holding steady inside of her throughout it. She could feel each contraction – every hot blast of his semen as it fired into her. Samantha rolled her hips against him, encouraging him to give her everything that he had. When he was finished, he pulled out of her, and on obviously wobbly legs, he stepped back and collapsed into a seat.

Samantha remained pressed against the window as she gasped and tried to control her breathing. She was shaky from her orgasm... shaky from *his* orgasm... but after a moment, she pulled off the glass and stood upright. She clenched herself, holding in what she could of his juice, and then sat down beside him.

"Your panties..." he said with a smile. "Don't forget your

panties."

"Let someone find them," she replied and shrugged. "I have more in my suitcase." She looked down at his member as it became flaccid and flopped onto his thigh. There was a pellet of his seed at the tip, and gingerly, she leaned down to him and licked it off. The hissing sound he let out make her nibble at it a bit more until he took it from her and tucked it into his slacks.

"It's so tender right now," he said and zipped up. "But... wow!"

"This definitely beats those tiny restrooms on airplanes," she admitted.

"Does it ever!"

For the rest of the ride, they remained in the observation car, watching the world go by through the large windows. Samantha was calm, even after her buzz from the alcohol went away. Don had calmed her the best way he knew how, and he had managed to turn this trip from hell into a train ride to heaven for her. Resting her head on his shoulder, she let herself drift off to sleep, and when she awoke, their destination was in sight. It was time for their vacation to truly begin, and if this ride was any indication, she knew it would be a vacation to remember.

*End*

# *After the War*

It had been three months since the war ended, and Kendra Matthews was ridden with angst over the fate of her husband Thomas. The last notice she received was over two months ago, when he was declared missing in action and presumed dead. Since then, she'd tried to cope with that knowledge, but she found it impossible. How did one cope without actual closure? She needed a photo or a body... something to let her know he was really gone.

Mostly, she needed Thomas to return home. That was the best of any scenario she could think of. She wanted him to come back to her, alive and well, so that they could spend the rest of their days together as they'd planned.

When they married, there was no active war to take him from her. They'd bought a small house and had planned on making a family together. They had been incredibly happy, living peacefully and with enduring love.

Then, the bomb hit, taking out an entire army base and beginning a new World War. Thomas had been a factory worker when the war began, but the draft was reenacted as the amount of willing new recruits quickly dwindled. Due to his age and health, Thomas was drafted almost immediately, and on the fifth week of the war, he was shipped overseas and into enemy territory.

Over the course of several months, Kendra received letters from him every other week. They were always the same – touching sentiments of his love for her and how much he missed her. He never told her of anything bad that was happening around him. She'd been thankful for that, as the idea of having her husband at war had terrified her.

The letters began to arrive further apart after a while. One a month… one every other month, and then finally, they quit coming completely. She became frantic with worry, fearing the worst but refusing to allow herself to believe it. Until she was told any differently, her husband was still alive and well… he *had* to be.

When the final letter arrived, it was delivered by two uniformed soldiers, who presented it to her with sorrow. She knew immediately what was inside the sealed envelope. It was news of Thomas's death, and for three days, she'd been too devastated to open it.

Finally, under pressure from her mother and his, she opened the letter and read it. While it mentioned he was MIA and that he was presumed dead, it did not state for certain that he *was* dead. That gave her hope – a thread to hang onto in this time of emotional turmoil. Thomas's parents began to cope with the news of their son, and a week before the war was declared over, they held a memorial for him. Kendra had not attended, as she did not want to believe he was dead. Attending that memorial would have finalized it… it would have made him dead to her in her mind and heart, and that was something she could not allow.

Checks from the government stopped reaching her bank account, as the war had crippled the government's financial status. She managed to find work at the factory Thomas had worked at, and for twelve hours a day, six days a week, she slaved to make ends meet.

Her parents offered the occasional financial support, as did Thomas's parents, but she hadn't wanted their money. She'd only wanted Thomas, and it was why she'd taken the job – to feel closer to him in the environment he'd worked in, and to keep the mortgage paid so that the house would still be theirs when he finally returned to her.

As time passed, she began to believe what her family was telling her – that Thomas was gone, and that she would eventually have to move on with her life. She didn't want to believe it; there was still a tinge of hope inside of her. Yet, that hope was lit like the flame of a flimsy match. Every now and again, an emotion breeze blew it out. When that happened, all she could do was light a new match and keep hoping and praying that it would guide him home to her.

Currently, Kendra sat in a chair near the fireplace, reading over the letters her husband had sent her. Tears rolled down her cheeks from the memories of him – from hopeful, promising days of love and togetherness. She'd read each of these letters dozens of times, but they never grew old to her. They were in her husband's handwriting, and when she sniffed them, she could actually smell him on them. They kept him near her, even if he wasn't physically close.

There was a knock at the door and it stirred her consciousness. She folded the letter in her hands and returned it to the envelope. Then, she set the stack of them on the table beside her and stood. Slowly, beaten down from long days of hard labor and the emotional turmoil that her heart and mind were suffering, she walked to the door and opened it. Her sister Janice stood on the other side.

"Thank God you're alive!" the older woman exclaimed and pulled Kendra into a tight, warm embrace. "I've been worried sick about you! I've tried calling, but it just goes to voicemail." She released her sister and entered the house. Kendra followed behind, closing the door as she did.

"I've had it powered off. I work long hours, you know. When I get home, sometimes I just need peace and quiet." She watched her sister sit and started toward the kitchen. "Can I get you something to drink? Tea or coffee? I've got some bottled water."

"No, I'm fine," Janice told her. "Come sit with me. I want to talk to you about something."

Kendra turned around from the kitchen and caught her sister's expression. Janice was smiling, and that usually meant she was up to something. She hoped she didn't plan on meddling in her personal affairs. Janice was known for that, and Kendra hated that aspect of her.

Regardless, she sat in the chair across from her, crossed her legs, and asked, "What's up?"

"I've been talking to Mom," Janice began, only to be cut off by her sister.

"Here we go," Kendra griped and rolled her eyes. "I've already told you and Mom and Dad. I'm not giving up this house."

"I'm not asking you too," she replied. "I've got something better in mind."

"I'm not moving anyone in either. You all have your own lives, and I have mine."

"You do?" Janice asked, raising her eyebrows. "Well, that's news to me. As far as I can tell, all you do is work from the time you get up until you're ready to drop into bed again."

"Do I look like I'm in bed?"

"No, but it's Sunday and the factory is closed on Sundays." Janice cleared her throat and adjusted in her seat. "Kendra, you can't keep living like this."

She rolled her eyes and uncrossed and then recrossed her legs. "Like *what*?" she asked. It was definitely meddling time.

"Like you're living with a ghost… or *for* a ghost." Janice smiled as sympathetically as she could manage. "You've refused to accept the obvious, but you're going to have to. Thomas is gone, Kendra, and he's not coming back."

Kendra swallowed and looked away from her sister. She gazed at the fireplace. There was no fire lit in it; it was much too warm for one. Still, it was more soothing right then than looking at her wide-eyed sibling.

"You can ignore me if you want, but I'm not going to shut up," Janice continued. "If you keep going at the pace you are, you're going to drop dead. Is that what you want?"

She considered the question, but she didn't know how to answer. If Thomas truly was dead – she shuddered at the thought – then the closest way for her to be near him would be for her to drop dead as well. Still, she had hopes that this wasn't the case. That he was still alive and trying his damnedest to make his way back home to her, and she needed to be there if and when he finally arrived.

"I'm not going to drop dead," she finally said and smirked, "but I'm not going to give up this house either."

"Again, I'm not asking you too," Janice replied, "but you've *got* to have a life outside of work... and away from those letters you keep your nose buried in." She looked at the stack of envelopes on the table and pointed at them. "Those are keeping you from being able to move on."

Kendra ignored the comment and asked, "Why are you here, Janice? Shouldn't you be cooking dinner for Ray?"

Janice laughed. "Ray does all the cooking. You know I can barely even boil water. Besides, you're just being snippy because you know I'm right. You need to *live*, sweet sister, and you can't do that if you're sitting here surrounding yourself with thoughts of a life that doesn't exist anymore."

She hated her sister for saying it. It was the absolute worst thing she could have said to her, even if Janice believed it to be true. "My life does exist," she countered flatly.

"Your life, yes, but not your life with Thomas. That life is over... Thomas is gone. You have to realize that and understand it."

Had she the energy, she would have stood from her chair, walked over to Janice, and smacked her right across her pretty little face. Instead, she looked away again and gazed at her enveloped letters.

"You're coming to my house for dinner tonight," Janice continued. Kendra currently hated the sound of her sister's voice. "You need a home-cooked meal and some time with family. If you don't show up, I'll send Mom and Dad over to collect you and bring you there."

While the idea did not please her, having her parents visit dissatisfied her even more. "Will Mom and Dad be at dinner?"

"Nope," Janice said and smiled. "Do I need to hang out for a couple of hours, wait for you to get ready, and drive you myself, or can I count on you to show up around sixish?"

"You don't have to wait," Kendra told her and stood from the chair. She walked to the front door and opened it. "I'll be there."

Janice stood and followed her. "You better be," she said as she stepped over the threshold and then turned to face her sister again. "I love you, sis. I just want you to be happy, and right now, you're anything *but* happy."

She couldn't deny it. Janice was right. She was miserable.

Her body was broken down from work, and her soul was in even worse shape without her husband. Janice hugged her one more time before starting down the walkway to her car.

"No later than six-thirty!" she shouted as she reached the car.

Kendra shut the door without a reply.

The last thing she wanted to do tonight was go to her sister's house for supper, but if it would appease her and keep her from meddling further, she saw no other choice. She'd have to buck up and show up, or else Janice would be right back at that front door.

On the fireplace mantle was a framed photograph of her and Thomas. It was the last picture they'd had taken together. He was in his army uniform, and she was in her blue dress – his favorite dress on her. She kissed his image and then held the photo close to her heart.

"I love you, Thomas," she whispered and felt tears well in her eyes once again. "I'll always love you." She kissed his image one more time before returning the frame to the mantle. Then, she took his letters and carried them into the bedroom, where she tucked them into the drawer of her nightstand – the place she always kept them. That way, if she missed him too terribly in the middle of the night, she could easily retrieve them and read them, imagining he was right there with her.

At five o'clock, she showered, brushed her hair, and applied a little make-up to add some color to her face. She was pale from spending so much time indoors at the factory. She also looked thin from it, and it didn't help that she never truly had an appetite anymore.

She dressed in a simple yellow dress, only because she never got to wear dresses out anymore. She was always in a pale blue uniform jumper that the factory required, and when she got home, she was always ready for sweats or pajamas. There was little reason for her to get dressed up anymore, but she felt the need to do it for this supper. If Janice could see that she could still make herself look presentable, maybe she would quit bothering her and realize she hadn't completely given up on life.

Kendra considered wearing pumps, but it had been so long since she was in high heels that she worried she wouldn't be able to walk in them anymore. Besides, being on her feet for twelve hours a day had formed hard calices on her feet. Heels would only make them hurt. Instead, she chose a pair of white flats and slipped into them. Standing in front of the mirror, she thought she looked pretty, but if Thomas were to return today, she wondered if he'd even recognize her. While pretty, she was far from the beauty that he'd often called her.

Janice and her family lived a good twenty minutes away, so Kendra climbed into her car at five-forty, just in case traffic was heavy. The last thing she wanted was to be late and for her sister to head out and try to hunt her down. She knew Janice loved her and was only trying to take care of her, but Kendra didn't want anyone's help. She wanted to be left alone, so she could be home and ready if and when Thomas returned home to her some day.

When… not if. She corrected the thought and pulled out of her drive way. At ten after six, she arrived. Instantly, she recognized Janice's car and Ray's van in the open garage. There was a third vehicle though – one she didn't recognize.

"It must be a dinner party," she muttered lowly as she parked and climbed out of the car. "Oh, joy."

She knocked at the front door and awaited her sister to answer. Instead, the door was opened by Tabitha, their young daughter of seven. Tabitha looked up at her from the other side of the screen door.

"Auntie Kendra, is that *you*?" the girl asked with an awe-inspired smile.

"Goodness, has it been that long since you've seen me?" Kendra asked as she opened the screen door and bent down to hug her niece.

"Yep!" Tabitha exclaimed and hugged Kendra tightly. "Daddy's been cooking all afternoon! I'm glad you're here. I'm hungry but they wouldn't let me eat without you."

"Well, now… that's no good is it?" She took Tabitha's hand and entered into the living room with her. "I guess now we can eat though."

"Yes!" Tabitha answered and then released her aunt's hand and rushed into the dining room. "Come on! Everyone's in here."

Kendra closed the door behind her and hung her purse on the coat rack. Then, ever cautiously, she followed her niece to the dining room. She worried about who would be in there. Janice had led her to believe she'd be the only guest, and she had hoped to be able to eat and run.

Even though Tabitha ran into the dining room without anyone stopping her, Kendra was not so fortunate. Janice met her in the doorway, blocking it from entry. She had a somewhat telling smile on her face, and it made Kendra cringe.

"You made it!" she exclaimed, but she didn't move an inch to let her enter. "And on time, too."

"I was afraid you'd call out the hounds to hunt me down," Kendra offered in a form of a joke. Sniffing the air, she said, "It smells delicious. What is it? Pot roast?"

"Yep, one of Ray's specialties. He also made some baby potatoes, green beans, and a really nice salad." She looked Kendra up and down and her smile widened. "You look nice. You got dressed up... I'm glad."

"Why are you glad? You're in jeans and a t-shirt."

From behind Janice, Kendra could hear Ray talking to someone. Even though she couldn't quite hear what was being said, she noticed the voice replying was also male. Her eyes widened and she took a step back.

"Oh, no..." she muttered and glared at Janice. "Why do I hear another man's voice coming from the dining room?"

Janice held her grin and walked toward her sister. She put an arm around her and began to escort her to the dining room. Once more, entry was stopped just before the dining room.

"Don't freak out," she told her, and Kendra felt her stomach sink. "I invited a guest."

"I'll kill you a thousand times over if you're trying to set me up," she warned.

Janice smirked. "Come on, now. Don't be like that. It's just dinner. All you've got to do is make light conversation, and if sparks fly, well… let them fly!"

"I don't *want* sparks to fly," she said in as hushed a tone as she could manage. "I want to go home, and that's exactly what I'm going to do." She turned around to leave, but her sister's next words stopped her.

"I'll call Mom," she threatened. "I'll tell her you're still depressed and I'll insist she stay with you for a while, to keep an eye on you."

Kendra turned back and faced her. "You wouldn't."

"Oh, I *would*!" Janice insisted. "Considering everything you've been going through, Grandma might even go with her. Wouldn't you love to learn how to knit? Bake cookies? Maybe take up scrapbooking?"

"I hate you."

"Hate me all you want, as long as you march into that dining room and eat."

"Come on!" she heard Tabitha yell from the dining room. "I'm starving!"

"She's *not* starving," Janice said, "but we really should get in there."

Begrudgingly, Kendra followed her sister into the dining room and stood at the threshold. There, seated across from an empty chair meant for her, was a man she barely recognized but remembered well. It was Brennan Welles, the quarterback from her high school days. In his teenage years, Brennan had been built like a Roman god. He'd had prefect blond hair, stunning blue eyes, and a body that made nearly every girl in her class melt. He'd also been cocky and arrogant, but that hadn't mattered then. Kendra had held a crush on him until graduation, when he went off to college on a football scholarship and she went to work at a clothing store. She hadn't seen him since.

Now, Brennan still had blond hair and blue eyes, but his sexy build was gone. He was verging on portly, and had grown into the meanest looking man she could imagine.

"Kendra," Janice said as she ushered her to her seat, "you remember Brennan from high school?"

"Wow!" Brennan exclaimed and stood to shake her hand. Kendra shyly accepted and then quickly withdrew. His grip was stronger than she cared for. "Look at you! You look amazing!"

She wished she could say the same about him. "It's good to see you again," she lied.

"Brennan was just telling me about how he's taken over the hardware store on East Street," Ray said, looking up at his sister-in-law.

Brennan sat again, and then Kendra did the same. "Yeah, I inherited it from Dad after his stroke. Hurt my knee playing college football, and after divorcing my wife, I decided it was time to come back home and take care of business."

He smiled. It was still a wide and full smile, but she didn't like it anymore. With his good looks gone, he was more threatening than attractive.

"What have you been up to?"

Kendra considered his question and forced a smile as she answered. "I work down at the old factory. Not much time for a social life."

"Well, now, that's a shame." She noticed his eyes leave hers and travel down to her chest, where her cleavage was exposed from the cut of the dress. "Such a shame."

Conversation through supper seemed to follow this pattern of Brennan asking too many questions, Kendra asking too few, and the former football player ogling her breasts at every given opportunity. It had been a long time since Kendra had felt this uncomfortable, and she made a mental note to pay Janice back for this sometime in the near future.

By dessert, the conversations had shifted. Brennan and Ray recounted old football games from high school and reminisced over their favorite plays. Tabitha kept Kendra and Janice's ears occupied with stories of tea parties with her dolls, her favorite cartoons, and the one time she kissed a boy named Billy Sandler on the playground. When she told them about how he had screamed and ran away afterward, both Kendra and her sister had to laugh.

Finally, when Tabitha had retired to her room to play with her toys and drinks were served to the adults, Kendra stood from the table and excused herself to the bathroom down the hall. She stepped into the room, turned on the light, and shut the door behind her. She didn't have to actually *use* the commode, but it had been a decent excuse to escape from the table. Brennan had chugged his first beer and was on his second when she got up and walked away. She just couldn't take the way he was staring at her any longer. It was lecherous, and she truly wanted to go home and be away from his company.

After several minutes of relaxing against the sink and trying to get her thoughts in order, she saw the door open. Quickly, she stood upright as Brennan entered, shutting the door behind him.

"No need to rush off," he told her as he walked to the commode. "I just need to drain the lizard." He turned his back to her and she heard his fly unzip. She wanted to leave the room, but he was a large man, and if she tried to go around him, she would surely brush up against him. That was more contact with him that she cared for.

He stood there for a moment, but Kendra didn't hear the sound of urine hitting the water. Instead, Brennan kept his back turned to her and started up conversation.

"Remember how you used to have the biggest crush on me in high school?" He asked and chuckled. His laughter made him sound creepier than he had seemed.

"I wouldn't call it a crush," she told him in a flat tone. "I thought you were cute, but that was a long time ago."

Brennan chuckled again. "Oh, I know you fantasized about me. All the girls did." He finally turned around to face her. He was holding his penis in his hand, and it was fully erect and staring up at her. Despite whatever she'd imagined in high school, it was much smaller than she'd ever thought. "Well... here's your big chance to have your turn at Beefcake Brennan. Isn't that what you all called me back then?"

He took a step toward her, stroking his member to keep it hard. Kendra took a step away.

"What are you doing, Brennan?" she asked him. She felt more than nervous or uncomfortable now. Suddenly, she felt frightened.

"Giving you what you've always wanted." He waved it at her like he was inviting her to take it from his hand and into hers. "Go ahead now. Get on down there and give it a kiss. I promise I won't take too long. You know you've always wanted this. Well, here it is, sweetheart."

She was more disgusted by him than ever before. "I don't know what you're expecting me to do, but..."

"I'm expecting you to suck my cock," he said, cutting her off. "Or would you rather me stick it somewhere else? That dress is pretty easy access. Did you leave the panties at home?" He smiled large and neared her again.

Before he had a chance to come any closer, Kendra walked

right up to him and punched him hard in the gut. He groaned from the impact, but it didn't seem to faze him much.

"I wouldn't screw you if you were the last man on earth," she told him and started toward the door.

"Come on, sweetheart. It's not like any other man will want you." His voice made her ears burn with anger. "I heard about your husband. Dead in the war. Let me slip it inside of you… give you a taste of what a *real* man can do. Hell, your husband couldn't even survive the Japs. I'm pretty sure he wasn't man enough to know how to handle a woman like you."

It was the last straw for Kendra. She turned around to face him again and then marched up to him. "Fine," she said, taking his member into her hand. "You want me to handle it? How's this?"

Before he could respond, she cut into his penis with her fingernails, drawing blood and making him scream from the pain. She let it go and he dropped to his knees, holding his bleeding tool with both hands as he burst into tears.

"No means no, asshole," she said and then opened the door to leave the room.

Janice and Ray were rushing down the hall toward her when she stepped out.

"What's going on?" Janice asked, worried. "We heard you scream!"

"You heard a scream," Kendra confirmed, "but it wasn't me." She looked up at Ray and added, "Your buddy in there just tried to assault me. You'll find him curled up on the floor, crying like a little girl. He may need medical attention."

She stormed past her sister and brother-in-law, into the living room, and collected her purse from the coat rack. Janice was right behind her.

"What on earth happened in there?" she exclaimed in as hushed a tone as she could so that Tabitha couldn't hear.

"He came into the bathroom on me, took out his junk, and tried to make me pleasure him," she said in a controlled, steady tone. "He's lucky I didn't rip it off."

"Oh, my god! Are you okay?" Janice's eyes were filled with honest concern, and a bit of shock and surprise.

"I'm just fine," she told her and opened the front door. "Brennan, not so much. He won't be using that thing for a long while, that's for sure."

Janice took a quick moment to consider things, and then a sly smile crossed her lips. "Good for you," she told her little sister. "I thought he might have changed by now, but he's obviously still a piece of shit."

Kendra ignored the comment and gave Janice a quick hug. "Thank you for supper," she told her, "but next time, please don't try to set me up."

"After this, I wouldn't dream of it," she replied. "Ray's libel to beat him senseless."

"He deserves a lot worse than that, but it's sure a start." She gave a thin smile and stepped outside. Janice closed the door behind her. Its sound nearly made her jump.

Kendra tried to calm down on the ride home, but she found it difficult. She hadn't been this worked up in a long time, but it had felt almost good standing up for herself. She hoped Brennan's penis got infected and they had to cut it off, or at the very least, she hoped it needed stitches. Never before had she felt so violated, but she couldn't blame her sister. Janice hadn't known what Brennan was going to do.

At home, she locked the door behind her and then made sure the backdoor was properly secured too. Once she was certain both doors were locked, she checked each window in the house to ensure the same. The last thing she needed was Brennan foregoing the hospital and making his way to her for revenge. If he did, she'd surely have to take stronger measures.

Checking the kitchen drawer, she took out Thomas's old gun and double-checked that it was loaded. It was, and she carried it into the living room, placing it beside her chair where it was easy to access. Then, she returned to the kitchen and boiled water for tea.

It took her a long time to get her nerves under control, but the chamomile tea helped. It also made her sleepy, and in the comfort of her chair, she dozed off. Sometime later, she was awakened by a knock at the front door.

With a jolt, she sat upright and opened her eyes. Worry once more plagued her. Was it him? Brennan? There to get revenge on her and to have his way with her? The knocking persisted and she stood, taking the gun in her hand. With slow, uneasy steps, she approached the door and readied the weapon to fire.

Cautiously, she unlocked the door, and readying her trigger finger, she opened it.

The gun slipped from her hand and landed on the carpet beside her as she saw her visitor. Thankfully, it did not fire.

"Kendra…" the voice whispered, and for a moment, she thought she was looking into the eyes of a ghost. But it wasn't a ghost at all. Although he was thinner than she remembered, and although he was unshaven and had a cane in his hand, she recognized him. It was Thomas, wounded but very much alive."

"Thomas…" she whispered in return, and she was unable to fight back the tears that suddenly began to storm down her cheeks. "Oh, my God! Thomas!"

Quickly, she threw her arms around his neck, holding him, feeling him, smelling the scent that was uniquely his own. She couldn't believe it was really him, and if this was some kind of dream hoping to trick her, she prayed it would never end.

"Careful there!" he laughed with a chuckle that came through as shaky and emotional as his words. "I've got a bum leg now, baby. You might knock me down."

She broke the hug and put her hands to his cheeks, studying his face… memorizing it all over again. He was in ill-fitting clothing, and it was obvious he'd been badly wounded during the war. She kissed him, repeatedly, and he kissed her back with as much energy as he could give.

After a moment, she led him into the house and to his old favorite chair near the fireplace – the very chair that she spent most of her time at home sitting in and thinking about him.

"I – I just can't believe it's really you!" she exclaimed through her tears. "You're really here! You've really come back to me!"

"I'm here, baby... I'm here." He wiped the tears from his cheeks as he stared into her eyes. Then, he looked toward the door and at the pistol on the floor. "Is that my gun?"

"Yes," she said and hurriedly went to the door and shut it. Then, she retrieved the gun and brought it over to her husband. "I – I was afraid you might have been an intruder. You always told me to be careful and protect myself." She didn't want to tell him about Brennan. Not yet anyway... not when he'd just gotten back home.

He took the gun from her and set it on the table beside him. "No, Kendra. It's just me... I finally made it back."

She crouched down beside him and gently touched the side of his face again. "They... they told me you were missing... presumed dead."

"I was," he said in a sympathetic tone. "I don't know how I survived... When the Japs came to make sure my troop was dead, I hit beneath their bodies... It was terrible, Kendra. Just... terrible." He broke down into tears once more, but he quickly made them end. A smile replaced them. "Once I made sure the coast was clear, I worked my way to a nearby village, but I was in no shape to continue. They nursed me back to health as best they could, and they took good care of me. It took a while for me to heal enough to leave there, and when I did, I had to go in disguise. I wasn't aware the war was even over until weeks later, when I finally made it to a US Embassy."

It was hard for her to comprehend what he was telling her, but she knew it was even harder for him to tell it. She had so many questions left to ask him, and she wanted to know why the Embassy didn't think to notify her that her husband was alive. Yet, she decided to hold all of her questions for later and simply to bask in the joy of having her husband back home and safe from war.

The made him a plate of food and brought him a tall, cold glass of milk. He ate heartily, and she could tell by the pleasured sounds he made that he was savoring every bit of it. When he was finished and had relaxed to let his food process, she led him into the bathroom and helped him strip his clothes for a nice warm bath. Thomas relaxed in the tub while Kendra cleaned him with a soapy sponge, taking care to not press against the several scarred wounds that she saw on his body – wounds that had not been there when he was drafted and deployed.

When he was clean and dry, she helped him into his favorite pair of flannel pajamas. She'd kept them clean and ready, close at hand for the day she knew would eventually come – this day… the day Thomas came home to her.

"What would you like to do tonight?" she asked him when they were back in the living room and in their chairs.

Thomas looked at her and smiled. "I'm just happy to be

here with you. To know you're still here, and that you never gave up on me. You don't know how much that means to me, sweetheart."

She beamed from his words and they elevated her heart to where it felt like she was floating in the clouds. She asked if she should call his parents and let them know he was home.

"No," he told her. "Not tonight. Tonight, I just want to be with you."

She didn't tell him that his family had held a memorial for him or that they'd truly believed him to be dead. She would leave that news for them to share. The memorial was something she'd refused to take part in, and now, she was gladder over that decision than ever before.

They spent the next few hours catching up through small talk. She told him nothing that would be emotionally hard for him, but she did let him know she'd taken over his job at that factory, and because of it, she'd been able to keep up the house. She also told him that she'd kept every letter he'd written her, and that she'd read them often. He talked about some of the people he'd met when recovering in Japan, but he never once mentioned anything to do with the war. For that and so much more, she was incredibly thankful. She knew that one day, he would need to talk about it, and when that day came, she would listen to every word of every story he had to share. Until then, she wanted him to be as relaxed and as 'at home' as he could be.

At bedtime, she helped him into their room, which he

commented hadn't changed a bit since he left.

"Of course not," she told him and kissed his cheek. "This is *our* room. We decorated it together. I would never change it without you here to help me."

She helped him into bed and then turned off the light. Climbing onto her side of the mattress, she snuggled close to him and kissed him softly on the lips. His pajama top was unbuttoned half way down, and so she caressed his hairy chest as she kissed him on his mouth... his chin... his neck. He moaned from the intimacy.

"I've missed the way you kiss so much..." he muttered as she kissed his earlobe, and then his pulse. "I've missed *you* so much... the way you smell... the way you feel..."

"There is nothing about you that I *haven't* missed," she confided. She unbuttoned his shirt the rest of the way and caressed his stomach. Even though he'd lost weight, his abs were still defined... enticing.

Coyly, as she kissed his neck down to his shoulder, she let her fingers slip beneath the band of his pajama pants. She felt his fur, untrimmed unlike he usually kept it. She didn't mind it though. She was just glad to have him home... to touch him. Her fingers crazed the base of his member. It felt thick, hard. She wrapped her fingers around it and squeezed. Thomas sucked in a deep breath and then released it with a moan.

Kendra moved her lips back to his and kissed him as she began to massage his manhood. It throbbed from her touch. It had been so long since she'd been able to touch him... to be intimate with him. She missed this. She missed *him*. He began to kiss her back and she felt his tongue slide between her parted lips, pressing against hers.

She slid her hand out from his waistband and then worked his manhood free through the fly of his pajamas. The tip of it was already sticky with his secretion. She wondered how long it had been since he'd had an orgasm. She knew how long it had been since *she'd* had one. It was time to remedy that matter.

Thomas moved slightly and brought a hand over, resting it on her hip. She was now in her nightgown, and he clutched it, pulling it up her thigh. Then, he grabbed onto her flesh and squeezed it gently. She felt his thumb graze her pubic mound. She, too, had not bothered to trim it during his absence, but that didn't seem to matter. He quickly moved his full hand from her thigh and pressed his palm against her mound. She parted her legs as he rubbed his fingers over her clitoris and her warm slit – aching for his attention.

"I've missed you so much," he whispered to her as he broke the kiss. "I've done nothing but think of you. Your memory is what got me through that war. You're why I survived... why I'm here. You're why I'm alive."

She felt his finger enter into her warmth, and she squeezed his hard member as she gasped. It throbbed again, and she loosened her grip, not wishing for him to orgasm too quickly... not without being inside of her.

Kendra became wet from the thought, and this new warm wetness made it easier for her husband to slide a second finger inside of her while rubbing his thumb over her clitoris. While his touch felt so good and so missed, she yearned to taste him... to remember his flavor. She broke the fresh kiss that he offered, and holding herself steady enough so that he stayed inside of her, she lowered herself down and grasped his erection with both hands. It was as gloriously big and as thick as she remembered it. She looked at it for a moment, and then she licked the underneath of the head, running her tongue over its hole and tasting the juices that covered it. He seemed more delicious now than she remembered him. She heard him gasp from the action. It was an encouraging sound.

Softly, she took the head between her lips and began to suckle it. Thomas began to whimper, and she felt the gentle thrust of his fingers as they freshly explored her inner walls.

It had been a while since she'd had him inside of her mouth, so she took him inch by inch, going slowly and pacing herself. She utilized only one hand around the base now, while the other reached for his scrotum and cupped them firmly. He did not try to guide her. Thomas knew very well that Kendra was skilled at this. After all, they'd had plenty of practice together over the years.

At one point, she felt him throb hard against her tongue and she worried again that she would make him orgasm too early. She pulled off of him and stood up on her knees. Thomas's fingers slipped out of her opening and his hand relaxed on the bed.

"Done already?" he asked her with a mischievous but loving smile on his face.

"Not even close," she replied. Then, ever so carefully, she straddled him and took his manhood into her hand once again. As slowly as she'd taken it into her mouth, she lined it up with her vestibule and carefully lowered herself down onto it.

It almost felt like she was losing her virginity all over again. Despite the work he'd done with his fingers, she was tight, and the head alone seemed to fill the girth of her space. Leaning forward, she locked eyes with him and kissed him as she sank down onto it. When she felt his pajama bottoms rub against her and every inch of him was inside. Thomas wrapped his arms around her and held her close, kissing her and softly thrusting into to her.

"I've missed you inside of me," she muttered through the kiss. To every thrust of his, she gave him a push of her own, ensuring the deepest and most electrifying penetration possible.

"I could spend the rest of my life inside of you," he admitted. "You're more than my wife, Kendra. You're my soul mate."

She rode him with this same gentle and full rhythm for the longest time. He managed to hold his orgasm at bay, and she managed the same, although it was not easy.

Finally, he looked into her eyes and asked her, "Are you ready to start building our family?"

That question was all the encouragement she needed. With

a Cheshire smile on her face, she arched her back and replied, "I'm ready."

She laid her face beside his head on the pillow. Thomas moved both of his hands down to her hips, and with her encouragement, he began to move inside of her much more swiftly… and then incredibly erratically. Despite his motions, she reached orgasm first. He'd located her g-spot with ease, and each punch against it had helped her edge closer and closer to ecstasy, until she caught herself screaming into his pillow and covering his manhood with her hot juices. She trembled in his grip, but she did not try to pull away. The electric current that surged throughout her made her yearn for him to experience the same.

Her fresh juices lubricated her vestibule further, and its slickness helped him to quicken his speed even more. Suddenly, he gasped and cried out. His cry was silenced by Kendra's lips as she kissed him through his orgasm. She could feel him holding steady, deep inside of her, unloading his baby juice into her burst after burst. When he was finished, she remained on top of him, kissing him and caressing him, keeping him inside of her until he had gone flaccid. Even then, neither of them were eager to pull away from this embrace. It was what they'd both yearned so long for, and now that they had it, they wanted the moment to last for an eternity or longer.

"I hope it takes," he told her with a boyish smile and bright eyes.

"If not, we'll just keep trying until it finally does," she

replied and brushed his bangs away from his brow. "I love you, Thomas. I'm so glad you came home to me."

"I love you, Kendra," he whispered and kissed her again. "Thank you for waiting for me."

They slept with their arms around each other, neither wanting to break the physical connection that had been kept from them for so long. And surely enough, Kendra soon glowed with a pregnancy that was the start of fulfilling their dream of having their happy little family.

### *End*

# *The Hunk*

Carrie Bryant loved her job. She worked for one of the top fashion companies in the country, and it was her job to photograph their models for magazine spotlights and advertisements. The best part was that the company specialized in men's fashions, and she was given the most gorgeous men imaginable to place before her camera.

Even with that perk, her job was still challenging. There was lighting to consider, poses, wardrobe, make-up, location bookings, set design, equipment management... the list seemed to go on and on. Fortunately, Carrie had a talented tight-knit crew that she worked with – a staff of five that she had personally handpicked and hired. It made her job easier, but not easy.

Every model that she was assigned to was different. They all had their good angles, and like any person, they all had their flaws. Some were easy going and willing to try most whatever she asked. Others arrived with an arrogance and tried to run the show. In the end, it was always what she wanted that ended up being done, but sometimes it was a fight getting there. For all of this and more, she was paid good money for what she did. The compensation helped, and she had little to actually complain about.

Checking a pose through the lens, she okayed a shot and

watched it digitally appear on a screen beside her. The model was posed exactly how she'd asked, but he looked timid and nervous. This had been the case for the last several shots she'd taken, and so far, she had nothing usable of him for the campaign.

"Joshua," she said and stepped forward, leaving the staff and equipment behind her and approaching her model. "What's up?"

He looked at her and smiled, but that nervousness was still written all over his face. "What do you mean? Is something wrong?"

"Yes," she told him. "You look petrified. Are you not enjoying this?"

He stalled and looked around the room – at the crew, at the lights, at the camera... "I – I guess I'm a little camera shy."

Carrie closed her eyes and shook her head. She wanted to laugh at him and ask him if he was crazy, but she didn't want to scare the poor man anymore than he already was. Instead, she said, "Joshua, you're a model, right? You've done this before?"

He swallowed and nodded his head. "Yes, ma'am."

"Don't call me 'ma'am.' That term makes me sound old. Do I look old to you?" She smiled, even though she knew her tone was a little intimidating.

"No, ma'am... I mean, no, Miss Bryant." He was starting to sweat. She noticed it and sighed. "I'm sorry. I've never done a shoot that was... this involved."

"How do you mean?"

He shrugged and looked down at his feet. She could tell he was trying to collect his thoughts before he said the wrong thing. "In my other shoots, it was the cameraman and a person handling a couple of lights. I – I feel like I'm on a movie set or something, and there are so many people here."

"Seven," she said. "There are seven people here, including you and me."

He swallowed and cringed. "That's a lot of people... and I'm in tight white briefs."

She looked down at him, noticing that he filled the underwear perfectly. They were indeed tight, but he also packed them just right. Looking him in the eye again, she asked, "Are you embarrassed by your manhood?"

Again, he shrugged. "No... not really. I don't know. Maybe?"

"You knew you'd be wearing underwear for this ad campaign, right?"

"Yes, ma'am... er... Miss Bryant."

She thought it was humorous the way he now kept correcting himself. She'd only been teasing him about calling her ma'am, but she was entertained by it now and she surely wasn't going to tell him any differently.

Instead, she needed to encourage him. She needed to make him think like he was worth his weight in gold – that he was by far the best choice for this particular campaign and that no one else could pull it off like he could. Likely, those were lies, as she'd had dozens of models in front of her camera that would have successfully completed this shoot by now and would have done so without a single issue.

She needed to make him comfortable as well. If there were too many people around for him to be comfortable, then she needed to send some of them out of the studio space. Perhaps everyone but her. Or... was it her that was making him uncomfortable? That was always a possibility.

"I've seen your work... your headshots, torso shots... You're stunning in them," she told him, and he gave her a bashful smile in return. "You're an absolute hunk, Joshua, and when this ad campaign goes live, you're certain to go viral. This shoot could catapult you to stardom. You could be in movies, television... The possibilities are endless."

She wondered if she was helping the situation or making him more nervous. By his expression, she couldn't really tell.

Joshua was quiet for a long moment as he considered her words. Then, he finally looked at her and said, "I don't want to be in movies or television."

Carrie sighed and raised her brow. "Okay, then. What *do* you want?"

"I – I just want to make enough money to be able to afford college. I want to get a good job, meet a woman I love, get married and start a family. I'm not here seeking fame. I just don't know any other way to make those dreams come true."

This was a first for Carrie. Every male model that she'd

ever encountered had been shooting for the stars with hopes of fame and celebrity status. Joshua had to be different, and this different outlook was throwing her way off schedule. Still, his response had been charming and, despite her better judgment, it was admirable.

She turned around and faced her crew. "Everybody, go home. I'll cut off the equipment and kill the lights. We'll pick this back up tomorrow at eight o'clock sharp."

As the crew obliged, Joshua's nervous smile grew. He asked her, "So, I'm done? I can go home?"

"No. You will stay. My crew is going home." She left him where he stood and walked to the table that had the monitors set up. There, she took her bottle of water and drank it down. She threw the bottle away and looked at her model again. "Go to the changing room and get dressed, but leave the underwear there. Wear what you came in. Meet me back here in fifteen minutes."

Without giving him the opportunity to respond, she followed her crew out of the space and walked down to her office. There, she locked the door behind her and collapsed into the oversized chair behind her desk. She was beyond frustrated with Joshua, but she was also sensitive to his problem. When she was seventeen, her parents perished in a car wreck, leaving her orphaned weeks before her high school graduation. They'd been a poor family, and she'd had to drop out of school in order to work and afford the rent.

Affording their house proved impossible. Within months,

she'd been put out on the street, but what little money she made had allowed her to rent a modest studio apartment. During the day, she worked at a department store as a sales clerk, and while that paid the bills, it allowed very little for food or other expenditures. She'd been forced to take a second job where she waited tables at night for modest tips. Half of the tip money was spent on food and necessities. The other half was stashed away for reasons that she didn't quite fathom then. Eventually, when she'd saved just over two thousand dollars, she realized the purpose for the money. Her studio apartment, while poorly decorated, had wonderful light and large blank walls. It was, truly, a perfect studio space for photography, and being a photographer was a dream of hers that she'd never before thought realistic.

She'd used the money to buy her very first professional camera, and it had taken nearly every penny that she'd saved. With the rest of the money, she ordered a stock of business cards advertising her services as a landscape photographer, a wedding photographer, and even a headshot photographer.

Business came slowly at first, but she worked cheaply and that helped to rake in a few clients. She began with a couple of small weddings, and she offered her first dozen or so headshot sessions for free. Eventually, word of her services began to spread, and she began scheduling more bookings than she thought she could keep up with.

One day, a young man who aspired to be a world-famous model contacted her for a photo shoot. He needed headshots, half-body shots, and full body shots. His budget was a hundred bucks, but it was a Franklin that she couldn't turn down. The shoot took only a couple of hours, and a week later, she provided him with a disc of his images and collected her fee. As fate would have it, the young man sent out several of his photos to various modeling agencies, and although several of them weren't particularly interested in his style or look, the quality and artistic feel of the shots caught the eye of an up-and-coming studio. They contacted her several days later, and after meeting with the studio head, she was offered a job that paid better than anything she'd made prior.

"And the rest is history," she muttered to herself as she reflected over her past and how her actions and taking chances led her to where she was now. Carrie knew that Joshua was hoping for something similar. He was taking a chance modeling so that he could go to college and land a normal career and settle down. There was nothing wrong with that, but unless he learned to loosen up a little, she knew it would never happen for him.

On her computer, she pulled up the headshots that had landed him this job and looked for the studio name. The studio names were never located on the photos anymore, as they were now placed in an attached file accompanying them. In Joshua's folder, she found the name Carter Studio, which she found ironic, as Joshua's last name was also Carter. There was a number for the studio, and quickly, she called it.

The call was answered on the fourth ring, moments before she was ready to hang up and try again later. "Carter Studio.

Danny speaking."

"Hello, Danny," she began. "My name is Carrie Bryant with Vander House Clothing. I'm calling for a reference on a model named Joshua Carter."

"Ahh!" the man on the line exclaimed. "Yes! My nephew Joshy! He's just a dear boy. Sweet, kind, and very easy on the eyes, I must say!"

A *nephew*, she thought and rolled her eyes. *It figures...*

"Say... Vander House... I thought he already got a gig with you," Joshua's uncle remarked.

"That's correct," she told him, even though she didn't feel like she needed to explain herself. "Everything is fine. I just needed to document a reference for the sake of paperwork."

"Paperwork. Well, isn't that stuff so worrisome? Don't you worry. Joshy is a good boy, and he'll work very hard for you!"

"Thank you for your time, Mister Carter." Carrie ended the call before he could further respond. He seemed like a nice enough man, but Danny Carter also seemed like one of those people who could talk an ear off if it was allowed. Carrie had no time for such conversation.

However, it explained why Joshua was so relaxed in his headshots. He'd been posing for his family, and he had nothing to fear from them. At Vander House, he was in a *powerhouse*. There was everything to fear here. It could make your career, or it could make sure you never had a career again. It made sense that, having never posed for a large firm, he would be nervous. It also made sense that Vander House's reputation in the field would add to those nerves.

At least now, she had some idea of what she was dealing with. She stood from her chair and walked to the door, unlocked it, and stepped into the hall. In the long-legged stride she always walked with, she made it swiftly down the hall and back to the studio room. There, she found Joshua back in his blue jeans and white t-shirt, sitting atop a black stool near the wall. He looked at her when she entered. His face was less nervous now but more fearful, as if he expected he was about to be fired.

"Follow me," she said and then turned back out the door, into the hallway. As the door started to close behind her, she heard Joshua catch it and push it back open, following her out.

"I'm fired, aren't I?" he asked as he trailed behind her. "I'm so sorry I let you down. If you could just give me another chance…"

"You're not fired," she cut him off. "Not yet, anyway."

She led him to the studio's south exit and out the door, into a parking lot that was beginning to shadow with the setting sun. Pulling her keys from her pocket, she pushed a button, triggered three honks, and found her car.

As she unlocked it, she instructed Joshua to, "Buckle up."

"Can I ask where we're going?" he questioned as he opened the door and climbed in.

"You'll see when we get there."

Once their seatbelts were fastened, she cranked the car and

pulled out of her space. She remained silent as she drove, and Joshua did the same. When they were a few blocks away, she finally spoke again.

"I used to be a lot like you," she told him and caught his glance at her out the corner of her eye. "Unsure and nervous about my future."

"Really?" he asked as he looked her over. "I never would have thought that."

"Why not?"

"You're so… in control. It's like, you know what you want and you take it. I don't know how to do that."

"Neither did I until I put in the work and had a little luck to help me out." She smiled. It was the first smile she'd offered him, and she glanced at him to see he was smiling back. "How old are you, Joshua?"

"Twenty-two," he told her. Her smile widened. He was just four years younger than she was, and a little older than she was when she got her big break. "Some people say I still look like a teenager though."

"Don't let those boyish good looks go to waste."

"Can – can I ask you something?"

She cocked an eyebrow and let her smile vanish. "What?"

"You called me a hunk earlier. Do you really think I'm a hunk, or were you just trying to… stroke my ego?"

Carrie's smile returned. "A little of both, I guess. You've got a body that could make a woman go weak in the knees, and you've got the face to make the heart melt right along with it." She turned right onto the next street and quickened her speed. "But yes, I was also trying to stroke your ego. Even if you don't want a career in this field, this campaign is a good opportunity, and a lot of professional models were turned down so that you could have the job. I didn't want you to blow it. I still don't."

She saw him grin again and nod his head, returning his stare straight ahead at the road. He was quiet again, but even though he didn't know where she was taking him, Carrie felt he was less nervous now than he'd been when she told him to get in the car.

A few more minutes passed and then Carrie turned into a parking lot beside a tall brick apartment building.

"Come on," she said as she stepped from the car.

"Where are we?" he asked, following her lead.

"The poor end of town, more or less, but status doesn't matter." She looked at him as he stood beside the car. "Come. Follow."

He cocked an eyebrow at her commands and then barked.

Carrie had no choice but to laugh. His reaction caught her off guard, and it was hilarious.

"Good boy," she told him once her laughter faded off.

She opened the front door of the building and stepped aside to let him enter. After closing the door, she led him to a stairway and began up it.

"We're going to the fifth floor," she said as she climbed.

"Stairs all the way?" he asked as he followed.

"It's good for the leg muscles."

On the fifth floor, she led him down to the seventh door near the end of the hall. She fished through her keys, found the right one, and unlocked it. Opening the door, she turned on the light and waved him inside.

"Where… where are we?" he asked as he stepped into the small and poorly decorated studio apartment.

"My home," she said, shutting the door behind him. Walking to a table, she dropped her keys into a dish, as she did every time she went home.

Joshua wandered forward a few steps, looking around questioningly. "You live *here*? It's so… small."

"My very first apartment, and the only home I've ever known since losing my parents," she explained. Joshua turned and looked at her. "You see, I may have found success in my chosen field, but I didn't let success rule me. This apartment is all I need for a home. Sure, I make *great* money doing what I do, but I don't need some big fancy house or a large elaborate apartment. This is my *home*. It keeps me grounded and in touch with who I am."

He smiled again and nodded. "I think I understand."

There was a small bar to the left and she went to it and uncorked two bottles of red wine. She carried them both over to Joshua and handed him one. "Here, have a drink."

He took the bottle and looked at it. "This is a full bottle of wine."

"You don't have to drink it all, but it's a small bottle and not really enough for two people." She took a long sip and sighed somewhat pleasantly. "If you want a glass, they're in the cupboard by the sink."

"Nah," he said, studying the bottle. "This will work." Then, he took a long chug – much deeper than the drink Carrie had just taken. "Wow!" he exclaimed, grinning from ear to ear. "This tastes fantastic!"

"At fifty bucks a bottle, it better."

"Fifty bucks?"

"My taste in apartments may be small, Joshua, but my taste in wine is rather extravagant." She winked at him and took another swig. Joshua followed suit.

"So… what are we doing here?" he asked, following her as she crossed the room and sipping from his bottle as he did. "Are you planning on seducing me?"

"Yes," she admitted as she walked to a shelf on the wall. "With my camera." She took a bag from the shelf, set her wine down, and then pulled out her camera from the bag. It was the very first professional camera she'd ever owned, and it was her favorite.

"You have quite a way with words," he told her, glaring at the camera. She noticed he was a little nervous again, and she watched as he drank heavily from the bottle.

"At the office, they call me a ball-busting business bitch, but Joshua, I'm not really that bad. In that environment, I *have* to be. It's how I succeed in my job there. It's how I *keep* my job there. But really, I love what I do. I love to take pictures and to help people look their best for whatever they need the photos for. I like to show the world who they really are, and let me tell you… you might be a gorgeous hunk on the outside, but on the inside, you're a really sweet guy. I want to capture both of those aspects, and I want you to get used to me being behind the camera and taking your picture."

There was a strap on the camera and she pulled it over her head, letting the camera hang from her neck. Then, she took her wine again and enjoyed another long sip. She was beginning to relax from it – to feel the stress of the day wash away from her – and she hoped that her model was feeling the same.

From across the room, she heard Joshua chuckle. Looking at him, she asked, "What's so funny?"

He smiled at her and shrugged. "You called me a gorgeous hunk." He laughed again – almost a giggle.

Carrie rolled her eyes, but she couldn't help but let a laugh slip out also. "Yes. Yes, I did. Have you *seen* yourself?"

He blushed a bit but kept his smile. "Yeah, but apparently not through your eyes."

"Oh, come on!" she chided. "I bet you have women throwing themselves at you."

He shook his head. "Nope. I've got female friends, and I've dated a couple of girls, but I'm pretty single. Been like this for nearly a year now."

"I find that hard to believe."

Joshua snickered. "The last one that dumped me told me I was too nice. Is it possible to be too nice?"

That was a good question, Carrie thought, and it was one she did not know the answer to. She set her wine bottle back down and began to fiddle with the settings on her camera. Finally, after a moment of pondering, she had an answer for him.

"A nice guy," she told him, "is a very rare and wonderful find." Glancing at him, she added, "Any woman would be lucky to have you." Then, she gave him one of her quick smiles and turned her eyes back to the camera.

Joshua said nothing, but she heard him take a big gulp of his wine and set the bottle down. It clunked lightly against the table. He walked over to Carrie and stood beside her, looking down at the camera as she toyed with it.

"This is the only side of this business I've ever really been interested in," he admitted. "That camera has a ton of settings."

"Have you ever used one of these things before?"

"Nah... they're way out of my price range. I've got a nice phone though, and it has a pretty good camera on it. I like to take a lot of nature shots with it. Birds, trees, storms, sunsets... you know, the basics."

She didn't tell him those were some of her favorite things to photograph also, but it would have been the truth.

"The cameras in the studio at work are so high tech that they're mind-boggling," she noted as she found her preferred setting and saved it. "So many settings... so many gadgets... all just to take a picture with." Looking up at him, she added, "They're extremely high definition though. I guess that's what they want and need."

"I guess... but doesn't that take some of the fun out of it?"

She nodded. "I'm not there to have fun. I have fun *here*. When I'm there, I'm there only to do what they need me to do, and to do it well."

He looked at her and grinned. She thought he had the most honestly angelic smile she'd ever seen, and it suddenly made her heart skip a beat. Nervously, she looked away from him and to the large blank wall across the room. Joshua followed her gaze.

"So, that's where you do your shoots here?" he asked.

"Sometimes. I have several backdrops I can hang on the extension rack, and when those don't work, I've got the rest of the apartment to play with. I've even shot through the window with my models posed on the fire escape before."

Carrie considered his earlier mention of his love for photography, and she knew she needed to build his trust. She'd never let anyone else handle this camera before, but if he was going to trust her, she needed to trust him also. Turning to him, she took the camera from around her neck and handed it to him.

Joshua looked at it before accepting. She could see confusion cascade over his face. "What do you want me to do with it?" he asked her, timidly taking the camera and holding it as carefully as if it was a baby bird.

"First, I want you to put that strap around your neck." She

winked, and he obliged. "I have the setting right for the room's current lighting, and you said this was something you've always wanted to try. Find something to photograph and give it a whirl. All you've got to do is aim and shoot."

He brought the camera up to eye level and peered through the viewer. Then, he took a few steps back and started taking photos of Carrie. Her eyes widened and her jaw dropped a little. A rebellious grin then appeared.

"What do you think you're doing?" she asked him. Her hands rested on her hips.

"You told me to find something to photograph..." He took another shot of her, changed his position a bit, and then took another. "I decided to photograph the most beautiful thing in the room."

She was immediately awestruck. It was, by far, the sweetest and most romantic thing anyone had ever said to her, and she couldn't believe she even heard it come from a man's mouth – especially this delicious specimen. Flattered, she blushed bashfully.

"That's a good shot too!" He snapped two quick repetitive shots of her bashful expression. "You look so soft and genuine right now... Almost *pure*."

Carrie laughed. "I *knew* I shouldn't have handed you that camera," she teased.

"It's only fair right?" he asked. His smile grew. Her heart thumped hard against her chest. "I mean, you're about to photograph me... probably here *and* at the studio. It's a little scary being on the other side of this, right?"

He had a point. She shrugged lightly and nodded, holding a slim smile on her face. "I get it. And I understand," she told him. "It is very different being in front of the lens instead of behind it."

Joshua stopped taking pictures for a moment and walked to his bottle of wine. She watched him chug... watched his neck muscles flex as he swallowed it down. A bit of red wine escaped the corner of his mouth and trailed down his chin and neck. Suddenly, she wanted to go over there and lick it off of him, but she knew that was just her buzz talking. It would have been incredibly unprofessional of her to do that. After all, they were still in a work relationship, and there was a company policy about intimacy with other people signed to the company. If licking wine off a hot guy's body didn't count as intimacy, she didn't know what did.

The wine continued its trail down his body, reaching his white t-shirt and staining it. As Joshua set the bottle down, he noticed the spillage almost instantly.

"Well... there's another shirt for the trash." He looked behind Carrie to the wall where she'd be photographing him. "This will show up in any shots you take."

She watched as he removed the camera from around his neck and carefully set it down on the table. Then, a little more seductively than he probably should have, he pulled his t-shirt up over his body, balled it up, and set it near the bottle of wine. As he took it off, every muscle on his rippling torso flexed. His pecs looked delicious, and she noticed that the chill in the room had caused his nipples to harden.

Carrie looked away as he caught her stare. He chuckled at her, walked to her, and handed her camera back. "I thought you were used to seeing men without their shirts on," he told her.

"Yeah, but it's impolite to stare," she countered, blushing again.

"Isn't it your job as the photographer to stare?" He winked and walked over to the large blank wall. There was a black stool there and he sat atop it. "So, what do you want me to do?"

Looking at him shirtless atop the stool with the light cascading over his incredibly defined chest, abs, shoulders and arms, she could think of many things that she wanted him to do. However, none of those would be appropriate for this shoot. Instead, she took the camera and positioned herself near him enough to block out the surrounding apartment so that only Joshua, the stool, and the wall were in shooting range. She crouched low, aimed, and found him in the viewer. Then, she took a few test shots to ensure her lighting was how she wanted it.

Carrie scrolled through the few shots she'd just taken, impressed with how photogenic he suddenly appeared. His expression was light and confident – happy and not nervous at all. It was exactly how she needed him to be in the studio in the morning, and she was thankful to see that he had it in him, away from his uncle's studio.

She had him go through a couple of easy poses atop the stool. Turning his face to either side, looking off in various directions, and then flexing his muscles while staring stone-faced into the camera. Those had nearly made her wet as she took them. It had almost felt as if he was looking through the lens and directly into her eyes while posing.

Then, she had him stand and go through a series of basic muscleman poses. His hunky form lit up the room more than her preset lighting did. Much more importantly, Joshua seemed to be enjoying himself. With every pose, he smiled proudly, flexing as strongly as he could while smiling or winking at the lens.

"This is fun," he told her as she snapped away. "I didn't think it could be this much fun."

"You're a natural," she told him, gazing at him through the eye of the camera and studying his every feature as she captured him.

After about twenty minutes of these standard but sexy poses, she had an idea. She needed him to be comfortable not only with her behind the camera, but with what he would be doing in the studio tomorrow morning.

Standing upright, she relaxed the camera around her neck, letting it hang against her chest. Then, she said, "Let's practice for tomorrow's shoot. Take off your shoes and pants, and we'll see if we can't break through that nervous barrier you had earlier in the studio."

He looked at her blankly. That nervous expression

reappeared. "You want me to take off my pants?" he asked and blushed.

"Yes, just like you were earlier today. Don't worry; you've got nothing to hide from me."

"I need to hit that wine again first." He left the big blank wall and returned to his bottle, where he drained the rest of its contents. Then, wiping his mouth on his forearm, he smiled. "Okay... That's better. I think I can do this now."

Carrie watched him as he returned to the bench and untied his sneakers, tossing them into the room and out of the shooting area. They were quickly followed by his socks. Then, he stood and turned his back to her. She watched his back flex as he undid his belt and then his jeans. She smiled, eager to move this along. However, as he started to lower his jeans and pull them off, her eyes grew wide and she became lost for words.

Joshua wore no underwear beneath his jeans. His tight and muscular rear flexed at her as he pulled his jeans down. She caught a glimpse of his goodies between his legs as he raised each knee, tugging the jeans away and throwing them to the side. When he turned around, his hands were covering his package and he was smiling bashfully.

"You... you didn't wear underwear," she noted, having to struggle to find the words.

"I only wear underwear when I absolutely have to," he replied. "I – I didn't know what we'd be doing when you told me to get dressed, and you said to leave the company's underwear in the changing room." He removed his hands from his package and flexed for her. "How's this?"

Her eyes locked onto his thick and lengthy penis and the heavy set of balls that hung behind it. His pubic mound was perfectly trimmed, and it was the most mouthwatering package she'd seen in person in years... if not ever. Joshua noticed that she was staring at him and he chuckled lightly.

"Do you want me to put my jeans back on?" he asked, relaxing his pose.

Carrie sucked in a breath and then released it in a sigh. "Not on your life," she whispered and lifted her camera in slightly shaky hands.

She tried her best to not focus on his crotch as she hunted for her shots in the lens, but she found this impossible. It was making her mouth water, and it had been so long since there had been a naked man in her apartment that she felt her clitoris throb in her panties. Still, after clearing her throat and taking another breath, she began to take the photos, hoping that this distraction wouldn't make her take poor images.

After a few shots, she glanced back through them and found herself studying his crotch more than his expressions. She had to find that professionalism that she knew was inside of her, and she had to make it come out so that this shoot would turn out decently. Most importantly, she had to force herself to believe that he was wearing underwear, even if he wasn't.

"How do you want me to pose?" he asked her as she looked

over her photographs. "Something like this?" He parted his stance and flexed both arms out at his sides. Carrie was lucky she'd strapped the camera on, as it slipped from her fingers and bounced against her chest. Joshua noticed and grinned. He seemed less nervous – less embarrassed now – but those emotions had simply transferred themselves over to her. "Is everything okay?"

"Everything is perfect..." she muttered without even realizing that was saying the words. She was almost in a trance as she stared at his naked beauty, and Joshua noticed this too. He folded his arms and changed his stands, but did nothing to conceal the largely endowed distraction that was occupying her eyes and mind.

"I have to get used to being in front of a camera," he told her in a cool and relaxed tone, "and you have to get used to my penis if we're going to get through this."

He was right. She knew he was right. She'd seen many naked men before in the studio. She didn't know why he was so different – why he turned her on as much as he did. Walking to her wine, she took it and chugged. The fresh dose of liquor helped soothe her, but her mind was still racing from the vision of his great bundle of treats.

"How's this?" he asked and turned his left side to her. He brought his left foot up and propped it onto the stool. Then, he put his elbow on his leg and rested his chin on his fist, giving her almost a studious pose. It would have worked, except she could still see everything. It was too large to be hidden in the pose, and it dangled down at a side view, but a clear and unobstructed view at that.

Nonetheless, Carrie composed herself the best she could, got back into position, and lifted her camera. Joshua smiled, and she began to shoot, focusing more on his upper body at first and then capturing the full pose.

"Is it relaxed enough?" he asked and stood upright when she stopped shooting. "I could maybe relax against the wall." He put his back against the wall and then lowered himself to a sitting position on the floor, relaxing back. With his legs parted, he brought his knees up and wrapped his hands around them. Then, he stared up and off toward the ceiling with a look of wonder and loss on his face. The pose was fantastic, but with him seated on the floor, his penis was draped over it and as relaxed as he looked.

Carrie captured the image though, shooting him at several different angles and, amazingly, finding herself more relaxed with every shot she took. Perhaps it was the wine that had brought back the photographer in her, or perhaps it was that she'd finally gotten over the initial shock of seeing Joshua's impressive manhood. Either way, when she looked back over this series of photos, they were much better than the others. She envisioned them in black and white, and she thought for a moment that they were among the best she'd ever taken in her home studio.

When she looked back up from them, he stood and positioned himself with his back against the wall, his arms, folded, and his stand casual. His was again looking dead at the lens with the most seductive expression she'd seen on anyone in a while. It nearly made her melt, and through the camera, it looked too enticing. He was more of a natural at this than he believed, and this series of photos came through golden.

As Carrie studied them, Joshua asked if he could borrow the restroom. She pointed him in the direction and watched his backside wiggle and flex as he walked to it. When he was out of her line of vision, she noticed that she was becoming wet between the legs, and she hoped to God she'd be able to control it.

A few moments later, she heard the toilet flush and Joshua reappeared. If it was possible, his manhood looked bigger than it had been, although it was not erect. It must have grown as he was handling it at the toilet, and she had to look away.

"Can I see some of the shots so far?" he asked and walked right up beside her. Nervously, Carrie removed the camera from around her neck, pulled up the images, and handed the device over.

"The arrows will let you scroll left or right," she said and watched his expression as he viewed them.

A couple of times, he raised his eyebrows, but the whole time, he smiled proudly. "These are really hot," he said and looked up at her. "You're excellent at this."

"It helps when I have a model as... *photogenic* as you." He handed the camera back and she returned it around her neck.

"Care for a lusty pose?" he asked as he returned to his spot in front of the wall. Then, he turned his back to her, climbed down onto his hands and knees, widened his stance, pushed his bottom up and out at her, and looked at her over his shoulder as he bit his bottom lip.

*Even his anus is gorgeous*, she thought as she eyed his winker and the heavy sack and large endowment that hung beneath it.

"Yes…" she whispered, getting herself in position. "Yes, a lusty pose is *fantastic*."

He didn't break from his pose to chuckle, and Carrie was impressed by this.

Once she'd taken a few shots like this, he changed his expression and looked beyond her again with his jaw slack and an almost virginal look on his face. The wetness between Carrie's thighs grew as she noticed this, and she took as many shots of this look from as many angles as she could.

"I've never been so comfortable with anyone before," he told her as he stood up and stretched. As he stretched, she watched his manhood bounce a little. "You make me feel… sexy and free."

"You *are* sexy and free," she admitted and took some general shots of him stretching and standing. "You're a freaking *god*."

He laughed at this. She kept shooting. "I don't usually feel this way, but there's something about you that's bringing it out of me. No other woman has made me feel as accepted and whole as you make me feel right now."

Briefly, she wondered if he was flirting with her, or if he was simply confiding his emotions to her. She decided on the latter and asked him to try a new pose – like a football player in position on the field, ready to catch the ball during a hike.

"That one's easy," he said as he faced her and crouched down, ready to grab the ball. He had a serious expression with it. "I played three years in high school."

She could tell. At least in this pose his crotch was not front and center. Through the photos, it blurred in toward the back, beneath the focus point of his readied hands and his warrior face. These shots, like the others, were amazing.

When she stopped shooting, he stood upright and stretched again. She glanced at him as he took hold of his member and stretched it down, but didn't outright play with it. He did the same with his scrotum, as if loosening and relaxing everything from the poses he'd been put through. They then did a few more general poses, along with some more explicitly creative ones that had been his idea. One, just for fun, included him wrapping his manhood around his wrist like it was a watch. Carrie outwardly laughed at that one, but she took the shots anyway.

"I can't think of much else to do with you," she said, and then added, "photo-wise."

"One more pose?" he asked pleadingly. "I'm having so much fun with you. I don't want this to be over."

She couldn't argue it. She was enjoying this just as much as he was, and perhaps even more. "Okay," she said in agreement. "You're choice of pose."

"Cool." He turned his back to her again and she noticed

*351*

that he was once again handling himself. She watched as his elbow moved at an almost erratic pace, and when he turned back to her, he was fully erect. Again, she would have dropped the camera had it not been secured around her neck.

Joshua's erection neared a foot in length and the thickness of his penis had doubled. It stood proud, straight, and upright, and he grinned mischievously as she eyed it. Then, he turned to his side, arched his back so that his member was aimed up at the ceiling, and pulled his arms down behind his back. He wove his fingers between one another and looked up at the ceiling. Then, he closed his eyes and held his pose.

Carrie shot this from every angle she could without getting too close to him. She didn't dare get close. If she did, she knew beyond a doubt that all of her professionalism would go out the door. Over the course of this shoot, she'd gotten to know Joshua much better, and he had grown on her. Nudity aside, she was starting to find him attractive and in an all too personal way. She didn't want to scare him off by making a move on him... by grabbing the bull by the horn. As far as she knew, he was just posing for the camera and having a little fun.

This was a habit of hers that she'd long tried to shake – finding men attractive and becoming interested in them, when they weren't interested at all in her. She didn't want to mess things up with him. They had a job to do together in the morning, and she needed him to show up for it, without fear that she'd molest him.

As she photographed, she became impressed by the

strength of his erection. It had not begun to soften or grow limp at all. It just stood there, perfectly upright, as if reaching for the stars. Again, her mouth watered and she licked her lips, doing her best to ignore the throbbing and ever-growing wetness in her panties.

She shot the pose facing him and on her knees, bent backward with camera aimed at him at an upward slope. As she did, he broke the silence of his pose.

"Would you ever consider dating somebody like me?" he asked.

Carrie instantly lost her balance and fell backward onto the floor. This caused Joshua to break his pose, and he rushed to her to give her a hand to her feet. As he helped her up, she felt his erection smack against her and press onto her side. The feeling lasted only a moment, as he stepped back once she was upright and sturdy again.

"Are you alright?" his tone changed to one of concern. "I – I didn't mean to make you fall or hurt yourself."

"I'm okay," she said, laughing about her tumble, even though she was highly embarrassed from it. "I promise. I just... lost my balance. It happens sometimes when I'm in an awkward shooting position."

Her response seemed to appease him and he smiled again. Then, catching her gaze and holding it with his, he asked, "So... are you going to answer my question?"

Generally, Joshua was *not* the sort of man she would have dated. She preferred men that were a few years older than she was

– not a couple of years younger. She also preferred men who were already successful in their chosen fields. Yet, those men had not worked out for her, and there was something different and special about this one – aside from his chiseled body and impressive endowment. As she considered the question, she powered off the camera, removed it from around her neck, and carried it to a table and set it down.

Turning back around, she faced him in all his glory, but it was no longer his manhood that had her attention. She looked him in the eyes and smiled.

"What about you, Joshua?" she answered his question with one of her own. "Would you ever consider being with a woman like me?"

"I've been considering it since we got here," he said bluntly. "And the answer is yes. I've been looking for a woman like you my whole life. Strong, independent, beautiful, talented… It's everything I've ever wanted in a woman, and I see all of that in you, standing right before me."

She saw the humor of the situation as he spoke – flattering her with beautiful sentiments while his hard-on bobbed at her. Yet, she noticed the erection was also fading, and it seemed to have nothing to do with what he was telling her. This, above all else, impressed her the most. He wasn't simply trying to woo her into bed. He was being honest with her, and that by far was his finest trait.

"I – I worry about our working arrangement," she confided

as a response. "It goes against my contract to have relations with people I work with."

"After the shoot tomorrow, you won't work with me there anymore, right? I signed on for the one campaign. It's all my contract requires."

"So, if they were to be so impressed by you that they offered you some insane contract with more shoots and an ungodly amount of money, you'd turn it down?"

"Yes," he replied, straight-forward and quickly. "I'll do any photo shoot you want me to do, but not contracted through them. Only through you. This face... this body... they're all yours after tomorrow shoot. Money isn't everything."

"Money will send you to college."

He shrugged and smiled. "I'll make enough off this campaign to pay for my first year at the local college. I can find a way to pay for my second year and earn my two-year degree. I'd rather be happy with someone I care about than well-off and miserable."

"Are you miserable, Joshua?"

"I was," he admitted. "But with you, I'm *elated*. You make me feel like I'm the best man in the world, and I want to make you feel like you're the best woman in the world. We can be the best of ourselves... together."

It was the greatest proposition she'd ever heard, and with all of her heart and mind, she considered it. Looking at him, she tried to imagine if she could spend the rest of her life with him –

happy and in love. It took only a moment to consider this. She knew beyond a doubt that she could.

"Yes," she finally told him and blushed a little at the announcement. "I think I could be incredibly happy with you."

"That's fantastic!" he exclaimed, and he punched a fist into the air to demonstrate his excitement.

"I just have one requirement for a man in my life."

His excitement quickly dropped a few notches. Looking a little worried, he asked, "What's that?"

"He's got to be a good kisser." She smiled teasingly.

Joshua smiled also – broad and daringly. "Yeah?" he asked, taking a step closer. "Let me know if this works."

She had no chance to reply as he pulled her into her arms and leaned into her. His eyes remained open, locked with hers, as he kissed her with soft delicacy and a tender passion that made that throbbing in her panties intensify. Normally, a man propositioned like this would have gone overboard, offering a wet tongue and a sloppy savageness. But not Joshua. His kiss melted her with deep satisfaction and a feeling of warmth and heart that the other men had lacked.

Against her stomach, she felt his erection grow again and he broke the kiss. Stepping back, he told her, "Oops… let me go put my jeans back on."

"Don't you dare," she said as he started to walk away. She grabbed him by the arm and pulled him back, kissing him this time and with enough passion that she felt him grow full hard again and a little weak in the knees. He let her kiss him how she wanted, and she felt his hand run down her side and onto her thigh. It felt incredibly good to be touched by a man again, but it felt even better to be touched by one who she truly believed cared for her.

When the kiss broke, she decided to be daring, and she locked eyes with him as she began to lower herself down to her knees, ready to take her prize in both hands and have her way with it. Surprisingly, he stopped her and brought her back up.

"No," he said in a soft tone. "I want to make love to you, and there's much more to making love than *that*."

His words nearly made her swoon. She'd never had a man refuse oral sex before, and she'd never had one refer to sex of any kind with her as *making love*. He pulled her close again, and much to her surprise, he lifted her off her feet and carried her over to the couch. There, he laid her back and slowly began to undress her, taking his time and studying her curves and all of her little imperfections as he did. Only, Joshua seemed to not look at anything about her as an imperfection. When her shirt was open and her pants were off and she was in nothing but her bra and panties, he softly kissed her all over, tasting her and enjoying her.

"Are you sure it's not just the wine?" she asked him as he pulled her panties from her body and flung them across the room.

"The wine was good," he admitted, "but you're even better."

She was going to reply but instead, she sucked in a breath as he parted her legs and licked the wetness from her vagina.

Although the heat of his tongue against that of her womanhood felt electric, she couldn't help but think of how unfair it was that he was getting to taste her prize but had stopped her from tasting his. Yet, when his tongue began to flick against her clit, making it throb with greater intensity than anyone had managed to bring to it before, the thought left her. All she could feel was deep, savage passion rippling throughout her.

His tongue moved from her clitoris and entered into her, and Carrie gasped roughly. He flicked his tongue inside of her with a skill she hadn't expected him to have, but what a skill it was. He went in deeper, sucking on her lips as he explored her vestibule.

Carrie opened her eyes and looked at his eyes and the top of his head as he fed on her. He was watching her – explicit eye contact with an unwavering focus. She smiled at him and she could tell he was smiling too… the best that he could considering the circumstances. Then, when he pulled his tongue back and took her clitoris into his mouth, he started to nibble and suck on it with heavy force. She couldn't smile anymore. All she could do was whimper and shout out. Joshua satisfied her like this for a long while before pulling away from her nether region completely. He stood – his manhood – slick and glistening with secretion.

She started to move but he instructed her not to. "I'm not done yet," he said and licked his moist lips, tasting her juices again. He held his tool in his hands and gently stroked it. She thought he was going to penetrate her, and she was beyond ready for it. Instead, he climbed onto the length of the couch with her, but facing the opposite direction. With careful positioning, he resumed feeding on her while he lowered his crotch toward her mouth.

*Finally!* she exclaimed in her thoughts, and as she looked at his massive erection, she reached up and took it, pointing it down to her. With a firm lick, she cleared the head of his early juices, feeling his whole body tremble from the touch. Then, she suckled the head between her lips, hungry for more of his deliciousness.

Joshua was gentle with her, allowing her full control over how much she took and how swiftly. Carrie definitely took her time. There was so much of him to enjoy, but she knew she wouldn't be able to handle it all in her mouth. Instead, she nursed on the first few inches while he mercilessly ate her out.

With a mouthful of him, she was unable to cry out as she orgasmed from his hungry feasting, and his licks and sucks against her only intensified as she felt the burst of intense electricity ripple through her and fill his mouth with her warm, wet love. He ate savagely, sucking down her moistness and alternating his attention from her orgasm to her now all-too delicate clit. He began to tremble too, and she prepared herself for a burst of liquid satisfaction to erupt from the manhood between her lips.

Joshua cut himself short. He pulled out of her and away from her and stood up, squeezing his tool as he looked down at her with lusty, gorgeous eyes.

"Not in your mouth," he told her and smiled. "At least, not the first time that we're together."

He crawled up between her legs and lifted them onto his shoulders. She felt his head line up with her opening, and she was ready for it – aching for it. He entered her, but only the head, and he held it there for a long moment.

"This might hurt," he whispered to her as he folded her legs back and leaned his chest onto hers. Looking her in her eyes, he added, "It's also part of why most women don't stay with me. They say it's too much to handle."

"Don't explain it," she whispered back. "Just do it... please."

He smiled again and kissed her with heated passion, sliding the first few inches into her. Yes, there was pain, but it was not a bad pain. It was a good pain – an intense and fulfilling pain that stretched her more the deeper he went and helped make their connection grow. Softly, he began to rock into her.

When half of him was inside of her, he broke the kiss and asked, "Are you okay? Is this alright?"

"This is *fantastic*," she replied, having never experienced a man fill her as he was filling her.

They kissed again, but only briefly this time. He once again broke it and asked, "Do I need a condom?"

"I've been on the pill for years," she replied and giggled. He giggled with her and went in a few inches deeper.

Eventually, she could feel his scrotum slap against her, letting her know he had entered his entire length and had found his rhythm. It was a strong but still gentle rhythm, and the more that he humped into her, the more amazing it felt. She wondered how long he would last – if he would soon reach climax and this moment of bliss would come to an end. But he seemed to be just beginning. Their kiss became a French kiss, but not sloppy like with the other men she'd been with. His was filled with heart and passion, and the rhythm of their tongues matched that of his internal strides.

Even though they did not change positions, she did not become bored with it. She found herself fully lost in their connection, hoping that he would somehow remain inside of her forever, thusly becoming a part of her. Eventually though, as she sucked his tongue between her lips, she heard him moan and tremble. His speed quickened, and as he sank deep into her, he held steady and released the powerful flow of his love juice.

When he was done, they held each other warmly, still kissing although much more gently. Indeed, he remained inside of her. She felt him as he started to soften and grow limp. Then, as their kiss broke, he slid mostly out of her, leaving just the head in until he sat upright on his heels.

"Was that okay?" he asked her with a slightly happy and slightly concerned look on his face.

"That was *amazing*," she responded, and it was true. She'd never felt so intimately explored and appreciated in all of her days. "Let's do it again."

He grinned at her once more, and their kisses resumed. It was only a matter of moments before they were again embraced in the heat of passion. His erection returned full force, and this time, there was no pain in his entry. Perhaps she'd become adjusted to his size… perhaps she just no longer recognized the pain, as she had finally found a man who appreciated her and cared about her, and she felt very much the same.

This second round lasted quite longer than the first, and they slept together on her oversized couch until her alarm awoke them in the morning. They got to know each other better, discussing personal triumphs and failures, their childhoods, and so much more over breakfast, and when she drove him back to the studio and their shoot resumed, Joshua was no longer nervous having other people in the room. His focus was solely on Carrie and what she needed from him, and he held her attention fully. This allowed for one of the best professional shoots she'd ever taken, ensuring the campaign would be a hit.

"That young man is amazing!" her boss told her as he looked over a few of the images. "I want to book him for another campaign immediately. Have the contracts drawn up."

"No can do, boss," she said with a smile on her face. "Mr. Carter is a one-time thing for this company. He expressed that very clearly to me yesterday and this morning when our shoot ended."

"A one-time thing?" her boss questioned in disbelief. "I'm offering him the job of a lifetime!"

She could see he was getting angry, but she didn't care. She held her smile steady and her eyes calm. "There are others who will be great for whatever you have in mind, but not him. He's just not right for this."

"How can you say that?" he shouted. "What the hell's wrong with him?"

"Just one little thing," she admitted. Her smile widened. "He's mine."

Carrie's boss protested this as loudly as he could, but when she pointed out company regulations and the fact that she could easily find another job at another company if he pushed her to it, he relented and stormed from her office. The door slammed shut behind her, leaving her in peace.

At the end of the day, Joshua met her at her apartment, where she showered and changed. Then, once she was ready and they'd taken a little time to cuddle on the sofa, they left the apartment, venturing off to their first of many dates. He was her kind-hearted hunk, and she was his ball-busting business bitch, but together, they made the ultimate pair of love birds.

### *End*

# *One Good Reason to Stay*

"God, I love you," he whispered to her as his orgasm caused his entire body to quiver. "I love you so much."

She moaned and whimpered, climaxing with him as he filled her with his hot flow. "I love you..." she told him, even though she was barely able to whisper the words. Her orgasm was intense and it took her breath away.

He rested his head onto her shoulder and kissed her tenderly on the neck as he pressed out the last few pellets of his juice. Then, as their bodies relaxed, they held one another close. Jasper and Kelley had been married for five years, and their passion for one another was just as intense and lively now as it had been when they were dating. She enjoyed the feeling of having him inside of her – being one with her – more than she enjoyed anything else in life. He was her soul mate, and she was his.

When he finally slid out of her, flaccid and slick, he rolled over and checked the time. "It's almost two in the morning," he told her and smiled. "You make time stand still for me."

"But it doesn't," she argued teasingly. "When we came to bed, it was just after ten."

Jasper chuckled. "Okay, well... time flies when we're having fun?"

"Yeah it does." Kelley reached over and took his member into her hand, squeezing it. "Wanna go again?"

"Yes," he replied, "but my alarm goes off in just over three hours."

"Can't you call in today?"

"Call in to whom? I'm the boss." He chuckled more and kissed her. Still, she continued to fondle him, feeling him thicken from the touch. "You're persistent."

"Can I help it if I'm a sensual creature?" she asked.

"Sensual creature? You're just plain horny." He slid his hand between her thighs and rubbed her moist vagina. "I can feel your clit throbbing."

"It loves the way you touch it."

His member throbbed in her grip. "The feeling's mutual."

They gave into this second round of urges. He grew erect from her fondling, and she grew wetter from his touch. He withdrew his hand from her flower and readjusted himself, taking his toy away from his wife's grip. With a bit of clumsy repositioning, he was now hovering over her with his masculinity just inches away from her face.

Kelley took hold of Jasper's horn and brought it downward and into her mouth as he lowered himself forward and pressed his face between her legs. She began to suck him, but as he slipped his tongue inside of her, she swallowed him deeper and held him there, muting the loud cry that threatened to escape.

Jasper was incredibly skilled with his tongue, and she loved it when he used it on her, exploring her and cleaning up the mess that he'd just made inside. He never complained about tasting himself on her, nor did she complain about swallowing him down after he'd just exited her lady pool. Together, they feasted and fed on one another until Jasper reached his second climax of the night, filling her mouth with a powerful burst of deliciousness. As she swallowed it down and suckled for more... as his tongue worked her libido and his lips massaged her clit, Kelley hit orgasm number three. She wrapped her legs around his neck, holding his face in place as her body writhed and thrashed against the bed in primal heat. When she was finished, she let her legs fall limp back to the bed and loosened her lips around Jasper's penis to let him pull out.

When he did, she smiled and said, "There's nothing like dessert."

"Baby, you're a full meal," he replied and climbed off of her, curling back up beside her and kissing her.

"You better get some sleep now," she told him and looked over him at the clock. "It's less than three hours until that thing wakes you up."

"I'm going to be dragging into the office..." He kissed her again and smiled. "But you're *so* worth it."

"Yeah, I am," she said teasingly. "You're worth it too, Jaz."

"Thank you, even though you don't have to get up with me."

"I will if you want me to," Kelley offered with sincerity.

"No... I want you rested for when I come home. We'll paint the town red together."

"So you *do* remember that it's our anniversary." She beamed with excitement. He'd never once forgotten their wedding anniversary, but she always feared he eventually would.

"Remember it? Hell, I *live* for it."

After another kiss, they snuggled together until they fell asleep. When the alarm went off, Kelley opened one eye to see Jasper silence it and then climb out of bed. He was still naked, and even through the dimness of the room, she could see his muscular, toned body flex as he walked into the adjoining bathroom. He turned on the light and she purred deep within herself at the sight of his magnificent firm bottom. It was the best butt she'd ever seen on a man, and it was all hers.

He shut the door behind him and she heard the shower as he turned the water on. This was enough to lull her back to sleep, and when she awoke again, he was gone.

Kelley yawned and stretched. She sat up and took a deep breath, smelling the aroma of the coffee that Jasper had made before leaving for work. It made her smile. He always made a pot for himself after his shower, and before leaving the house, he made a fresh pot just for her. It was one of the many things she loved so much about him.

The scent of the coffee led her from the bed and into the kitchen, where she poured herself a full cup, blew on it to cool it a little, and sipped. As always, it was strong, perfect, and made her toes curl and her eyes open fully.

She sipped the first cup at the kitchen table, drinking it slowly and letting it wake her up enough to pour a second. By the time that cup was finished, she was mostly awake and ready for a shower.

Kelley's least favorite part about showering was washing Jasper's scent from her body. Up until that point, she could always smell her on him – a scent that was one she cherished above all others. Because of this, she had a habit of putting a dab of his cologne behind each of her earlobes after drying and dressing. This kept a version of his scent with her throughout the day and until he returned home, when she would be able to have his full scent on her once more.

Once she was showered and dressed for the day, she returned to the kitchen, feeling the hunger pangs gnaw at her stomach. Opening the fridge, she took a good look around and saw nothing that looked appealing. She could cook some eggs, make a sandwich, or have leftover pizza that had been in there for nearly a week. Kelley shut the door and walked away from it, empty-handed.

Checking the time on the stove's clock, she sighed and muttered, "I'll go out for an early lunch after a while. Then, I guess I should do some grocery shopping."

She passed some time catching up on the morning's headlines on her laptop, and then she settled down in front of the television and watched a talk show. The host was a comedy legend, but she didn't find him even the least bit humorous today. His guests were an actor promoting his latest film on some streaming service, a fashion model discussing her premier line of clothing, and a former politician who had a new book out that promised 'inside dirt.' None of the guests interested her, and she flipped the station to an old rerun of *Laverne and Shirley*. Kelley loved this show, even though she hadn't been around for its original broadcasts. She fancied herself as a Laverne, strong but troublesome.

When the episode ended, she checked the time again and decided to gather her purse and keys and head out for something to eat. Then, she had a thought and grabbed her phone to call Jasper and see if he wanted to join her.

The call went to voicemail, but instead of leaving a message, she hung up and tried again. Once more, voicemail instantly picked up. This meant one of two things – he was either on another call, or his phone was turned off. She considered Jasper could have sent her call to voicemail, but it would have ringed at least once for him to have been able to do so.

Thusly, she called his office. This line rang four times before it went to a recorded message and asked for her to leave a message of her own. Looking at the time again, Kelley found this most unusual. Mateo should have been at his desk, answering the phone like a good secretary. She hung up, waited a few minutes, called again, and received the same results.

"Well, that stinks," she muttered, deciding her husband was

likely in a meeting with a client, and that Mateo had taken advantage of the situation to go on a coffee break or to the restroom.

Either way, Kelley's hunger pangs were not lessening, and she decided lunch would have to be a solo occasion today. With her purse, keys and phone in hand, she stepped outside and locked the door behind her. In her car, she made it about a half a mile before she saw the remains of a really nasty wreck. There was a towing vehicle pulling a nearly flattened vehicle onto its trailer. She thought the vehicle looked familiar, and as she was waved to pass through in the next lane, she caught a glimpse of the tag: JAZKEL.

It was Jasper's car, practically destroyed. Dangerously, she braked quickly and pulled off to the side of the road. When she rushed back to the scene of the wreck, she was informed that her husband had been killed by a truck that had lost control. The driver of the truck also perished.

First, she went numb. She couldn't speak. Her eyes stared off into the distance at absolutely nothing. Then, her mind began to race through what she was told and the wreckage that she'd seen. Finally, she dropped to her knees and began to scream in hysterics through heavy sobs.

****

The funeral was held four days later. It had been a closed

casket, which she was thankful for. She had been able to see him though, as she'd been asked to identify the body at the morgue. Jasper's face had been unrecognizable and missing most of it, but she was able to identify him by a tattoo on his right bicep – one that had her name written inside of a red heart.

Attendance at the funeral was massive. All of Jasper's colleagues, clients, friends and family had been there, as well as most of Kelley's family and friends. She'd dressed in all black with a wide-brim hat that had a lacy black veil covering her tear-stricken face. There were several people who spoke, but she paid attention to little that any of them said. Instead, her eyes shifted between the flower-covered casket and the large portrait of Jasper that his corporate headquarters had commission in honor of him.

She had seen his body... she'd seen the remnants of the wreck and his totaled car... She knew he was really gone, but everything within her fought to believe it. When the procession left the funeral home and arrived at the cemetery, she felt lightheaded and nearly fainted – held up by the support of the people nearest to her. Then, as they began to lower his coffin into the six-foot deep hole in the ground, she rushed to it and dropped to her knees, begging them to stop. When they wouldn't, she tried to throw herself inside of the hole with her husband, but she was pulled away, kicking and screaming.

Her sister Alexandria drove her home. There was so much food in the kitchen that had been dropped off by strangers and familiar faces alike. Despite Alexandria's insistence, Kelley

wouldn't eat a bite. She had no appetite. Her husband was gone –
taken from her on their wedding anniversary. It wasn't fair. He
should have come home to her that evening. They were going to
paint the town red. Jasper had said it himself. Instead, that
anniversary had been the darkest day of her life, and the night had
been spent in hysterical fits of crying, screaming and cursing.
She'd sworn that night that she'd never forgive him for leaving
her, but she knew it hadn't been his fault. Some speeding asshole
had taken him away from her, and that asshole was dead and
unable to be punished for it.

"I'm going to stay tonight," Alexandria told her as she tried
to make room in the refrigerator for all of the food. "I don't think
you should be alone tonight."

"I'm fine..." Kelley muttered as she sat blankly at the
table. She was staring through the open doorway to the living room
at the television, even though the TV hadn't been turned on since
the morning of Jasper's death.

"I don't believe you," her sister remarked. "You're in
mourning and that's normal, but no one in mourning should have
to go through it alone." From the wine rack near the pantry, she
took a bottle of merlot, uncorked it, and poured two glasses.
Alexandria carried the glasses to the table, kept one in her hand
and set the other in front of Kelley. "Here... have a glass of wine.
Heaven knows you could use it."

Kelley looked at the glass but she didn't take it and drink
from it. She knew there was only one bottle of merlot on that wine

rack. It was the bottle she'd picked up the day before her anniversary, for her and Jasper to celebrate and enjoy together on that special day. Now, it was the last thing she wanted, as she didn't wish to drink it with anyone but her Jaz. For all she cared, Alexandria could drink the whole bottle.

"What about your kids?" she asked, looking at Alexandria. "Don't Janey and Tommy need their mommy tonight?"

"Nope. Mom has them for the night. Harrison has a report to write for work, so he's happy the house will be empty."

Kelley groaned. She didn't want her sister there with her – she didn't want *anyone* there – but she couldn't exactly tell her that. As far as Alexandria thought, she was doing a good thing by staying with her and keeping her company.

Standing from the table, she looked at her older sister and said, "I'm going to change out of these... death clothes and take a shower."

Alexandria smiled and sipped the wine. "That sounds great. Do you want me to pick out something for you to wear?"

"No... I think it's a pajama day."

In her bedroom, Kelley chose her most comfortable pajama bottoms and one of Jasper's oversized t-shirts. She brought the t-shirt to her nose and sniffed it. His scent was heavy on it and she could tell he'd wore it for something and then took it off, folding it and putting it back in the drawer. Normally, she would have gotten onto him about such an act. Once something was worn, it was considered dirty and meant for a laundry basket. In this instance however, she was thankful he'd done it.

She carried the clothes into the adjoining bathroom and turned the shower water on. As it heated, she stripped away her black dress, stocking and underclothes and kicked them into a pile near the hamper, where normally she would have instantly put them *in* the hamper. She just didn't feel like it. She had no energy – like there was now a major part of her missing.

When the water was hot, she stepped beneath it and let it run down her body. Knowing that she was alone in there – that Alexandria was still in the kitchen and enjoying the wine – she broke into tears again and slid down the shower wall, crouching low and letting her tears fall like water toward the drain.

Kelley was inconsolable and she believed she had every right to feel that way. She and Jasper had their whole lives still ahead of them before he died. They'd only been together a few years, and they'd had plans to make a beautiful baby together. They'd written out a bucket list together of places they wanted to travel to, and even though it was summer, they'd already planned on what they would wear for their annual Christmas card photo.

She was more than just inconsolable, she thought. She was miserable... heartbroken. Life for her would never be or feel the same again; she was certain of it. At the funeral, she'd been assured by Jasper's company that she would have no financial worries. Their insurance plan ensured she would be well taken care of, but it wasn't their money that Kelley wanted. She wanted her husband back, and no financial security could begin to compare to that need.

Until the water ran cold, she stayed beneath it. Then, feeling achy and exhausted, she stood and cut the water off. Just grabbing a towel from the rack beside her had seemed like the most torrential chore, and drying off made the level of her exhaustion mount. Finally, she began to dress, pulling on the pajama pants first and then holding Jasper's t-shirt to her face, inhaling his scent for a long time. Begrudgingly, she took the shirt from her face and pulled it on over her. Then, as was her tradition when her husband wasn't there, she took his favorite cologne and dabbed a bit behind each earlobe.

The scent of him swam over her. For a moment, it was like he was right there in the room with her, but she knew that idea was impossible. He was gone, and he would never be coming home again.

When she opened the door, she stood on the threshold and stared at the bed that they'd shared. It made her tears resurface, and she let them fall freely. Kelley walked to it and sat on Jasper's side. Then, she took his pillow and hugged it close. Looking down at it, she saw a few strands of his hair clung to the pillowcase. She let them stay so that a part of him would always be there on the bed… at least until she was forced to wash the sheets. When that time came, she decided she would collect the few strands and save them. She couldn't bear to lose them, as she'd already lost him.

Even though the bedroom door was open, Alexandria knocked on it and stepped inside. Kelley looked at her and fought her tears back as best she could.

"How you doing, kid?" her big sister asked as she approached the bed and sat beside her. "Did the shower help any?"

Kelley shook her head. "Nothing will help me right now."

"I know it's hard, but you'll push through this." She put a hand on Kelley's shoulder, but the widow pulled away and stood.

"I don't want to *push through* anything!" she yelled, although she hadn't meant to raise her voice. "I *want* my husband back."

Alexandria stood with her and hugged her close. "I know, sis. I'm sorry... I wish there was something I could do." As she hugged her, Kelley felt her sniff her. "You smell manly."

Kelley couldn't help but smile. The grin was quick and faint, but it didn't help to make her feel better. She appreciated her sister for trying – even if she didn't *want* her to try.

The night was quiet from then out. Alexandria spent much of it in the kitchen snacking on the various foods. Kelley lay on the couch, staring at the television but paying no attention to the movie her sister had turned on. All she could think about was her sweet and wonderful husband, taken from her all too early. No big budget flick could distract her from this.

The last thought in her mind – the last image her mind's eye saw – was of Jasper. She focused on him, on how he'd looked when he was still with her, and how his smile had always helped to lift her spirits. With that image, she was able to fall asleep.

When she awoke, it was morning and to the sounds of

Alexandria gathering her belongings.

"I made coffee," she told her as she hunted around for wherever she put her missing shoe. "I hate to run off, but I've got to pick up the kids from Mom's and take them for their check-ups today. They've got to have all of their vaccinations before I can enroll them in the academy for the fall term."

"Still sending them to private school?" she muttered, attempting to make light conversation even though she was groggy and half-asleep.

"Of course! They're already way more advanced in their reading and math levels than children their own ages in public school."

Kelley rolled her eyes. The only reason her niece and nephew were in private school was because Harrison's job paid for it. Otherwise, she was certain they'd be in public school, just like she and Alexandria had been.

Her sister gave her a quick peck on the cheek and told her she was just a phone call away. Then, with a quick wave, she headed out, locking Kelley into seclusion.

Now alone, she allowed herself to sit up and wander into the kitchen, where the coffee was indeed brewed but it didn't smell like it did when Jasper brewed it. It smelled weak, and one sip confirmed this suspicion. She poured out the entire pot and considered making more, but she quickly decided she didn't need it. After all, what was there to wake up for? Without her husband, Kelley had no purpose anymore. She was a widow, living in a big house all by herself. Her financial security had been ensured, but that didn't help any. What good was money if it was just her? There was no one to spend it with… to enjoy it with. There would be no more dinner dates or movies at the theater. The weekly pizza night had been Jasper's favorite, and she couldn't imagine doing it without him.

That enormous feeling of mourning swooped over her once more as she realized exactly how alone she was. She wanted nothing but her husband to be there with her, to kiss her and love her and tell her how wonderful their life was and that they'd be together forever. Instead, all she received was the silence of the house.

Walking upstairs, she went into the room they'd shared and refused to look at the bed. Instead, she went into the bathroom and stripped, placing her clothes atop the toilet seat so that she could wear them again. She looked at the shower and then at the bathtub. While a shower would have been faster, she wanted the warm and confined comfort of the tub.

Her motions were slow as she went to push down the plug, then turned on the water. When it was mostly filled, she turned the water off and stepped in, sitting carefully and stretching her legs out as she rested her back against its inner wall. The warm water began to sooth her achy muscles, but it did little to calm her mind. She shut her eyes and let it replay that fateful day over and over again. She saw it all so clearly – the remains of the wreck… the license plate with their combined names on it… She saw Jasper's corpse laying atop a steel gurney in the morgue, unrecognizable except for the tattoo on his arm.

Once more, she began to weep for her husband. She couldn't imagine life without him; she couldn't bear it.

As the tears fell, she slunk deeper into the tub, letting the water cover her face. Slowly, she released all of the air she held. It blew upward in bubbles, popping against the water's surface. With her lungs empty, she fought the urge to pull up and decided to let her body die so that her spirit could be reunited with his.

There was a sharp tug on her hair, and with a gasp and a start, she jolted upright and breathed. First, she touched a hand to her hair, and then she looked around the room for whoever had tugged it. The room was empty except for her, but there was something in the air... a distinct scent that she recognized immediately, even though it was faint.

"Jaz?" she asked, searching the room for a further sign of her husband. Standing, she grabbed a towel and wrapped it around her as she stepped from the watery tub. "Jaz, is that you?"

She walked to the door and opened it, looking into the bedroom. It too was empty. Walking back to the tub, she sniffed the air again. There was no longer a trace of her husband's scent there, and she sighed with somewhat controlled desperation.

"Just my imagination..." she muttered and reached into the tub, pulling the plug and letting the water drain out.

Smelling Jasper's scent – or imagining she had – did two things to her. Firstly, it made her mourn him further, as she could feel the emptiness inside of her grow. Secondly, it made her realize that his death was making her go crazy. She had literally walked around the bathroom, asking her dead husband if he was there. If that wasn't crazy, she didn't know what was.

After redressing in the clothing she'd just taken off, she went back downstairs and found that the television was on. It was tuned into her favorite sitcom, but she knew she hadn't turned it on. It had been off from the moment she awoke, or at least she thought it had. Perhaps Alexandria had turned it on this morning, and through her dark and groggy state, Kelley simply had not noticed. Nonetheless, she was in no mood for *Laverne and Shirley*. She was in no mood to laugh.

Powering it off, she left the living room and went to the kitchen, where she opened the refrigerator door. There was so much food in it, but nothing looked appetizing. That was of no fault to the food or the people who had made it; she simply had no appetite. Quickly, she shut the door and looked at the table, where the glass of wine Alexandria had poured for her still sat, awaiting her.

Kelley sat and pushed the wine glass away. She still didn't want it – not without Jasper sitting across from her enjoying a glass as well. That would never happen, and so her glass would remain full until she poured it down the sink later.

Suddenly, she felt the urge to scream, and so she did. It was a loud, horrific scream that attempted to release all of the pain trapped inside of her. It failed in its attempt. When the scream was over, she laid her head against the table and wept for her lost love.

"I can't do this!" she shouted through her crying and slapped her hands on the table. "I can't live without him!"

Jasper had been the best part of her, and she'd lived for him, just as he had lived for her. Without him, she found that life was no longer worth living. It was a miserable place where the people most cared about were snatched away without even an opportunity for a proper goodbye. It was a terrible thing and it was something she decided she no longer wanted to be a part of.

Lifting her head, she wiped her tears away and stood. Walking up the stairs, she went through the bedroom and returned to the bathroom. There, she stood before the medicine cabinet and opened it. Last year, Jasper's bike chain had broken while he'd been out on a ride. He broke his ankle in the fall, and the doctor had prescribed him some incredibly strong pain killers. They had been too strong for Jasper's taste, and he'd only taken two before deciding he'd rather deal with the pain. He'd placed the container in the medicine cabinet, where they still remained.

She took the orange bottle, unscrewed the top, and looked inside. There were twenty or so round white pills within. That would be plenty, she knew, to take her away from this miserable life and to hopefully reunite her with the only person – the only soul – that mattered.

Kelley carried the bottle downstairs into the kitchen. Sitting at the table, she poured them all out into a pile before her. Then, she leaned forward and grabbed the glass of wine, sliding it to her.

She decided she would swallow them a few at a time, washing them down with the anniversary merlot – a tribute to her fallen husband.

Briefly, she considered writing a note to explain why she was doing this, but she decided against it. She had nothing to explain. Everyone knew that she was in a state of mourning that she could not shake, and surely, they would all understand. If they didn't, well...

"Tough shit," she whispered and took a handful of pills in one hand and the glass of wine in the other. Just as she was about to pop the pills into her mouth, she heard something startling from behind her.

"Please... don't."

Now, she knew she'd gone crazy. That had been Jasper's voice, which was impossible. He was dead. She'd seen him herself.

Looking behind her, she saw him again – a faint and somewhat transparent image of her husband, looking at her with a soft but sad smile upon his face. He looked so handsome – like he'd never been in the wreck... like he'd never died. Immediately, she felt tears well in her eyes again. The pills and the glass of wine slipped from her hands, spilling back onto the table.

"Jaz?" she asked, unable to believe her eyes. It was staggering and beyond belief.

"The one and only," he told her and stepped toward her. His whole aura seemed to glow a hazy white all around him.

She stood, shaky and nervous, but she felt no fear – only

the love that seemed to radiate from him. Standing still, she looked at him, letting her jaw fall slack, still in a state of disbelief. The one thing that helped her realize it was really him was his undeniable and unique scent – the scent she loved so much and missed even more.

"I miss you..." she whispered to him and wiped the tears from her eyes. "I miss you so much, Jaz."

His smile remained steady, but it was still filled with a bit of sadness as he eyed the pills on the table. "You should throw those away, love. You don't need to take them."

She shook her head and took a step back. "No... I won't throw them out, Jaz. I need them... I need them so I can be with you again."

"But you're always with me, just as I'm always with you," he offered and took a step toward her. "Please... don't do this. Don't kill yourself just so we can be together. I promise, we *will* be together again, and we will hold each other again and love each other again... when the time is right. But not now. It can't be now."

Kelley understood his words, but she was having trouble fathoming them. She needed him so much – to be with him for all eternity. Yet here he was, telling her she couldn't have what she most wanted.

"Why not?" she asked, almost bitterly. "Why not, Jaz? You're the one who left me. Why can't I leave this place and be with you?" Her voice began to rise as she grew defensive. "One reason, Jaz. Give me one good reason to stay here."

He walked closer to her and put a hand over her belly. Chills overcame her and goosebumps rippled across her skin. She could feel him... she could *actually* feel him.

"Right here in your womb is the reason, my love," he told her and caressed her stomach. "You may not know it yet, but within you, a baby is growing. *Our* baby. We created this new life together the night before I died." He moved his hand from her stomach and placed both hands on her shoulders. They were inches apart now, and his scent was stronger than ever before. It nearly made her woozy as it overcame her.

"I – I'm pregnant?" she asked him. Fresh tears rolled down her cheeks, even though she had no idea they were falling.

"Yes!" he exclaimed, smiling proudly. "You're going to be a mommy, and I'm going to be a daddy."

"You're not here to be a daddy," she countered through her emotional state.

"I've never left you. You may not always be able to see me, but I'm still here, Kelley. I'll be right here when that baby comes into this world, and I'll be here through every step of its life and yours... every moment until your time here has passed and we are together again, in a brand new life."

"I need you with me, here... *really* here," she said, begging. "Please... please don't make me do this alone."

"You'll never be alone. If you ever have any doubts about that, just close your eyes and inhale deeply. You always said you'd know my scent anywhere, and when you smell it, you'll know I'm there with you."

"But, Jaz, I...."

She couldn't finish her statement. He wouldn't let her. Midway through, he pressed his lips to hers and kissed her with such love and intensity that she felt his warmth wash over her. She closed her eyes through the kiss, letting it enrapture her and transport her out of her misery. In that moment, she was no longer scared of the future... she no longer felt alone.

"I love you, Kel," he told her as the kiss broke. "Always and forever."

"I love you, Jaz," she replied. Opening her eyes, he no longer stood before her, but she knew he wasn't gone. His scent still lingered, and this time, it didn't fade away.

\*\*\*\*

Jaz had been right. A trip to her doctor confirmed that Kelley was pregnant, and when the baby was born, she looked into his precious face and saw that he was the spitting image of her beloved husband.

Her life began anew as she raised her son, and when things got hard and she thought she couldn't take it anymore, she closed her eyes and breathed in deep. Each time, she smelled her beloved Jaz and knew he was there, watching over her just as he'd promised. She knew he'd been right. One day, they would be fully reunited, but until that day, she had his legacy to care for and raise, and so that was what she did. She became a mommy and it was the most wonderful feeling she'd ever know.

## *End*

# *About the Author*

Best-selling novelist (*Restless*, *Where the Demon Is*) Jae El Foster is a world-building visionary residing in Middle Tennessee. His gay romance *Once Upon a Christmas* has been translated into multiple languages across the globe, and his epic horror novel *She Rises at Night* was praised as '*...a bloody good read to be enjoyed time and again,*' and '*...superb in so many ways.*' His breakthrough hit with DCL Publications *Restless* was proclaimed '*... another must read penned by Jae El Foster,*' and '*...something that happens very rarely.*'

With *Remember to Breathe*, Jae El Foster returns to his more sensuous roots nearly 20 years after his last collection of erotic fiction, *Dirty Little Secrets*. Now, older and wiser, he has crafted this brand new collection of romantic erotica '*...with more maturity and a softer voice.*'

"*I am incredibly proud of this collection,*" he says of *Remember to Breathe*. "*Dirty Little Secrets was meant to be a triumph for me after the small success of Nothing: A Tale of Terror. In my early twenties, I was too young and too immature to understand the true meaning of romance when mixed with erotica. I was not proud of the final product, but that's fortunately not the case with this one. Maybe I'll pen another similar collection in another 18 to 20 years. Who knows?*"

# *Other Works by Jae El Foster*

## *with DCL Publications*

- Restless
- Where the Demon Is
- Forever: Shaded Whisperings Book 1
- Playing Saint Nick: Shaded Whisperings Book 2
- Beauty Within
- Restive
- Madame Howell's Book of Very Bad Things: A Baker's Dozen of Frightful Fairy Tales Vol. 1
- She Rises at Night
- Remember to Breathe: A Collection of Contemporary Erotic Fiction

## DCL Publications, LLC

http://www.thedarkcastlelords.net

*Find our books at any fine online retailer.*

www.ingramcontent.com/pod-product-compliance
Lightning Source LLC
Chambersburg PA
CBHW030353030726
47497CB00002B/322